how to survive a holiday fling

ISABEL JOLIE

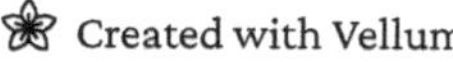 Created with Vellum

one

Oliver

December 23

Visibility maxes out at about thirty feet. The gray haze blocks what should be an expansive view across two thousand acres of winter wonderland. Light ice and snow fall steadily, prickling any exposed skin. The darkness on the horizon promises a full-on blizzard. In other words, it's not only frigid, but this weather is for shit.

Drew, the frat brother we called Loki for solid reasons back in the day, is long gone. The notorious troublemaker whipped down the infamous canyon with a rebel yell and not one glance back. *Fucker.* The guy lives near Jackson and skis all the damn time. In all fairness, I'm an expert skier, too. But there's a snowboard currently attached to my feet, and that's giving me pause. I'm not a newbie boarder, but I'm not great, and I've got a sinking feeling this blasted canyon demands great.

On a normal day, there'd be a crowd of onlookers gathered to gawk at anyone foolish enough to attempt Corbet's. Folks from the lift could get a good look at any epic crash and burn. On the bright side, the current storm system stops the lookie-loos. If I smash into one of the imposing rock walls on either side of this canyon, there will be no video posted on YouTube.

I hop forward and peer over the edge. The invisible lift is somewhere out there in the haze.

I'm too fucking old for this shit. Why the hell did I let Drew talk me into this? What the hell am I going to do if I break a limb? I live on a fucking ranch. A vision of my sorry ass riding a horse in a cast has me cringing.

We knew conditions wouldn't be great today. Why the hell didn't I pick skis? What the hell was I thinking? I'm a good snowboarder, but am I Corbet's Couloir good?

My hands sweat in my gloves, but a deep freeze stings my toes. My quads burn, a solid reminder I'm no longer in my twenties. Yes, this might qualify as one of the stupidest things I've done in my thirties, and that's saying a whole helluva lot. *Fucking Drew.*

"You okay?"

The voice comes from out of nowhere. It's almost like I imagined it. Tips of skis appear. My gaze follows up loose black ski pants to a helmet, goggles, and a black face and neck cover.

"There are other ways down. You don't have to do it." The voice is distinctly feminine, and I'm just man enough that I won't ask her about those alternate routes.

Drew left me here, and I assumed this was the only way down. An alternate route is damn attractive, but there will be a blizzard in Texas before I admit that to a girl. Even one in shapeless ski pants and a matching shapeless black ski coat that falls mid-thigh, with winter gear that completely hides her face.

"Are you scared?"

Now, that question just pisses me off. Never ask a Texan if he's scared. "No, ma'am, I'm good. You go."

"I don't want to leave you up here if you...that storm's coming in. Lifts have stopped."

Visibility is now about ten feet. This has to be the stupidest thing

I could possibly do. I can't even see the rock walls I need to avoid. Flakes fall, dusting my gloves and my coat.

"There's no shame in fear." There's a hint of a smile in the way she lassos those words.

"That sounds like a dare."

Her muffled laugh travels over the packed snow. "Take it how you want."

The twenty-foot drop taunts me. The stranger mocks me.

"I can call ski patrol—"

"That's quite all right." My southern drawl comes out with the statement because that's what I do to calm a situation. It's instinctual. A slow southern drawl relaxes all things. But southern drawl and all, that cliff in front of me is still a straight fucking drop.

"What level snowboarder are you?" There's an air of authority in her tone that makes me suspect she's an instructor. She's not wearing the signature ski patrol red jacket, but she is up here on what's widely considered one of the most difficult routes at Jackson Hole. "If you—"

"I'm fine, promise," I lie. "Just go on."

"Nuh-uh. You first." She pushes forward on her poles so she's a whole helluva lot closer. She's probably one of those college kids on holiday vacation with her parents and knows the mountain like the back of her hand. I recognize her type because I used to be that type. Know-it-all. Fearless. It's not that I'm fearful, but I have responsibilities that will be a shit ton more complicated if I'm sporting a cast on one or both legs.

The snow falls heavier now, further diminishing visibility. Once I go, it's going to be a blind fall.

"Ladies first," I tell her. She shakes her head like she's annoyed with me and she's tired of my shit. That would be entirely understandable. But I'm not giving in, and I gallantly gesture with my arm for her to proceed.

"I'm gonna go, but I'm waiting for you. It's a regular expert run after you get through the pass. When you land, do a quick right to avoid smashing into the rock."

Smashing into the rock? Fucking great. "No problem, got it," I lie again.

"Do you have a phone? To call ski patrol? In case we get separated?"

"You taking me under your wing?"

"Do you have a phone?" Her gloves wrap around her poles, but she sounds like those hands are on her hips.

Visibility is piss-poor. A wall of blurry white exists behind her. Snowflakes plaster to my goggles, and I use the back of my glove to wipe them, only for new flakes to replace old ones.

"I do," I grunt.

Satisfied, she raises one ski, pushes on a pole, lines up on the edge, and *whoosh*. I get one glimpse of a long dark braid down her back that lifts from the base of a sticker-plastered helmet as gravity claims her. And...she's gone.

Ah, shit. The next person to come around will be ski patrol.

I hop until the tip of my board hangs over the edge, lean forward, and freefall.

The scream that rips out is half terror and half thrill.

"Holy fuuuuck!"

two

Kate

December 23

The snowboarder performed a handful of rolls and one epic garage sale. His speed bordered on reckless, but he maintained acceptable control. The whole way down, I could imagine Hudson, a professional snowboarder and my older brother, egging him on. My whole life Hudson egged me on, mocking me for inadequate speed and hesitation. So as much as I wanted to give the boarder a well-deserved razing, I bit it back.

The Corbet run is one I need to master for my training. Out of respect for the mountain and the community, I checked on the lone boarder.

Most people hang a bit at the top of Corbet's. But I watched him hovering for at least five minutes. I'd hoped he'd go so I'd have it all to myself. I wanted the exhilaration of being the lone soul on the mountain. Then it became apparent he was probably in over his head. Which is dangerous. If you don't know what you're doing, severe injuries, even death, await. Corbet's is no joke. But, like most dudes, he couldn't admit he might be out of his depth. He wouldn't back down, and I'm not ski patrol. I have no authority.

With more luck than skill, the guy conquered Corbet's, albeit shrieking like a little girl the whole way down. I led him to what I think of as the intermediate middle. But, in these near-whiteout conditions, the intermediates are technically advanced slopes.

The descent took forever, leading a boarder. But I finally got him to Sundance, a pretty benign slope. From there, ski patrol was all around, and I lost patience. With a straight shot down, he didn't need me pointing the way. If it wasn't for the boarder, I might have gotten in two runs after work. But, under these conditions, it probably all worked out for the best.

"Oak!" The shrill shriek cuts through the base crowd. Through the heavily falling snow, I can barely make out my roommate, Nash.

Nash possesses the soul of an eternal wild child. He's loud as fuck, brash, and daring. He's the embodiment of the frat boy from movies. The kind of guy I didn't know in college because I studied too hard and avoided the frat scene. But he's a lot like my older brother, so I get him.

We met three months earlier when I applied for his roommate posting. I'd applied because he said he was a ski school instructor, and I thought that would be an in to jobs on the mountain. And he had been. But I didn't accurately estimate his penchant for a good party.

"Oak!" There's a pause. "Lee!"

Nash waves his pole back and forth in the air. He's far down the dip, toward the restaurants and the path that leads back to lodging.

A couple of skiers approach him. They look like an older couple, probably parents of a kid he taught today. I wave my glove, letting Nash know I see him and I'm headed down.

My braid gets caught on something, and my head pulls back. I raise my arm, attempting to free my braid from whatever coat snagged it, and come face to face with the boarder. His bright orange coat is hard to miss. It's part of the reason I could keep an eye on him as he coasted down behind me.

"Made it down," he says.

"I see that." I bite back a snarky comment. Something like 'do you want a medal' comes to mind, but that's my brother's world coming out to play. I want the mountain life, not the asshole vibe. "Nicely done."

Another skier skis up, close enough I assume the two are together. The snowboarder taps a hand on my shoulder. "She stayed to make sure I got down."

"You took him up to Corbet's?" I gape at the skier. I really cannot believe the audacity—or perhaps stupidity is the better word. His friend could have died.

The skier shoves his gator, a thick black cloth that covers his entire neck and part of his face down, revealing a wide, schmucky smirk.

I glare at the guy, not that he can see me behind my reflective goggles. Friends don't take friends up to Corbet's unless they can handle it. And you especially don't do it in severe conditions and leave their ass.

"Tell me. How scared was he?"

"Not," I say. "Took it like a pro." The lie rolls easily off my lips. "Later," I say as I leave the two guys, heading toward Nash.

"Wait, can I buy you a drink?" the snowboarder calls from behind me.

Nash is a good twenty feet ahead, and the couple he was talking to has moved on. He's not about to climb up the slope to me. Instead, he just yells out, "See you at Mangy Moose!"

"I saw that. That's down across from the resort hotel, right?" the snowboarder asks.

"Straight ahead," I answer with a polite smile, not that they can see it because my facemask covers from my goggles, down my face and throat, into my jacket, which is zipped up tight to my jaw. I push forward, gliding easily down the gentle slope.

Ski people are friendly people, mostly. The guests are on vacation and in good moods. The people who work at the resort are thankful to be here because it's a fantastic place. The vacationers tend to hang in the group they travel with, and the locals hang with locals. But, on the mountain, there's a spirit of camaraderie. When you see someone down, you help them.

The Mangy Moose is packed, as evidenced by the overflowing ski racks out front. I recognize Nash's skis and set mine near his. A flash of orange catches my attention.

The snowboarder has his board slung over a shoulder, but he sets it down against my skis. He's in his comfy snowboarder boots. He holds an arm out, as if he's directing the way.

"Shall we?" He pushes his gator down and leans in. In a conspiratorial tone, he adds, "Thanks for not selling me out."

"No problem." I lower my gator, and the icy wind bites my skin. "What happens on the mountain stays on the mountain."

He barks out a laugh. We step through the doors, and we're met with a blast of heat. The threadbare carpet mat is soaked with melted snow. The boarder opens the second door. I peel off my gloves and scan past the hostess to the bar area. Sure enough, Nash has commandeered a high-top table across from the bar. I lift my goggles up on my helmet, unsnap the helmet clasp, and lift. On instinct, I breathe in deeply, released from the confines of the goggles, helmet, and facemask. The tip of my nose drips, and I wipe it with the back of my glove.

"See ya'," I call to the boarder who's in line at the hostess stand.

My ski boots clomp on the hardwood floor. Families are packed at tables. Skiers, snowboarders, and a few folks who don't look like they went out at all today fill the bar stools, and others hover. The jammed après-ski scene in Jackson is par for the course. They don't quite have enough bars for everyone to get their hot toddy with ease. But those of us who work here look out for each other, which I'm sure is how Nash scored us this table.

When I moved here two months ago, I applied for ski patrol, and they handed over a list of the requirements and told me, "Not this year, kid." One requirement is to possess the skills to traverse every single foot of this mountain. I'm working on it.

"How was ski school?" I ask him as I unzip my coat. My toes burn from the cold, but my body is quickly reaching hot tub-level heat. Because of the extremely low temps, I layered up today with an additional wool sweater. Good for outside, but it has to come off the minute you step indoors.

"Groovy," Nash answers, glancing up from the menu on his phone. "You up for nachos?"

The wicked high prices deter me. Resort prices are fine for those on vacation. For those of us living here and working the hourly jobs, it's not such a great thing.

"I've got food back at the apartment. I was just going to get a beer. Cheapest one."

"If we can sit with you, I'll pay for dinner and all the drinks."

"These two seats are yours, my man," Nash belts out.

My heavy ski boots are resting on the rail of the empty stool beside me, and I have to brace myself on the table to turn and see who is behind me. But, without seeing him, I kind of already know. It's the boarder.

His helmet and goggles are off, and his orange jacket lies draped over an arm. His helmet hair spews back and forth in bursts of blond and brown pieces. He's got a couple of days' dark growth along his jaw that gives him a rugged, manly vibe. He's pared down to a form-fitting long-sleeve top that augments muscular arms, a chiseled chest, and tapered stomach. That's no dad bod. Which is what we see a lot of on the mountain. Especially over Christmas break. Almost everyone packed into the Mangy Moose is married, and a vast majority have kids with them. The throngs of college students at the bar tonight are most likely also here with parents. It's the Christmas season.

"Thanks for the seats. It's an hour wait for a table. I'm Oliver. And this is Drew."

"I'm Nash." Nash smiles good-naturedly. "And this is Kate. My buddies are stuck at work. Running late. Do you guys live around here, or are you on vacay?"

Oliver slides onto the stool next to me, and his friend claims the seat next to Nash.

"God, I'm starving," Drew says as he hunts for waitstaff.

"Menu's here," Nash hands him his phone.

"I'm visiting this guy," Oliver says. "He lives on the Idaho side."

"Oh, are you from around here?"

Drew mumbles something about not originally, but he and his wife moved to Idaho recently. After placing a food order, Nash and Drew launch into an intense discussion about the surrounding towns and which places are growing and which aren't. Nash aims to buy a place, and it won't be in Jackson. Not too many of the folks who work for Jackson Resorts live in Jackson. There are several towns on the outskirts with more affordable housing. Nash lucked into the current rental we occupy, but he let me know up front it's a year-to-year rental agreement and he never knows when it might end.

"What about you?" Oliver asks in a deep, slow drawl that's definitely not local.

"What about me?" My brain muddles next to this attractive man. It's a symptom I am familiar with. Hudson has some friends who stir the same clueless reaction. My fingers shred the paper napkin on my lap.

"Are you on vacation? From here?" Oliver clarifies his question to assist my addled brain. It would be easier if Nash and Drew led the conversation, but they're wrapped up in the Wyoming dispatch.

"I live here. Right now, I work at the ski rental place." I also wait tables and am searching for an additional part-time job, but this random doesn't need to know that. "Is your family here?"

Christmas is in a couple of days, so the question rolls off my tongue, even though I just learned he's visiting his friend, Drew. This is the first Christmas I won't be with my family back in Vermont. I couldn't get the days off, and even if I could, I couldn't afford the flight.

"Well, funny thing about that. I'm supposed to be in Aspen. My brother's family normally hosts. But his kids came down with something called hand, foot, and mouth disease. Have you ever heard of that?"

"It sounds…" My nose scrunches automatically.

"The photos on Google are every bit as bad as it sounds. It's also highly contagious. So, I sent out a mayday. Drew and I went to UT together. He's been asking me to visit, so here I am."

"Did he know you were a boarder when he invited you out?"

"Oh, I can ski too. And I'm a better skier. I just had my headset on boarding. Now, what about you? What's your story?"

"I ski and board. I chose skis because of the conditions."

Boarding isn't more dangerous, but in near whiteout conditions, it's a challenge to keep pace with a friend. It's hard for a boarder to keep pace with a skier, if not impossible, on a good day. Given the weather conditions, they should've chosen the same sport.

A server arrives and fills our table with nachos, wings, mini burgers, and four hot toddies loaded with whipped cream. It's a smorgasbord of food. She also unloads four small shot glasses filled with amber liquid.

"I ordered a lot," Drew says to the table. "We'll get more if we need it."

I can't afford all this. I always order the cheapest on-tap beer.

"They're paying. Stop frowning, Oak."

Drew smiles and clinks his glass against mine, supporting Nash's announcement with yet another friendly, silent toast.

"Thanks," I mumble.

Nash often has parents of his students offer to pay if they see him at restaurants. He also gets big cash tips. I don't get cash tips, and I also have student debt. As much as I might like to refuse to accept their generosity, I really have no choice.

"Oak?" Oliver asks beside me as he digs a nacho into a pile of meat and cheese.

"It's for Oakley. My last name. Nash loves to call me Oak. I have no idea why. If you hang out with him long enough, you'll get some sort of nickname, too."

"Gotcha."

The Mangy Moose is loud, packed to the brim, and music blares from speakers all over the room. The result is that Oliver and I are paired off and pretty much in our own world of conversation.

The alcohol keeps coming. Toasty warmth cocoons my cramped toes. Oliver's southern drawl strengthens with each drink. He rests one elbow lazily on the table, and he's got a welcoming, warm smile that lights up his face. You can tell he's an entertainer by nature.

Funny stories roll out. Our knees touch, and he presses his hand to my thigh or my arm to highlight a punchline.

I've always had a thing for men's arms, and the black Thinsulate top hugs the curves of his biceps. The corners of his eyes wrinkle with every chuckle. Over dinner, he traverses the line from stranger to friend. He brushes loose hair back behind my ear, and my skin lights. His touch reverberates down the curve of my neck. As we talk, my mind wanders to his age. I'd guess from his weathered skin he's in his mid-thirties, but he possesses a boyish quality, an effervescent love of life that's unexpected for a middle-aged man. Unlike my brother's dyed blond highlights, Oliver's are real. He's not looking to draw a crowd around him. The only person he's lavishing his attention on is me.

"So, tell me, Kate, what was it like growing up on a mountain?" He's leaning forward, grinning. His upper teeth drag across his lower lip, and he's looking at me with avid interest. Yes, he's learned I grew up in Vermont and I've been skiing since my toddler days.

"Overrated."

He barks out a laugh and rests his elbow on the table. An electrical charge flows between us, fueled by alcohol. The rest of the world becomes background noise, and there's only this man who keeps ordering wicked expensive hot toddies. This man with a deep-throated laugh who shows an interest in everything I say.

"Are you going to be here for Christmas?" Christmas is in a couple of days. It's pretty obvious I'll be here. But the alcohol buries my snark, and I simply nod.

"My brother will be home with my parents. It'll be my first Christmas away from my..." I sigh. The room spins a bit, and I chug down some water. He's still staring at me like I'm catching air off a jump. "I'd like to pretend it's not Christmas. Just skip this one this year."

"Skip it? You can't skip Christmas. What are you? The Grinch?"

"No." There's this silly, super-wide smile I can't wipe off my face.

"Okay. In the Duke family, we're allowed one Christmas wish. Just one." He holds up his finger. "Now, as kids, that wish was always some big-ticket item, but it was clear, we got to wish for one thing." He rubs his hand over his mouth. He may have forgotten where he was going with his story. "Now, if we all skip Christmas, think of all those boys and girls who wouldn't get their wishes."

"They can still get their wish. I just won't." I'm not getting a wish, anyway. My parents already sent me a check for my Christmas gift, which this year I wholeheartedly appreciate.

"No." Oliver's thick eyelashes flutter closed. When he opens his eyes, I notice his eyelids are half-shuttered, and I giggle. "You gotta make a wish. Tell me. What's your Christmas wish this year?"

With one discreet glance across the table, double-checking Nash won't weigh in, I say, "I'm giving myself one year to make ski patrol."

I don't share that this is a big life change for me or that no one in my life approves.

"Ski patrol?" He verifies that's my wish, and I nod. "Awesome. Let's drink to ski patrol."

His index finger bats my nose. He leans in like he's going to kiss me, and I tilt my chin up, receptive. But he slowly leans back, lifts his beer glass, clinks it against mine, and swallows.

When he waves away the next shot glass, his whiskey eyes are pouring over me in a way I recognize. He's over the alcohol. He's interested in a different kind of post-ski party.

The question is, am I interested? Sure, he's cute. Nice. But he's a vacationer. Here one week, gone forever. But it's Christmas. And in the spirit of Christmas, sharing the time with someone feels more than a little right. And all that alcohol swirls and warms. My heart rate hitches when he leans in, and his fingers press against the back of my neck, sending tendrils cascading down my spine.

"Let's get out of here." He pulls back and smiles a slow smile. "It's too loud. You probably want to get those boots off."

He's right. I do. The bones in my feet throb inside the ungiving ski boots. Nash and Drew are no longer sitting at the table with us. They are over talking to a group at the bar.

"I have a fireplace. Let's go get comfy."

My insides curl, and I can almost hear Claire, my other roommate, chastising me. This is so cliche. Hooking up with a resort guest.

He brushes his lips across mine. Just a light touch that whips flurries through me and heats me from within. He pulls back, and those whiskey eyes probe, questioning. I reach forward, digging my fingers into his unruly hair, and take the leap. He tastes like cinnamon and bourbon, and the combination spins and whirls. My heart rate skyrockets the same way it does the moment I push off, let go, and sail through the air at the top of a run.

When he breaks the kiss, he swallows, smirks, clasps my hand, and scrunches his nose as he says, "Come on. Let's get out of here."

three

Kate

December 23

Claire: Where are you? I'm here.

Claire: Nash said you left. Where did you go?

Paisley: Nash says you left with a guy. Who???

Hudson: Hey, sis. Back home. Sucks without you here.
How's the snow? Looks like you're getting a dump.

I scan the texts on the sofa in the living area of Oliver's hotel room at the Four Seasons. I've always wondered about this hotel but have never been inside. It's as gorgeous as expected. He flipped a switch, and the fireplace roared to life. Then he excused himself to go to the bathroom, but not until he offered me a bottle of water. My ski boots are over by the door on a warming pole. And I am sitting here in my flannels and only my flannels. It felt good to get rid of the heavy outer layers, but now I'm feeling naughty. I wish we'd just stumbled in kissing and I didn't have to sit out here and second guess myself.

Me to Paisley: A guy I met. Vacationer. 🫠

Me to Claire: Already left. Sorry! See you tomorrow?

A text comes through.

Paisley: Woo hoo! Holiday fling! Have fun girl! 🥒🍑

Me: 🫠

Paisley: Have fun! 🎉 *Like my grams says, you're only young once! Merry Christmas to you!*

Yes, indeed. Merry Christmas to me. The weight of my recent decisions has crushed all remnants of the Kate I once was. And for what? This is the new leaf I supposedly turned over. What's the point of life redirects if nothing changes? This next year, I am going to enjoy life, and that starts now. What's the point in waiting until New Year's Day?

"Would you like another hot chocolate? Or water?" Oliver shuffles into the living area and waffles between the small kitchen and the sofa. He's wearing a form-fitting athletic shirt and black flannel bottoms, and he truly looks delicious.

"Water would be great."

The buzz from our earlier alcoholic beverages permeates my cheeks and blurs the edges of the room. But nerves fray my peaceful, happy state. The high altitude and frigid temperatures require hydration, and I know this, so I down about half the bottle in several gulps.

He plops down on the sofa beside me and kicks his socked feet up on the coffee table. Thick gray cotton socks have replaced his ski socks, and they climb almost up to the bottom curve of his calf.

Behind the sofa is a separate bedroom area with a looming king-size bed and crisp white comforter. The curtains on the window are open, and outside the lights along the ski lift twinkle in the otherwise dark, snowy night.

"Your feet sore?" Oliver's left-field question draws me back into the room.

"A little. I'm pretty used to my ski boots, though."

"Kick 'em up here." Oliver presses his back against the sofa and taps his thigh, asking for my throbbing socked feet. Most of the guys from my past would've moved on to the next step the moment the hotel room door closed. And there's definitely a part of me that wishes for that heated, mindless rush.

"Right here," he repeats, tapping his thigh again.

"You're offering to massage my feet?"

"You're a quick one, aren't ya, darlin'?"

I swivel so my back is against the side of the sofa, and my feet land on top of his thigh. He presses his thumb into my arch, and I lurch forward.

"Ow."

"Less pressure?"

With a lighter touch, the heel of his hand kneads the sore area. Warmth permeates the bottom of my foot, and I slowly relax back against the sofa. He kneads the knots away, and the comforting sensation travels up my ankle, calves, and thighs. I tilt my head back and close my eyes. A moan escapes, and my eyes flutter open.

Whiskey eyes pour over me, the corner of his lips turned up in clear amusement.

"You like that?" He's worked through the initial soreness, and my limbs are now transitioning into loose, satisfied extensions.

"So much."

"Yeah?" That slow, deep drawl does things to me. It's suggestive and teasing and wraps around me.

"It's better than sex." Heat rises in my cheeks, and I bite back a giggle as his eyebrows raise in mock dramatic shock.

"If you think this is better than sex, then you haven't been doing it right, darlin'."

The flames flicker orange in the fireplace, and I sigh in contentment. The quiet of his hotel is so much more relaxing than the raucous noise of the Mangy Moose.

"How long are you here?" Most vacationers flying in stay for anywhere from five to seven days.

"I head back on the twenty-ninth."

"And you're not staying with your friend?" It didn't sound like Drew lived too far away.

"Nah, he's married. It's Christmas. They've got stuff to do."

I didn't notice a wedding band on Drew's finger, but I also wasn't looking. No, I'd only been looking at the man sitting beside me with a tousled helmet head mix of chocolate, caramel, and honey-colored strands. His southern drawl and half-cocked smile, and whiskey-brown eyes pulled me right in—well, along with the alcohol. His weathered tan skin speaks to years outside in the sun, which makes me wonder exactly what he does when he's not on vacation.

"Tell me about yourself, Oliver."

"What would you like to know?" He digs a thumb into my arch, and I squirm and stifle a moan.

"Last name."

"Duke."

"Where are you from, Oliver Duke?"

"Texas." He's got the swagger and the drawl. "Outside Austin. Ever been?"

I shake my head then reconsider. "Well, I might have had a connection in Dallas once or twice. That airport is enormous. No snow in Texas, right?"

"Not much to speak of. And the tiniest bit causes all hell to break loose."

"What's going on outside would—"

"End the world." He drops my foot and waves his hands for comedic effect. "Electricity would frazzle. Cars would crash. Empty shelves in the grocery store. End. Of. Days."

We grin at each other as he switches to my other foot.

"Tell me about Vermont. You said you grew up skiing?"

"And boarding. Did it all."

"And then?"

"Went to college at the University of Vermont." A satisfied sigh escapes. The relaxation permeating my body softens this next admission. "Moved here this past fall. Where'd you go to school?"

"University of Texas." He smiles his wide smile that wrinkles the corners of his eyes. "Best school on the planet. Go, Longhorns."

I'd rather not talk about college. I glance around the room, looking anywhere but at the hot, sexy Texan blissing me out with his handiwork. This hotel is probably the nicest hotel I've ever been in. And it must cost a fortune.

"Do you visit Drew often?"

"First time, other than his wedding a couple of years ago. That's how I knew about this place. When my plans changed, I called, and they had a cancellation. All these places sell out over the holidays, but there's usually at least one cancellation. It's a traveler's secret." He winks at me, and I swear that wink travels to my clit.

"Did they give you a deal because of the cancellation?" I've never researched the cost of a hotel at The Four Seasons. Given technically I can't afford the cheapest beer on tap, it goes without saying a night here isn't within my means.

"Nah. I don't think they give discounts. But when you get to my age, a good hotel ranks as worth it."

"An old man, are you?" He smirks and moves up to my ankles and calves. I scoot down so he doesn't have to reach. He doesn't offer more, but now I have to ask. "How old are you?"

"Thirty-five in January." His hand wanders higher up my calf near my knee.

"Wow."

"Wow." He jerks on my leg, and I laugh. "You don't say 'wow' when someone tells you their age. How old are you?"

"Old enough." My cheek muscles burn from the width of my grin.

"What kind of answer is that? If you mean you are legal…" His brow wrinkles. "You're older than eighteen?" His jaw drops. "You have to be. You said you went to college."

I laugh at the dismay written all over his face. I'm pretty certain if I answer eighteen or even nineteen, I'll be escorted out of the hotel in a hot second.

"Yeah. I'm twenty-four," I go ahead and share to settle his consternation. "I'll be twenty-five soon."

"You know what they say, don't you?"

"About what?"

"You have until twenty-five to do something crazy. Then it's all downhill from there."

"I'm a skier. I live for downhill." My bravado laugh might be as much for my benefit as his. My life isn't exactly following the path I expected, but I do my best to not dwell on it. I have a plan. He kneads the muscle on the side of my knee, and I jerk, lifting my leg so his hands are lower.

"Does that hurt?"

"Sore ITB band."

"You should roll it."

"I do." Sometimes. I hate rolling it. Hurts like hell.

"Do you do the forever winter thing?" I tilt my head, questioning, although I suspect I know what he's referring to. "Australia next season?"

"No. I'll be here in the summer." Only the wealthiest and most well-sponsored athletes can compete year-round. My brother doesn't even get to do the Australia circuit every year.

"What'll you do?"

"Oh, I don't know. Work at a golf course? Something outdoors." I'll be doing everything I can to get hired for ski patrol, but he doesn't need the details.

"I'm the same way. If given a choice, I'm outside."

"You look like it. You've got that weathered tan. What do you do?"

"Ranch work."

"A cowboy, huh?"

"Something like that." He tugs on the end of my sock and pulls. It glides off. Cool air wraps around my skin. Then he repeats the action. His gaze travels up my body, and my skin heats. "God, you are scrumptious."

He takes my fingers and toys with them. The pad of his finger traces the ends of my short nail, but his heated gaze stays locked on me, warming me more thoroughly than the nearby fire. He shifts and leans over me, one hand braced on each side of my body. My thighs spread, making room for him to rest. He holds himself above me in a plank position, and time slows.

He scans my face. I reach up for him, and my fingers weave through that mess of hair. His lips brush across mine, and his breath flutters over my skin. My fingers roam the curves of his corded, flexed biceps. His mouth covers mine, and this time, his tongue flicks across my lower lip. I open for him, and his body lowers, creating much-needed pressure over my core, and my hips buck up into him as our tongues explore in a slow sensuous rhythm. Mint with a hint of chocolate combine.

This kiss is so much more than a kiss. A thin layer of cotton covers us from our wrists to our ankles. An extremely thin layer reveals every curve, every hard and soft inch. We might as well be naked. Bared to each other. There's no doubt where this kiss will lead.

His hips rock and press back and forth, ratcheting up an instinctual need. I tug on the bottom of his shirt and skim his smooth, firm stomach. The cotton bunches as I continue moving forward across the plains of his chest. There's a light fuzz of hair, and I scratch my nails through it. I feel the rise of his nipple and pinch. He breaks our kiss. We're both panting, sucking in oxygen.

"Bed." He says it like a command. But he lifts, and cool air breaches the chasm. Am I really doing this? A one-night stand? The unnerving thought hits like a spray of sleet.

"I don't know your middle name." It's a weird thing to say, but it's what comes to mind.

"It's Carson." He grins a slow grin and presses his lips against mine.

The press of his lips is electric, and my hips rock forward.

"What's yours?" The tip of his nose brushes against mine, and I exhale. The top layer of worry disseminates as visceral reactions overtake thought.

"Hannah."

"Kate Hannah?" There's the sexy half-smile.

"Katherine Hannah."

"Oakley." He breathes out my last name in a way that makes it sound better than it ever has.

I tug his head down and kiss him with abandon, throwing caution to the wind. I'm twenty-four and still have time to be stupid and crazy. Cool air surrounds my back. He groans, and I giggle.

"I can walk."

He stumbles, and I squeal. His hand slaps my ass, and he picks up his pace. He tosses me down on the bed, and I bounce on the comforter.

"Well, now that we've got the middle name thing out of the way." He gives me the absolute sexiest, most panty-melting grin. I swear my panties go from damp to dripping. How lucky am I? A sexy Texan cowboy. This is one experience I must journal about so I never ever forget it.

He grips my waistband and tugs. My ass rises off the bed a few inches as my flannels and my panties leave my body and find their way to the floor. He stands and soaks in my thighs appreciatively. I sit up and pull off my top, revealing a jog bra. There's no way to take it off in a sexy way, but I go ahead and remove the breast flattener. I toss it past him to the spot on the floor where the rest of my clothes lie.

By the time I've gotten the jog bra over my head, he's removed his shirt, and I gawk at his lean muscles. It's the kind of corded muscle earned with an active lifestyle. The weathered tan skin on his chest and shoulders is lighter than his arms, neck, and face. Somehow, he wears the farmer's tan well.

He reaches forward, behind my neck, and clasps my braid. With one hand, he undoes the band.

"Loosen that." He stands above me like a lord or master.

My fingers unravel the wavy strands.

"You." He swallows, and I cover one breast with my arm. "Gorgeous." He blinks. "Fuck. Lean back."

I do as he says, leaning against the stacked pillows. He climbs up on the bed, and my lungs cease functioning. It's as if his dark gaze has simultaneously sucked the oxygen out of my lungs and halted my bodily functions. He spreads my legs, and his fingers lightly graze my inner thighs. He bends before me, and his lips follow the path his fingers blazed all the way to my exposed and needy pussy.

I watch, mesmerized, as the tip of his nose hovers above me. He bows, and his soft, warm tongue dips in. His palms press against my thighs, creating more room, and his tongue traces my seam. My hips buck.

What I want is him. Foreplay can be nice, but a need burns to have him deep inside me, filling me up, and his tongue is merely serving to tease. And what he's doing also threads the line on a deeper intimacy.

As if sensing my unease, his finger penetrates me, and he presses down harder, his tongue circling my most sensitive nub. My thigh muscles tighten and quiver. Any uneasiness melts away.

"Please," I gasp.

A second finger stretches me, and he thrusts them in just the way I need. His teeth graze against me as his tongue works me over. I lean forward, reaching for his waistband. I want to tug him up, but he pushes me back.

"Nuh-uh," he grumbles. And then he attacks me with his tongue and fingers like this is his life's work. My thighs squeeze against his ears, my hips rise, my back muscles tighten, and all of my muscles quiver.

"Fuuuck," comes out of my mouth as I gasp for air and the room goes momentarily black. "Oli—" His name is too fucking long. I might not be able to say it, but it's one I will never forget.

When the room returns and I am panting against the pillow, his grin comes into view.

"That was sexy as hell."

Then he gets up off the bed, reaches for a wallet, takes out a condom, and tosses it on the bed beside me. He removes the remainder of his clothes within seconds. His erection salutes me, and as he returns to the bed, I reach for it. Pre-cum covers his tip, and I smear it with my thumb. Then I take my thumb and taste.

"Fuck, Katie girl, you're going to be the death of me."

He grabs the condom and bites the corner of the wrapper as I grip his shaft, moving up and down. He bats my hand out of the way and rolls a condom down.

"I need inside you."

I only nod. After what he just did with his tongue, he's earned it. Hell, I need him.

He hovers over me and blinks. He reaches down, and his palm slaps the side of my thigh.

"On your knees."

I scramble onto my knees, thrust my ass out at him, and look over my shoulder. My hair pools onto the comforter.

"Like this?"

"Fuck," he grits out, his hand gripping his covered cock. "Just like this."

He positions his tip at my entrance, and I rock back, ready for him, eager. His palm circles the side of my ass. Rough callouses graze sensitive skin, and I arch my spine. I'm on the verge of whimpering, pleading for him to stop with the teasing and hesitation. His palm slaps hard. The sound echoes in the room, and with one thrust, he fills me.

"Fuuuck," he says and stills. I need him to move, and I rock back.

That palm slaps again. My throat stretches as my head snaps back at the crisp sound.

"Still. Give me a minute. Fuck. You are tight. And wet. So fucking..."

I can't wait. I inch forward, then back, begging him to move. He grabs a fistful of my hair, my back dips, and my chest angles out. Fingers massage my tits and pinch my nipples. The tug on my scalp burns. The added sensation threatens sensory overload. And then he moves. Hard thrusts, pounding into me, and I rock back, matching his beat.

His thighs slap against me over and over, and I push back on my arms. My muscles clench, and I lower onto my forearms. He abandons my nipples and finds my sensitized mound and kneads it, circling over the pulsing nub as he hits deep within me.

It's wild, and it's crazy, and it's absolute insanity to be doing this, and it's also fucking awesome. My muscles seize. His hips buck into me, losing rhythm. Deep inside me, he pulses as I quiver.

"Fuck," he breathes out. I collapse, and he falls over me.

"Damn, girl. You are something."

I chuckle. "I hope they don't charge you extra for what we did to this comforter."

"If they do, it's worth it."

He trails kisses along my shoulder and back. The distinct smell of sex fills the air. The stretch of my bladder reminds me that there are less sexy things that need to be taken care of, and I make my way to the bathroom. When I open the door, I scan the floor for my clothes.

He slips by me for his turn. When the toilet flushes and the door opens, I'm fully dressed, hopping as I pull on my last sock.

"Whoa. Where do you think you're going, missy?"

"I have to work tomorrow." I didn't think he'd want me to stay.

"Where do you live?"

"Not far. About a mile away."

"Then stay." My disbelief must be transparent. "There's a snowstorm outside. Stay."

The bulk of the storm should pass in the early hours of the morning. And tomorrow will be mayhem as everyone rushes to get their powder time. If I were on ski patrol, I'd be the first one out. But that's not me...yet.

He pulls back the comforters and lifts the hem of my top and tugs, forcing me to raise my arms. The top hits the floor, and he bends and presses his lips to my breast. Then he swirls his tongue around my nipple. It tickles, and I bite back a laugh. He bends and removes my flannel bottoms, patiently waiting at my feet for me to step each leg free.

In the bed, he pulls me up against him. It's warm and cozy. The wind howls past the window. The wind, the strange bed, and the late-night surge of adrenaline combine to chase away sleep. Oliver's breathing evens out, and his arms loosen around me. The time on my watch shows it's after midnight. There's no way I'll sleep in this strange bed, and tomorrow I have a full day of work.

With the stealth I once used to sneak out of the house in high school, I gather my clothes and carry them as far away from the bedroom area as possible to the entry door near my ski boots. I dress and carry all my ski paraphernalia out into the hotel hallway. In the corridor, I force my heated ski boots on and freeze all the way home.

Kate

December 24

"Merry Christmas!" I shout for the umpteenth time over the course of the day. The stitching on the discount Santa hat itches, and my eyelids droop with the weight of exhaustion.

Thoughts of the night before have circled my head all day, and a goofy Looney Tunes perma-grin has been planted on my face. His deep drawl has been on constant mental replay, mixing in with *Jingle Bells* and *Last Christmas* and all the upbeat holiday pop songs. Flashbacks from last night periodically heat me from within, and a random daydream overrides the cash register at unexpected moments. The fantasy that has populated my overactive imagination is of Oliver riding along on a horse, wearing a cowboy hat, jeans, and no shirt. There's a stick of grass hanging out of the corner of his lips, and he flashes that sexy grin. *Gah. I hope I never forget him.*

It's Christmas Eve, and everyone's smiles are bigger, so my omnipresent smile fits right in. There hasn't been a single irate guest all day. It could be the Christmas magic in the air. It could also be the two feet of powder at the top of the mountain. A snow dump like that is pretty much the skier equivalent of winning the lottery on vacation, especially early in the season.

One might think we'd close early on Christmas Eve, but we won't. We do, however, get to open a full hour late on Christmas Day, and our boss has claimed a hospitality room at a nearby hotel restaurant for an employee holiday party this evening. Almost all of us are away from our families. It's the busiest week of the year, and not working isn't an option. Mom isn't so happy about it, but it's just one Christmas. There will be more.

Paisley enters the shop and promptly stomps snow off her boots. We have a big mat near the door that remains permanently damp and nasty because everyone does exactly what she's doing. We close in five minutes, and at the moment, there are no customers, so I leave my station behind the register to preempt her from embarrassing me by shouting a question about last night.

I love her to death, but she's loud and possesses a subpar filter. Paisley is younger than I am and just out of college. She's doing a hospitality internship and currently works as a cashier at one of the Jackson Resort spas. But before she finishes her internship, she'll work in several businesses within the resort.

Her straight blonde hair practically glitters under the lights. Because she works in hospitality, she always sports perfect, blown-out hair. Those of us who work on the mountain don't bother. We all wear helmets. Primped hair and helmets don't mix. The most I do is braid my hair.

"Tell me." She beams.

My cheeks warm, and I glance around the shop. I'm the only female working here, and while the guys carry on about their sex lives like they are up for medals, my preference is to keep my adventures under wraps.

"Was it good?" She grins and playfully elbows me, and her mouth drops close to my ear. "Did you get the Big O?"

"Would you hush?"

The guys I work with are behind the counter, double-checking the organization of the ski boots to prep for the morning rush. They show zero interest in what Paisley is going on about. The lifts closed two hours ago, and we're all ready to close up shop. At this stage of the day, we're wasting time as we clock gaze, wishing for the minutes to drip quickly.

My phone vibrates, and I tug it out of my back jeans pocket. I'm expecting a text from my family because it's Christmas Eve, and we normally spend the day making cookies and playing board games. But the text isn't from anyone I know. It's from an unknown number.

> Unknown: Merry Christmas Eve! Hope you don't
> mind I'm texting. Ran into Nash on the slopes,
> and he gave me your number. What are you up to?

Paisley reads the text over my shoulder. She's taller than I am and grins down at me with irrational excitement.

"Is that last night calling?"

I let out a sigh and shove the phone back into my pocket.

"It is. Walk with me to the register. I have to close it down, and then we can go."

Paisley is my plus-one to the shop holiday party. Not that anyone will be monitoring attendance. My boss, Harvey, is a pretty laid-back guy with an anything-goes attitude. He's fully aware that I'm here with the goal of getting a job with ski patrol, and he's one hundred percent okay with that. He says he knows when he hires young kids they will not be lifers. For my part, I like that I'm almost twenty-five and he calls me a kid.

Another text comes through, and after I close down the register, I surreptitiously check it while I'm grabbing my coat.

Unknown: *Oh, this is Oliver. The guy from last night.*
Unknown: *Oliver Carson Duke*

Paisley grins and wiggles her eyebrows.

"Oliver. I like that name."

"He's from Texas. He's leaving in a few days." I shove my phone into a coat pocket.

"So? Who cares? It's a fling. Have fun. Enjoy it. And trust me, you hit the jackpot. Not sure if you've noticed, but mostly couples vacation here. And the hard-core boarders and skiers are..." She twists her hand back and forth, giving a so-so hand signal.

I laugh. I get it. My brother and his friends are an unruly crew, as are a lot of the guys who live for sport.

"Stoners who never want to grow up." She expands on her hand-waffling sentiment. I shrug, and my perma-smile miraculously remains in place, even with her insult to my brother and his kind.

As I tug on my coat, the sting of her comment settles into my chest. Paisley sounds too much like my mother. While Mom supports Hudson, she lets everyone know she'd prefer he choose a real career. When it comes to my goal of wearing the red snowsuit, she doesn't remotely support it.

A refusal to grow up? That's bullshit. Life's short. This is spending your days doing what you want to do. And not getting stuck behind a desk or spending decades soaking up fluorescent lighting with a shit boss.

Harvey holds the door for us, and we all trudge across the snow to the hotel. Several walkways in the resort area are heated, but the temperature dips so low in Wyoming that at times even the heated walkways are still coated in slippery ice. All of us have our facemasks pulled up and gloves on to protect from the frigid, icy wind, and we half-stomp to avoid wiping out on an ice patch.

They expect another system tonight but are only forecasting a few inches. We expect another big dump in a couple of days. That one has everyone humming. It's an enormous system coming through near New Year's that portends mind-blowing conditions on the mountain. It'll snarl travel, but when you live on the mountain, that's not a concern.

Inside the doorway, we all begin the process of unbundling. Gloves first, then throat and facemask, then coat. Paisley strikes up a conversation with Harvey, and I follow them both into the banquet room. There is a bar set up in each corner of the room, a Christmas tree with multicolored lights and red balls all over it, and a center table with an assortment of food. There's also a big sheet cake with "Merry Christmas" scrawled in icing with an image of a Santa Claus snowboarding. *Walking in a Winter Wonderland* sifts through the speakers in the ceiling.

I spot Bill Woodland, the director of Jackson Resorts ski patrol, standing in a corner alone. I've met him once before, briefly, when I first came in hoping to interview. His secretary handed me a list of requirements for the role and smiled as she told me to come back when I was qualified. He half nodded at me as his secretary told me his name and role.

His brother, Harvey, is worlds friendlier. After doing my homework, I sought the job at one of Harvey's businesses, hoping for a reference that would help me with next year's application process. Harvey owns two rental shops, a storage building, and a tubing facility just outside of Jackson.

The two men couldn't be more different. Or, at least, that's how it appears when I've seen Bill out on the mountain. He's always stern, whereas Harvey is almost always smiling and laughing. Of course, there are no life-and-death matters in Harvey's world. The safety of thousands of visitors falls under Bill's jurisdiction. Deaths on the mountain are rare, but they happen.

"Go over and talk to him. He's not going to bite." Paisley has a small plate in hand loaded up with carrots, bell pepper slices, and ranch dressing.

"I don't think he likes me."

"Does he know you?"

The surly man surveys the room with a beer bottle in hand. I'm surprised members of the ski patrol aren't here at the party, but a lot of the patrollers have families, even kids. Christmas Eve is probably spent back home.

Almost all the patrollers are men. The physical job requires strength. It's open to women, and there have been women in the ranks, but the physical requirements are daunting. It's why I go to the gym and lift weights every other day. As it stands, I couldn't maneuver a toboggan down the steeper areas. We have areas a snowmobile can't go safely, so it comes down to one skilled skier to get the injured down. Skill is a definite requirement, but so is strength. I'm working on it.

"Go on over. No one likes standing alone. Introduce yourself." She gives an exasperated sigh. "You need me to hold your hand?"

She tugs me over. I don't have a beer or food or anything to occupy my hands. Bill is in his fifties. Both Bill and his brother sport shaved heads, but Bill has a long beard that gives him a mountain man aesthetic. With a little white and a pillow under his flannel, he could fill in for a Santa. As it is, his steel gray beard and thick mustache build a gruff, intimidating exterior.

"Hi. You're Bill Woodland, right?" Paisley asks. He lowers his beer and looks down at us. He's a big man. Bigger than his brother and no doubt stronger.

"Yes, ma'am." He doesn't smile. His dark eyes size us up, probably wondering why two twenty-something girls are coming by to chat. He clinks his wedding band against the glass bottle in his hand. It could be out of habit. It could also be to warn us away. *Lovely.*

"Hi. I met you before. At your office. I'm Kate Oakley. I'm planning to apply for ski patrol next season."

His bushy eyebrows lower, and his eyes squint. "You're Hudson Oakley's sister, right?"

"I am." I smile, and my heels leave the floor, which probably makes me look like a goofy teen.

"Why not ski school?"

"Ah..." My brain malfunctions. I fumble for an answer, bouncing from saving people, like my mother the doctor, to spending days outside. Ski patrol is the hardest job on the mountain, but it has perks. "You get the first morning runs. Before anyone has marred the snow."

I look up at him, hopeful my response works. It's the biggest truth I have. I'm going to get the same breathtaking photographs that Hudson gets. I'll do videos too. To me, ski patrol is both a badge of honor and an enviable life. It's the pinnacle. The ski patrol life is huge. Big enough to justify all my decisions.

He chugs his beer. When he lowers his beer, he says, "Good luck," and steps away.

"That didn't go well," I say to Paisley.

"I don't know why you want ski patrol. I think that job sucks. You have to go out in all kinds of weather, and it's a lot of shit grunt work."

"Yesterday you told me you spent the day dusting." For someone who plans to kiss asses for her entire career, she's not really in a great position to throw darts at my career choice.

"Well, yeah. I'm starting out. But in hospitality, I can move to cities that don't require snow tires and plastic bags over the side-view mirror at night."

"Let's get a drink."

I head over to the beer and wine bar. The other bar is for hot toddies.

As a Vermont girl, cold weather doesn't faze me. But we did have a garage growing up. And, unfortunately, it might be years before I can afford a place out here with a garage, so those plastic bags over the side view? Yep, I need to remember to add those to my car.

My phone vibrates against my butt cheek. It's pretty late on the East Coast, but just in case, I check it. There's a photo of a hot chocolate drink stacked with square marshmallows.

> Unknown: Handcrafted mallows. You can't say no to this, can you? I'm lonely. It's Christmas. Come join me.

"Is he at the Four Seasons?" Paisley asks. I'm not sure how to decipher her open mouth and wide eyes.

"Yeah."

She grips my arm and shoves me out of line. "Are you an idiot? Go. Better food and drinks."

I scan the party. The room is emptying out. The Christmas Eve party seems to be more of a 'stop in and say hello' soiree rather than a full 'let's spend time together' party. I imagine many of our colleagues have family to spend time with. And for those of us who don't, it might be Christmas Eve, but when you have another full day of work on Christmas Day, it's just another weekday.

"What are you going to do?"

"I'm headed to my sister's tonight, remember? My parents are staying at her place. After brunch I'll drive back in."

"You're working tomorrow afternoon, right?"

"Yep. Double pay!"

That is the one fantastic thing about working Christmas. Holiday bonus pay.

A group of loud guys laughs, drawing my attention. Harvey is with them, and the white ball on the end of his green elf hat bounces around as he rocks back and forth, laughing hard. The TV on the wall plays a collection of cannonballs off the mountain. Fun times. If I stand around long enough, Hudson will probably appear. He's a legend of sorts and has a role in most of these indie films.

My phone vibrates again. I check it, but it's not a text. Oliver is calling.

"Hey," I answer.

"You're not gonna half-night stand me, are you? It's Christmas."

Oliver

December 25

There's a woman in my bed. Her dark hair fans out behind her, and when I roll closer, I pick up a faint trace of mint. The sheet covers us both to our waists. My gaze traces the slope from her chest, down her waistline, and up to her hip, over her tight ass and down her thighs. Her ribcage expands and contracts as she softly breathes, deep in sleep.

Out the window, snowflakes fall. It's a light snow, most likely remnants of the system they expected to come through last night. It's supposed to clear out early, but it makes for one picturesque, movie-worthy Christmas morning. And she's sleeping through it.

Last night, Kate declined dinner, claiming she'd already eaten. Yet by our third drink, her eyelids were half closed and her words got the slurs. If she really did eat dinner, then she's a lightweight. We made out in the elevator and fucked like rabbits the second we entered the hotel room. Afterwards, she curled up on the sofa while I dug out some Kahlua for another round of Christmas Eve spirits. By the time I got the drinks mixed, she'd fallen asleep.

With the fire roaring, it wasn't a bad Christmas Eve at all. I put the drinks away, curled up behind her and watched her sleep. She didn't get much sleep the night before, and then she worked all day. So, youthful or not, cliff-jumper or not, she was tired. I scooped her up and brought her to bed, and she slept the whole night through.

She rolls onto her back, and the right side of her body lands against mine. She stretches out an arm, and it crosses over my stomach. Her skin warms mine in every place she touches. Her nipples point upward, firm and erect. I curve my fingers around her breast, caressing her. My morning wood throbs, on the verge of painful.

I'd like to roll her back onto her side and slide into the warmth I couldn't stop thinking about yesterday. Yeah, I should have taken her departure in the middle of the night without a note or a phone number as *hasta la vista*. But when I saw her friend out teaching a couple of kids, it felt like divine intervention. Like the gods above blazed a path for us to reconnect.

Her head lolls onto my shoulder, and I skim the smooth, flat planes of her stomach, over the dip of her belly button, to the line of the sheet. Those long lashes flutter. Her lips curve up.

"Morning," she mumbles.

"Merry Christmas," I drawl. "If you've been dreaming of a white one, your wish came true." I twitch my head in the window's direction.

"Hmmm." She stretches as she hums, and the vibration filters through my ribcage and down to my groin.

I press my lips to the side of her neck. She clasps my painfully erect dick through the sheet. I close my eyes and send gratitude out into the ether because that is exactly what I want.

"A very good morning, indeed." She lifts the sheet, and her warm fingers greet me, and a deep groan of gratitude rips out of me. Her grip is fucking perfect. "Did I fall asleep on you?"

"Ah, yes, you did." Her thumb circles my tip, spreading my pre-cum, and I swallow hard. "Hope you don't mind. I moved you to my bed."

She shifts down the bed. Her dark hair trails along my side. Dark chocolate eyes gaze up at me. Her warm, wet tongue laps my cock, and my hips thrust up. Fuck. I gather her hair out of the way of her mouth. Those full lips open wide and take me in. The sight of those lips swallowing me is enough to almost get me off all on its own. Merry Christmas to me.

The urge to shove her down and take control has the arm holding her hair quivering from restraint. Her cheeks hollow as she sucks, moving up and down. I'm getting closer. My lower back muscles clench.

"Jesus," I praise. "So fucking good."

My balls tighten. I watch, mesmerized, desperate to let this continue as long as fucking possible. But I can't.

"Close," I grit out.

Her hand replaces her mouth. I could whimper.

"Condom?"

I look to the side table, and she reaches over me. Cool air circles my abandoned dick. Her soft breasts graze my chest as she pulls back, having retrieved what she wants. She rips the condom packet with her teeth. *Hot. Damn.*

Mesmerized, I stare as she glides the condom down my length, then swings a thigh over me, positions me at her entrance, and takes me. *Holy fuck.*

"That's it, baby. Ride me."

That dark hair falls over her shoulders. Her perky breasts peek through the strands. And those rich chocolate eyes lift from watching us join, to locking on me. Her palms flatten on my chest, and she rocks over me, up and down, warm and tight. She's every man's wet dream.

"Fuck. Talk about being on Santa's good list. I must have done something fantastic last year."

She grins, but then her face transforms into one of focus as her hips flex against me. Her teeth sink into that lower lip, and she tilts her head back. I take the cue and thrust my hips up, hitting her right where it must feel good. My thumb massages her apex, adding pressure with each downward thrust.

Little noises escape from her mouth, and her pace quickens. Her chest lowers closer to mine, and I grip her hips, guiding her, helping with the pace. She quivers and her hips still. She cinches me, her muscles tightening and loosening, fucking milking me, and I hold her tight, as tight to me as possible as my release follows hers.

She collapses onto me, breathing heavily. Some of her hair falls into my mouth, and I blow it away. My hands roam her back and, I grip her close. Fuck, that was amazing. A damn good way to wake up.

She pulls herself off me with a groan and heads into the bathroom. My phone vibrates on the side table. I can see it's my parents calling, but given I've got a used condom on my dick, I decide to hold on answering that call.

The toilet flushes, and I call out, "There's an extra toothbrush and toothpaste if you need it. It's in one of those drawers." The sink turns on, and I sit up.

My phone vibrates again. It's my brother Sam. Not taking that call, either.

A text comes through from Maggie, my brother from another mother's wife. Jason leaves all social calls to Maggie. The photo she texted shows their kid in Jason's arms, and Jason is wearing striped pajamas that match his kid's, and I'd bet also match Maggie's. I plan to mock him sufficiently.

But first, I need a bathroom, a toothbrush, and coffee.

When I exit the bathroom, Kate is dressed and by the coffeemaker in the kitchenette.

"How do you take your coffee?" she asks.

"One sugar pack." She nods, and my phone vibrates again.

Here's the thing about the Dukes. They are not gonna stop.

"Mind if I take this?"

"Go ahead." She glances over her shoulder with a soft smile. Her skin is flushed, alive, her hair in tangles, and I'm struck by how beautiful she is, how natural. My ex also had a natural beauty, but it was a rare thing to see because she rarely came out of the bathroom without her face on, as she called it.

Kate returns to watching the coffee shoot out of the coffeemaker, and I suck in a breath and press accept.

"Merry Christmas!" A chorus of the same sentiment echoes through the background. "Did you think we were going to let you sleep in?" My brother's face fills the phone screen, and while he has yet to shave, he looks wide awake.

"Never." I chuckle at Sam's shit-eating grin. But this call isn't about Sam and me. "Was Santa good to you guys?" My question goes out into the ether.

The phone screen jerks up and down, and I hear my niece screaming, "Uncle Ollie!"

"I take it the hand, foot, and mouth disease is under control?"

"Can you tell?" Sam's wearing a long sleeve T-shirt with a Vineyard Vines logo, and I'd bet he's got on matching flannels. A little less Ralph Lauren than I'd expect of my sister-in-law, but they are on a ski vacation.

"Merry Christmas, Ollie," my sister-in-law Olivia says from somewhere in the room.

"Merry Christmas to all of you." I say it louder than I probably need to, but my view is a closeup of my brother's nose, and I don't have a good sense of how close everyone is to the phone.

"Hey, you mind if we switch to Zoom? Mom and Dad want to see what Santa brought the kids."

"That's fine. Let's get it done." I get up to find my laptop. "Ian's with Mom and Dad, right?"

Given the disease outbreak with Sam's kids, my parents stayed back home. I tried to get Ian, our youngest brother, to come to Jackson with me, but he begged out. He's one busy bastard. Both of my brothers are serious workaholics.

"Pretty sure he's with Mom and Dad," Sam says. "Hold...okay... sent you the link."

Olivia's voice comes across the line, but she's not in view. "Your mom said he got in yesterday. He's there."

I click the link and go through the motions until I see a different closeup of Sam's face.

"Okay. I'm on."

"Here. I'll get the others," Sam says as my adorable niece crawls on the sofa and sticks her face close to the laptop.

"Uncle Ollie, was Santa good to you?"

I catch Kate's brown eyes and grin. "Yeah, I'd say he was pretty stellar."

"What did you get?"

I choke on my coffee because my four-year-old niece has stumped me. Thankfully, my pre-coffee brain doesn't have to come up with a PG answer because my niece takes charge.

"I got a car!"

"You got a what?" I ask.

A screen opens, and my parents appear, sitting tight together so they are in the same frame. Ian is nowhere to be seen, but I'm sure he's nearby. Then another screen opens, and it's Olivia and Sam. Apparently, they let my niece have her own camera. My two-year-old nephew toddles by with a life-size doll of Buzz Lightyear. He's repeating one word, as he tends to do. His word this morning is "Buzz."

A coffee is carefully placed in front of my laptop, and I reach for it. Kate stands to the side of the coffee table where I have my laptop perched. For a second, nerves strike. It would be no big deal to introduce them to my ski buddy, but it's early enough here on Christmas morning I'd raise eyebrows and some knowing snickers. And then, Jesus, Patty would be all over that like flies to honey.

Kate drops to her knees and crawls behind the sofa, remaining out of view of the camera. She's a smart one. That's what I should have expected. Hell, she pulled a half-night stand two nights ago.

She's choosing to live the ski bum life. And I am one lucky bastard to get to enjoy a little carefree holiday fling.

Another box opens on the Zoom call, and Jason and Maggie join in, and there's a chorus of greetings. I glance back and see Kate crouched down, carefully reaching on top of the bed, searching for something, unsure of where the camera frame ends and begins.

"Is someone there with you?" My bastard brother Ian's voice calls me out. So, he is with Mom and Dad.

"No. Just me. What did Santa bring you, Uncle Ian?"

"A lump of coal," he says, and that brings giggles from my niece, and a touch of annoyance flashes because my little bro stole my line.

Kate crawls all the way to the tile in front of the door. I angle the laptop toward the window, where it's snowing, and in the opposite direction from Kate.

"Can you guys see the snow?" I ask and jump out of the frame.

Sam and his family are at their place in Aspen, and their screen wobbles as someone scrambles to show the view out their window.

"It snowed here yesterday, but we might get snow later today, right, Daddy?"

I leave the laptop and my outside view and reach Kate right as her hand falls on the door handle. She's dressed for the cold. I loop my arm around her and run my nose along her neck and breathe her in, getting a lungful of delicious.

"See you later?" I whisper.

She pulls the door open with a bright smile and pushes against me, wiggling out of my grasp. "Merry Christmas," she mouths, and then she's off down the hall.

"How much longer are you there?" someone asks. I think it's Olivia.

"Just a few more days."

"You can come here for New Year's. All of you can," Olivia says. "The kids, as you can see, are apparently cured."

"Oliver can't. He's got a hot New Year's Eve date here in Austin."

I'd like to reach through the screen and give Ian a solid wedgie for dangling that carrot in front of Mom, but there's no need. The days when my brothers and I dominated Christmas morning are long gone. My eldest niece takes over by shouting, "Wanna see what I got for Christmas?"

The Duke family chaos show plays on my laptop with happy, bright voices talking on top of each other because the Dukes don't mute shit. A chill falls on my skin, and it hits me. My flannel pajama bottoms aren't quite enough, and I search out a thermal top and some socks. The snowflakes outside the window swirl with a gray overcast haze so thick I can't see the mountain that's a stone's throw away.

six

Kate

December 25

Christmas music plays through the speakers, and yes, it's actually Christmas Day, but on the mountain, it's just another day where people paid an exorbitant amount for ski lift tickets. I got called in as an emergency ski school fill-in, so here I am, shuffling between cheeseburger and taco lines.

Whatever gifts Santa carted to Wyoming have been shared, and all the kids have put that joy aside and set out for downhill thrills. As a kid, that's what we did, too. Admittedly, we were in Vermont, but pretty much every year we'd get something snow-oriented on Christmas morning. Some years it was just ski clothes, but other years Santa delivered snowboards or ski boots or new skis. No matter what fell off Santa's sleigh, we were on the mountain after lunch.

This morning my brother texted a photo of his brand-new snowboard gifted to him by our parents. My parents and I caught up as I trudged back to my apartment. Mom swore she had gifts that should have arrived yesterday, but she got a notice my package wouldn't

44

arrive until the twenty-seventh. I assured her it was absolutely fine, and they thanked me for the framed photographs I sent them.

Given my finances are strained these days, I got creative with the parental gifts this year. I went through old photographs and found some of my brother and me when we were young. The photo I picked is of Hudson beaming with a goofball jester hat. I'm gazing up at him, laughing. Laughter and Hudson go hand in hand.

"I forgot about that photo," my mom gushed. Hudson apparently spent the big bucks on them this year. He bought them both expensive watches and new ski sweaters and goggles. But he just signed a new sponsorship contract, so he can afford to splurge.

"Excuse me, sorry." The person I'm apologizing to leans forward and inches his chair up but never bothers to turn around as he's mid-conversation with the guy across the table.

The hot chocolate spills, and the heat singes my skin. Somehow, the hot chocolates, burgers, and chips remain on the tray as I squeeze through the narrow divide between chairs while clopping along in clunky ski boots. The tray clatters as it hits the table in front of my students.

We should be out skiing, but Charlotte informed me she is starving. Her parents made her ski all morning and didn't get her lunch. They thought ski school would provide lunch. And her parents are correct. On a full day of ski school, we offer lunch. On a half day, we plan for breaks. But Charlotte and her sister Catherine apparently hate skiing and have zero intention of doing jack until we feed them. These two are a living personification of all the reasons I have no interest in teaching ski school.

"Where's the whipped cream?"

"They're out," I lie.

"On Christmas?"

Two tables down, there's a hot chocolate with whipped cream in between helmets and gloves. There's no way Charlotte and Catherine will not catch sight of it, so I plaster on a fake smile and say, "I'll go check for you. Maybe I can work some Christmas magic."

"You doing ski school today?" One of the older instructors, I think his name is Stan, asks as he snags napkins from the dispenser.

"Substitute." I pick up a can of whipping cream and test it on a napkin. The can emits a fart-like whiz. Empty.

When Harvey came in after the morning rush and asked if I'd cover for an instructor who called in sick, my response had been a no-brainer. Ski school pays way better than my hourly rate at the ski rental place, and sometimes you get a fat tip. Given it's Christmas, as long as these two girls don't complain loudly when their parents come to pick them up in a few hours, I should make bank.

"Don't let them spend the whole time inside. Their parents will be pissed."

I offer Stan a half-smile and a nod. *Thanks, Stan.*

A force hits me on my back, and I career into the side of a trash can.

"Watch where you're going," a deep, gravelly voice says. I tilt my head, mouth half-open in disbelief.

Stan chuckles. "Merry Christmas."

I love the ski community. On the whole, it's a truly good one. But there are a few specials out there that grind my goat. A woman who looks as frazzled as I feel speeds toward us, and in her arms are six cans of whipped cream.

"Bless you," I tell her.

"It's a madhouse today," she says as she lifts the empties, testing them with a quick shake before tossing them in the trash.

With one full can of whipped cream secured, I return to my two students perched on the end of a long table with two other families sharing the space.

"Look what I found," I tell the girls.

"Now our hot chocolates are cold," Charlotte whines. She's eight years old, and her sister is six. They aren't bad girls, per se, but it's supremely clear if given a choice they wouldn't be spending Christmas afternoon perfecting their turns.

"How about this?" Both girls look up at me, waiting for my

proposition. "We ski down to the base, then go up one more time, then I'll take you for hot chocolate at the ski school. We have marshmallows there." And that's where they are supposed to break, anyway.

"I still want my whipped cream," Catherine says. "I don't care if it's cold."

I fill it all the way to the top, then add a small blob to the tip of her nose. She laughs, a full-on laugh accompanied by a Christmas-worthy smile.

"So, Catherine," I say as I spin a chair around and straddle it. "Did you know my name is also Katherine? Only I'm with a K."

"We've got the same name." She grins up at me, and I'm pretty sure I secured a friend.

That friendship scores a couple of hours of conflict-free skiing time. Catherine has the snowplow down by our third run, and Charlotte is testing parallel skiing. The system has cleared out, and blue skies are overhead. These two aren't anywhere near ready to head higher up the mountain, but I don't need to be up there to envision the spectacular view across the Tetons.

With thirty minutes left, Charlotte asks if she can take a little dip through a couple of trees. It's a green, and she can do it.

"Watch how I go through. Then you follow."

It's pretty self-explanatory, but I show them the best path through the winding turns. Then I wait. Catherine weaves through and throws her hands up in the air as she pops up the last little hill at the end of the trees. Then we wait for Charlotte.

She's standing there, poised as if it's a cliff. It reminds me of Oliver staring down Corbet's. This little novice trench winding through six trees isn't anything at all like the twenty-foot drop Oliver couldn't see down, but every drop bears subjective relativity. To Charlotte, this is her Corbet.

And I've been in her ski boots. My brother cascaded down everything and anything. I've been told I'm adventurous. I had a coach who used words like "gutsy" and "spitfire" to describe me. But I have a hitch. It's a delay. A split second of terror that rips through me. I always push forward, but that split second of self-preservation instinct kept me out of the competitive running my whole life. Prevented me from winning. Ripped any chance of living Hudson's life out of the realm of the possible. Ski patrol offers the closest thing I'll get.

"It's okay, Charlotte. You can do it. Do the pizza wedge if you need to."

"That's what I did," Catherine calls out helpfully, but there's a bit of shitty younger sister's glee coating her words. She's fully aware her older sister fears doing what she just did. I recognize that shit-eating look because my brother gave it to me all the time.

"You got this, Charlotte." There's no easy way for her to back away from this little trench. If she climbs about ten feet, she can change course and head down a wide-open green.

The fronts of her skis dip down, and she's off. Fast. *Way too fast.*

"Slow down. Pizza wedge!" I shout as she rises, catching air before dipping back down.

Her arms flail out. She screams. Her skis career off the path and slam into a tree. *Fuck.*

I unsnap my skis and take off as fast as one can in ski boots, which is, by any measure, not that fast. When I reach her, her face is soaked, and she's sobbing.

"Show me where it hurts."

The poor girl cries so hard she can't speak. I touch her arms and hands and don't get any reaction. No jerking back. But she's bawling. It's the bawl that kids do when they didn't sleep well the night before and exhaustion and fear and a sugar crash all collide.

Stan, the fellow ski instructor from earlier, watches the three of us approach. Catherine pizza wedges straight up to her waiting parents, but Charlotte howls. Heads turn to the bawling girl. Her mom can't get her arms around her quickly enough. I can't see past Stan's reflective goggles to see his eyes, but I feel the judgment. And worse, I see Judith, one of the top dogs in ski school, watching. I'll never be called in as a substitute again.

"Just be a ski school instructor," they say. "Ski school is way easier than ski patrol," they chant. Chalk it up to one more failure. One more of my skills that needs improving. Or no, scratch that. One more thing I suck at.

With Mr. Berryman's one-hundred-dollar bill in hand, an extremely generous tip given his daughter wouldn't stop crying, I head to the base. Harvey told me not to bother coming back to close up at the ski rental place, so I'm done for the day.

I need alcohol isn't an emotion I regularly feel, but today it's hitting me strong. I can't get out of my ski school jumper fast enough. With the outfit I wore to work at the ski rental place back on, I find my way to the Mangy Moose.

For some sick reason, I check Instagram on my walk down the slope. Hudson's video plays in my feed. A full three-sixty maneuver in the air off a pipe. It's a move I've never come close to achieving. One of my parents probably recorded the video. Actually, knowing my parents, they probably both taped it on their phones, then compared footage to see who had the best angle, and that's the one Hudson posted for his feed. Logos adorn his helmet, and he's wearing a Soloman jacket. Gotta keep the sponsors happy.

Inside the Mangy Moose, the après-ski crowd is at max capacity. There's a line out the door from the hostess stand for tables, but I locate a lone stool at the bar and claim it.

"Darlin', you look like you need a drink." The drawl wraps around me, and a little of the crap day slips into the past.

Oliver's sandy brown hair flops over his forehead, and his crooked grin brings out my smile. Those eyes are more topaz than brown, almost the color of bourbon. And I'd really like some bourbon about right now. He's holding a highball glass of the amber liquid, and I snag it and sip. The smooth, rich taste curls over my tongue, and I close my eyes, homing in on the velvety feel.

"Damn." I open my eyelids, and Oliver has his hand raised in the air, catching the bartender's attention. "She'll take a glass of her own."

"You don't want to share?" I offer him his glass back, but he holds his hand out, refusing.

"Aw, naw. I'm a sharer. But with you looking that fucking sexy when you sip Double Eagle, I'm buying you your own."

I relax my side against the bar so I can better see the good-looking guy standing before me, using his body to give us our own little ecosphere.

"I'd offer you my stool, but my legs are too tired."

"Psst. What do you take me for? A man who would take a woman's stool?" He brushes some of my hair back behind my ear and caresses my cheek as he does it. Exhaustion weighs me down, and I want to fall against him. "I've got a stool over there." He points to the farthest stool in a back corner. "Allowed me to keep an eye out for one particular girl who I thought might come by the Moose at the end of her shift."

"You got lucky," I tell him. He raises his eyebrows and smirks, misunderstanding me. "I don't always come here." I can't really afford drinks every day. "But today, it's Christmas."

My glass hasn't arrived yet, so I lift his again, swirl it, and sip. Damn, it's like dessert in a bottle.

"Tough day?"

Flashes of sticky hot chocolate and Charlotte's non-stop wailing come to mind. "Got called in to sub for ski school. Let's just say it was a reminder of all the reasons I want ski patrol and not ski school."

"Ah." The bartender slides my glass across the grimy wooden bar, and Oliver thanks him. Then his attention returns to me. He inches closer, and his long fingers curl around my thigh. He squeezes and kneads my quads. A moan erupts. Those muscles are sore after today's workout, and what he's doing feels divine.

"Spoiled kids?"

"Charlotte and Catherine with a C," I share. "But their dad tipped well, so there's that."

"Oh," he says suddenly and whips out his phone from a ski pants pocket. "That reminds me. I need to complete my contact information for you. Now your name is Katherine with K, I take it?"

"Why?" I drawl it out the way he likes to drawl out words.

"Just the way you said with a C. Figured you must be K. A hunch." He scrunches his nose. "My hunches are usually pretty good." My cheeks and toes warm under his sexy grin. Sitting on this stool is the most contented I've been since I woke up in his bed this morning. "And how do you spell Hannah and Oakley?"

"Oh, my god. We've been sleeping together, and you don't even know how to spell my name."

He waves his phone in my face. "But I'm getting it now. Spelling?"

My hand shields my eyes in mock embarrassment, but I answer him.

He flashes his phone to me. "Correct?"

"Yep."

"Birth date?"

"Why?"

"It's a field. Oh, and address. Put it all in there, baby."

I hesitate. He reaches up beneath my sweater, and his thumb flicks back and forth across my hip.

"You wanna become my pen pal?" My thumb grazes the rough growth along his jaw, and he dips his chin and playfully bites. The sensation travels through me more swiftly than the bourbon and goes straight to my center.

"Give me your deets, Kate. I wanna see you again."

"You visit frequently?"

He shrugs. "Stranger things have happened."

It's ridiculous. He's gone in a few days, and I'll never hear from him again. But it's not like it hurts to share my contact information.

"Now, your phone," he commands. "Hand it over, little darlin'.

I'm putting my info in." I punch in my code and do as the man says. The alcohol works its magic, warming me from the inside and loosening me up. Anything that might have flustered me gets flushed with the golden sweetness.

When Oliver passes my phone back to me, I read his full name again.

Oliver Carson Duke.

"This morning, didn't your family call you Ollie?" I grin, remembering that adorable kiddie voice. "Uncle Ollie."

"I go by Oliver." His whiskey eyes tease, but he forces a mock-serious expression. Jeez, this guy is so fucking sexy. My fantasy of him in a cowboy hat, on top of a horse, a la western romance novel style returns, complete with a blade of grass jutting out of the corner of his mouth.

"Oliver sounds stiff for someone like you."

"Someone like me?" His big hands clutch my hips. Those whiskey eyes hover inches away. My skin heats from his intoxicating gaze. It's all a bit much, so I reach for my glass of bourbon.

"You seem casual. Laidback. Easygoing. Oliver sounds..." I search for the words.

"Like a suit? Someone with a desk job?"

"Exactly."

God, those eyes. The weathered lines in the corners make him that much more attractive. Like the sun has baked into his skin and no amount of winter can remove the golden effect.

He mock-shivers. "A desk job is something I'll never do. Not for me. At all."

"Me too. That's exactly how I feel."

He knocks back a swallow from his glass. Or maybe it's mine. He inches forward, and the inside of my knee rubs the outside of his thigh.

"Growing up, they called me Ollie."

"But you don't like it?"

"It's not that I don't like it. But in grad school, I started going by Oliver."

"Grad school." For some reason, I didn't expect that. "What'd you go to grad school for?"

He sucks in air, mouth wide open in a large, entertaining smile. "I went to grad school so I could stay at college. That's what I went for."

I could easily see him loving college. He strikes me as the type of guy who didn't take school seriously. That's the reason I didn't see him as a fellow grad student.

"How many years in undergrad?" I ask.

"Four. Sam Senior didn't let his boys enroll in the five or seven-year undergrad plan. Pops was pretty clear on that. Sammy takes no shit." Somehow, my hand finds its way to his chest and roams upward. My fingers coax the slope where his neck flows into his shoulder. "I got my JD-MBA, which allowed me three more years at the most wonderful place on Earth." He pauses for dramatic effect. "The University of Texas."

"I'd always heard it was Tijuana."

He laughs a full-bellied laugh. It's the kind of laugh that has other people looking at us and forces me to drop my hand. It's a full-throttle laugh that brings on my laughter and, like the bourbon, warms from the inside out.

"What about you?"

"What about me?" I don't want to talk about college.

"Did you do the desk job thing and decide you didn't like it, or did you just know right from the get-go?" His question curves around me and relaxes the temporary tension that popped back up at his initial inquisition.

"Never really done the desk job thing. I guess I always knew?" I scrunch my nose. I give myself such hell for not being like Hudson and having it all planned out, but that is one thing I have always known. I thought a life on my feet would be enough. Movement. Action. But I misstepped.

"Not everybody gets that, you know?" His question is quiet. His expression thoughtful.

Oh, do I know it.

"But I'm lucky. Both my brothers kick ass on the professional desk scene, so my folks aren't too upset they have one that won't leave the rodeo." An image of Oliver flailing on the back of a bucking bronco surfaces.

"What exactly do you do?"

"Work on the family ranch." He seems proud. I wish I had that kind of pride.

"Like cows?"

He chuckles. "And horses. But yeah, cows that go moo." He's grinning down at me. "And you? You're all about the mountain, right? Ski bum all the way?"

Ski bum. I really hate that term. That's the kind of thing my mother would say.

"Thank you for the drink." A small amount colors the bottom of the highball glass, and I sling it back.

"You ready to get out of here? We can get dinner—"

"I'm exhausted. I've got to head home."

"Let me buy you dinner."

It's tempting. All I have back at the apartment is spicy ramen.

"Hey, I didn't mean anything by the ski bum comment." His thumb caresses my cheek, and he angles my chin so I'm forced to look up at him. "I understand loving something no one else really gets."

There's an honesty in his eyes. My body leans into him, into those whiskey eyes and his leathery scent, and without any thought, I kiss him like we're the only two people within miles. My head whirls with the alcohol, and my body hums with frenetic energy and an intense need for release.

I'm delirious with need and tempted to jump him right here against the bar. He throws dollar bills down, and we stumble out into the cold, jackets unzipped, gloves off, and hands and mouths all over each other. The need between us is all we need to keep warm.

We stumble, and I giggle, and then he holds my hand and we take off running for his hotel like two teenagers. The icy wind tingles my exposed skin, but it's not enough to melt the inferno inside that he set off, or maybe this is just me letting go. I promised myself that this year I'd let go and live. Well, what better way to kickstart a year of living than a carefree fling?

His hotel door opens, and we stumble through it, our hands all over each other. The coats hit the ground, and we frantically rip off clothes as if there's a timer and when it buzzes, we have to stop. I tug off my shirt as he pulls his over his head. Freezing fingers touch my breasts, and I squeal.

He pulls back, and we're both panting.

"Fuck, you're beautiful." His stare is so intense I have to look away, but my fingers continue roaming the lines of his chest.

"I'm not even wearing make-up." I bite my lip in acknowledgment that, yes, what I just said is way too girly, but I blurted it out because no one looks at me that way, and it's awkward.

"You don't need it. You've got a natural glow. A natural beauty like the wildflowers back home."

His lips fall softly onto mine. The tips of our noses rub, and the rise and fall of his chest slows. His eyelashes flutter closed, and his thigh presses between my legs, stoking all my desires.

My wandering fingers find the buttons on his pants. He bows his head, and his hot breath coats the tender skin along my ears and neck as my fingers wrap around his very hard erection.

"Fuck, that feels good."

"Not too cold?"

"No." His hips thrust up, and he props his forearms against the wall, caging me in. "Perfect. Absolutely perfect."

His lips capture mine, and our tongues meet again, less frantic but more intense. I break our kiss, gasping for air, and his lips trail below my ear, along my neck.

"Fuck me."

He expels air in a half laugh and gives me that sexy fucking grin. "Yes, ma'am."

He falls to his knees and tugs my pants and panties down to my ankles. My bare ass presses against the cool wall as he struggles with one snow boot, then tugs my bulky winter pants over one ankle. His tongue swipes through my center, and my skin lights up in a whirl of sensation.

All the urgency that lit our stumbling walk back here roars to life, and all I want is him inside me, pounding me against a wall, half-dressed and totally free. I tug on his hair, and he looks up, perched below me, one bare leg over his shoulder, his mouth kissing me intimately. "Now."

He presses his entire face into my stomach, and my thighs clench. With a grunt, he rises off the floor, lifting me with him, my legs around his waist, and he fills me with one thrust.

"Fuck." His arms strain, lifting me a touch higher, and then, positioned perfectly, we find our way. Every stroke hits my clit right, and all my muscles tighten as I strain to help hold myself up and around him as my hips rock against each thrust.

We're a mess of limbs and sweat and need to climb higher and higher until my body quivers uncontrollably, and I cry out from the overwhelming riot of sensations, freefalling into the abyss. With two more thrusts, he joins me over the edge, pulsing inside me. The side of his face brushes against mine, and I cling to him, our chests melded against each other, hearts pounding, gasping for air.

He presses his lips to my temple and lets one leg down at a time. Awareness of my mixed state of dress has me grabbing at clothes on the floor until his hand slaps my bare ass.

"Get a T-shirt or flannel from my clothes. I've got thick socks too. We'll get cozy on the sofa and order in."

"I can't stay tonight, but I'll stay for dinner."

I stumble into the bathroom and, behind the closed door, struggle with my one remaining snow boot.

"My brother is coming in tomorrow. You sure I can't convince you to stay? I might not get to see you for a couple of nights. He's staying with me."

"Which brother?" I remember the one brother with a cute boy on his lap.

"The king of Houston." He says it as if that should mean something. The door cracks open, and he places a green and navy flannel shirt and two enormous gray cotton socks on the counter. He closes the door in a flash, leaving me to my privacy.

My leg muscles ache and burn. I wince as my knees straighten. If one afternoon of ski school does this, I've got to find more time to hit the slopes. And the gym for weights.

As I do my bathroom thing, he takes my dinner order through the door. When I re-enter the room, he's in flannel pajama pants, sitting on the sofa before an electric orange fire with low blue lights. He pats the sofa for me to join him.

"I know nothing about Houston." I take a seat on the sofa and kick an ankle out to lean forward to stretch my hamstring.

"Just something I tease him with. He's succeeding at his desk job." His nose crinkles, amused at his own reference.

"Ah." I smile. "Seems we have something in common."

"What's that? Other than a disdain for desk jobs and a love for good bourbon?"

"Brothers who kick ass in their respective fields."

He cocks his head. "What did you say your brother does?"

He positions a throw pillow behind my back and pulls my feet up onto his lap.

"He's a professional snowboarder." He grips my calves, and I squirm. "An athlete."

Hudson is big shit in Vermont. And in the snowboarding community. But I expect no one from the outside world knows him.

"What's his name?"

"Why?"

"I wanna look him up." His hands continue working the tight

muscles in my legs, and I lean back and breathe in and out deeply in hopes my muscles relax into the borderline pain.

"You can follow him on Instagram. He's always looking to grow his following." The more followers, the more he can charge sponsors. "His name is Hudson Oakley. His handle is The Flying Oak."

It's a cheesy moniker, but he passed a million followers last year. He's an international sensation. Some marketer coined that expression. Or maybe a journalist.

Oliver kneads up to the outside of my knees, and I almost leap off the sofa, eyes wide.

"That hurts?"

"Like a mother. Not so hard."

His face twists. "You gotta roll these muscles."

I sag, knowing exactly what he's talking about. Any good athlete rolls their muscles to increase blood flow and work tight muscles. Any good athlete also stretches. I need to do more stretches.

"Hhmm." With a lighter touch, he continues kneading my legs, and I relax back into the cushion.

After dinner, with a full belly and loose, relaxed muscles, it takes a world of willpower to force myself into my winter gear. Oliver doesn't help at all, given he looks incredible barefoot in only his pajama pants. But an early workday tomorrow beckons.

"Have fun with your brothers." His foot props the hotel room door open, and he's looking down on me in a way that heats me from within, readying me for the long, cold walk home.

Those whiskey eyes pour over me, looking me up and down like he has x-ray vision and can see right through my bulky winter clothes. It's a hungry look loaded with desire, the kind of look a girl could get used to.

Leveraging every ounce of self-control in my possession, I push myself up, press my lips to the side of his jaw, and spin away. He's only got a few days left of vacation. I wish I could let loose and join him, but I'm a working girl. And it's the busiest week of the year.

seven

Oliver

December 29

The frigid thirty-below temps kick up my craving for Texas heat. Back home, folks wear jackets and sweaters when the temperature dips to sixty, our January average. That's ninety degrees warmer than here in Jackson. Nine. Zero.

My clothes are top-notch, the best available for skiing on a mountain. But it's still fucking cold. I would check the time, but that would require removing my gloves and loosening the coat binding on my wrist. I pulled my goggles down and my face mask up to reduce exposed skin. Heating inserts warm my toes and my palms.

It wasn't quite this cold on the mountain earlier, but the sun's gone down, and there's another storm system blowing through. It's a big one, and the excitement on the mountain borders euphoric. Temps should lift, albeit still well below freezing, before the mass of precipitation hits. My flight out tomorrow isn't canceled yet, but the airline sent a text with options for rescheduling.

Ian and Sam got out of Dodge first thing this morning, afraid the cancellations would begin rippling through. Sam's arrival had been wholly unexpected, but awesome. His in-laws showed up in Aspen after the sickness passed through the kids, and Olivia encouraged him to get away. But the guy has it bad for his wife and can't stay away too long. A couple of years ago, he declared he'd never go on another ski trip without her. So, yeah, when Ian called and said he'd come join me, and we extended an invitation to Sam, we didn't expect a yes.

Now, why couldn't Ian stay longer? I'm not so sure. He says the week between Christmas and New Year's is prime time to get caught up on research studies. He's a surgeon, but he's also an investor on the medical scene. The Texas Medical Center is the biggest in the world, so he's as happy as a pig in shit over there.

We tried to get Jason to join us, but he had things planned with his wife Maggie's family. I can't even remember the last time I saw the guy without Maggie.

As for me, I probably should've moved my flight up and gotten out. But I want to see Kate again. And if my flight gets canceled, I'll take it as a sign. The only thing I've got going on back home is New Year's Eve plans, and it's no skin off my back to cancel those. In order to nab the room I'm in, I had to book it for the week anyway. Might as well get the full use of it.

My phone vibrates, tucked away in one of my many coat pockets. It's most likely one of my brothers telling me they arrived home safely. Ian might text a screenshot of Houston's mild weather forecast. Sam would likely send a photo of his kids. Either way, my curiosity doesn't overpower the blinding cold, and my gloved hands remain ensconced in my pockets.

As I huddle by Kate's apartment entrance door, minuscule snowflakes twirl. The fringe of the storm has arrived. Where the hell is Kate? Her text said she didn't have plans after her shift ended. Showing up here unannounced might be a dumb ass plan. She could be sitting at the Mangy Moose.

I haven't seen her in three days. My brothers preferred The

Handle Bar, which conveniently sits inside the Four Seasons and offers reservations to guests. As we have aged, my brothers have evolved into hoity-toity pansies. Given drinks start at twenty dollars a pop, I didn't expect to run into Kate or her friends the last three nights.

The wind picks up, sending the flakes into a horizontal flight path and obscuring visibility. Two minutes. I'll give it two more minutes, then I'll traipse down to the Moose.

I'd like to see Kate. My brothers, Drew, and I had a great time out on the mountain, egging each other on as we are prone to do, but that doesn't mean I didn't keep an eagle eye out for one thick dark braid beneath a white stickered helmet. Didn't mean my thoughts didn't keep going back to one homespun athlete with chocolate eyes and an All-American smile with full, cherry-red lips. Didn't mean I didn't text her photos from the top of each slope, and she didn't text me back photos of the garbage can she had to empty or a broken ski some chump mangled.

"Shit. My fingers. Set it down."

The voice draws my attention to two bundled bodies lugging a cooler up a path. One sucker wears jeans, and his arm wraps around himself as he bounces up and down.

"Jesus F'ing Christ. It's cold as the Arctic out here."

"You guys need some help?" I offer. It doesn't take a rocket scientist to tell the one guy isn't adequately dressed, and while his hand might be gloved, it's probably frozen.

"Hell, yes. Thanks, man. We'll give you a beer."

"No worries." I lift the sucker's end, and the adequately dressed guy lifts his end. With bowed heads, we push through the icy air.

"Seriously, man, we'll give you first choice."

"Nah. Here we are. You almost made it."

The adequately dressed guy enters a code and opens the door.

"But we got stairs. Elevator's out."

"Oh." I look back over my shoulder. I'd hate to miss Kate, but once I'm inside, I can call her. "Let's go."

"Man, I think my hands have frostbite."

"What the fuck are you doing going out in jeans? There are warnings all over." His friend says what I'm thinking.

We reach the first level on the stairs, and my cooler-carrying partner lowers his end.

"Let me unsnap my helmet. Lower my gator."

I lower my end of the cooler, lift my goggles onto my helmet, then lower my gator. I might have been freezing outside, but the heat inside my layers builds up fast. The guy before me looks familiar. I've seen him before. And he's looking at me like he knows me, too.

"You're the boarder who bought Kate drinks."

I break out into a grin. "Hell, yeah, man. You're her roommate."

"Nash." He grins wide and bends down to grip the handle of the cooler. His buddy is two stairs down. He's cuddling his gloved hands like they might shatter.

"Oliver." I grip the handle again and lift. "How many flights up?"

"One more. Thanks for helping, man. We got weed too, if you'd prefer that. We were supposed to get a keg, but with Anaconda blowing in, a lot of folks aren't coming tonight. Figured a few cases would do." Anastasia is the name The Weather Channel has bestowed on this storm, but I like Nash's name twist.

"Big party?"

"Nah. Just another night."

When we reach the door of apartment 2B, Nash sets his end of the cooler down, and I follow suit. He removes his gloves and searches through pockets for keys, checking me out as he does so.

"You here for Kate?"

"Thought I'd swing by."

"You live here?"

"Nah. Just here for the week."

He finds his key and unlocks the door.

"Huh." He lifts his end of the cooler, and I follow him in.

The apartment reminds me of my apartment back in undergrad. Compact kitchen that opens into a den area. Sliding doors with metal frames and a stick of wood wedged for security. There's a small deck off the sliding doors and a good three to four feet of snow on it. There's a long hall with faux wood panel doors and brass knobs that presumably lead to bedrooms. The sofa is a plaid blend L-shape with a couple of rips in it and threadbare corners. The worn indoor-outdoor carpet might be responsible for the mildew aroma that permeates the place. A few presumably empty pizza boxes are stacked on one end of the kitchen counter, but the sink isn't filled with dirties, so it's a step up from my college pad.

A long, narrow table butts up against one wall, and framed photographs line the top. While Nash and his friend get down to taking off snow boots, I lean that way, checking out the frames. All the photos are of groups of kids partying. Most wear winter clothes, but there are some in tanks and shorts with broad-leaf trees behind them. I pick up one such photo.

In the center, there's one photo with a girl who looks a ton like Kate, but her hair is blonde. The yellow hair spills down over her shoulder in waves that strongly resemble Kate's in every way except the color. There's a guy with his arm over her shoulder on one side, and two guys on the other side crowded next to her. I study her face. It's a dead ringer for Kate.

"Is this Kate's sister?"

Nash grins from the floor where he sat to wrangle out of his boots. "That's Kate in college. She's hot as a blonde, right?"

I nod and study the photo. The tank top she's wearing molds perfectly to her breasts. Her skin is pale, but the guys in the photo sport solid tans. Her legs are almost too skinny, her knees borderline knobby. When I look closer, I can see the emergence of dark roots.

"Did you know her in college?"

"Nope. Met her when she moved here. That's her brother with her. Hudson Oakley. Have you heard of him? He's a pro boarder. I've followed him since high school."

"You're a ski instructor, right?"

"Teach it all. Boarding and skis. Whatever they need. Keep trying to tell Kate that's what she needs to do. Ski patrol." He grimaces, as if to say that's a bad thing. "But she won't listen to me."

His last ski boot tumbles forward after he shoves it off with his toes and stands.

"You want to hang, or you need to get out of here?"

His friend sits in the corner armchair, gloves off, fingers circling a glass bong.

"There are a couple of girls coming over. Ones that live in the apartment building. No one wants to drive tonight."

The sweet tang of marijuana overtakes the mildew scent. It strikes me this is a distinctly different life than I lead now. I pride myself on being the laidback one, but this vibe is like a trip back in time. And yet, *this* is Kate's life.

Nash continues to strip in the hallway. It's not until he's shimmying out of his long underwear that I realize he's planning on going full Monty.

"I'm gonna slip on trunks. Grab a beer."

"Dude," his friend grunts. "I don't wanna see your junk."

Nash laughs and turns, showing us his hairy bare ass.

"Not better." His friend leans back and closes his eyes.

I return to looking at the photos, searching for more of Kate. There's a couple of boarders against a blue sky backdrop, but you can't tell who the person is. Mostly, the photos are of groups of partiers. And they took a lot of the photos on that plaid couch. This place, I realize, is party central.

The apartment door opens, and Kate clomps through, the sound of her heavy ski boots muffled by the mildewed carpet. Her helmet, goggles, and gloves are tucked up underneath one arm, and her gator is bunched below her chin. She frowns when she sees the guy in the armchair, then those dark eyes widen when her gaze falls on me.

Nash steps into the hallway in swim trunks and flip-flops.

"Hot tub, baby. No suit for you. Let's go."

"Nash." Kate's glare would scorch most men, but Nash is unfazed. "Where's Claire?"

"She's back at Montclair's place. So, you know what that means? Hot tub's calling!"

"You know, Claire isn't the only one who doesn't like you smoking up this place."

"Oh, quit your griping." He waltzes over and slaps his palm against her ass.

A not-so-friendly feeling toward Nash rises. He's standing too close to Kate, and he's way too chummy. I am frozen in place, watching the scene play out like it's Netflix.

"Hot tub! I wanna see your tits."

Kate pushes him away and tilts her head back, looking at the dingy ceiling. She steps forward, and her snow boot kicks the cooler. She bends and lifts the lid.

"How many people do you have coming over?"

"Not that many. Promise." Nash seems to finally absorb the daggers she's shooting at him. "I'll clean up."

"Nash, I have work tomorrow."

"No, you won't. They're calling for blizzard conditions. The rental shop won't open. Lifts will be closed."

Nash grabs a beer out of the cooler and heads into the kitchen. Kate closes her eyelids, and her facial muscles tighten. She looks annoyed as fuck. When she opens her eyes, she addresses me.

"What're you doing here?"

"Was waiting outside for you when these two needed cooler help. Thought I'd see if I could persuade you to have dinner with me."

Laidback or not, if she invites me to hang here, I won't. I like Kate and have had a good time with her, but this isn't my scene.

Kate glances down at her outfit. She's wearing loose boarder pants, a ski sweater, and snow boots. She didn't take her boots off at the door, which in my experience with ski lodging, is unusual, but given the damp state of the carpet, it's logical.

"Pack a bag. Stay the night. Unless you want to make it back for the party?"

As if on cue, the guy on the armchair leans forward to pick up his bong, lets out a loud fart, then sighs dramatically as if he feels worlds better now.

"Dude," Nash says from the kitchen. "Good one."

Nash comes around, arms out, standing in his trunks. His jaw and a sliver of his forehead have a weathered tan, but his chest and arms are as bright white as they come. "Am I going to the hot tub by myself? You two look like you're about to jet."

Kate tugs on my pinkie finger, and I follow her obediently down the hall. She opens a door to a room that is markedly different from the rest of the apartment. It's a small bedroom, and the queen-sized bed fills up most of the space. The bed is neatly made with colorful pillows thrown across it. Over the bed hangs a framed photo of a snowy mountainscape. On the dresser, there's a photo of four people taken by a ski resort photographer, something I recognize from all the photos my family took with us growing up. The ski resort logo gives it away. Because of the helmets and thick clothes, you can't tell much, but they're all smiling and holding boards.

She opens a drawer and pulls out some clothes, tossing them in a bag.

"You sure you don't mind if I crash at your place? When Nash brings Frank around, it can get a little crazy."

"Are you seriously asking if I mind you staying in my bed tonight?" Color flashes across her high cheekbones, probably from the transition from the cold outside to the indoor heat. No matter the origin, the blush is damn attractive.

"If Claire were here, she'd keep him from going crazy. She'll be pissed when she comes back and our place reeks in the morning."

It sort of reeks now, but that's immaterial. "Claire whips him in line, but you won't?"

Kate's back is to me, and her right shoulder lifts, then falls, and then the same thing happens on the left side. She shuffles into the tiny bathroom.

"Nash is a lot like Hudson and his friends. It's best to just lie low and let crap pass."

"What do you mean?" I can't see her, so I step closer to the bathroom. "Do they hit on you?"

"No. Nothing like that. I'm more like a little sister to them all." She steps out and dumps a small zipped bag into the duffel on the bed. "But there's no point in making a fuss. Those guys don't change."

When we re-enter her den, there's a fog of smoke on one side of the room. She tosses her hand in the air as a goodbye and doesn't respond when Nash tells her to have fun and be naughty.

Outside, the wind is howling, and the snow is coming down at a quick pace. It's so blasted cold that we both bundle up, covering all exposed skin, and trudge with our heads down. By the time we reach the Four Seasons, my pinky toes sting. The high winds slice straight through the fabric to the skin.

We both clomp our feet on the welcome mat, shaking off the excess snow. I love a good ski week as much as the next person, but as we go through the rigamarole of removing goggles, facemasks, and gloves and unzipping our thick outer coats, I can't help but wonder how anyone lives through this for months at a time. I suppose the world takes all types, but severe winter would wear me down.

"You got snow tires? Chains? How do you get around?"

"Well, that's one reason I'm in Nash's apartment. It's close, so we can walk. Only have to drive if we want to go into town. He lucked into that and subleases the two extra bedrooms. Most of the people live away from here, even in Utah. Like as much as thirty minutes away."

"People drive in this?" Outside, yes, it's night, but visibility is crap with the amount of snow coming down.

"Not if they don't have to." A lazy smile crosses her face as she tilts her head up at me. "But yes, I have chains. And I hang plastic bags around my side-view mirrors. I strap down a cover over my windshield too to save me scraping time. And if I needed to drive tomorrow, on a night like tonight, I'd oil up the door handles and a few other places on the car so they don't snap in the morning."

"You park outside?" *Mind. Blown.*

"Nash's apartment is close, but it's kind of crap." By crap, she's not referring to the mildew carpet. She's talking about the lack of covered parking.

If I continue down this conversational path, I will offend her with my impressions of her living situation, so I close my eyes and shake like a wet dog.

She half-laughs. "It's not forever."

My stomach growls, reminding me I failed to nosh after the lifts closed, given I was alone.

"You want to eat in the restaurant down here or do room service?"

There are two restaurants in the hotel. I'm not sure I can get us a table, but since I'm staying in the hotel, there's a good chance I can.

Snowflakes cover the shoulders of her jacket, and I brush them off. She scrunches her nose. "Room service sounds more comfortable."

"I agree. Just know I offered to take you out to dinner."

"You don't think room service counts?"

"Well, let's put it this way. If you ever meet Patty Duke, also known as my mother, it's a phrase you best not mention."

eight

Oliver

December 29

The gas fireplace lights a warm flickering orange. It doesn't roar like a real fireplace, which is what the storm outside calls for. But, on the flip side, the only thing required to turn it on is flipping a switch. It's something to consider in the house I will one day build down in Texas.

Our phones have been lighting up and vibrating with alerts for the last hour. Blizzard warnings are no joke in Wyoming, and this storm is a beast. They're saying it'll lighten up in a few hours, but then the bulk of the storm will hit midmorning. Whiteout conditions will combine with thirty-mile-an-hour gusts.

After returning to the hotel room, I reschedule my flight for New Year's Day. Also send a quick text to Cindy back home canceling our New Year's Eve plans.

Kate comes out of the bathroom as my phone lights up and vibrates.

> *Cindy: Oh no! I'm not sure I should go to the party
> without you.*

> *Noah: Dude. Seriously? They've been announcing the
> storm for days. You didn't leave?*

"Everything okay?" Kate asks.

"Yeah. Just letting people back home know about my change in plans." I pass her the leather-bound notebook with the room service menu. "Pick out what you want."

Kate and I both stripped out of our snow clothes and boots when we entered the place. She's in form-fitting silks, the kind everyone wears these days below ski clothes. The thin material highlights every curve, and all I can say is score one for ski clothes. She's also put on thick marbled gray socks that give her a relaxed vibe and highlight the curve of her calves and the lean shape of her legs. I come up behind her and snag the band at the bottom of her braid. My fingers unravel the braid, marveling at the silky-smooth feel of her strands. The end result is wave after wave of luscious locks.

My phone buzzes again.

> *Drew: Noah just asked if you're with me. You need a place
> to stay? The storm's already started. Not sure you can
> make it here.*

Drew and his wife live about forty-five minutes away. He's already told me he was weathering the storm with his wife. I'd, however, been nonchalant about moving my flight when I spoke to him earlier.

Me to Drew: Got the hotel room until New Year's Day. I'm good. Stay safe.

Me to Cindy: Definitely still go. You'll have a blast.

Me to Noah: Flight canceled.

That's all Noah needs to know. He's the one who pushed me into inviting Cindy out on New Year's Eve. She's one of his wife's friends, and she doesn't have a date to some extravagant shindig that I don't have one iota of interest in attending.

Me to Cindy: Can't get a refund on the tickets. Definitely still go.

Cindy: K. Do I get a rain check on our date? Maybe I should say snow check...

Patty Duke: Sam said you're snowed in. Our flight to Aspen was delayed, but we're about to board. Cannot wait to see my grandbabies. Let us know if you need anything.

"I think I'll take the grilled cheese and tomato soup." Kate pushes the menu book my way. She settles down on the sofa and pulls a throw blanket over her lap.

I order, set the phone face down in the kitchenette, and join her.

"You looked good as a blonde."

"Oh, lord. You saw that picture?"

"Yeah. Was one of those guys your boyfriend?"

"No. The one with his arm around me is my brother, Hudson. The other two are his friends."

I lift the hem of her silk top to reach her smooth, bare skin. The energy flow between us surges.

My palm flattens across her stomach, and I feel my way up, over her soft, full breasts, to the narrow neck opening, to her throat. The fabric bunches and she sucks in air. My lips find hers. Our kiss is soft and warm. My sore muscles relax into the kiss as she opens for me. She tastes sweet, like candy canes and hot chocolate.

Our bodies align and press against one another. One thing about long silks, it doesn't hide much. My erection presses against her. I cup her ass and knead. Her fingers curve around my erection. *Fuck.* The pressure she places against my dick unlocks a feral need.

I break our kiss and lift my shirt up and toss it. She does the same. Garment by garment, we peel out of our clothes in a wicked-fast striptease. No words pass, just small smiles and knowing looks. She's the first to wrangle everything off, and she lies back on the sofa. Her dark hair falls over her shoulders, and the long strands tease her nipples. Her thighs spread, showing me one delicious, turned-on pussy. I am so fucking hard it hurts.

I kiss a path from her inner thigh to my destination. She tilts her head back and closes those eyes. She pinches her own nipple, and her hips thrust up in anticipation.

"Watch," I tell her.

Her eyelashes flutter. She rises on her elbows, and I place a kiss above her sex. Her tongue laps her lower lip, and her chest lifts on an inhale. Hooded chocolate eyes obey.

My tongue dips inside. Her thighs squeeze inward. I shake my head, silently communicating *no.* Not yet. Then I set my tongue to work. She tastes so damn sweet, smooth, and silky. I add a finger into her tight core, curling it up, and press over and over, searching for the one magical spot. The one that will render her incapable of moaning my full name. I suck and lick. Her hips flex. Over and over.

"Ol…lie." She groans. That nickname has never really done it for me, but hearing it broken apart on her lips, gasped out as she fights the brink of orgasm, well, I could hear that all night long.

When she curls up and her thighs clamp against my ears, I can't hold back. I am throbbing. I snatch the condom off the coffee table where I dropped it earlier, roll it on, and slide home.

"Fuck, you feel good."

Remnant quivers from her orgasm force me to take a moment. Her fingers tug on my hair, and she brings me to her mouth. She sets the pace, and my hips follow her lead, thrust for thrust. I lift her leg, placing the bend of her knee over my shoulder. Her eyes widen, and all kinds of little noises spill out of her. This position allows me to go deeper. Our skin slaps, and I'm close, but so is she.

I let her leg down and reposition myself. With every movement, my pelvis rubs her magical bundle of nerves. Her breathing picks up, matching the pace of my hips. The grip of her muscles tightens around me. Our eyes lock, and the intensity rachets higher. I'm torn between those eyes and the need to kiss her. Our tongues wrangling wins out.

That party scene that's rocking her apartment right now? Fuck that. This right here, this is my scene. This is where I want to be.

She breaks our kiss with a deep moan and a drawn-out "Ol" that sends me over the edge without warning, a little too fast for my liking. I collapse over her, and she wraps her arms around me, holding me close. Her lips press to the side of my face, and my hips roll forward as I continue to spurt out my release.

Afterward, I hold her close until our breathing levels off and the slight perspiration on our skin gives way to chill. The condom on my dick grows uncomfortable, but I don't want to leave our warm fireside cocoon. Unfortunately, nature calls, so I force my lazy ass up.

After room service arrives and we chow down, instead of pulling her into bed, I take the comforter and pull it over us on the sofa so we can watch the fire. I let my wandering hands massage her sore muscles, which leads to another round of fun. Much later, we fall asleep, our naked bodies intertwined, snug and warm, as Anastasia howls outside.

In the morning, the alerts ping in a steady stream. They canceled all flights in and out of Jackson. Lifts are closed due to strong winds and dangerous mountain conditions. My phone buzzes with texts from the ranch. Nothing too bad. One of my horses is limping. Jerry, the ranch manager, agrees to watch it for a day before calling the vet out. I let him know I'm snowed in and get a thumbs up in response. I don't bother responding to any other texts.

You can barely see outside the massive window. The storm rages in a haze of white. Room service takes longer than normal to deliver our breakfast, but other than that, Anastasia can rage all she wants. We are more than adequately sheltered. I flip on some tunes, and Kate taps away on her laptop.

"What'chu working on?" I ask her, curious. Her gaze falls to her laptop screen, and she sucks on the side of her bottom lip. "Don't want to tell me?"

"I write articles for extra money." She pushes her laptop away. "Do you mind if I get a shower?"

This morning when I woke with her naked ass pressed against me, we had the best kind of wake-up call. So, yes, it's safe to say we could both use a little cleaning.

"Want company?"

"Give me a few minutes? Come in when you hear the shower going?"

I grin in answer. This snowstorm may turn out to be my all-time favorite.

The bathroom door closes, and curiosity wins. I turn her laptop around to read what she's got going on. The headline packs a punch. It's a whopper. There's no doubt it will pull in readers.

"The Benefits of a Fling."

75

nine

Kate

December 31

Winter Storm Anastasia dumped three feet of snow, spreading holiday cheer for the lucky travelers who rolled the dice by coming out early in the season and promising one stellar snow season ahead. Locals, which includes anyone within a day trip radius, fill the parking lots. And for Jackson Resort employees, after one slow day for a lot of us, it is now all hands on deck.

My morning at the rental place might have been the busiest yet. I went hours without a breather, the line at the register constant, me more or less floating through the mindless task of ringing up customers and instructing them on how to insert their credit card.

Yesterday, I holed up in Oliver's hotel room. We ordered room service, watched movies, and did a lot of other things that flare through my mind, delivering hot flashes, and at almost twenty-five, I am nowhere near menopausal.

Hudson: How's the snow?

He attaches a video of him clearing a hurdle over machine-generated snow. Vermont didn't get the dump we got, which has me feeling a tad smug. Even if I am relegated to the rental shop all day.

"The best snow ever, man. Un-fucking-believable. Like, waist-deep powder in the bowl." The guy entering the shop has the biggest grin.

While others hang on his every word, the soreness between my legs has my thoughts going in an entirely different direction. Me bent over the sofa. His shower. The cold glass biting my nipples when he pressed me up against the window. The awkward laughter when he suggested we attempt sixty-nine. And then the not-so-awkward moment after we got the position going.

It's a good thing Oliver's leaving tomorrow, because otherwise I could totally fall for this guy. He's not a stiff, but he's mature. He's settled in life. Nothing seems to bother him, and he's simply fun to be around. When I'm with him, all the crap that typically fills my head and weighs me down disappears. But that's sort of the point of a fling. It's a temporary escape from reality.

I have a running tally of the benefits of a fling. My contact with a source at *Juice* says they might be interested and to send it over when I'm done. If they don't bite, she's pretty positive I can earn some money from an online site like *Metropolitan*. Or maybe I'll submit to *Ski Health*. They don't run a lot of articles like that, but they should. Listicles are the bomb.

So far, my running list of benefits is five long. I'd like to get to ten.

1. Lifts the mood. We're talking massive amounts of oxytocin, dopamine, and serotonin. Your body's feel-good cocktail sends you on an all-natural, hangover-free high.

2. Exercise without the gym.

3. No girlie what's-happening-tomorrow concerns, because it's a just-for-now thing. Good riddance, insecurity!

4. Research shows sex boosts immunity. Face sniffly noses sans fear!

5. It's FUN.

6. No strings, no serious talks.

I added numbers five and six when I realized we spent the entire day alternating between 'bang bang shoot'em' movies and romcoms. He hadn't seen *Must Love Dogs*. We both love *Office Space* and plan to watch it late night before he leaves. Everything we do is fun. All the movies we watch are mindless. It's fantastic.

My hot flash day gives me another one to add to my growing list.

7. Sex is way better when it's new.

Holy shit. I've never had sex like this. Maybe it's that Oliver is older. Maybe all men in their mid-thirties are insanely skilled. If so, that's fantastic news. But for my article, I'll focus on the newness. The thrill. The tingles and electrical connection. Jeez, I look straight ahead at a wall of snowboards and his face appears as a haze. His angular jaw, his cinnamon taste, which I now know is due to an apparent addiction he has to Big Red gum. The rough texture of his fingers and how he can find just the right spot with his longest finger while he does that lick, suck, and graze with his teeth combo.

So, yeah, way better when it's new. My college boyfriend and I had frantic, fantastic sex when we first started dating. But then, months later, it fizzled. And he began to really annoy me. And I suppose my flighty personality exposed itself because I noticed things like his nasty feet, and when he ate, I heard his teeth. With a fling, there's an expiration date. There will be no opportunity for annoyances to creep in.

My mom says I'm the queen of dropping things. She says I go gung-ho, dive in, and then quit. Throughout my life, I picked up sports and dropped them. I changed majors four times in undergrad, and my mother will never forgive me for my most recent career change. But there is literally no reason to focus on the negative.

I pull out my phone and edit the growing list in my notes app.

8. Built-in expiration date. No heartbreak.

Oh, and...

9. He's not around long enough to become annoying.

The bell on the door twangs. It's been twanging all day, but this time a flash of red catches my attention. It's Bill Woodland. I imagine he was out on the mountain early this morning, checking for hazards and avalanche risks.

"Hi, Bill." He's standing at least six feet away from me, and he narrows his eyes like he's trying to remember who I am. "I'm Kate." His face is a blank slate. "Kate Oakley. We met at the Christmas Eve party."

"Is Harvey in the back?"

"I think so." There's an office in the back where Harvey mostly works. He prefers to work from the mountain, but he has an office in Jackson too.

Bill pushes past the counter. Several of my colleagues utter hellos, and he responds to all of them with a gruff nod.

The line at the register has dissipated. In a few hours, the tide will switch for returns. We can regroup, straighten, and stand around waiting for malfunctions to walk in the door. We sell a lot of goggles and gloves in the middle of the day, either from people dropping them or deciding the old pair they have needs a tech upgrade.

Bill returns from the back. Harvey trails him. He calls out to one guy who is restocking boots. In a rush like we just had, sizes can get out of whack.

"Harvey says he can spare you this afternoon. I need an extra set of hands at the base for speed monitoring. You up for it?"

"Absolutely." The lucky bastard beams.

Harvey points in my direction. "If you need anyone else, I can spare one more. Kate here is getting her patrol certifications."

Bill spares me one quick glance. "We'll see if she's around come fall."

He turns to the other guy, whose name I don't know because he grabs whatever name tag is free in the spare drawer. Today his name tag reads Lucy. "Let's get you tricked out."

I didn't think my mood could deflate, but Bill Woodland's brushoff effectively dials it down. This isn't personal. He barely recognized me. Maybe he's a sexist prick. That's possible. But, deep down, I know ski patrol is a physically intensive job. It takes muscular legs to get an injured three-hundred-pound man down a steep incline. But that's why I lift weights and force down protein bars. I can do it. It'll take time, but I'll prove myself. And it'll be worth it because I will spend my days outside. Helping people out in the sun and on the snow. I'll be the one sending Hudson GoPro video clips because I'll be the one having a fantastic day, every day.

As if on cue, an alert comes across that Hudson is going live on video. I'm about to stick my phone in a drawer when it lights up with my mother's name.

"Hey, sweetie," she says in greeting. "Wanted to wish you a Happy New Year's Eve."

"Are you out with Hudson?"

"Your dad is. I'm taking a break. Saw you got a dump."

"Yep."

"Have you been out in it?"

"Working." A huff slips out, unwittingly showing my dissatisfaction. To avoid the I-told-you-so rant, I add an upbeat, "Next year."

"You know, Hudson says he doesn't know why you're so gung-ho on ski patrol."

The unstated judgment that if Hudson can't understand it, then it must be irrational, hangs over us.

"Well, I don't understand why he wants the pro life, but I still support him." Of course, Mom sees through my bullshit statement. If I had my brother's athletic prowess, I'd be competing on the same circuit in a heartbeat.

"He can't do it forever." She absolutely loves to say shit like that.

"Sure he can." There are boarders who continue competing into their forties, right into retirement.

"At any rate, his point about ski patrol is that he believes your personality is better suited for ski school. Or even event planning. There's a lot of opportunity in event planning."

"That's what Hudson says?" She's so full of shit. This is some theory she's concocted and she's sugarcoating it as Hudson's opinion.

"I'm not calling to argue, sweetie. I really just wanted to wish you a happy New Year. I don't plan to be up at two in the morning for our annual phone call." The time difference is a drag.

The door swings open, and a blast of cold air knocks over the point-of-sale piece, sending the index cards touting Harvey's tubing business scattering across the shop.

"Mom, I gotta go. Happy New Year to you and Dad. I'll give you a call tomorrow. Love you."

Hours later, as we prepare to close, my phone vibrates. We're not busy at all. I suppose all the folks who rented earlier are keeping their rentals and planning to use them again tomorrow to enjoy another powder day. The name on the screen reads "OL...Lee."

I laugh out loud. He changed his name on my phone and told me that's how he wants me to pronounce his name every day.

"Hellooo." One guy behind the counter gives me a weird look, and I step away for a little privacy.

"There she is. How's the day been?" The combination of both his Texan drawl and the anticipated call has me grinning like a school-girl and my insides doing a three-sixty.

"Good," I blurt. Then add a more truthful, "Insanely busy."

"Sounds like my girl needs some TLC. Where are we bringing in the New Year?"

"I thought we'd check out a little place called Thai Me Up."

ten

Kate

December 31

There's a pause and a deep, husky chuckle. "What did you say?"

"Get your mind out of the gutter, cowboy. It's a bar. Thai Me Up. Spelled T-H-A-I."

"Ah, I'm thinking there's some subliminal context going on here. If that's what you're into..."

My face is on fire. Absolutely burning. But he can't see me. And there's something fun about the tease.

"Like what? You want to tie my wrists above my head? Spread my legs and strap them down? Fuck me with your mouth?" A low, groaning gargle comes across the line. He's out in public, so he can't easily respond. "Or do you want to flip me over so my ass is in the air? Spank me?" His breath sounds like static. This is all talk, but imagining his response urges me on. I'm having way too much fun with this. "Are you into ass play?"

A loud throat sound ricochets loudly. That sound isn't from my phone. I slowly turn.

Please let it be one of the guys I work with.

Not one man, but two stand behind me. One wears the coveted red ski patrol outfit, the other is in jeans and a crewneck sweater. The Woodland brothers. Harvey is grinning ear to ear. Bill is as stern as ever. The man missed his calling as a high school principal. *Fuck.*

The phone pressed against my ear scalds my skin.

"Damn, girl—"

"See you at seven." My thumb ends the call. The two men stare me down.

"Did you need something?" I ask my boss, Harvey, the one smiling brother.

"No. You're off the clock, right?"

"Yes. Heading out now."

"Have fun. That's one helluva way to bring in the New Year." Harvey chuckles, and I can't bring myself to look at Bill. Now he thinks I'm into BDSM. And ass play. I never, ever say anything like that on the phone, and then the one time I do, the guy I want to hire me is in the fucking room? What are the fucking chances? Only in my fucked-up life would that happen.

When I enter the local bar called Thai Me Up, Oliver is unmissable. He's in faded blue jeans and a cream sweater. His snow boots rise to mid-calf, and the bottom of his jeans crowd the top of the boot. He's animated, talking to a man wearing dress pants and a button-down dress shirt. The man has to work here because only an employee would wear dress pants to a place like this.

I watch Oliver from afar, appreciating his off-kilter smile and his slow drawl. From what I can tell, he hasn't shaved since he's been on vacation, and his scruff has grown into a short beard with hair a slightly darker shade of chestnut than the rough-and-tumble light brown strands on his head. His unkempt hair is longer on top and falls over his brow. When he laughs at something the man says, he tilts his head back and brushes the hair off his forehead.

In a perfect world, Oliver would live here in Jackson. The mountain life looks good on him. But I'd bet he's at ease everywhere he goes.

When Oliver sees me, his gaze flows through me in sparks and waves. Thirty feet of busy restaurant separates us, but everything else fades to black. Familiar whiskey eyes lock on me as he talks to the guy. Seconds later, there's a handshake, and he's striding my way.

When he reaches me, his hand covers the back of my neck, his fingers weave through my hair, and he angles my head just right, granting himself access for a heated hello that sends an avalanche of need thundering down that nearly smothers the crash and burn fall out from my Woodland brother embarrassment.

A catcall from the bar prompts us to break apart. He smirks, looking supremely cocky, and he possessively claims my hip. Without hesitation, I cuddle into his side. Tomorrow, he leaves, but we have tonight. If we're standing on the edge of our proverbial Corbet's, I'm going to charge it for maximum air and chase the adrenaline. Tomorrow is not only a new day, it's a new year. I've been a planner for too much of my life. A fling is about flying on the edge of your blade without a plan, and that's what I'm going to do.

"Our table is ready. Come on." Once we're seated, he asks, "Was the day okay?"

Bill Woodland comes to mind. The man doesn't think I really want the job. He doesn't think I'll stick around. Apparently, my family doesn't think it's for me. All these know-it-all judgmental pricks surround me. The funk descends like a foreboding storm cloud. And of course the mortification from the end of the day adds to the mire.

"It was fine." This is New Year's Eve. I need to get out of my head. "Who was the man you were talking to?"

"Restaurant manager and part owner of this fine establishment. I love the name. Trying to talk him into franchising. If he won't, or if that route doesn't make sense, I might just nab the name. I think a Thai Me Up would make hay in Austin."

"Is make hay an expression for do well?"

"Yeah." His sandy brown eyebrows crowd his nose. His calloused hand covers mine. "What's the matter?"

"My boss overheard me on the phone with you." Heat rises from my neck.

He grins wide, and I want to smack that grin off his face.

"It's not funny. The head ski patrol guy was with him."

"I wondered why you hightailed it. Figured somebody walked up. Looks like I was right." He drawls out *right* in a light, exaggerated southern drawl, his smile in place. "Don't worry about it. You think those two are saints? They've lived the mountain life for decades."

"You know the Woodland brothers?" He's right about them having a wild past. But now they're both married.

"There's an article in the Jackson magazine back at the Four Seasons profiling them. I guess they are local celebrities."

"I don't know about celebrities, but personalities. Everyone knows them."

"Like I said, I wouldn't worry about it. I doubt they're thinking twice about it, other than maybe if listening to you turned them on. How much of the call did they hear?"

"Enough to know it was a personal call." My palm slaps my forehead, and I scrunch up my face. "Ass play."

My mortification has him laughing out loud. "They're ski bums. Seriously, don't let it worry you."

Ski bums, huh? Oliver loves that fucking phrase.

I agree to whatever he suggests on the menu, but the second our server lifts the menus from our hands, I let it rip.

"Why do you say that about ski bums? Everyone acts like they're a joke. But both of those men are highly accomplished. They didn't get where they are without a shit ton of work."

"Hey." He holds a defensive hand up in the air. "You don't need to tell me. Some people have the same view on ranchers. Men who don't want to grow up. That's what you're getting at, right?"

I give a quick, hard nod.

"I come across like a laidback goofball. Never wanted the respectable job. Don't want what either of my brothers have. Yeah, I have to sit down at a desk. But I'm not chained to it. Most of my days are spent outside, on a horse, exactly how I like it. I have the utmost respect for those brothers. They saw a life they wanted, and they did what they needed to make it happen."

"Right." All that bumbled annoyance simmers, and after a beer, it completely evaporates. With a second beer, the Woodland brothers incident finds cover in the deep recesses of my mind.

Alcohol courses through my veins, and all the tension of the day vanishes. The oversized fireplace weaves oranges and yellows over iron logs. Music blares, and the television plays alternate ski scenes from around the country.

"You missed a great powder day."

I groan. "Trust me, I'm aware."

"My legs are toast."

"I can imagine." My legs and feet aren't feeling particularly fantastic after being on them all day, but I'd give anything to feel the muscular burn from a full day sailing through powder.

"Excuse me?" An older woman in her fifties or sixties leans into our table. She's wearing a snowy white sparkly sweater and dark jeans, and her blonde hair has been blown out to perfection. She's attractive, but there's a slur to her words. A man comes up behind her, his hand on her waist.

"Honey, let's leave these kids alone."

"No. I had a vision. I have to tell them."

"Honey." The man's weathered hand grips her hip, and it looks like he's pulling on her.

"It's okay," I say.

"What vision?" Oliver asks with a wide smile. "Are you a fortune teller?"

"I am a seer."

The man behind her rolls his eyes but removes his hand and crosses his arms over his chest. He stands behind her, close enough he can catch her if she falls, but giving her space to carry on.

The woman waves a nail back and forth over my face.

"Saw your future. Struck me like lightning. Only happens in very special cases."

"Like when there's a run-in with tequila," the man behind her says.

"Oh, hush up, Frank." She straightens and almost falls back against the man she called Frank. "You," she says, her finger pointing straight at me, "are going to fall in love with a mountain man. And you," Her finger whips around within an inch of Oliver's nose, "Are going to fall in love with a southern girl. And..." her eyes widen as if announcing a proclamation, "you will do the two-step at your fifty-year wedding anniversary."

"The two-step you say?" Oliver grins up at her. "So, I'm going to be highly mobile at a ripe old age."

"You are." Her thick eyelashes flutter and she points back at me. "You too."

Then she stumbles, and Frank catches her as her palms plant on the sticky barroom floor. Oliver gets up and assists with getting her to her booth, where several people, presumably her friends, are in hysterics.

Oliver returns to the booth and says, "Maybe we should have what she's having."

I laugh, but I can't help but think for an inebriated woman, she might have gotten it all right. After all, I always assumed I'd end up with someone who loves the mountains as much as I do, and I'm sure Oliver, Mr. Texan, expects to end up with a southern woman.

His fingers graze mine, and the light touch sets off a flurry of sensations. That woman might be right about our future, but his whiskey eyes and sexy smile are mine tonight.

Tendrils curl around me, lighting up crazy notions. Our knees touch under the table, and over the table his fingers continually play with mine. I'd like to get out of here, but we're fifteen minutes shy of the Times Square apple dropping.

Folks on the mountain get tired early after an active day, and most revelers here celebrate the New Year when the apple drops on the East Coast. Patrons sit at every single table, and the bar area is packed to capacity. The annual New Year's Eve ski down the mountain parade with lights finished earlier in the evening. There's a buzz of energy, and all the television sets show Times Square.

The restroom line extends down the hall and merges into the bar crowd. We're approaching the midnight hour, and it seems the whole restaurant jumped at the chance to relieve themselves before the big countdown.

"You know of any other restrooms?" Oliver asks.

"Yeah, I do. Come with me."

There's a bathroom on the backside of the building. I'm not sure which business put it in, but several of the front retail shops in this building use it for employees. It's tiny, and there's a punch code, but I know it—6969. All the locals know the code.

It's cold outside, and I attempt to warm myself by briskly rubbing my arms while he goes in. When he's done, he holds the door for me, asking if I need to go.

It's dark in the back of the building, but strung lights from out front blanket the fresh snow in glittering light. Edison bulbs swinging from tree to tree add to the festive holiday atmosphere in this winter wonderland. A winter wonderland that, for tonight, in this moment, is ours.

I press my palm against his sternum and push him back into the restroom. There's a toilet, a urinal, and a sink. And one wall of planked wood.

Fiery amber eyes bore into me. I reach for him, tugging him closer. His cheeks are cold to the touch, but his mouth is warm and sweet. He tastes like bourbon with a hint of cinnamon. With a firm grip, he presses me up against his crotch.

"You want me? In here?"

Our noses rub, and he traces kisses along the side of my neck. His palm cups my core over my jeans, and the warmth is like a match to cinder. He bites at my lower lip, and hands slide on bare skin beneath my sweater. I tremble as his cool skin collides with my warmth. He pushes my bra up over my breasts and cups them, pinching my eager nipples.

I fumble with the buttons on his jeans. It's a struggle, but I finagle the top few buttons and reach inside, curving my fingers around his stiff erection.

He groans, and his warm breath tickles my ear.

"Yes. Just like that." He bites at my earlobe as I tug on him, taking care to toy with his sensitive tip. "Fuck, you feel good. I like your hands on me."

My teeth run along his jaw, echoing his playful bites on my ear. "Good. I like holding you. Claiming this." I squeeze, and he kicks his hips up.

"In a bathroom?" He questions this, but why not? Our time is limited. His vacation is coming to an end. We'll probably never see each other again. Hell, a fortune teller basically just told us our future involves fifty-year marriages with other people.

"Now." The location feels irrelevant when my core is burning, craving a release I know he can give.

"You're coming back with me tonight, and we'll do all of this a lot more slowly."

"Promise?" I raise one eyebrow, and he shoves my pants down.

"How do you want me? Against a wall, or with your hands clasping that sink and me taking you from behind?"

'Your choice' is on the tip of my tongue, but I choke it back. I debate my options. As hot as it would be to watch him pummeling into me from the mirror, the sink itself is a turnoff, and I'd rather not stare at it the whole time.

"Wall."

He grins, bends his legs, tugs my pants all the way down my legs, and glides them over one ankle. He gazes up at me, those amber eyes electric. "We'll only release one leg."

He bites and nips his way up my thigh. He lifts my free leg and places it over his shoulder, and his tongue slips between my slit. Soft, warm, and wet. Fuck, he is good with his tongue. My head hits the back of the wall as I kick back from the sensation.

"You are so wet. Were you this turned on all through dinner?"

"Yes," I admit. Need pooled the moment I entered the restaurant and saw him standing there looking hot as fuck in his creamy sweater and rough-and-tumble hair.

Oliver licks me, spreading my lips with his fingers. He drives a finger up, and I curl forward from the sensual intrusion. He pounds deep, finding that spot he has learned, drawing out a mewl from somewhere within me.

"Ol...lie," I beg.

"Oh, baby, I think you are ready for me."

He stands, bends his knees, positions himself just right, and pushes inside.

He's right. I'm ready. I want him. I lift my free leg, opening more for him, wanting him to move.

"Ah, shit. Condom."

"It's okay. I've got an IUD."

Those three letters are all he needs to hear. He pounds up and slides down, over and over, creating a rhythm that has me panting. He grips one arm, holding it high against the wall. My other hand is free, and I squeeze his ass, clinging to it, pulling him into me. With each upright thrust, pressure builds on my clitoris, almost to the point of pain against my pubic bone. My one standing leg goes weak as I both hold myself up and writhe against him.

Blowing off steam has never felt this good. But this is more. It's me throwing myself out there without hesitation. This is me getting over all the shit that's held me back. This is me going for it, not second guessing, not overthinking.

There's a dull chant from the crowd on the other side of the bathroom wall. "Ten. Nine."

His fingers dig into my ass, and I slide up off the floor. He holds me, pressed against the wall, suspended in the air.

"Wrap those thighs around me." It's awkward, but I do as told. His arms loop beneath my knees, and the angle shifts. He's deep. Pounding so hard my nether region vibrates. The hard wood against my spine aches. It feels so fucking good.

"God, this feels good."

"Me inside you?" He grunts, pushing me higher. "I agree."

"Four. Three."

I tense up, my muscles on the verge.

"You close?" His jaw flexes, and his rhythm breaks, becoming erratic.

"Two. One." He pulses within me, and the sensation, combined with the roar from the other side of the wall, sets me off, quivering my release.

My legs slowly fall to the floor. I would collapse, except he's pressed against me. His lips press against my cheeks until he finds my lips.

Hovering over me as I cling to his shoulders, he whispers, "Happy New Year."

eleven

Kate

January 1

Last night, we sang all the words we know to *Auld Lang Syne*, laughing and kicking out our legs, all the way back to The Four Seasons, where the New Year's party continued in full swing. Inside the fancy hotel, sequins and blazers mixed with shrill paper horns and shiny pom-poms. Oliver and I bypassed the group celebration, choosing our private version instead.

We celebrated a second time in our unique way when we crossed the line into the New Year in Mountain Time with the bittersweet *Auld Lang Syne* lyrics flowing between us. The seas between us broad will roar, but last night, we allowed no distance between us.

My heart thumps heavy in my chest as I braid my hair. But there's no reason for a heavy anything. This fling has done me a world of good. For one, I've never had better sex. Two, I made a friend. There's no romantic future for the two of us. I'm a realist. I accept reality. But I believe months from now I could call Oliver, and he'd have me laughing in no time. He's one of those guys who can be your friend after sex. Even lots of sex.

My brother is the same way. There are so many girls he considers friends, and I'm pretty sure he's slept with all of them. It's all part of his competitive touring lifestyle. Snowboarding fans show up to watch and hope to hang out after events. I imagine it's like the rock star life but on a significantly scaled-down level. Instead of groupies, Hudson feeds the snow bunnies.

Oliver places the earrings that I left here days ago on the bathroom counter. He's packing, and with each item he drops into the suitcase, a piece of me drops too. But that's the silly girl within. The one who read books with titles like *P.S. I Love You* during middle school.

Oliver loves Texas, a state I've never been to and have no desire to enter. Their governor is a lunatic, and their politics are atrocious. Gun-toting extremists thrive in that whacked-out hillbilly state.

Aside from all of those issues, Oliver loves heat. I love snow. My fantasy is the never-ending winter, spending half the year in the northern hemisphere and the other half in the southern. Blizzard warnings get my blood pumping like nothing else. Well, other than an orgasm.

"You working late today?" Oliver asks while diligently folding clothes.

"I got a text from Harvey when you went down to get coffee."

"And? You have the day off?" One eyebrow lifts, like it would be a good thing. And I suppose it might be nice, except I need the money and a day off would be pointless. He leaves this morning.

"No." I return his smile. Leaving isn't fazing him at all. He was scheduled to leave two days ago. He's jonesing to get home. "I'm going to work the morning shift at the rentals, then someone called in sick, so I'll be subbing again at ski school."

"Does Harvey run the ski school?"

"No. A friend of his does. I registered as a sub at the start of the season. I don't know exactly how it works, but I imagine Janessa calls Harvey and asks who he can spare. Several of us are on the sub list."

"Waiting to get a permanent spot?"

"Not me. I want ski patrol." How many times do I have to fucking say it? Sometimes it feels like banging my head against a wall.

"Right." His barely-there smile softens the irritation simmering.

He steals a quick kiss before bypassing me to check the bedside table drawer. He lifts a box of condoms, the ones we didn't use, and drops it in his bag.

Yep, he'll be needing those. And we shouldn't have gone last night without one. Hell, we shouldn't have fucked in a bathroom with a gross urinal. I'll add it to my long list of shouldn'ts. Only, as long as he's clean, it won't fall into my list of regrets. No, I loved feeling him inside me, bare. I loved being that close to him, as close as humanly possible, just once. And, well, the other times last night in this now rumpled bed.

The zipper zipping across his bag announces his readiness to depart.

"I wish I could see you off at the airport." It might sound like an obligatory statement, but there's a part of me that would really love to drive him to the airport. Thirty more minutes of car time, selecting music and holding hands, appeals, but no matter how much my insides wish for it, it's simply not meant to be. And I am a realistic girl.

"Airport goodbyes aren't what they used to be." He wheels his suitcase into the living area, and I follow.

"What do you mean?"

"You're probably too young to remember this, but there was a time when you could hug someone right at the gate."

"Did you do that? Hug someone right at the gate?" He's only ten years older than I am. Times haven't changed that much.

"Well, I was a kid. But my folks would sit right with us and watch us go down the hall to board the plane."

"You flew by yourself as a kid?"

"To go visit my mom's parents. Sure did. Every summer. Not after 9/11, though. My parents didn't feel the same about sending us off for a while, and then I was just older."

"No summer visit at grandma's?" I'm smiling, but inside there's a torrent of sadness swirling. He's about to leave. Nothing gold can stay. All good things must fade. And so goes our fling.

"Nope." He weaves his fingers between mine as I scan the hotel room.

The beautiful hotel room with enormous windows and a fireplace and a fuchsia orchid on one small table. "Room 248, you've been good to us."

"She has been good to us. A week I'll never forget." He opens his wallet and drops several bills on the kitchenette counter. His long lashes flutter as he looks my way. He appears almost thoughtful. "If you ever find your way to Texas…"

He lets the sentence trail. All the sad emotions swirl with hope. But that's not how flings work. And if I let myself get wrapped up in hope, then I'll be losing out on one of the good things about a fling. No girly emotions weighing me down. No concern about tomorrow.

"No snow. No mountains." I lift my shoulders and smile. I check my wristwatch to avoid looking into whiskey and amber. "Texas isn't my kind of state."

"Ouch."

His phone vibrates. He reads it.

"Car's here."

"But if you come back to Jackson," I offer. I shouldn't be harsh with him. If things go well, I'll be in Jackson for years to come, and skiers and boarders love to vacation here.

"We normally go to Aspen. This year is an anomaly thanks to contagious children."

"You only go skiing once a year?"

His bottom lip juts out, and he nods slowly.

"Once is enough. I'll be paying for days after a week on a board."

"How?"

"You come down and ride in a saddle, and I'll show you. Different muscles. I'll be in some serious pain."

"You ride every day?" I haven't asked him a lot about his day-to-day life. It felt like infringing and maybe venturing into dangerous ground for a fling.

"Every day I can." He opens the door and holds it for me. After I pass through, he calls out, "Goodbye, Room 248."

We ride in the elevator and pass through the lobby without saying a word. He reaches for my hand and toys with my fingers. My gaze falls to the tiled floor the whole way out to the black Cadillac Escalade.

A driver in a black wool coat and black leather gloves awaits. He takes Oliver's suitcase, confirms the destination, and rounds the vehicle to stow the bag.

My chest constricts. Girly emotions win out and threaten to spill over, and I fight them down.

His large palms cup my jaw. I lean in, loving the feel and the warmth.

"Hey, look at me."

I force my gaze up. I barely glimpse the golden amber before his lips press to mine.

That's all it is. A brush of lips. He doesn't ask for entrance. He doesn't push to deepen our last kiss. His forehead presses to mine, and in that moment, our souls mingle.

For this one brief moment in time, our lives overlapped. It's such a girlie thing to think and feel, but I'll never be the same.

"Take care, Ms. Oakley."

He climbs into the back seat and shuts the door. The dark tint on the glass prevents seeing into the vehicle. The back passenger window rolls down. I take a mental picture of his barely-there smile and his unruly sandy brown hair. He slides on his sunglasses and gives me a two-finger salute.

The Escalade's chained wheels grind the icy patches out to the main road. I stand there, gathering my emotions, until the black Escalade turns out of the hotel, airport bound.

One lone tear rolls down my cheek. I swipe it. There will be none of that.

An idea for my next article comes to mind. When I return to my apartment, I type out the headline—How to Survive a Fling.

End of Part 1

# *twelve*

Oliver

January 5

The meteorologist on the muted television set points at a national map. There's blue over the Tetons and green all over the southern half of the country. The blue over the Tetons is good news, I expect. Kate loves snow. Maybe she'll get a chance to hit the slopes on one of those powder days.

Of course, those national maps are deceptive. Rain's generally spotty in Texas, but they green out the whole blooming state when a system rolls our way. The local forecast pops on, and we're looking at a thirty percent chance of showers this afternoon.

With a steaming cup of joe in hand, I step out onto the deck to catch up on the news. The sky outside is a hazy gray. The air bears a clean, fresh pine scent with a hint of earth. I love my life.

This land has been in my father's family for generations. At forty-five degrees, it's a chilly morning, so I click on the patio heater and kick back. Off in the distance, my Appaloosa swats her tail and shakes her neck, then trots away from whatever horsefly is after her.

From my folks' back screened-in porch, I can see across two pastures. Off yonder, behind the woods line, there's a family cemetery. No one's been buried back there since my great grandparents' generation, but I keep up with it just the same out of respect for my elders.

The Duke ranch encompasses twenty-four hundred acres. That's a lot of fence line. We're what's called a working ranch. Most years, we eke out a slim profit. When I was growing up, my parents lived off income from my dad's construction company, not from this farm.

When the land passes on to us, I hope to buy out my brothers' shares and keep the ranch whole. We've talked about it some, and I don't expect they'll object.

My older brother, Sam, married a Yankee, and I don't see him ever finding his way back to Texas. He's got his multibillion-dollar company to look after. And my younger brother, Ian, is firmly rooted in Houston. It's like pulling teeth to get him out of that sinking, over-populated cesspool.

Jason spent a few summers with us after his folks passed, and while he's always welcome here, he made it clear he's more of a city boy. Jason prefers academic life, and I completely get his desire to live in Chicago. But I'll never understand Sam's and Ian's willingness to leave this place. We had one of the best damn childhoods imaginable. Tons of land to roam, hunt, and fish. Neighbors out of sight and sound.

I love this land. Seems crazy to say you love land, but I do. There's no peace like the peace I feel looking out over the freshly cut pastures. The moo of the cows and the neigh of the horses give me those sounds any day of the week and twice on Sunday over the honk of a horn.

Kate mentioned she loves the expansive view from the top of the mountain. Well, I understand her. This is the top-of-the-mountain view I crave. Rolling green augmented by lush broadleaf trees as far as the eye can see.

I haven't seen or spoken to Kate since I got back, but the ski girl has entered my thoughts time and again. What a stroke of luck to run into her. My Christmas would have royally sucked, but instead, I had a fucking great week. A little bit of family, a sprinkling of time with an old friend, and a shit ton of sex. Most spectacular holiday I've ever had.

Too bad she lives so far away. She and I are a lot alike. I'd bet she'd love the wide-open spaces here. At least, I think she would. I've been wrong before thinking a woman would like it here.

She's probably off on her next fling. I never clued her in that I'd read that little article she was working on. Mainly because I didn't want to let her know I'd snooped. Also maybe because that invited a discussion, and by her own accounting, that was number six on her list of fling benefits. Who am I to deprive her of one of the benefits of a fling?

The screen door creaks and the noise catches my attention.

"You look like you're king of the world sittin' on your throne."

I tilt my mug to Sandra in a mock salute. Sandra is a neighbor, or what we consider a neighbor in these parts. Her family's place is a couple of miles down the road. She's also my older brother's ex-girlfriend. She's a couple of years older than I am and a friend for the ages. I swing around to take in my auburn, leggy friend. The girl still puts her hair in rollers on most workdays, but this morning her mane is all kinds of wild, like she maybe brushed it out and didn't bother to do more.

"How you doin', girl? Can I get you some coffee?"

"Already had mine. Heard from Bo you got back a couple of days ago."

Sandra sets down a large basket filled with red and green tins and crinkled paper straw. The basket partially covers the latest industry report on automatic car washes. I'm considering building a few of those. I like businesses that earn income with minimal ongoing effort. I'm a partner in a restaurant group, a real estate development group, and I own storage facilities throughout Texas and all along the Gulf. My goal is to set enough aside so that when the day comes to buy my brothers out, I can do so with ease.

"Didn't get your holiday gift to you before you left." I scratch the back of my neck and hope Mom got Sandra something from all of us. "How'd the Duke Family Vacation go?"

"It didn't this year."

She sits down in an armchair and rests her forearms on her knees, leaning forward, her face one big question mark. I chuckle.

"Hand, foot, and mouth disease hit."

"Well, I know about that. I was here on Christmas with your folks and Ian. But I thought you guys all got together? Were you sick?" Her nose scrunches up, and there's a touch of shock. Not surprise that I'd be sick, but probably more surprised I didn't call her for help.

"I didn't make it to Aspen."

"So, when you were snowed in, where were you? Still in Jackson?"

"Yeah. I thought you knew that. Ian and Sam came out for a couple of days."

"I did know that. I just thought, for some reason, you headed to Aspen with Sam."

Here's the thing about Sandra. She's never gotten over my brother Sam, and I don't know if she ever will. There was a window of time when I thought she came by all the time because maybe she had set her sights on yours truly. But she walks a careful line asking about Sam, and from time to time those blue eyes go misty, and it's clear she's still got it bad for Sam Bo. And that's a tragic thing because Sam is one fish that is caught, hook, line, and sinker.

"Nope."

"I knew you canceled on Cindy." Her hand falls over her sternum. "Were you alone on New Year's? And Christmas?"

"Look at you getting all dramatic. I was not alone." I think back to Kate in my bed on Christmas morning. A white Christmas I'm not likely to ever forget.

"Why are you grinning? Who were you with?"

I roll my eyes at Sandra and pass her my phone, opened to the folder with photos from the week in Jackson.

"Wanna see the photos? There are a few of Sam and Ian in there." Yeah, it's sort of like tossing a bone to send the retriever off in a different direction.

As expected, those photos absorb her. I don't miss how she slows on the photos of Sam. The two of them split when I was a freshman at the University of Texas. I never asked for the details because my head was firmly parked up my own drunken ass. But sometimes I wonder what the hell happened.

My phone lights up while she's holding it. It's on vibrate, so there's no sound.

"It's Liam." She holds the phone out for me.

Liam Sheffield is one of my frat brothers from UT and a business partner in Artisan Homes Incorporated. We started out small with custom builds, moved into specs, and now we have a multi-million-dollar neighborhood development on the outskirts of Austin.

"Hey, bro." I haven't spoken to him since the holidays, so I add, "Happy New Year."

"Not so much." Liam is your average business guy. Never too jovial, but never too stern, either. He typically walks it right down the middle. Makes him a natural for real estate as he can adapt to any kind of customer. With me, given our long, sordid history, I don't get an adaptation. I get real. And his solemn tone says shit has hit the fan.

"What's up?" Or down. I take my kicked-back feet off the table and set them on the ground. Sandra tilts her head and tosses me concern.

"Lawsuit. Damn kid at Coronada was running poolside and slipped. Ended up in the ER with head trauma."

"But the pool and club area are closed."

"Closed, yes. They say the gate was unlocked. Probably one of the pool cleaners left it open. Do they have a case?"

"In our damn litigious society? Probably." *Fuck.* We are a stone's throw away from raising another round of capital for Phase II. The last thing we need is a suit hanging over our heads.

"Can you pull any strings to get us before a good judge?"

I can't help pulling my phone back to look at it. My insides churn. "Let's not jump the fence. With luck, this will never see the inside of a courtroom. Are you at the office today?"

He confirms he is, and I tell him I'll stop by. In exchange for keeping my pretty face out of the office, I offer my legal services to my partners. But I'm not a litigator. If this goes to court, we'll need to hire resources. Which means we'll need to raise even more money.

What a fucking mess. Unlocked fucking pool gate.

Weather doesn't get wicked cold in Texas, but it gets too cold to swim year-round. And we have trouble staffing through those winter school months, so we close it down November, December, and January. Damn gate should have been locked.

"Everything all right?" Sandra drawls, pulling me back to my deck.

"Yeah. Kid fell at Coronada."

"And he's suing?"

"It's America, baby." I grin, but I don't feel it. I told them that travertine was too damn slippery. *Fuck.*

"Your photos there." She points at my phone, which is still tucked tight in my hand. "Who's the girl?"

I didn't snap a photo of Kate. I should have, but I'm damn positive I didn't.

Sandra busts out laughing. "Your face. There's no photo in there. But you stayed out there for a week. You could've left when Ian and Sam did. But you stayed. There's gotta be a girl."

"Nope."

"I don't believe you." Skepticism coats her face. She knows I'm no monk. But I'm smart enough to know nothing good will come from telling Sandra about my adventures. She's the sister I never wanted, and she'd grate my nerves with incessant teasing, the way any blooming sister would.

"Cindy really was bummed. I thought you'd just decided to join the fam in Aspen." Her grin has me mentally rolling my eyes. She slaps my leg. "Look, I think it's great. But Cindy is hoping you'll make good on that rain check."

I shrug. It's not really something I'm itching to do, but who knows how I'll feel about it after some time elapses. She's a nice enough girl. And, unlike my ex, she seems to genuinely like country life.

After I tell Sandra to have a good day, I check in on the ranch. It's BAU and running smoothly.

In the Artisan offices, a cursory review promises this lawsuit will be a thorn. And there will be a lawsuit, because it's pretty damn clear the father of the boy is aware how much we raised in our first round. He referenced it when saying we could afford to pay for pain and suffering.

Pain and suffering for his ten-year-old running off where he shouldn't've been. Gotta love America. It'll all come down to whether or not that gate was left wide open. Worst case, it was. In such a situation, I'd prefer to settle, switch out that travertine, and call it a day.

Back home, with a beer in my hand and the same view that started my day, the sunset catches my eye. Pinks, roses, yellows, and golds paint the horizon above the tree line. I whip out my phone and snap a photo because our sunsets are nice here, but this one is a spectacle. The moisture in the air from the scattered rainstorms generates an optical delight. Kate's brother sends her snapshots all day. On a whim, I hit forward and send this one on.

Under the setting sun, the deep greens of the expansive pasture will be a sharp contrast to the bright whites Kate loves. As the sun sets behind the tree line, a chill blankets the air. Not the kind of chill that requires gloves, neck and face warmer, plus goggles, but it's too chilly to sit outside comfortably. I head on in and call it a night. While I'd love to have a certain brunette to keep me warm, I've got my memories. And I fully expect those memories will occupy my fantasies for quite a bit of time to come. At least until I meet my next Kate.

thirteen

Kate

February 5

"What are you doing?"

Claire, my roommate, collapses onto the bed beside me, lying on her stomach, socked feet up in the air, just like me.

"Picking the best photo. Which do you think?"

She enlarges the photos and thumbs through.

"Is this for that guy you've been sulking over?"

I have not been sulking. I've just had a lot on my mind. It's frustrating because I absolutely loved my holiday fling, but I apparently am not built for carefree flings. My heart and mind are not in sync. Or they haven't been. I'm a work in progress. Small steps every day.

"He's a fling. Let it go." She bumps my arm. Claire means well. She's got everything together in her life and she wants the same for me. "In your article, didn't you say the best way to get over someone is to get under someone else?"

"No." I curl up onto my side and grin at her. Claire proofs my articles before I submit them. Actually, that particular one I posted on

Medium as a listicle and it did quite well. "In the article, I said the act of searching for a special someone focuses your mind on the future."

"Same thing." She shrugs and gives me a grin. "Which online dating app did you choose?"

"I just put that in the article. I have zero intention of actually doing it. And I can tell you did not notice, but dating others was last on the list. The other self-care items are much more important."

"Why?"

"Because."

She gives me a look that basically says I've got serious issues.

"Kate…the whole world uses dating apps." Oh, she's stuck on that.

"It's just not me."

"How can you promote something to your readers and then not do it?"

"Easy." I roll onto my back and take in the ancient popcorn ceiling. "My advice was hand-curated from a selection of well-respected and educated psychologists."

She rolls her eyes.

"And I don't have time to go on dates." I've picked up several bartending shifts, plus I'm working pretty much every single day. "I'm focusing on career. Number one on the list. Remember? There are three aspects to everyone's life. Love, work, and family and friends. Right now, I'm just at a phase of life where work is all-consuming."

"Why do I get the feeling you've always been like this?" She squints, and her expression grows thoughtful. Claire is the kind of person who has her life together. "Have you?"

"What?"

"Always been like this? That work box is everything."

I'm only twenty-five. Of course, my primary focus has been career. Up until last year, no one questioned me. If anything, they admired me. Saw me as driven and goal-oriented. Now everyone looks at me like I'm out of my mind. But I don't care what other people think. This is my year to pursue a life I enjoy, and I don't owe anyone explanations.

"Did you pick a favorite picture?" I ask, redirecting her. She isn't that different from me, so I don't get her attitude or her assumption I'm doing things wrong.

She lets out a sigh, scrolls, and picks a bland nothing photo of a blue sky with one small fluffy cloud. "What kind of photos does what's-his-name send you?"

"Mostly animals. Horses. Cows. Birds."

"That's cool. Is he coming back to visit?"

"Nah. He's one of those who goes skiing once a year. His brother has a place in Aspen, so if he goes once more this season, it'll be out there."

Oliver and I send snapshots to each other. It's no big deal. He's become a friend. A connection. I select a photo from the top of Corbet's, a much better image than the one Claire selected, zip it off to him, then click on the folder of images he's shared.

"This is his ranch. It's gorgeous, isn't it?"

Claire's head rests against mine as she leans in to get a look. She doesn't enlarge the photos but scans the rows of three squares.

"Nice," she says and straightens. "Look. There's something I need to talk to you about." She pushes up off her hands and sits with her legs crossed. "I got an apartment."

My stomach plummets.

"It's a great deal, and I can't turn it down. With my personality, I will be happiest living alone. It's not a thing against you guys. It's just me. And I got a raise in January and can afford it. But I want to help you find a new roommate. I don't want to leave you guys stranded." She clasps my hand. "Say something. Don't be mad. I don't have that many friends here."

Claire, like me, moved here last summer. A lot of us moved here last summer. The seasonal employees are always in flux.

"I totally get it," I tell her, and I do. But I didn't get a raise in

January and can't afford to pay more rent. Who on Earth are we going to find mid-season?

"Honeys, I'm home," Nash calls from down the hall. A door slams, followed by heavy clunks as he removes his boots on the wood.

Claire grimaces. I squeeze her hand and whisper, "He's the reason you're moving out, isn't he?"

In a perfect world, we could kick him out, except we're subletting from Nash.

Nash appears in the doorway, shirtless and barefoot, with a big, drunken grin.

"Why did you guys skip après-ski?" His eyes are slightly blood-shot, and he's louder than normal, but he's not stumbling. Nash, as he proudly tells anyone, can hold his alcohol.

"Claire's moving out." I barf the words. He might as well know as soon as possible. We need to brainstorm roommates.

Nash's smile dims, and his eyelids half-close. His reaction makes me question exactly how intoxicated he is.

"No problem," he says, and his full smile and bright white teeth return. "It'll just be the two of us, babe."

"Nash. I can't afford to split this place." He should know that. I have debts on top of rent.

"No worries. I'll tell my folks. They'll cover it."

Nash is my brother's age, and he's still leaning on his parents for subsidies. Just like my brother. It burns me up. I won't do it. Yes, I turned twenty-five last month, and not a damn thing in my life changed. But one thing is certain. At twenty-five, I'm not taking money from my parents. Or from Nash's.

"I'll help you find a new roommate. I promise," Claire says in this pleading tone that forces me to internally cringe.

"Carlos," Nash says. "I think he might need a place."

Carlos is a bartender boarder who has a social life that makes Nash's look positively boring. If he needs a place to stay, it's only because he got kicked out of his apartment. His parties are legendary.

"I don't think Kate wants to be out-gendered," Claire says, shooting a glare at Nash. The glare sobers him, and his smile fades.

My phone vibrates, and Oliver's face shows on screen. It's a selfie he sent me a few weeks ago while horseback riding on his ranch. He's tan and smiling, and the sun highlights the golden tones in his left eye. The shadow from his cowboy hat shades the other eye with a chocolate glaze. And yes, I gave him hell for wearing a cowboy hat. I mean, yeah, I'm in Wyoming, and technically it's cowboy land too, but not here at a ski resort.

He told me the hat protects him from the sun. Judging from his tanned complexion, I think he needs more sunblock, but that's me, a doctor's daughter.

"Look at you." She nudges my ribs. "He calls, and you start smiling and go all goo-goo."

"I do not."

"Who's that?" Nash asks, stepping closer to the bed.

"Can you two get out of here?"

Claire grins as the phone continues vibrating, but she does at least get off the bed and pull Nash out of my room. She wags her finger at me as she pulls the door closed. "Tell lover boy I said hello."

"Lover who?" Nash says, and the door clicks shut.

I wait a beat, breathe in deeply, and answer.

"Hey there," I say.

Nash, for whatever insane reasons, shouts, "Hey, Kate, we're gonna be the Nash and Kate Show. We'll YouTube it."

"Did you recognize the spot in my photo?" I ask Oliver while hoping Claire will quiet Nash down. I assume Oliver's calling because of the photo I just sent him. He sometimes calls after I send him a photo, especially when it's later his time and he's at home.

"What's the Nash and Kate Show?"

I plop back on my bed, phone to my ear, and lay a hand over my eyes.

"Nash is drunk. Ignore him. What are you up to?"

"Sitting out on my deck beneath the heat lamp."

"Heat lamp? I thought it's always hot in Texas."

"Goes to show how little you know. We're getting down to forty-two tonight."

I bark out a laugh. "That sounds positively sultry. I think we'll be at negative eighteen."

"Dang. I don't know how you do it."

"Tell me about it. Two days ago, my car door handle snapped off in my hand. Almost sent you a photo, but it was too much of a hassle to dig my phone out."

"Are you serious? How do you people live like that?"

"There are tricks." I'm from Vermont. This isn't totally new to me, but Wyoming is a singular brand of cold. "I forgot to grease up the handle. I should've known better."

"You need a garage."

"Right?" I'd rather not talk about my life. "Any movement in that lawsuit?"

"Not really. Those things move about the pace of a tortoise. The meeting with the insurance company's legal team is on the calendar. Nothing's going to happen until we have that meeting." I hear him swallow and visualize the movement along his tanned throat. In my mind's eye, he's sitting back with fuzzy slippers, jeans, and either a flannel or a sweater, with a blanket draped over his legs and a beer in his hand. There's a symphony of crickets and horses neigh off in the distance.

"Have you been skiing this week?"

"Not this week. Working too much. I had two substitute sessions with ski school, but that's lower mountain." It's a problem, actually. I need time on the advanced slopes so I can prove I can do it all. It's a catch twenty-two. I need money to live, so I need to work. But if I don't get time on the slopes, Bill Woodland will cut me from consideration. And rightfully so. People entrust their lives to ski patrol's ability to get them down the mountain safely from any point within the resort.

"Have you got much planned for the weekend?"

My breathing slows as I wait for his response. If he tells me he's going on a date, it would be fine, of course. There's a good chance our paths will never cross again. The chances are good he goes out on dates regularly. Unlike me, he lives a more normal life and has his evenings and nights free.

Oliver and I don't talk on the phone often, but when we do, our conversations ramble. We talk about all kinds of things...music, movies, books. Our families. But we never directly inquire about each other's love life. Given how we started, it would be too much.

"Let's see. This weekend. Planning on taking it easy. Not a lot planned. Might go hunting."

"Hunting? For what?"

Knock. Bam. Knock.

My bedroom door swings open. I'm still reeling from the unsavory idea of Oliver out there killing innocent animals.

Nash bounds into my room and loudly announces, "Great news. Mom says they'll cover the rent. No need to stress."

Nash grins, proud of himself.

"Nash. I'm on the phone." I point at the device pressed against my ear, and he does a weird salute with his hand and closes the door behind him. After I get off the phone, I'll have to talk with him, as I have zero intention of letting his parents subsidize my share of the apartment.

"What was that?" Oliver asks.

"Claire is moving out."

"The Nash and Kate Show. I get it now."

"I'll find a replacement roommate."

"Doesn't sound like Nash wants you to."

"Nah, he's just like my brother. Happy to lean on his parents. He's a good guy. He's just..." I trail off, searching for the right words. I love my brother and Nash. I don't want to slam them.

"He just doesn't want to grow up," Oliver supplies.

"Yep." And the fact is, until the parentals cut Hudson and Nash off, they'll be content with things as they are. My parents look at it as supporting their son in a competitive sporting world. And if he keeps these sponsor deals, it looks like it's going to pay off. For all I know, my parents don't even support Hudson anymore. I'm not sure how Nash's parents justify it. He's off the competitive circuit. "What kind of hunting are you doing?"

"Old Nash has heart eyes for you, so he's stoked. It's gonna be just the two of you in a love shack."

"What?" Oliver's country twang makes that sentence sound like it's out of some old nineties flick. "There's nothing romantic between Nash and me. Please tell me you're not going to kill Bambi."

"You can't honestly tell me you don't see that he has the hots for you."

"Not at all," I insist.

"Isn't that a love trope? Best friend's little sister? Roommates? Friends to lovers?"

"Are you going to tell me what kind of hunting you're doing?" This is something I did not know about Oliver. And now I'm wondering if he's one of those men who collects guns and pretends there's a rational reason for an assault rifle.

"Come on, Kate. You know the tropes." Why is he going on and on about this? My hand falls over my forehead, but I'm grinning like a loon. "One day, my friend Sandra walked me through her favorite love books." He drawls out the word love, and my grin grows wider. There's something about talking to Oliver. He always brings out my smiles, even when he goes on a tangent and won't answer my freaking question. The world feels better through the lens of his Texas lilt. He's mentioned some of his friends, but never a woman other than his mom.

"Who is Sandra?"

"Come visit me in Texas. I'll introduce you."

Yeah, right. I can afford a flight to Texas like I can afford a new handle for my car door. I won't say that, though, because that would sound needy or like I'm asking him to pay.

"Come visit me in Jackson, and I'll introduce you to my new roommate."

"You got someone lined up?"

"No. But I will."

"Not if Nash has anything to say with it. Mark my words."

"You are wrong about Nash."

"I wish I was, Ms. Oakley, but I'm not."

Oliver

February 10

"Mom, you did it again. Fantastic meal."

Mom and Dad returned home after an extended trip to Aspen and then to Connecticut to spend time with her precious grandbabies. All the Christmas stuff had to be put away, and while I love all the free meals and laundry service that come with my folks' return home, Dad's annoyed, perma-frown lets me know he's about to put an end to Mom's extended holiday checking on her chickadees. He's ready to get back to the beach house and his retired life. Sam Senior makes himself pretty easy to read.

"Honey, have you talked to your brother?"

"Which one?" I've got a good guess which one she's inquiring about, given she just spent over a month with Sam's family, and she got to see Jason and his family on that trip too, but I like seeing her get a little flustered that I'm not reading her mind.

"Ian."

"We've texted."

"I'm worried about him. I'm thinking about maybe visiting him this weekend." One glance at Sam Senior, and it's abundantly evident what he thinks of that plan. "We could stay at one of those nice hotels in Houston, and we wouldn't need to bother him."

"Didn't you see him at Christmas?"

"Yes, we did." Dad's hands rest on his belly, and he's giving mom a stink eye if I've ever seen one, but she completely disregards him as she busily clears the table and rinses the dishes.

"He seems pretty good to me. Busy like normal."

"Something was off at Christmas. I'm worried about him."

"Not sure you need to be, Mom." She acts like she didn't hear me, and Dad grunts. "He's basically working two full-time jobs. He's just busy."

"No. It's not just me. After Christmas, Sandra checked in on him to make sure he's doing okay when she was in Houston visiting a friend. She's such a sweet girl. I know she was just checking on him as a favor to me."

Mom puts some elbow grease into the stainless steel pot she's working on, and her focus gives Dad and me a chance to exchange knowing glances. Sandra keeps close to this family because she's not over Sam. We all know it. I think Mom does, too, but she doesn't readily acknowledge her son broke 'sweet Sandra's' heart.

Bang. Bang. Bang.

The loud racket is coming from the direction of the front door.

"Who is that?" Mom asks at the same time my Dad asks, "What's that?"

The racket pretty much guarantees whoever is at the door is there for me and not my parents. My parents' generation would pretty much always ring a doorbell.

"Someone's at the door. I'll get it." I wave a hand at Dad and say, "Stay seated."

I swing the door open, and Noah Alden, my childhood friend, fraternity brother, and business partner, stumbles inside. The guy reeks of both alcohol and cigarettes, and he's not a smoker. It's also barely seven in the evening.

"What the hell?" He heads down the entry hall toward the kitchen.

I catch up to him as Dad enters the hall.

"Mr. Duke." He snaps back, looking at me, like we're teens and he's been caught.

"They're in town." Visiting is on the tip of my tongue, but that's not right. This is their house. It's a fresh reminder to me that it's time I build my own house. They're gone so much it's easy to settle in, and the reality is, this is still my parents' house.

"Noah," Dad says in his customary deep voice. He's a good ten feet away, but by the flare of his nostrils, I'm guessing he can smell him. "Good to see you, son."

Noah somehow trips, and I leap forward, catching him and leaning into him to help.

"I'm gonna take Noah to sit on the porch."

"Sounds good," Dad says. "I'll ask Patty about getting some coffee together for you boys."

"Thanks, Dad."

Yeah, we're both thirty-five, but we could be sixty-five and Dad would refer to us as boys. That's the way it is.

On the back porch, Noah moans as he lands on the sofa and rubs his hand all over his face.

"What's going on, man?" I take the chair near him and lean forward. Something is royally fucked up.

"Jocelyn's pregnant." That's not remotely the answer I was expecting.

Jocelyn and Noah have been together since high school. Years of on-again, off-again drama that we all thought would simmer down when he finally proposed, but their marriage followed the same tumultuous path, given some years Jocelyn wanted a baby, and Noah didn't, and other years the situation flipped. Given the state of my drunken friend, I surmise Noah is currently in the no-baby camp.

"That's not a bad thing," I say. "Babies are good. Might be the best thing that's ever happened to you."

Noah leans over his legs, arms on his thighs, head in his hands, hair falling forward. Dad arrives at the glass door and gives me a questioning glance. I throw him a thumbs up and wave him away. Dad gives me a thumbs up back and retreats.

Noah slowly lifts his head. His eyes are a bloodshot mess, and I can't help but wonder how long he's been drinking. And how the hell he got to our house.

"It's not my baby."

Aw, hell. Shit.

"Bourbon? That's what you want?"

I get up and leave the porch, heading straight to the liquor cabinet in the den. Mom and Dad stand in the doorway.

"Everything okay?" Mom asks.

I look Dad in the eye as two glasses clink together.

"Jocelyn and Noah are going through a rough patch."

"Well, honey, let us know if there's anything we can do. Are you sure you want more of that stuff and not coffee?"

"She's pregnant with someone else's baby."

Dad loops his arm around Mom's shoulders, steering her down the hall. "We'll make sure the guest room's ready. Don't let him get alcohol poisoning."

As I set the bourbon and glasses down on the coffee table outside, my phone buzzes.

Kate: You around?

"Who's that?" Noah asks as he sloshes bourbon onto the table. About half of the golden remedy spills into his glass. "If it's Jocelyn, tell her to fuck off."

Since I'm not sure if not being Jocelyn is a good or bad thing, I respond with, "You got it."

Me: N. Will try you tomorrow.

Tomorrow for Kate and me doesn't really mean tomorrow. It just means another day. Sometimes we talk. Sometimes we don't. Tonight, it looks like I'll be on vomit duty.

"I can't fucking believe it." Noah leans back on the sofa, and his head hits the wall. "Should've fucking known."

My phone vibrates.

Sandra: Have you seen Noah?

"Is that Josie?" Hearing him drunkenly use his wife's nickname, the one only he uses, tears at some heartstrings in a completely unexpected way. What a fucked-up situation.

"Nah. It's Sandra."

He closes his eyes, and that's when I notice his damp cheeks. *Fuck.*

Me to Sandra: He's here.

Sandra: Do you need help?

Me to Sandra: Nah. He'll be lights out shortly.

Me to Sandra: Who else knows?

Three dots appear and disappear and then appear.

Sandra: Everyone.

Well, fuck.

Me to Liam and Sandra: I've got Noah tonight. Swing by in the morning if you want coffee and breakfast.

That's another nice thing about Patty Duke being in the house. She'll cook us up a spread.

Noah's eyes are closed, and his bourbon glass tips to the side. I lift it out of his hands, but his fingers remain in holding position. "She's kicking me out of the house."

"You can stay here."

"Patty," he utters. "Sam."

"They're leaving in a day to two. This house is plenty big enough for the two of us."

I should probably tell Drew. He won't hear about this bullshit through the normal friend circuit.

"Kicking." His breathing slows. "Out."

I sit there watching my old friend, reeling from the bullshit. There was a time when I admired Noah for sticking through thick and thin with Jocelyn. A time when I'd been so damn jealous they made it and Collette and I didn't.

Country tunes play through our Siri on the deck, and the song that comes on is one I played a shit ton back when Collette and I split. She never did return her engagement ring, and that's still a sore point for me. But Garth Brooks' words pack meaning like they never have before as he drones on about unanswered prayers. Things for Noah are mighty bleak now, but maybe, just maybe, this will be the best thing that's ever happened to him. God knows I express gratitude every single day that I discovered Collette's true desires before we walked the aisle.

Noah's passed out, but it's still early enough I don't stand a chance of sleeping. I get on my laptop and search around. There's a *Medium* article about a thirty-five-year-old who may have lost the rest of his life. Being thirty-five, I naturally click on it. Turns out he has colon cancer, but there's something else about the article that gets my wheels turning. He mentions he hasn't posted an article in a while. That gets me thinking about if Kate might have published her little fling article. Is that why she wrote it? Do you get money from this?

So, I search by the title "Benefits of a Fling." A ton of links surface, but there's one from an Annie Oakley that catches my attention. I click it and read. Word for pretty much word, it's her article and a silhouette of a girl I know intimately. That's interesting. She's got herself a *nom de plume*. There's a link to another article.

It's titled "How to Survive a Fling." Since when did survival become necessary? She seemed to be doing just fine, from what I can tell. I skim her points and close the laptop after reading her last survival tip. *Get out there and date.*

Kate

March 5

Mom grips my arm, the crowd cheers, and Mom buries her head into my shoulder.

Dad screams, "Go, Holden!"

My brother's body twists as he performs a stunning airborne three-sixty, catching air, spinning over the embankment, and lands.

"Three corks! Yes!" It's not the back-to-back double cork he's been working on, but this also isn't the Olympics. This is Jackson, and his score will be high. This performance may earn him a place on the Olympic team.

"He did it?" Mom asks, slowly lifting her head and peering toward the judges' stand.

The crowd cheers. Nash belts out an earsplitting "Wooooooooooooh."

Music blares out of speakers set up near the base. It's a mix of old-school Fu Fighters and newer Chainsmokers and bands I've never heard before.

"Nine point seven five," Dad says, so proud you'd think he completed the run himself.

"Will that put him in first?" I'm pretty sure it will, but I don't follow the scores as intently as Dad.

"It should. Three more to go."

Mom twists her hands together. She's wearing reflective goggles, but the tension in her jawline reveals her concern. "I hate watching you kids do this. If you guys saw what I see come off the mountain."

Mom hasn't worked the ER in decades, but to hear her talk, you'd think she treated a spinal injury patient minutes ago. You'd also think boarding is the most dangerous sport on Earth, or perhaps right behind jumping on a trampoline. She forbid trampolines, and the mention of one sends her into a flurry of gruesome, tragic stories.

Dad grins at Mom and slaps his gloved hand against her snow pants butt. The cushion on cushion creates a swoosh sound. Dad never seems to worry much about Hudson.

Given that's not the case for me, I might be more like Mom than I'd care to admit. I've held my breath and closed my eyes more than once.

But Hudson is a natural. Dad knows it and therefore doesn't worry. Somehow, the natural ability genes were front loaded with Hudson and skipped me. I've wiped out thousands of times. My multiple wrist fractures prove it. In middle school, I broke both of my arms when I cascaded into a tree. Mom put me in gymnastics, thinking that would help develop my coordination, and I ended up injured. One could argue the muscular injury from gymnastics is preferable to broken bones, but injury aside, the consistent issue is I suck.

Hudson approaches us, his smile as wide as ever.

"Did you see that?" he shouts.

Our group claps and whoops. We each resemble seals, flapping our flippers, hoping for a sardine to be tossed our way. Hudson bypasses all the others and picks me up, making me squeal.

"Gaining weight, sis." He's grinning and places his hand on his lower back for dramatic effect. I slap his jacket, and he laughs.

"Awesome job, bro," I say as he hugs Mom and high-fives Nash.

"Not perfect."

"No one ever gets perfect," I answer.

Two boarders have received perfect scores in the Olympics. Only two. Shaun White, who is a legend, and Chloe Kim, who is a badass.

It's more common in competitions like the one out here, but still rare. I love how my brother pushes himself. He's an inspiration. He makes it all look so easy, but he's dedicated. Over the years, I've heard his coaches call him a hard worker. You'd never know it from the plethora of stickers and tattoos and his wild hair.

A group of Hudson's friends approaches, and my parents and I drift to the side.

"Did Hudson tell you he's signed on for Australia? And he's got events in Italy, Spain, and Switzerland."

"He's big time now," I say.

Dad squeezes my shoulder, and Mom's lips wrinkle. It's her serious expression. If there was a mirror in the vicinity and she saw the result of her serious thoughts, she'd stop it.

"He's working on an indie film, too," Dad continues. I'm aware of the film. Hudson and Dad have talked about it more than once.

Back in high school, these competitions crushed my self-esteem. And as I observe the small clusters of spectators, the tangible thrill in the air reminds me of those days. As the announcer's booming voice cuts through the commotion, a flash of memories of Holden on the podium passes. Me, with the participation award, if they had one, and him with a trophy.

No one really knows what to say to the losers. Mostly I got the standard "you did a good job out there" mention if someone remembered I competed after they slapped Holden on the back and congratulated him on his incredible win.

I tag along with my parents, smiling at the regulars who know my parents as Emmett and Elizabeth. They greet them, chat about the event, and congratulate my parents. Sometimes they talk about upcoming events and compare lodging notes. It's been years since I've attended all of Hudson's events, so most everyone approaching my parents today doesn't spare me a second glance.

On the ride back to the airport, Mom scrolls through Instagram and Facebook to read the live-action commentary on Holden's win. Back in the day, only family and friends posted. But now Holden has a following, and the congrats roll in.

Just as the Jackson airport comes into view, and I think the visit will end without any mention of my life, Mom drops her phone into her pocketbook.

"Kate, do you need any help with financial aid? All that should be coming soon for next year, right?"

My sunglasses hide a lot, but they don't block my uncontrollable scowl.

"Honey, she'll let us know if she needs us to do anything. Isn't that right, sweetie?" Dad reaches across the seat to pat my shoulder, but he doesn't shift enough, and his palm slaps the pleather seat.

"Mom. I told you—"

"You're taking a year." Through the rearview mirror, I glance at her in the back seat, clutching her pocketbook to her stomach.

I'm not "taking a year," as she likes to call it. Well, I am taking a year in that I'm working on getting my foot in the door at one of the most challenging ski resorts in the country. I'm not taking a year to decide if I want to continue medical school. I pull up to the front of the airport and let relief flow through me. We don't have time to argue about it.

By the time I return from dropping my parents off, it's too late to get a good run in. But there's time to hit the gym. I return to the apartment, change, and am halfway across the snow-packed court-yard when the door to the Mangy Moose opens.

"Kate? Where are you off to? I thought you were joining us." Hudson has a beer in one hand while his leg props the door open. He must've seen me passing by.

"I've got to be up early. Can't party tonight." I give Hudson an apologetic shrug. The truth is watching him all day has stoked the fire within. Just like Hudson, I have dreams, and I need to work for them. He's worked all day, therefore he deserves his beer and nachos. However, I stood around all day watching him. It's time for me to put in some effort.

The door to the Moose slams closed. Holden catches up to me and slings an arm over my shoulder.

"Did you say goodbye to Mom and Dad?"

"Yep."

"They were pretty bummed you didn't make it home for Christmas."

I stop and peer up at him. *Seriously?*

"Christmas week is one of the busiest weeks at a ski resort. If not the—"

"Hey, I get it." He chuckles. "Just wanted you to know you were missed."

"Thanks." In some ways, Hudson is the glue that keeps our family together. I don't know what our parents would talk about if he quit competing. Maybe me, and that would depress both of them.

"Hey." He tilts his head, and long, crazy curls fall forward over his eyes. He brushes the hair off his forehead and licks his lips. An unusual expression flits across his face. Hudson doesn't do serious.

"What is it?"

"I can get you a job at Killington. If you want. Zander said he'd hire you."

As a favor to Hudson, his merry band of fans would do anything. Even take on a weak link. While I appreciate his willingness to help me out, living in my brother's shadow is exactly what I don't want.

"Thanks, but I like it here."

"Damn better mountain." He squints at me, and I think he's going to say more, but instead he bear-hugs me and lifts me off the ground. The faint smell of whiskey fills my nostrils, then he swivels and trudges back inside. It's brutally cold out, and he didn't bother with anything on his head, so he wraps his arms around himself and brushes his arms rapidly for heat.

Music pours out of the Mangy Moose when the door opens, and silence descends when it closes. A heavy sadness blankets me as I trudge along in my running shoes, attempting to avoid ice patches on the shoveled path.

My phone vibrates deep within my coat pocket. I dig it out as it goes to voicemail. It's Oliver. Sometimes the man's timing is impeccable.

I shove my glove into one of my coat pockets to free up a hand to call him back.

"Hey, there. Couldn't get to your call fast enough."

"Let me guess. Had to take off those gloves and then remember which pocket in your coat or ski pants held the phone?"

"Let me guess, you're currently sitting in shorts and flip-flops outside?"

"Nah. Not shorts. I keep tellin' ya. It gets chilly here in the winter. If it gets below seventy, we've gotta jacket up. But we do keep the flip-flops."

"Of course you do." A lot of that sadness and general yuck feeling still weighs me down, but I smile into the phone.

"If you ever come down here to visit, I'll win you over. It's nice here. We got good barbecue."

With the setting sun, the temps have fallen well below freezing, yet there's a warmth oozing from within. It's something that happens every time Oliver calls. Claire mocks me all the time, telling me I basically wrote an article on forgetting a fling, and then I've gone and done nothing on my list, but that's not really fair. I keep myself incredibly busy, which was number one on my list.

And it's not like I'm mourning him. We're friends. Maybe one could accuse me of crushing on him, but that's only because I spend too much time looking at his photos and texting him. Even if it's a crush, even if the mushy stomach and warm buzz his phone call delivers are a sign I haven't forgotten him, who cares? We live in different states. A fortune teller told us we'd end up with other people. I'll probably never see him again. If there's a crush, nothing's going to come of it. Ergo, harmless.

Yes, when I researched that article, one expert recommended a digital detox or deleting him from my contact list. That's extreme. He's not an ex who broke my heart. And not following on social media has been a breeze given he doesn't have any social media accounts.

The sound of shoes crunching some refrozen snow in an uncleared section of path fills a lengthy silence.

"How's my favorite ski patrol girl?"

"Not Ski patrol yet." After the almost confrontation with my mom, I do appreciate Oliver's enthusiasm for this crazy endeavor of mine. It's good to have someone who backs you. Keeping him in my life has been a good thing, experts be damned.

"Have to put it out there," he says, and an image of him kicking back, watching the sunset comes to mind. "That's the way the universe works. You say what you want, you believe it, and it comes true."

"Is that so? Then I guess I don't need to go hit the weight room. Let me get off the phone, and I'll just go join the others at the bar." I'm smiling and playing it light, but guilt nags me. My brother isn't in town often, and I probably should spend this evening with him.

"No. It's a two-part universe rule. Put in a little effort every day. Weights are probably a good idea. Avoiding Nash is probably another one."

Oliver hasn't let the whole Nash thing go. But every time he brings it up, I fight a grin. His comments feel protective and border-line jealous. But they're also fun and light.

"How's that going?" he asks. "Found a roommate yet?"

"Claire has someone for me to meet. So, maybe. I hope so. Claire paid this month's rent, but starting next month, Nash is planning on taking money from his parents. It's his place, and he can do what he wants, but it hits me wrong."

"I get that. Of course, I'm currently living in my folks' house."

"You live with your parents?" I am floored by this. In all our conversations, he's never mentioned this.

"It's the house I grew up in. They retired to San Pedro. It's an island in the Gulf. I'm taking care of the ranch, so I've been living in their house. But I've been working on plans to build a house on the far north side of the ranch. There was an old—and I mean really old—abandoned gin mill on the river. I'm exploring converting it into a home. Doing a wall of glass. If I'm successful, it'll feel like you're outside, but you'll be in the nice, cool air conditioning."

"Nice. Send me photos."

"I've sent you a few. Just of the view. You know that photo from the riverbank?"

"Where the trees butt up to the river?"

"Yep. Not a neighbor within shoutin' distance."

"Wow. That sounds awesome."

"You think?"

"Wouldn't anyone?" Back in Vermont, my dad was always big on not having a house too close to us. If he could, he'd buy land with a breathtaking view and not a neighbor in sight.

"Not anyone, no. There are some out there who wouldn't go for it at all."

I can picture Oliver sitting on a wooden dock, swinging bare feet, humming and grinning. I could see him cannonballing into the river on a whim.

Oliver's disposition blends with pretty much any personality, so it's curious he seeks solitude. If asked, I would have categorized him as an extrovert.

I arrive at the gym and stand outside beneath the overhang.

"How big is the house you're envisioning?"

"Downstairs is an open floor plan. Upstairs, I'm putting in three bedrooms with baths and a living area. And on top of that—"

"Holy shit. That's a big place."

"Well, I have the space. On the top, it's the master with a big open deck. I'm torn about how to build out the deck. Current plans include some shade and fans. And in the bedroom, there's a skylight open to the stars."

"That's some bachelor pad."

"Eh, I like architecture. I keep watching all those shows about interesting homes around the world. And we have all this land. I'm the only one of the Dukes keeping it up. If I do the renovations myself, it'll take me years."

"That's a long time."

"Yeah, but it'll come together. That's what I mean. A little at a time adds up to something real. A little each day will eventually get you there. Like ol' Tim Robbins. A little each day dug him right out of prison."

"*Shawshank Redemption*." Oliver loves old films. Half the time I haven't seen his film reference, but I saw that one. "Took him over ten years or something crazy, right?"

"Yep. But he ended up on a Mexican beach. A little, each day, and you'll get there." His analogy is quite similar to the second point in my getting over a fling article. Do something every single day that works toward long-term goals. Claire wanted me to push it under the keep busy point, but I kept it out as its own point. "Why is it, exactly, you want to be ski patrol?"

A man exits the gym, and I wait until the stranger is outside of hearing distance before answering.

"The slopes. First man out. And it's a way of helping people. My mom, she's a doctor. She helps people every day she goes to work." Ski patrol will allow me to use some of my med school learning. Two years is such a waste to throw away. But I'm not up for sharing that much, especially after a day of watching my brother crush it. "It's helping people with the bonus of being outside and doing what you love. It's a dream job."

"Emmett and Elizabeth agree?" He's referring to my parents, and I grimace as I remember the airport drop off.

"No. Can't say they do."

No one agrees, actually. In a perfect world, I'd be a coordinated, skilled athlete, and I'd be living Hudson's life. But it's not a perfect world. In another version of a perfect world, I'd be a third-year med student kicking ass. But we live in this world.

"Well, with a little each day, you'll catch that dream."

You've gotta love an optimist. The bare hand holding the phone has turned raw from the burning cold. I should head inside to the gym, but instead, I ask him about his friend Noah. He's another person who doesn't live in a perfect world.

sixteen

Oliver

April 5

Snow overflows off a balcony in my most recent photo from Kate. There's so much snow stacked up against the sliding glass doors that I'm surprised the balcony doesn't fall off the side of her apartment building. I'm pretty sure you're supposed to shovel the snow off those things from time to time, but she's living the twenty-something life.

When I was her age, I was finishing up grad school and researching how to finance a diamond ring. My dad encouraged me to hold on the ring until I got my feet on the ground. Told me if it was meant to be, a couple of years wouldn't make her run. When I look back on everything that happened, that might've been the best advice Dad ever gave me. She still ran, but not because of the years. We split when it became crystal clear Collette and I wanted different things. She wanted a life in Austin. The city life. And I wanted—well, hell, I wanted the same thing I've always wanted. Life on a ranch.

I've often thought Dad must've seen it. He must've known she wouldn't be happy with the life I had planned.

I flick to the photo folder on my phone. Then I click on the private Kate folder. It's where I file away all the photos she sends. Every now and then she sends a selfie. She's a beautiful girl. Shiny, dark hair. There's a glow to her skin. Every time I look at her photograph, my mind clicks on, and I remember all the things. The feel of her skin, her moans, her scent and taste. How she felt as she pulsed around me. The thought gets me semi-hard, and I flip the phone over. *Enough.* It's been months.

Admittedly, we've all been rotating Noah duty. He stayed with me for a couple of weeks until he moved into one of the small spec homes in one of Liam's neighborhood developments. Turns out Jocelyn had been seeing someone else from work. All those business trips weren't quite as businessey as Noah had believed.

The guy's been taking it hard. When you make plans with him, you never know what you're gonna get. Sometimes he just wants to drink at home. Sometimes, he wants to prowl. Many times he cancels last minute.

The bar crawl isn't my favorite maneuver, but I'll be his wingman any day. When we do go out, I'm open to meeting ladies right alongside him. Only problem is, I've always been a one-woman kind of guy, and Kate checks so many fucking boxes. When I meet a woman, I don't feel anything, and I'm pretty sure it's because I've got Kate on my mind. But it's time for me to jettison her out of my head.

Our dreams don't sync - at all. It's a big reason I haven't hopped a flight back up to Jackson. I'd love nothing more than to spend a couple of days with her again. Preferably naked. But what's the point? Noah and Jocelyn are a case in point that when it's really hard, it's a sign. Hell, my ex is a blaring sign that when dreams don't align, you gotta walk the fuck away.

I flip the phone back over to a photo of Kate on moving day in tight jeans that cup her ass. She's looking back over her shoulder at the camera, smiling, carrying one end of a box. Her smile lights up the photo, and my memories of her ass and curves and how good she felt fill in all the photograph's gaps.

It's tempting to suggest I go up and visit. I talk with her more than any other person. Most nights, she's the last person I speak to. In the morning, I'll shoot her a good sunrise shot. But we're in two different stages of life and want different things. Yeah, she might not be a city girl like Collette, but there are no mountains on the ranch. You can't build mountains or haul in snow.

These are things I know. I should let it go. If we didn't chat so much, she would've vacated my head by now. Yet, here I am, sitting at a Torchy's picnic table with a beer, drooling over a photograph. It's April. I last saw her on New Year's Day. But she still frequents my damn dreams. I'd love to say it's all good, but it's not.

My boys and I are meeting up for tacos on this nice spring day. Afterward, even though it's a school night, we might man up and hit a few bars now that Noah is back on the prowl. And god knows I should be looking for a distraction, too.

"Who's that?" Noah asks, leaning over the table and checking out my phone because he is one nosy son of a bitch. I swipe the phone and flip it over on the table.

"Did you order yet?" You order up at the restaurant window then find a table. As a general rule, we wait so we can all order together, but these days, Noah can get away with doing anything he wants.

"Liam said he's running late." Noah sits down across from me, raises his beer, and takes a swallow. "Why don't you want to tell me about her?"

"She's no one." This is my fault for scrolling through photos. But as I watch Noah take a long swallow of beer, it hits me he's kind of connected to her. "Remember when I was in Jackson, and I called and told you about Thai Me Up?"

"Yeah. I'm making headway on that, by the way. I have a lead on a potential location in the university area. There's a bar that's three months behind on rent. Rusty Wallace owns the building. Met him for lunch last week. He says if he kicks them out, we've got first dibs.

I'll take you down there. It's not the best location, so I'm still looking."

"Great."

The heat is building, but it's not so hot and humid yet you can slice it like cheesecake. It's that perfect temperature where everyone wants to sit outside and soak up some rays. There's a nice breeze blowing, strong enough to gently sway the nearby tree limbs.

"You were saying?" Noah asks, his eyes narrowed, head tilted. *Nosy.* "What's the girl on your phone got to do with our new restaurant?"

"She's the one who took me to the place in Jackson." My body reacts as my wayward brain returns to the bathroom she pulled me into that night. I shake my head to keep from going down that frequently traveled memory lane. "New Year's Eve."

"You still keep in touch?"

"Yeah." I take a swallow of my beer. "Sandra told me you went out on a date with Becky."

"My mother." He rolls his eyes, frustrated with the communication flow in our neck of the woods. All our mothers love to gab. "And no, we're not going out again. And no, you don't need to report back to Sandra."

"I don't report shit back."

"Yeah, right," Noah says.

"Hey, guys, you ready to order? I'm starving." Liam's standing by the counter, a good twenty feet away.

Noah and Liam are two of my closest friends and couldn't be more different. Noah's a lot like me in that he eschews ties and a traditional desk job. He's worked every job in a restaurant, from dishwasher to owner, and he'll be the first to hop in and pull any shift that's needed if one of his restaurants is short. We now have eight restaurants in our portfolio, all under his management. He's about my height, rides horses, loves to go camping, and drives a pickup truck.

Liam is a pretty boy, and he's got a few inches on me. The guy prefers suits and clothes that require dry-cleaning. He's my real estate development partner, and he's all about wining and dining clients and schmoozing with investors. He's a visionary with all the big ideas and switches out his vehicles on the regular. Last I saw, he drove a Porsche convertible. I don't have him out to the ranch often because when I do, instead of seeing pastures and rolling hills, he sees a high-end development and dollar signs in the sky. He's always been like that, though. In our fraternity, he was the one creating and selling T-shirts. He had a pretty solid income stream by the time we graduated. He's one big, Black, well-dressed man. He's also married.

For years, Noah and Liam would go out with their spouses, and I'd only join them if I had a date. But, given the Noah and Jocelyn debacle, all that's changed. We do way more boys' nights now. Noah's divorce isn't final, but it's in progress. With no kids and dual incomes, it should be pretty easy. At least from a legal perspective. Nothing about this has been easy on Noah.

The crowd at Torchy's isn't too bad for a Thursday after work. After we all place our orders and refill on salsa and chips, we return to our outdoor table. Noah and I get a second beer, and Liam orders a margarita. We all toast, and the second our glasses clink, Liam gets his serious work face on.

"I can't believe they fucking turned down our offer." The set of his stern lips shows he's pissed. Noah questions me with only a look.

"I told you about the kid who fell and hit his head?" Noah nods. "We're dealing with the lawsuit now. Insurance company made a settlement offer. But it seems they got wind of someone's PR article all about how much money we raised."

This is where Liam really irks me. He tries to get press on every damn thing we do. Says it's good for business. But if he'd kept that capital raise on the down low, then maybe the kid's family wouldn't have gotten dollars in their eyes.

"It's called investor relations." He glances down at a text he received, taps away, sends, then directs his attention back to me. "What're our next steps?"

"Given the lawyer they've hired, we're preparing for court. They won't get everything they want, but they may get more than what our insurance company offered. Such a crap shoot when it comes to juries awarding compensation." Noah has nothing to contribute to this conversation, nor does he have skin in the game, but he's paying attention, as he should. He hasn't been sued yet, but as an owner of a restaurant group, it's only a matter of time.

"There's a Republican Party fundraiser next week. We should go," Liam says.

"Why?" I ask. I hate that bullshit.

"Influence. With the right contacts, maybe we can sway which judge gets the case. There will be judges at the fundraiser. Hell, we could end up breaking bread with the judge assigned to us. Besides, it never hurts to be friends with congressmen."

"That's not my shindig." Liam may like to schmooze, but I do not.

A server drops off our orders, and I dig in. Noah scans the crowd, and I'm pretty sure he's searching for single women. I've already scouted the scene and came up short on age-appropriate single women.

"We should all go." Liam says it like he didn't just hear me. "A Duke will be the hit of the barbecue. They'll be swarming over you."

"No," I bark. Duke comments tend to raise my blood pressure. What he's saying is they'll swarm over me because I have connections to Sam Duke, the Austin-raised billionaire.

"We'll either lose this case or win it, but it will not be because I gave money at some god damned barbecue to Joe Crook or Bill Asswipe. I'm done with politicians. All two-faced schmucks. Maybe some of 'em are good. Like Beto. I like him. But even he's got to make compromises to get where he is. They all do."

"If you vote for that fucker, you're voting for taxes." The venom in his tone reminds me once again that he and I have no business talking politics.

Noah bows his head. His grimace warns we're veering into

treacherous territory. But he's pushing my buttons when I'm in a semi-foul mood.

"Will you shut the fuck up about taxes?" Liam drives me nuts. He's a one-issue voter, and that issue is his wallet. Meanwhile, the orange orangutan passed tariffs that did exactly what they always do and contributed to inflation. "You know, sometimes I feel like you Republicans never watched *Ferris Bueller*."

Noah chuckles. He'd rather not be having this conversation, but he gets my reference. There's a whole scene where the actor reads about tariffs in a boring, monotone voice, but if anyone listens, he's giving a damn good history lesson. "Bueller, Bueller, who can tell me what another word for tariff is?"

"What's wrong with you, man? You used to be a Republican."

Noah shoots both of us a look that warns us equally to drop it.

"There was a time when the difference between being a Republican or a Democrat pretty much meant different economic policies. But now, if you're a Republican, you've gone off the ranch."

"There are crazies on both sides." Liam waves a hand, dismissing me.

It's not like this is our first rodeo on the topic. He believes the left is all about social welfare and that Antifa wants to kill us all. But he's not interested in a debate.

"Fine." He knocks his beer against mine and pauses for effect. "We'll schmooze both sides. But this barbecue is one we need to attend."

"How much are those tickets?" I ask, knowing it's going to be an obnoxious answer.

"Like, five a head."

"Five thousand?" I ask for confirmation.

Liam shrugs. The fucker knows I get worked up about this shit.

"And then my money goes to the Republicans, which will go to more ads. And I give to the Dems, same shit. I'm not a Torchy's. I don't cater to everyone, no matter how different they are." My frustration exits in a loud huff.

"Guys." Noah's harsh reprimand aims at both of us. "Stop it. No politics. We don't see eye to eye. Never will. How about we talk about the Rangers? Or, hell, the Longhorns? You guys catch any baseball games? Or, if you want, we can compare notes on Jocelyn's baby bump. Did you see she's posting profile shots every single goddamn day?"

With that little tidbit, Noah successfully changes the conversation. Dinner passes, but I'm still riled up, and I head back to the ranch instead of out to the bars. Noah and I have gone out loads. Liam can cover tonight.

Back home, I don't go out on my deck. I head into my bedroom, undress down to my boxers, and collapse onto my bed. It's late, but not as late, Kate's time. So, I call her.

"Hey there." There's a smile in her voice.

"Hey to you." I close my eyes and revel in the connection. There's something about her voice. It flows through me with the calm of a winding creek. "You guys got more snow, huh?"

"Can you believe it? And we'll be shutting down soon for the season."

"Never-ending snowstorm there, huh?"

"A banner year. My new roommate, Paisley, is moving in tomorrow. Hope the weather stays clear."

"Nice. You sound excited." And she does. When Kate's excited about something, her voice rises a couple of octaves. Enthusiasm bursts through. When she's not so happy, her words come out a little slower in a deeper tone.

"I am. Ready to get another girl in this apartment. How're you doing?"

"Well, I'm better now that you've got a new roommate. And she's a girl." She laughs, but I'm not blowing smoke. It's totally nonsensical, but the idea of her and Nash living there alone together didn't sit well with me. The tension from earlier vacates my muscles, and I cross one leg over the other.

A burning desire to see her, to look into those chocolate eyes and watch her rosy lips spread into a wide smile, hits me hard.

"Hey, Kate, any chance I could talk you into a video call?" There's a pause. "I just...I'd like to see you."

"Sure. I'll call you."

The call ends, and the phone rings. I answer and push my arm out so my face isn't quite so large and in charge.

"Everything okay?" She sounds concerned, but what I fixate on is those eyes. Her dark hair is loose and flows over a pink polka-dot pillow.

"Just another day in Texas."

"Hhmmm." Her upper lip projects over her lower lip, and god, I wish I could pull her to me and taste those lips once again. "How's Noah?"

She's been so concerned about Noah. Hell, everyone has been. We still are.

"He's hanging in there. Went with him for tacos tonight."

"Tacos cure all."

"Hellz, yeah, they do." We stare at each other. It feels so much more personal than just talking to her on the phone. "You not waiting tables tonight?"

"Not tonight." She rolls onto her side, and it feels like we're both lying in the same bed. "Something's off. You want to talk about it?"

She's right. Things are off. Frustration points in multiple directions, and it's hard for me to decipher why. It's not Liam. No matter our differences, he's my friend. I stare right into those chocolate eyes and breathe deep.

"I miss you. That's ridiculous, right?" Her pale skin flushes an attractive shade of pink, and those lips I miss spread into a smile. It's not one of her wide smiles that flashes her pearly whites, but it's subtle and sexy and really all kinds of perfect.

"Is it hard watching your friend go through a divorce?" My chest snags over her duck of my question, but I suppose it's not so much a duck as a maneuver to dive into the heart of the matter.

"Yeah, it is. But probably not for the reasons you think."

"What do you mean?" She juts her angular chin out, and I want so much to reach through the phone, touch her cheek, and brush that thick strand of hair behind her ear.

"It's just…" I struggle with how to explain. "I came pretty close to being in his shoes. And it's just…"

"You see how easy it is for a relationship to end?"

"Yeah. I guess?" I'm not sure that's exactly right, but it sort of is. "Have you ever been in a serious relationship?"

"Never married. But I've had boyfriends."

"Hhmm. What's the longest you've ever dated anyone?"

"About a year. I guess I've always had other priorities."

"Priorities like ski school?"

"Or school." The phone flashes a back wall and then returns to her face as she adjusts on the bed. "What about you? Any serious relationships?"

"Well, I was engaged. I suppose that counts as serious."

"Yeah, I think I agree." She half-laughs, and it's cute, but then she grows serious and some of that concern comes back. "What happened?"

"We wanted different things." It's the simplest way to describe it. "The kicker is if her folks hadn't wanted the wedding of the century with like six hundred in attendance, I'd probably be married to her now and one of us would be miserable." Kate's quizzical expression begs for more. "We were working on house plans. If anything is a test of a couple's mettle, it's building a house. She wanted this traditional monstrosity. That was my first warning. But then, she found the lot. About three months before our wedding date. I'm not sure how we could have been so off. I think I just assumed if we built her monstrosity near the ranch, it would be a compromise."

"Do you still love her?"

"Honestly, Kate, I'm not sure I ever loved her. How's that for a kick in the pants? I think things with us were easy, and we had all the same friends, and it flowed. Until it didn't."

"Where is she now?"

"Oh, she's married. But she's in Dallas." There's not much to say about Collette. A few years ago, I probably would've gone on and on, but now I don't feel much. I suppose one could describe what I feel as unsettled. Uneasy about how close I came to disaster. "What about you? Still in love with any of your exes?"

"No." Those brown eyes flash to mine.

"You need to tell me when it's a good time to come visit."

She rolls her eyes, and it seems she's staring at the ceiling for answers, but she's smiling, so it's all friendly and light.

"Did you know I wrote an article about how to survive a fling?"

"Am I the fling in question?" She full-on laughs, and I laugh right along with her.

"You're my only fling. But here's the thing. We're supposed to move on."

"No visits?" She shakes her head, and I hate that. But she's absolutely right. Visiting doesn't make a lick of sense. Although, for the record, that point wasn't on her list. But my thoughts go to that last little point. The bombshell point. Dating other people.

"Have you been moving on?"

She slowly shakes her head, and her tongue licks that lower lip, and holy shit, my insides are like a firework explosion, all sizzle, and boom. She's saying she hasn't moved on either.

"But I mean, I've been working a lot. So, in that regard..."

"But you haven't been with anyone since January?" She doesn't answer me with words, just the shake of her head, but that's enough to pretty much make my month. Stupid, I know, but I can't deny that answer of hers has me feeling like I just won something huge, like the lottery or something.

I've gone on an inconsequential date or two. My New Year's cancellation did claim that snow check. But I didn't kiss her goodnight because I didn't want to see her again, and in this small suburban town, you don't lead friends of friends on.

"What about you?" She sounds hopeful and maybe a little scared.

"Nope. I've had this brunette in my head. Can't get her out." And she smiles. It's that gorgeous smile, and for the first time, I don't feel like kicking my sorry ass for having a girl four states away stuck in my head. No, there's a whole lotta gratitude filling me up that I can share that bit with her and bring out that smile.

seventeen

Kate

May 15

My boots squish in the mud as I cross the quad area. It's officially spring, and the melt has begun. I snap a photo of the muck and send it off to Oliver with the caption *Spring time*. This time of year, Mother Nature shoots down periodic cold bouts from the north, but today we should reach the high fifties.

With the season change, our jobs do too. It's end-of-season inventory time at Jackson Rentals. Paisley, my new roommate, hooked me up with a job at a nearby golf course for the summer. I'll be both a golf cart driver and a cashier at Claire's spa, and I'll continue bartending. I pretty much enjoy all the jobs and the people interaction. The hourly wage isn't so great, but bartending certainly helps with that.

My journal pages are chock full of alternative career ideas. Writing articles offers supplemental income, but there's no way I could live off of it. Nash promotes ski school as an option pretty much daily. I can see his points. It's outdoors and offers plentiful access to the mountain on off days. The pay is great, or at least with tips, it is. If I don't get ski patrol this fall, it's not the worst Plan B.

Oliver tells me to "just keep livin'" and that I'll figure things out. He says he doesn't have everything mapped, but when doors open, he gives the door a good look-over. Sometimes he walks through. Sometimes, he passes by. But, in the words of the great Buddha, "The only real failure in life is to not be true to the best one knows."

"Kate."

Thanks to the bright sun overhead, I can't see the man calling out my name. I shelter my eyes with my hand, squinting at the dark, shadowy shape approaching.

"Headed in for cleanup?" It's Bill Woodland. We haven't crossed paths in months.

"Yes, sir," I say and cringe, because *sir* isn't a word we typically use within Jackson Resort.

"Heard you aced the medic training. Impressive."

The world slows. The sun grows magnitudes brighter, and a flock of birds breaks out into song in the recesses of my brain. A compliment from Bill Woodland, the man who selects the ski patrol members.

"Does that have anything to do with your time in med school? Was training ridiculously easy for you?"

And my insides crash. My gaze drops to the mud. He's a heavy man, and his boots rest about two inches deep in the quagmire. I'm a med school dropout. That's why he assumed I wouldn't stick around.

"Hey, I meant nothing bad." His hand lifts but then falls back by his side, as if he thought about touching me and then second-guessed it. "I just meant I may have misjudged you. You've got to improve your strength, but Harvey tells me you've been hitting the gym regularly. Says you've just about got the mountain mastered. I think it's clear I expect the same from the women on my team as the men. Lives depend on our skills. Your frame is slight, but with the effort you're putting in, you can do it. If you're looking at training this summer, I can give you the name of someone good."

My brain reels, going from a high to a crash to a rebound, but I manage a smile and push out, "I'd love that."

At the end of my shift, I call the number Bill gave me and speak to Willy. He offers to meet me at the gym tomorrow. When I ask about his rate, he says not to worry about it. He'll see what I can do and map out a plan for me. He won't charge unless I want him to be with me at each of the workout sessions. My legs have been sore, but I can't believe my luck in having someone knowledgeable to discuss what stretches I should be doing.

When I push through the apartment door and trip over Nash's muddy boots, my humming continues. Because this is a glorious day.

Paisley calls out from her bedroom, "Those flowers are for you. Is it your birthday or something?"

An enormous bouquet of wildflowers fills our small, round kitchen table. Reds, blues, oranges, and yellows overflow. I think the reds are poppies, but I'm not familiar with the others. They're stunning.

I open the small white envelope addressed to Kate Oakley as Paisley joins me, reading over my shoulder.

We're crossing into full-blown summer here, but since you're still getting snow, I thought maybe you could use a blast of spring. When I thought about what kind of flowers to send to someone who might just love the outdoors more than I do, it had to be wildflowers. Resilient, steadfast, and true. From your one and only fling, O. Duke.

"Who's O. Duke?" Paisley asks.

There's a knock on the door, and it pushes open. Claire still has her key, and she drops by every now and then.

"Whoa." Her gaze drops to the folded white card in my hand. "Who sent you flowers?"

"A friend." The skin along my throat and cheeks warms. Friend fits better than any other word. How else would you describe Oliver? He's not an ex, we're not exclusive, but he's someone I really like keeping in touch with.

"Some friend," Paisley says as she heads into the kitchen to refill her water bottle. "Wish I had me one of those. From back home in Vermont?"

"No. He lives in Texas."

Claire's eyes widen. "That guy? From the holidays?"

"Yeah. We still keep in touch." I shrug and slide the card into my pocket, full of as much nonchalance as I can manage without thespian skills.

"Huh. Well, tell your friend he has amazing taste in flowers." Paisley dips her nose into the flowers and turns the vase on the counter for a three-sixty view.

"He does, doesn't he?" My little fling turned into something completely unexpected. A friend. A really sweet, thoughtful friend. One day, he'll tell me he's dating someone. He's such a great guy. It's inevitable. When that day comes, it will absolutely suck, but there's no point in plunging into a funk over the future.

"I want a friend like that." Paisley grins and her eyebrows wiggle.

"I thought he was nothing more than a fling?" Claire crosses her arms, looking simultaneously skeptical and amused.

"Things evolved." I shrug. "We're friends now. I'm gonna go call him. Do you guys mind?"

Claire leans against the kitchen counter with a 'cat ate the canary' kind of smile. "Go right ahead and call your friend. Paisley and I can hang, right?"

"Absolutely." Paisley snaps her fingers. "We should make a new cocktail. Get your phone out and let's look up recipes."

Their heads bend over Paisley's phone, and I quietly slip down the hall. If voicemail picks up, I'll leave a message. Right after I snap a photo of the flowers and send it to him.

"Hey there." I can literally hear his smile through the phone, and my grin, that he can't see, full on matches what I'm hearing.

"Oh, my god, the flowers are so gorgeous."

"There's no way they touch the beauty of the girl. Wait. Was that cheesy? You can tell me. Feel free to call me out."

Moo.

"What was that? A cow? Where are you?"

"You caught me out riding the property line."

"On a cow?"

His chuckle is deep and brief. "No. A horse. We had a storm roll through, so I need to check the fence. Check for fallen limbs. Fence line damage. All in a day's work."

"How big is the fence?"

"You mean, how much land does it cover? We've got about twenty-five hundred acres. Couple of miles of fence."

"Yowza."

"You want to see it? Not sure how long we'll have a signal, but we can switch to video. Since you refuse to come to—"

"Yeah. Show me."

We switch to video, and less than a minute later, my phone screen shows a tree line to his left. To his right there are rolling green hills. A couple of cows graze along the side of a grassy embankment.

"It's beautiful." It is. His ranch is idyllic. There's no house or buildings. Just wide-open natural space. We have that here in Wyoming, too, but Texas is ahead of the seasons. Based on the foliage of the trees and the thick grass in the pasture, it looks like he's sitting in the middle of summer. The camera view rocks back and forth in a lulling motion.

"Well, I don't want to take up your time. I just wanted to thank you—"

"Don't run off. Sit and talk to me for a while."

An old wrought-iron fence comes into view. It looks like it's in the shape of a square, and there are headstones.

"Is that your family's cemetery?" In Vermont, out in the country, you sometimes come across small plots just like the one on screen.

"It's the Duke family cemetery from a few generations back. They buried my grandparents at a church in Austin, and that's where my folks bought plots. These here headstones are from the late eighteen hundreds and early nineteen hundreds. My great, great grandfather and his ten kids."

"Ten?" It's crazy to me how big the families used to be.

"Yep. We come out and scrub the stones now and then. Put in a new fence about twenty years ago. I have a dog named Otis who's also buried in there, but we buried all of our other pets in a plot up closer to the house. There used to be a house out closer to here. Long time ago. Before I was born."

"Wow. So, you are truly Texan."

"Truly am."

"It's amazing it's still in your family."

"That it is. We had more land. Over the generations, it gets split up. Family members inherit land and sell it. Don't want to live here or pay taxes on it. The ranching way of life doesn't pay well. Constant work. Lots of reasons. We're down to what's considered a mid-size ranch. I think I told you I'm hoping to buy my brothers out. Keep what we have together. But up on the opposite end of the property is where I'll build. If we end up splitting the land, I'll take that northern piece. That's another problem with splitting land. Deciding where to draw the lines so it's all even-steven."

"Your brothers were willing to leave. But not you?"

"Why would I leave this?"

I have to give it to him; the view is stunning. And peaceful. The fence line trails into the line of trees, and the shadows darken. The faint sounds of gurgling water, the fuzz of wind, and heavy footfalls mix.

"Do I hear a creek?" My original impression of Texas had been one of a dry state, almost like a desert. Oliver's daily photos revealed land much different than expected. Having grown up in Vermont, and having parents who spent every vacation skiing, I have never been to the southwest. Everything I know about it comes from television or textbooks.

"Yeah, we've got a couple of creeks that wind through the property. One's just through those trees. And then you saw the water near the old gin mill. That's a stream that spun off from the Colorado River."

The horse neighs loudly, and the view shifts. In quick succession, I see the tips of brown horse's ears, tree branches, and blue sky. There's a loud shuffling. A horse whinnies.

Then the screen goes black.

"Oliver? Oliver?"

eighteen

Oliver

May 15

Fuuuuck. My back. Hot damn, Sylvester, what the hell?

Sylvester, my quarter horse, stops about twenty feet away, nostrils flaring. I sit up, grab my hat from the ground, and the scoundrel turns and trots off to the barn.

"Sylvester!" One of his two pointed ears flicks back to me, but he continues trotting home. It's a full-fledged equine fuck you.

I scan the area, searching for what spooked my horse. I suppose this is why you shouldn't gab on the phone while riding. Up ahead, through the trees, I see a furry something skedaddling into the brush. Whatever critter sent Sylvester into a tailspin is just as scared as my scaredy cat horse. This is what I get for gabbing on the phone while riding the fence line with a young colt.

My phone landed on a patch of grass. I pick it up, brush it off, and call Kate back.

"Oliver?" Sheer terror vibrates through Kate's tone.

"Kate."

"Oh, my god. You're okay." There's a pause as she inhales, the sound coming through like static. I scan the area and the sky, cursing. My ass aches, and I rub it. "Are you okay? I didn't know if I should call nine-one-one or what to do. Holy shit. Are you all right?"

"I'm good. Horse spooked. Caught me off guard."

"I didn't know what to do. The video call cut off, and you didn't pick up. If I called nine-one-one, I wouldn't know what to tell them. I don't even have your address."

"Yeah, you do."

"I do?"

"I entered it on your phone when I gave you my number." Come to think of it, I never do that. Seems even back in January, I suspected Kate would be more than a short fling.

"I didn't know. So, are you okay?"

"Yeah, I'm fine. Landed flat on a tree root. My back's sore. Will probably have a weird bruise."

"Holy shit." She's practically panting. "I didn't know what to do."

"Nothing at all. You ride long enough, you're gonna take a fall. And hell, never call nine-one-one for me falling from a horse. I'd never hear the end of it."

"But you don't know what that was like. To hear that. And then you were gone. Oliver, like, I actually started crying. Tears. I felt so helpless." Her voice cracks, and then I just feel like shit. "And you didn't say anything for the longest time. What are you doing now?"

"Well, since my dang bloom ride trotted off to the barn, I'm hoofin' it back home on my own two feet."

There's a pause. And she laughs. Of course she does, and I have to say, it's damn good to hear her laugh. If my brothers had been out here with me, they'd still be laughing. But Kate's laughter has me smiling. It's a good sound. Better than any country music song.

"But you're okay?" she asks again, as if she needs reassurance.

"Other than my ego taking a hit? Sure. But you know, if you're really worried, you can come on out and check me out yourself. You know, to be absolutely certain."

"If I could get away, I would definitely come down. But with my work schedule…Does this happen often?"

Using the sternest voice I possess, I answer, "No. It does not." I kick a rock, and it sails two feet in front of me. "I don't remember the last time I fell off a horse. But most of the horses around here are dependable. One day, Sylvester will be too. He's just young."

"Oh. How old is he?"

"Under two years. But he shouldn't have done that. I think a fox or something caught his eye, and he freaked."

"Huh." She sounds thoughtful. There's nothing to be thoughtful about. Sometimes these things happen. "You wear a helmet, though, right?"

"You mean one of those little black hats?" I'm teasing her. I totally know what she's talking about. All the English riders wear them. I rent out a couple of stalls to some jumpers, and they are always strapping on their helmets. Not a bad idea when you're going jumping.

"Do you remember Christopher Reeve?" I roll my eyes. Every single person in the equestrian community knows what happened to Christopher Reeve. He was jumping, fell, and ended up paralyzed. Freak accident that skyrocketed helmet usage.

"I do. How do you know about him? Aren't you too young?"

"I grew up reading *People* magazine. I never watched him in Superman, but I knew him."

"Yeah, his version of Superman is an old one."

"But you wear a helmet, right?"

"No." I shake my head. Not that she can see me. "I ride Western. We're not as big with the helmets."

"Are you serious?" She's a skier and boarder. Helmets have overtaken that sport too. I get it. And appreciate her concern. It's sweet.

"See, here's the thing. You've never been to Texas, so you might not comprehend this. But in the summer, you can slice the heat like it's pound cake. I'd be at a bigger risk of heat stroke with that helmet strapped on. Cowboy hats help with the sun. Fights that other little enemy known as skin cancer. Out here, we pick our battles."

"You wear a cowboy hat?" There's a smile in her voice.

"Does that turn you on?"

"It kind of does. And cowboy boots?"

"Wearing 'em right now."

"And faded jeans?"

"Yep."

"And no shirt?"

"Nah. Got a T-shirt on."

"I have the best visual right now. Maybe we should try a video call again?"

"No can do. I need to watch where my feet are steppin'. Plus, if I come across one of the other ranchers out here, I'll never hear the end of it if I've got a phone held out and I'm video chatting." After being thrown off a horse, no less. Jesus.

I travel about twenty yards, holding the phone to my ear, walking the narrow path stomped into the ground by the horses on their daily trek back to the barn. Her voice is cutting in and out. There are spots out here where the signal is for shit.

"Hey, Kate...can you hear me? I think I'm in a bad signal patch. I might need to cut it short."

"That's fine. Claire is over, and I should go and visit with her. Want to talk later tonight?"

"Unfortunately, I've got plans."

"Saturday night plans." She's speaking softly, and I can't tell if it's a question or a statement.

"Me and the boys are going out. What about you? Any Saturday night plans?"

"We're all going into Jackson."

"Not hanging out close to home, huh?"

"No. It's easier to go into town now. Roads are clear."

"No fear of a door handle breaking off into your hand?"

"Exactly. But I shouldn't be out that late."

"I'll call you if it's not too crazy late, but with the time difference, there's a good chance…" I let my words trail and leave it at that.

When we hang up, my mood tanks. She's going out, and she'll be hit on. Hell, I'm going out, and I might hit on someone else. It should all be fine, but discontent rumbles. I don't like thinking about her going home tonight with some random. It's the macho male in me coming out. There's not a damn thing I can do about it. About her or about me or about my piss poor mood and sore ass.

* * *

"Heard we got Judge O'Brian." Liam cracks the shell of a peanut and tosses it in his mouth, crunches, then swallows it down with a gulp of beer. "What's with you?"

"Nothing," I answer, fully aware I sound like a sulky teen. Liam squints at me. Noah is off talking to a woman at the bar. I wish I'd invited Sandra. She'd keep the conversation away from business.

"Judge O'Brian is going to be at the upcoming Diamonds and Studs Golf Tournament. We should go." Now it's my turn to give Liam the squint eye.

"He's a judge. He's not going to tilt the tables in our favor just because I let him beat me at golf." And he will beat me. I don't particularly care for golf. "You're making my stomach curdle with what you're suggesting."

"You don't think that's the way business works?"

"Business might work that way, but the law shouldn't." I dig into the peanut bowl and scan the pool tables for an open one. They are all full. "I met with the kid."

"You did?"

"Last week. He's doing good."

"This lawsuit is such bullshit." Liam's statement isn't wrong. These are the kinds of lawsuits that drum up the cost of everything under the sun and give the US litigation system a bad name. But one good thing about Texas is our chances of getting a jury who sees right through a family looking to game the system is pretty high. Yes, the gate was open. But the kid knew he shouldn't have been running by the pool. He knew the pool was closed. There were signs up. He passed one, and the kid can read. I doubt we'll actually get to court.

"The family seemed almost apologetic. Nice people. I think they've got a lawyer who convinced them to see what we'd come up with, hoping we'd be desperate to settle while we're trying to raise capital. They signed on with a legal firm taking a contingency fee, so they can't back out now." With a contingency fee, they don't owe their lawyers any money unless they win the case. Their lawyers get a percentage of any settlement or reward. Read: Greedy, bastard lawyers at play.

"It's not gonna hurt to attend that golf tournament. Let Judge O'Brian get to know us. See that we're upstanding citizens."

"Our personal character will not be a factor in the case. And like I just said, I don't think we'll actually make it to court. It's a small law firm that took the case. I don't think they'll invest the money in litigation unless they believe they have a strong chance of winning. And, in this state, it's not a given."

"Even with an Austin jury?"

Austin is one of the liberal bastions of Texas. All the cities are, really. Same as most cities in the US. It's the rural areas that bleed red. There's a lot you can extrapolate from that, but in this case, Liam is afraid the blue jury will hand out a nice reward to a boy who hurt his head. But it's not like the boy is a professional athlete. He had some medical expenses, which we offered to cover. It'll be a mighty task to prove any kind of lifelong impact. They have us on negligence. We left the gate open. But I don't see them taking us to the cleaners.

"Like I said, I don't think it'll get to the jury stage." I take a long swallow of ice-cold beer. Wheels are turning in Liam's head. "And, for the last time, even if we go to trial, I'm not trying to schmooze our way into a favorable verdict. That's sleazy as all get out."

"What is up with you?"

"What do you mean?" I have always been like this. Integrity is something I value.

"You've been a grump ever since you got here. Do I need to get a round of shots over here? Loosen you up some?"

"No." Tomorrow, I've still got to finish riding that fence line, and I do not want to be doing it hungover. Plus, a tree fell over a portion of the creek, and I need to clear that up before it becomes a bigger problem.

"I think I know what will make you happy." Liam slides off his stool before I can ask him what the hell he's talking about. I flag down the bartender for a second beer while he sidles up to Noah.

"Ladies, this is my friend and business partner, Oliver."

Noah pulls up two stools and sets them in front of ours, creating our own little circle. Liam and Noah are introducing a blonde and a brunette. They're cute. But neither of them is my type. When the bartender returns with my beer, I ask them what they want and buy them both drinks.

They're dolled up with glossy lips and stiff hair. My type runs more along the lines of Kate. Her idea of lipstick is cherry ChapStick, and when she does her hair, it's in one thick braid.

There's a conversation going on between the four of us, but my heart's not in it. I can't help but wonder what Kate's doing. If she's sitting in a similar circle. And if she is, is she into the conversation? Is she giggling like these two? Asking tons of questions like the men are the most fascinating creatures they've ever come across?

The thing that bugs me the most is that I'm looking at these two women, but I'm seeing Kate. I wish Kate were here. And it's a futile wish. Her heart's on the slopes, and I can't handle that cold for longer than a week. I'm not bred for it. Not raised for it.

I'm into a woman who's my polar opposite. Sam, my older brother, once told me I always want what I can't have. He said it when he thought I had a crush on Sandra. And at the time, I had a crush on Sandra. But was he right? Is the reason I can't get Kate out of my head because I can't have her? Do we have easy conversations because there's no risk of a future? No pressure? No obligation?

Elsie Travis draws a heart over her lower-case I. Below her phone number, there's a cursive scrawl that reads, "Hope to hear from you."

In the parking lot, Liam follows me out. Noah left about thirty minutes before us with the woman he met at the bar.

"You sure you're okay to drive?"

"Only had the two beers. I'm good. You need a ride?"

He shakes his head. "You gonna call her?"

I don't bother answering him as I reach my truck.

"She seems like she'd be your type."

"Oh, yeah," I say, amused. The pretty boy thinks he knows my type.

"Nice rack. And ass."

"Night, Liam. Get home safe. Give Natalie my love."

The night breeze blows through the window on the thirty-minute drive home, and I let the music flow. Once I reach my destination, I don't bother turning on any of the lights. It's not that late. I could call Kate. I open my phone and look at a photo of her. It's one she texted to me.

She is a gorgeous girl. Easy to talk to. Adventurous. Headstrong. The current star of my favorite fantasies. I'm her only fling, and she's my only fling that counts. And she lives in Wyoming.

I take out the slip of paper with Elsie's number on it and set it on my dresser. I'd been in a foul mood when I met her, and she still dug me. And Elsie lives right here in Texas.

nineteen

Kate

May 21

Matt Marrero, the expert Bill Woodland connected me with, hops on his snowmobile, guns the engine, and grins as he offers a friendly, "Hop on."

Matt's forty-three years old and has been a patroller for an astounding fifteen years. If he didn't wear his age like a badge of pride, I'd assume he was in his early thirties. There's some gray sprouting through his thick dark beard, and I noticed on the drive out to the backcountry the lines along the corners of his eyes are deep. But his selection of blaring alternative bands, the tattoos on his fingers, and his near-constant smile and bounce set him solidly in the realm of twenty-something snowboarder.

On the ride out to the backcountry, I learn he's a divorced father of two, and given his abundant youthfulness and zeal, it's an unexpected reveal. He's what I imagine an older version of Hudson will be like—an energetic kid trapped in an adult body.

Yesterday, we got a late-season dump. Matt called and said he was going out to Togwotee Pass and asked if I wanted to join him. Said there are some steep inclines I'm not familiar with that will be good practice. Said he'd get in the toboggan and let me have a go at assessing the situation and figuring out how to best get a patient—Matt, in this case—down to the base.

The snowmobile engine, combined with my piggyback position, makes conversation difficult, so I hold on to Matt's waist and revel in the fresh snow. Winter Storm Wyatt provided a late-season burst of winter that delivered one last fantastic dump. Reports said as much as five feet of snow dropped in parts of the Tetons, but in Jackson, we received closer to a foot.

The clean air bears a tingling mix of fresh snow and pine. Tree limbs bow down, heavy with the weight of late-season snow. The temps will rise as the day progresses, and that snow will drip, eventually forming rivulets below the draining snowpack.

When I asked Matt what his favorite part of being a patroller was, he beamed. "Hands down, the awareness runs."

That's what I imagine will be my favorite part, too. Many people think of ski patrol as the folks who scout the mountain searching for speeders. But it's so much more. They're like the firefighters on the mountain. They have to be prepared for all emergencies. And when an emergency occurs, whether it's a dangler from the ski lift or an injury in an almost impossible-to-reach location, they have to respond quickly. In a place like Jackson, where temperatures can easily exacerbate shock symptoms, life-saving care may depend on speed.

Saving a life can be stressful. But the awareness run is part of the prevention. Early in the morning, before the run is open, patrollers check for hazards. This includes some boring duties, like checking signs and fencing. Of course, checking fencing reminds me of Oliver checking his fence.

Oliver likes the solitary ride around his property, scouting for potential dangers to his herd. It's similar, I suppose, to the role of a patroller. Surveying the slopes for changing conditions or any potential danger. He has views of green, blue, and brown, whereas the views here are crisp, pure white and stunning mountain cross sections.

Oliver never called last Saturday. I kept my phone out on my bedside table. I couldn't sleep. Kept staring at the phone, willing it to ring long after I knew he wouldn't call. Continuing to talk to Oliver defies the fling survival techniques I outlined in my listicle. Our friendship defies logic. Yet I rely on Oliver for support and camaraderie. He's the person I text the most. My only fling. And he engenders out-of-bound emotions. Those emotions I shouldn't feel, but they seep in anyway. It's dangerous in the same way a skier traversing out-of-bounds territory is dangerous.

I know full well when Oliver went out Saturday night, he met someone. He chose in-real-life action over calling me on the phone. As he should. He's gorgeous and friendly and a genuinely nice guy. The real mystery is how on Earth he's still single. And as frustrated as I might be with the sick, nauseating sensation from thinking of him with someone else, and my crush-like fixation watching the phone for it to ring, well, it's all understandable. He's fantastic. If I were a smart young woman, I'd cut ties before this crush becomes too painful. Or maybe I won't need to cut ties at all. Saturday night might have led to Sunday brunch and an afternoon riding the ranch. He could be with her right now.

Matt stops the snowmobile and cuts the engine. He points skyward.

"We're going to hike up there." He points to a summit too steep for the snowmobile. It occurs to me that because of the forty-minute hike before us, I'll be able to analyze the slope and pick my best way down without the required speed of a real-life situation. But that's a good thing. I'd like to impress Matt. He's one patroller Bill Woodland relies on. He'll undoubtedly ask Matt's opinion of me when he's weighing hiring decisions in the fall.

I don't go out into the backcountry often, but there's a wildness here that speaks to me. The scene out beyond the trail is untouched by any human. You could travel back two hundred years and the scene would be the same. There's not a building, a road, a telephone wire, or any trace of a human, as long as I position my body looking forward. To my back, there's a trail and a snowmobile. But facing forward, it's like we've jumped out of a helicopter into a land untraveled by the human species.

I pull out my phone and snap a photo. Out of habit, I send it to Oliver with the caption, *Day in the Tetons. Training Day.*

I add a smiley face emoji for good measure, although it's not needed. The photograph of the resplendent Tetons in all their glory is frame worthy. If he's with whoever he met Saturday night, it won't matter. He'll just tell her I'm a friend from Jackson.

A friend in Jackson, doing a little something each day to work toward her dreams. Number two in my article. Number one in pretty much any self-advancement guru's strategy.

Matt points at the ground as I hitch my skis in place on my back. "Paw prints. See 'em? I think a fox."

The snow is light and powdery, so even an animal as light as a fox sinks. The slide-like path through the snow is clearer to me than the shape of the paw. I'd need to hover over it to get a good look at the print.

Matt points at the toboggan. "You gonna haul it?"

"You bet," I say with a smile I don't feel. My muscles are sore from my gym workouts. The sides of my legs are killing me. I haven't been rolling my legs like I should.

Matt points in the general up direction. "You lead. Pick the way."

"We're headed up there?" I point to confirm. The drop from the summit is steep. I'd bet steeper than anything in Jackson. Nerves fire. What if I screw up and hurt Matt?

My boots sink into the snow to my knees. The wind kicks up snow flurries, blowing the loose snow. I might have dressed too warmly, as within five minutes, I'm sweating. My goggles fog. It's imperative I not get too close to the edge, as one wrong step could mean tumbling down the side of the mountain. I loop straps from the toboggan around each arm, hauling it as if it's a backpack. On top of the weight of my skis, the hike is slow going. My quads, hamstrings, calves, and lungs burn.

"So, Kate, why did you decide you want to be a patroller?" Unlike me, Matt isn't winded from this hike. I can barely breathe, and he's speaking as clearly as if he's pressing the accelerator on his truck.

"Same as you," I huff out. "First one out," I gasp. "Every day." Hudson's videos flash before me. I want that, but there's no way I'd admit that to anyone. Besides, ski patrol is a solid number two behind a professional snowboarder. It's just as close as I can get.

"There's a lot more to the job."

I know that. Why does everyone feel they have to tell me that? Why does every single person I come across question me? This is my life. Mine.

"You know, I'm not one to judge, but you don't look like you are enjoying this." *Would any sane person fucking enjoy this?*

"I," gasp for air, "love it." Rivulets of sweat drip down my temple. Sweat drenches the foam on the border of my goggles. While my muscles are on fire, my toes are oddly frozen solid, and the accompanying freezer burn aches.

If someone was injured, they'd be in serious trouble waiting for me. This thought gets my thighs rising higher and faster, attempting to cover more ground at a quicker pace.

Fifty-five minutes pass, and I'm at the peak. We pause, taking in the sweeping blue-sky view across the Tetons. Objectively, it's like the views I see all the time. But this is one I earned, and as I suck in the thin air, elation circulates.

I snap a photo, but I have zero signal, so I don't send it. The zero signal gives me pause.

"Matt, do you have a geotracker?" There are several tracking devices that help locate people when out in the backcountry.

"Smart to ask." He pats a coat pocket. "Never leave home without it. But don't you worry. You're going to do just fine. Now, get me set up in this bad boy."

"How much do you weigh?" I tug the straps along his legs,

getting him tied in as tightly as possible. Patients are tied in and, if needed, we cover their face, but I have him cocooned in below his neck. "What do you do if someone is claustrophobic?"

"I've had that happen."

Of course he has. Fifteen years of experience. He's seen it all.

"You gotta work through it. It helps if someone they know and trust is nearby and can help talk them through it. In that case, she'd broken her leg. She wasn't getting down the mountain any other way. Reality helps too."

Once I'm ready, I get in front of the toboggan. I've got a steep slope, then several trees I've got to maneuver around. It's fresh, untouched snow in the wild. This means there could be an unexpected hole or rock. Troublesome nerves fire all cylinders. We should have others with us.

"Are you sure about this?" I ask back over my shoulder. Matt's goggle coating shines bright yellow, reflecting the golden sun.

"You got this, Kate. Show me what you can do."

The guy is putting his life in my hands. I suppose that's what he's trying to teach me today. When I'm out on the mountain, I have someone's life in my hands. And maybe it won't always be in the wisest of situations. But the Kate that has held me back my entire life whines.

This isn't smart. If you wipe out, he's tied in and can't get out. If you are injured, you both could die on this mountain. It would take far too long for rescue to make it up here. And that's assuming you are conscious and can get the word out.

"How much do you weigh?" He never answered before.

"About two-twenty."

Fuck. This is all kinds of new for me. I'm not used to hauling that kind of weight down in a toboggan.

The whining voice speaking to me is the voice that halted me for a fraction of a second at the top of every half pipe. The pause that slowed me down and prevented me from earning a top trophy. I hate that voice. Cautious Kate. It's time to bury her.

twenty

Oliver

    May 21

The white-capped mountains shimmer under the overhead sun. She's happy as a jaybird, whereas I'd be pissed beyond belief if we got more snow in May. I snap a shot of my view. The golden sun sitting at not quite noon overhead, a few funky-shaped white clouds dot the horizon, and the trees full of green leaves in summer prime. She can't breathe the air from a photo, but the scent of fresh-cut grass blows strong since Archie is up on the north side mowing the pasture.

Kate's my enigma. Can't get the girl out of my head, but she and I, we're like night and day. Meanwhile, I never got around to calling Elsie. Even ran into her one afternoon in Austin. Told her I'd call. Never did.

Sam Junior might've hit the nail on the head when he diagnosed me. I always want what I can't have. At my age, I need to get myself over that pile of crap.

I slip my phone into my pocket and head out. There's a cow in labor up on the east corner, and I need to go check on her.

The moment the screen door slams behind me, I'm hit with a wave of Texas heat. Sure, it's only May, but we're in the midst of our first heatwave. After flirting with the eighties for weeks, we're headed to ninety-seven today. Meanwhile, up in Jackson, they got a surprise May dump in under twenty-four hours. Their temps are climbing today, but it's still unreal when you think about how different our temperatures are. Hell, how different our lives are.

I take in a big whiff of the outdoors. Freshly cut grass, crisp, clean air, a hint of lingering pollen, and pine all mingle. In the barn, the stronger stench of manure and urine fuse, but I don't mind it. I don't mind it one bit. It's all-natural, and I love it.

We might have a scorcher today, but I'll take that over a foot of May snow any day. If I could ever get her down here, I think she'd like it out here, too. But galloping a horse is a different thrill from downhill skiing. A flash of Kate's wide smile at the top of Corbet's, confident and headstrong, comes to mind. She taunted me that first moment we met. I mean, sure, she'd been concerned I might be a foolhardy bastard about to kill himself. But she'd also goaded me. Whipped down the pass and showed me how it was done. Yeah, she's a natural on the mountain. It's her domain.

I ride across the pasture, the tree line in front of me, horses' tails swishing, and the buzz of the crickets and cicadas intensifying like a string quartet. I see her like an overlay over the scene. It's insane. *I can't get her out of my head.*

Dwayne, one of the ranch hands, flags me down, telling me to hurry it up. I urge Yoda, my chestnut quarter horse, a mature, reliable steed, and his pounding hooves provide a reprieve from the girl I can't jettison.

As I approach, it's clear I missed the magic. A baby calf on wobbly legs hovers near his mother. There's nothing quite like seeing a newborn, fresh out of its mother, control wobbly legs. Mother Nature is awe-inspiring. The newborn nuzzles its mother's side until he finds the udder and nurses all on its own, with no help from us. We like to be here for births, in case there's any issue, but we don't need to be. Mother Nature's got it all under control, at least most of the time, and has been doing so for eons.

A humming sound mixes in with the quiet awe of the baby's first suckling. Yoda lifts his back hoof and kicks out. His black tail swishes. I slam my palm down on the horsefly that landed on his rump, then dig out my phone from the saddle pack. The humming sound didn't sound like a text or a phone call. There's a notification on my phone from my weather app.

Avalanche near Togwotee Pass. Road closure. Search and Rescue underway.

Togwotee Pass isn't a part of the Jackson Hole resort. It's a part of Teton County. An uneasy feeling roils through the pit of my stomach. Dwayne scratches the mother cow's ears, and I dial Kate. I get her voicemail, which makes sense. When a person is out on the mountain, it's difficult to stop everything and answer the phone.

"Hey, Kate. Read about the avalanche out your way. Call me when you get a chance."

We rarely leave voicemails for each other. When she gets my message, she may think I'm a worried mother hen. I'm not worried, though. The Tetons are enormous. The chances she'd be involved in an avalanche are about the same as getting struck by lightning.

I snap a quick photo of the minutes-old calf and shoot it off to Kate.

"Avalanche?" Dwayne asks.

"Near Jackson."

"Texas?" He sounds mystified.

"Wyoming."

"Oh." He chuckles. "That makes more sense. You know someone up that way?"

"A friend." It rubs wrong to describe her as a friend, although that's exactly what she is. A friend with a passion for snow and downhill thrills.

Back at the house, I flip on the television while I fix myself a sandwich. I flick to the Weather Channel. On the bottom of the screen, the scroll reads, "Breaking: Two Missing After Avalanche."

I check my phone. Still no message from Kate.

Me: All okay up there?

I look again at that photo she sent me. Read the caption again. Day in the Tetons. *Shit.* She didn't spend the day at the Jackson resort. She went out somewhere else. A shiver chills my skin like frigid AC, mixing in with that turmoil in my gut.

I locate Drew's name and give him a call. He answers on the second ring.

"If it's not my favorite Texan."

"Shit. You went to UT. And I'm your favorite Texan?" I grin into the kitchen, but inside there's no grin.

"Well, if you knock out all the sorority girls from the running."

"Hey, so, I saw you guys had an avalanche up your way."

"It's bad. Local news is all over it. They shut down the highway down there."

"What happened? Isn't this late in the year for an avalanche?"

"Yeah, it is. But we got that big dump. It was a slide. I think there was melt and then freeze and then fresh snow. Some folks were probably up hiking or doing something at the top and set it off. How'd you hear about it?"

"I've still got the weather app set to Jackson."

"Yeah. It's pretty scary. You know, when someone's trapped in snow, they say you've only got about eighteen minutes to find them before they die. It's a combination of suffocation and death by your own carbon monoxide." Nausea mixes in with the turmoil in my gut. "Sick way to die. And search and rescue have been at it for a couple of hours now. We had a pretty good season this year with no avalanches. A few years back, by December, we'd had, like, three. This is—"

"Drew." I cut his rambling off. Black spots flick across the room. "Do you remember Kate?"

"Oakley. Yeah, I remember her. Did I ever tell you that my wife is friends with her old roommate? Claire? I've seen her a few times out and about. Small world. You and her...you two were tight."

"We're still tight." I'm fine working his euphemism. "She sent me a photo of where she was this morning. She's not answering her phone. If I send you this photo, do you think you'd recognize the spot that she took it from?"

"Dude. I mean, send it on, but you get it's a big damn mountain range, right?"

I open the text exchange with Kate, click on the image and forward it to Drew. "You see it?"

"Hold."

I spread bread and Duke's mayonnaise out on the counter, along with my sandwich meat, but I can't fathom eating. The nausea kills any appetite, and I open the fridge door and put the meat and mayonnaise away.

"She could be over that way. I can't really tell. I don't go off that way often. I've got a season pass at Jackson. Let's see. Based on this angle, it appears she's high up. Did she take a helicopter?"

"I don't have any idea. Her caption said it was a training day in the Tetons."

"She's not returning your calls?"

"No." I draw the unnerving answer out.

"Look, the chances that she's involved in the avalanche are slim. But it looks like she's in the vicinity. Maybe she's helping with the search and rescue."

"But she's in the vicinity?" I ask for clarification. My fingers and palms tingle.

"That would be my guess from the photo, but like I said, I don't head up that way, and when I do, I'm usually cross-country skiing. I don't make it up that high, so I don't...I mean, yeah, she's in the area."

After I hang up with Drew, I dial her number again. Again, I get voicemail. I don't have her roommates' numbers. I don't have her family's numbers. The one number I can easily get is the Jackson Rental Shop, where she works. A kid answers and tells me she's not on the schedule today.

I check the flights to Jackson. There aren't as many flights out there in the offseason. I could get a connecting flight, but it would take forever. I'm not one to call in favors from my billionaire brother, but I've always been one to listen to my gut. And a burning need to get my ass to Jackson rips through me. Call it instinct.

"Sam Duke's office. How may I help you?"

"Hi. This is his brother, Oliver. I'm trying to reach him. It's important."

Only my high-powered executive brother would forward his cell phone calls to his assistant.

"Ollie Duke." Shirley's voice is full of warmth. "How are you doing?"

"Not that great. Is Sam around?"

"He's in a meeting." *Of course he is.* "Let me get him for you."

There's a beat of silence. I stare out across the stretch of rolling hills. The tree limbs rest heavy, unmoving in the still heat of the noon sun.

"Ollie?" Sam's hushed timbre tells me he's not alone and he's concerned. I've never pulled him out of a meeting before.

"Do you still have a company jet here in Austin?"

"Small one. What's up? Everything okay?"

"Can I use it? I'll reimburse you."

A door clicks shut. "It's yours to use. What's going on?"

"There was an avalanche in Jackson."

"Drew? He okay?" Sam's known Drew as long as I have.

"It's Kate. She's a girl I'm seeing. I can't get her on the phone. She was out doing training exercises this morning."

"All right. Let me make some calls. It might take a few hours to locate a pilot and get the flight plan."

"Sam, thank you. I've just got this bad—"

"Hey." He cuts me off. "She's gonna be okay. Let's get you out there so you can see for yourself."

twenty-one

Kate

May 21

"Sir, please stand back. We're keeping this area clear."

Red flashing lights blink in an eerie silence. The sirens have been turned off, but the lights remain on rotation. Pickup trucks with emergency lights on the dashboard, three fire trucks, and police vehicles sit in the blockaded section of highway.

We'd been halfway down the pass when the deep rumble vibrated from the mountain through my legs.

Matt yelled, "Look behind you. Where's it coming from?"

I couldn't see. The tip tops of trees swayed.

"Get me up. Unstrap me."

Matt twisted in the toboggan. I hadn't completely covered his head so he could observe me. His nostrils flared as he sniffed the air.

"Avalanche. Not far away. We need to get off the mountain. Go! We're almost to the snowmobile. Go!"

I pushed forward, using all my might to control the toboggan while flying down the mountain. A pop in my right leg hurt, and I knew it couldn't be good, but I kept on, burning pain and all. The ground vibrated, and my heart pounded so hard and rapidly that I feared it would explode.

Tears broke from my eyes, pooling in my goggles. But we made it to the snowmobile. The quaking ground calmed. My knees hit the ground, and I tore off my gloves to unstrap Matt. He helped, too, and within seconds, he was up. I tried to get up, but pain ricocheted through my right side and I fell forward.

"What's wrong?"

"My knee. It's...I might've pulled a muscle."

Matt unsnapped my skis, tied them to the mobile, and lifted me like I was a flour sack onto the back of the snowmobile.

As we flew down the mountain, he called the avalanche in. Matt offered to remain on the trail to ward off unsuspecting hikers. But dispatch informed us we were too close and could be in danger.

Search and rescue vehicles beat us to the base. The slide stopped just short of the highway and had taken with it tall pines, roots and all.

Search and rescue set off. Local police cordoned off the highway. Another team headed out to assess the situation. One avalanche can set off additional avalanches and slides.

"Keep people back," Matt ordered me. He knew several of the search and rescue members and took off with them. If anyone got swept up in it, they had to find them fast.

I had one mission and one leg to do it. Bright lights flashed, spiking my adrenaline. I watched the time, and with each passing minute, emotion seeped in. But Matt gave me a mission. That's how I find myself leaning on a ski pole, using it like a cane, standing guard.

A woman jogs up with her German shepherd, passing me with a steely determination. The search and rescue dog is more likely to locate a person than any of the human searchers.

The first media vehicle pulls up, and I check the time. Search and rescue has been underway for about an hour. A reporter approaches, the first non-official person on the scene.

"Sir, I need you to stay behind the barricade."

Additional media vehicles approach, but none give me a hard time. They understand lives are in danger. They also understand the snowpack isn't stable.

Another hour passes. The handful of media at the base are somber.

A dog's bark pierces the air. The rapid barking intensifies. A heavy dread accompanies the shouts mixed in with the barking. Too much time has passed.

Matt returns. His grim expression says everything. Quietly, he gives me the update. He's careful the media doesn't hear, as he has no official capacity.

"Search and rescue found a man and a woman. Late twenties to early thirties. They're digging them out now."

After an avalanche, the snow packs like concrete. The Teton Search and Rescue team is currently checking out the rest of the snowpack and flagging off areas for danger.

Two bodies. The numbness settling around me drowns out my feet, aching in ski boots. My right leg won't straighten. I think it's swollen, but I can't really tell. The whole scene is surreal. Cops and firemen swarm the area.

Matt pats me on the back and mumbles about going to speak to someone.

A car pulls up. An older man, I'd guess in his mid-sixties, gets out of the car. He stumbles along the snowpack.

"Sir, we're asking everyone to stay back."

"My daughter. I got a call. You found her?"

Matt didn't mention this man. He didn't tell me what to do.

His big hand latches onto my jacket. "Where is she?"

He looks dazed. His cheeks are blistery red from the cold air. I step aside and point through the maze of cars. Someone with more information will direct him.

They load two bodies on gurneys into an ambulance. I don't see the man from earlier, but I hear his wracking sobs. The sound of a grown man sobbing is more than I can handle. My eyes burn with the emotion welling up.

The lights on the ambulance flick off and the taillights flicker as it drives slowly away. The speed of an ambulance is inversely related to hope. When it speeds along, there is hope for survival. When it crawls by, there is no hope. A slow-moving ambulance performs the functions of a hearse.

By the time I return to my apartment, I am beyond numb. Matt asked if I wanted to go to the bar with the rest of the crew for a beer, but I can't stomach beer or conversation. I am gutted. Shocked.

Matt said we didn't cause it. My training day didn't claim two lives. But it could have. Why did Matt take me up there?

In the shower, the hot water singes my cool skin. The pale flesh glows red. I wiggle my toes, and pain reverberates up the side of my foot to my ankle. Tears fall and blend with the water cascading down from the showerhead.

The fear when my legs vibrated. The uncertainty. The destruction. The heavy weight of locating bodies. Not lives, not humans. No, search and rescue found bodies.

After showering, I plug my phone into the charger and crawl into bed. The phone vibrates as it comes to life. I am depleted. My arms are heavy, as if strapped with iron weights. The vibrations continue.

With a monumental force of effort, I lift the phone. Ten texts. Twelve missed calls. I click to the texts. Hudson, my parents, Nash, Paisley, and Oliver.

I click my family group text.

Me to family: I'm okay. Spent the day with search and rescue. Will call later.

Me to Nash and Paisley: Back home. I'm okay. Not going out tonight.

Oliver is the one who seems panicked. I dial his name.

"Oh, thank god. You're alive."

If death hadn't taken up residence inside me, I might laugh at him. But instead of laughing, I inhale and look at the ceiling as my lips tremble.

"Are you okay?" Concern paints his every word, and I press my lips together, hard, and swallow down the lump in my throat.

"Tough day. But yeah, I'm okay."

"Hmmm." The deep rumble across the line expresses skepticism in my assessment. Or maybe that's how my skepticism colors his low-key response. "Here's the thing about okay. It's a half-hearted shield we wear to avoid sharing what's really going on. It works with colleagues or strangers on the street. But I hope we're more than that."

Shit. He's right. My bottom lip trembles uncontrollably. I swipe at my eyes and sniffle. I try to pull my knees up to my chest, but the one leg hurts when it bends, so I wrap my arms around the leg with the phone tucked between my shoulder and my ear.

"Tell me about it. Tell me what you're going through." Again, he's right. It's not over. I'm still going through it. My insides ache.

"There was a deep rumble. I've never been in an earthquake, but I think that's probably a close analogy. Matt, he shouted—"

"Who's Matt?"

"A patroller. He was helping me prep. Took me out on a snowmobile. We had this big dump. Late spring snow."

"I know. I get Jackson's weather reports. That's how I got the alert."

"We were so close. And, you know, I can't help but wonder if we didn't set it off. When the snow is unstable...you just don't know."

"Does Matt think you set it off?"

"No. But..." How could he possibly know? "I spent hours down at the base with the ambulances and the patrol cars. Pretty quickly everyone knew we wouldn't find them alive, and it was just the most sickening..." A sob breaks out. How do you describe that kind of heaviness? "I'll never forget the bodies being loaded into the ambulance, and the ambulance slowly pulling away."

"How many died?"

"Two. Young, too."

"Kids?"

"No. Twenty-nine and thirty-two." Not children, but so much life left to live. "I saw one father. He just...crumbled." The phone beeps from being pressed against my ear so hard, and I have to set it down on the bed, wipe the front dry, and get myself back under control. I set it to speaker, so I don't have to hold it up against my wet face.

"Were you...did Matt take you to a restricted area?"

"It wasn't a trail, but it wasn't restricted."

"Then it's not your fault." I know what he's saying. Some people ski in restricted areas without regard for consequences. And when they cause an avalanche, any deaths truly are on their shoulders. But Matt and I didn't do that. But we also didn't check for avalanche risk. Or at least I didn't. So late in the season, I didn't think.

"It might not be my fault, but inside..." I choke back another sob. "It's just...I feel dead. I didn't know them, but it feels like I did."

"I'll be there in the morning." Snot wells up in my nose, and I reach out for a tissue. *Honk.* I'd normally be choking on laughter after releasing such a gross sound, but I'm not anywhere near a normal state of mind. "Where will you be? At the apartment?"

His questions bring me back to the conversation, and his meaning registers. "You're coming to Jackson?"

"I couldn't get you on the phone. Set about figuring out how to get up to you."

"You were coming to check on me?" Fresh tears spring. He cares enough to come up here. "What were you going to do? Join the search and rescue team?"

"If that's what it took. Jesus, Kate...Drew told me that, well..."

"He told you what happens during an avalanche?" I collapse onto my side in a fetal position. The phone rests on the bed, inches from my face. "It's not pretty. If anything like that happens again, don't come up. There's no point."

The father crumbling, tears, mouth turned down in agony…the vision returns, and I close my eyes, trying to block it out, but it doesn't work.

"Well, there's a point now. I can be there for you. And I need to see you. Need to see for myself you're okay."

That's sweet. He's so sweet. A truly good friend. I'd love nothing more than to hold him close and to cry into his shoulder.

"I hurt my leg."

"How?"

I remember the pop. I don't know what the fuck I did. "My knee is swollen. Really swollen."

"What did you do?"

"Not sure. Pulled a muscle?"

"What did the doctor say?"

"I didn't…I haven't."

"When I get there, we'll get it checked out. Unless you think you should go tonight?"

"I'm hoping the swelling will go down." I don't have health insurance. I'd definitely rather wait and see. It's not like I broke my leg.

"Well, if it doesn't, we'll get it checked out." He's insistent, and god, it's so comforting to hear how much he cares. "I'd love to see you, but I have work tomorrow."

"On the mountain? I thought ski season was over?"

"For the resort, it is. We're switching over to things like mountain biking and hiking. I have to work at the golf resort tomorrow."

"Is that mostly on your leg?"

"Yeah." I sniffle, and my brain begins connecting dots that work might be really hard for me if my leg is messed up.

"How are you liking that?"

"It's good." This change in conversation has me breathing more easily because I don't want to think about the ramifications of an injury or what happened today, and I dab the tip of my nose with a tissue. "I'm actually really enjoying it. Our roles float, so I'm getting to do different things. Tomorrow, we're brainstorming ideas for an upcoming tournament. It's fun. Different."

"What time do you get off tomorrow?"

"My shift ends at six." I sniffle, but the torrent of emotions has quieted. Talking with Oliver, hearing his voice, it helps. I would truly love to see him, which might be an odd thing to feel about one's fling. But he became more than a fling when we continued our friendship. He's grown into one of my closest friends.

"I'll be there." He's adamant, and the thought might be the sweetest consideration ever, but it's unnecessary.

"You don't need to do that. I'm going to be okay." I half-laugh at the shield word. "Really. I just...this talk...I'm already feeling better."

"Kate. I'm glad you're feeling better, but I need to see you. I need to touch you and know you are...Kate, the universe needs you in it. My universe needs you in it. I need physical confirmation."

"That's so sweet of you to say, but...I'm pretty far away."

"If we're talking the scale of the universe, you're a hop, skip, and a jump away."

"I'd love to see you, too." My voice cracks and my lips scrunch up as another wave of tears fills my eyes. I get what he's saying. I only had a couple of minutes when he fell on the horse, and I'd been terrified. But with my work schedule and... "The feeling on the mountain is suffocating right now." I'm not the only one rocked by unexpected senseless deaths.

"All the more reason for me to come."

"This would be a miserable time to vacation here."

"Kate, it's all planned. I'm gonna see you. And I'll bring some first aid for that knee."

twenty-two

Kate

May 22

"I don't know, girl. That's pretty gnarly." Paisley stands before me, looking down at my leg. A dark bruise now accompanies the swelling. It's mostly on the side of my leg, which is odd. "Let me fill in for you."

"Would you?"

"Sure. You can cover for me when your leg's better to make up some of the time."

Nash sticks his head on. "Yowza, girl. Did you take a tumble?"

"No, actually." It's confusing. I never fell. It must have been the strain of maneuvering a two-hundred-twenty-pound man down a powder embankment.

"Nash, don't you know a nurse?"

"Yeah, I do. She works at urgent care."

"Do you know her well enough to do a house call?"

"Guys, I'm not going to a doctor. The swelling's already going down." Paisley and Nash exchange a glance.

"I'll go call her."

"It's not necessary," I shout after him.

"What's not necessary?" Claire enters the bedroom, and her eyes widen. "What did you do?"

"She doesn't know, and she doesn't want to go see a doctor," Paisley answers before I can.

"I'm fine." I hobble into the bathroom and shut the door. Shit. I was in med school, not that they know that. I'm not an idiot. I don't need a nurse. No, I don't have an MRI machine, but I don't need one to know there's nothing they can do for me. Chances are I pulled my ITB band. I should've been better with my stretching. If it doesn't get better, it might mean it's a tear, but I don't need to pay the money yet. They wouldn't do surgery with this much swelling, anyway.

There's a loud knock at the apartment door. If that's the nurse already, then she's one of Nash's hotties on speed dial. It sounds like Paisley and Claire both left to answer the door, and I rest my hands on the counter and give myself a good once-over.

I feel like I've been run over by a Mack truck. I'm too lazy to braid my hair, so I pull it back into a ponytail. It is a good thing Paisley will cover for me. I don't have any business being on my leg. Even if it's a pulled muscle, I need to let it rest. I'm such a moron to have let my insurance lapse.

"Hey, Kate," Paisley calls out.

"Yeah?" I call back.

"You've got a visitor." There's a sing-song quality to Paisley's tone that has me searching for my watch to check the time. Did he really come? How could he be here already? Why would he be here? I told him I have to work.

I hobble out into the hallway, and his deep, soothing southern twang wraps around me like the heat from a toasty warm fire.

"Such a small world. Can't believe you're friends with Drew's wife. I was at that wedding."

"Kate, look who—"

"Ouch. That's not good." Oliver's statement sends everyone's gaze down to my leg. I'm wearing pajama shorts, and I really should've changed.

"It's fine. A pulled muscle."

"Are you in pain?"

My leg has been in a perma-bend since yesterday. It hurts too much to straighten it, and I can't put weight on it, but it will be fine.

"Not too much. I've already taken Advil."

"I left my bag at the hotel, but I did bring some wraps." He's wearing faded jeans, brown leather cowboy boots, and a navy crew-neck lightweight sweater. His tan is darker than when I saw him last, and his blond highlights are brighter. His unruly hair might be a tad longer. He looks absolutely delicious.

Paisley and Claire stand on each side of him, and their presence is the only reason I haven't thrown myself at him yet.

He shifts and those whiskey eyes pour over me, from my bruised leg and up my torso, hovering near my breasts, and up my neck to my lips, and finally my eyes. My throat tightens, and my breathing becomes shallow.

"Well, I suppose I should head on out since I'm taking your shift today." Paisley's comment breaks me out of the stare fest.

"Thanks again, Paisley."

"What's your schedule tomorrow?"

"I'm cashier at the spa. And bartending."

"I'll cover you tomorrow at the spa, but you've gotta find someone to bartend."

"I can—"

"You know there's too much walking around. You have to give guests tours of the facilities after they check in. Take it easy, Kate. You don't want whatever that is getting worse. And besides, even if you weren't injured, after what happened yesterday, folks would understand you taking some time off." Claire steps forward and gives me a warm hug, then pats my back. "What happened yesterday is a lot. You don't need to pretend it's not."

And just like that, tears spring up, and I flutter my eyelashes, willing the unexpected flash of emotion away. She leans forward once more, her nose practically in my ear, and whispers, "I knew you'd see him again."

She grins and heads down the hall. Paisley spins and follows her.

"Make her relax, Oliver. Keep her off her feet." From behind Oliver's back, Paisley starts with hand and tongue gestures, and I roll my eyes, turning back into my bedroom.

Oliver follows close behind me, and he kicks the door closed while capturing me in his arms. There's a whiff of cinnamon and his earthy cologne, and I fall into his embrace, placing my head on his shoulder.

His arms tighten around me, his heart beats against me, and I close my eyes, feeling him, letting his presence sink into me. I really can't believe he's here.

"Jesus, Kate. If something had happened to you..." His lips press against the side of my head. "I thought I'd never see you again."

He shifts back, and his thumb caresses my cheek. I press the side of my face into his palm and close my eyes, relishing the touch. His hands are rough but warm and strong.

"But I'm okay." I pull back and take him in. "I can't believe you came."

"Wild horses couldn't keep me away." He presses his lips against mine. It's a fleeting kiss, and he backs up in an awkward way. "Can I use your restroom? I dropped my stuff back at the hotel reception and came right here. I've also got this gum." He snaps it between his teeth a few times as visual evidence.

"Go ahead."

Bathroom sounds trickle through the hollow panel door, and I press my palm against my sternum, surprised by the rapid beating. Nerves unsettle me, and I step forward, but pain ricochets up my thigh. So, I sit down on the edge of the bed, facing the bathroom door, waiting.

I thought I'd have more time to get ready if he was really coming. I haven't shaved in a couple of days, I've had a cup of coffee since I brushed my teeth, and my hair is like a rat's nest since I fell asleep last night with it soaked.

The faucet turns on, and I know he's washing his hands. He's going to taste like cinnamon, and I'll have foul coffee breath. I can't remember when I last shaved my legs. How early was his flight?

The door opens, and I attempt to get up, but my damn leg aches, and I twist to use both hands to push up off the bed.

"Hey, what are you doing?"

"I wasn't expecting you this early."

He hovers over me, then drops to his knees. He tenderly touches the sides of my calf, the pads of his fingers lightly pressing up to my injured knee. My knee jerks from his touch, and his whiskey eyes, a deeper brown in this light, study me as he roams my injury.

"There's not much heat. Just swelling. Have you had ITB band injuries before?"

"No." It comes out like a whine, and his eyes flash to capture mine. "But that's what I think it is, too. How do you know about injuries?"

He shrugs. "Just do. Comes from being on a ranch, I guess. And in a fraternity with intramural jocks. Why don't you lie back on the bed?"

"I need to shave. I—"

"Don't you worry about that."

"But—"

"Trust me."

I position myself back against the pillow on my bed, and the mattress sinks as he gingerly climbs up beside me. He lies on his side, his head propped on his hand. The bed dips a little with his weight and squeaks as he leans into me. He cups the side of my face and slowly lowers his lips to mine.

Cinnamon fills my mouth as he kisses me soft and slow. All the annoying nerves drift away as I lose myself in this kiss. He lifts my sweatshirt, and his calloused hands graze my stomach. I roll into him, on my side, needing to be closer.

"You let me know if something hurts, okay?" He rubs the tip of his nose over mine.

"Okay." He grips the bottom of my sweatshirt and lifts. Obediently, I raise my arms. I'm not wearing a bra, and he sits back on his heels.

"God, Kate. I had wanted to get you back to the hotel. But I don't think I'm going to be able to wait. Are you okay with that?"

I nod and reach for his sweater, but there's no need. He lifts it over his shoulders and removes it. Then he grips my pajama shorts and gently tugs them, along with my panties, over my hips and down my thighs, slowing in the vicinity of my injury, then down over my calves and ankles, and he tosses them. He takes my healthy leg and slides it to the side, positioning himself between my legs.

"That's...I haven't shaved or..."

He traces kisses along the inside of my healthy leg, careful to avoid my injury. There's no point in saying more. He can see what a mess I am, and he doesn't seem to care.

His tongue slips inside me, and my hips buck up. A riot of sensations course through me, and I tilt my head back, reveling in everything he's doing. It's been so long since anyone has touched me. Given me this level of attention or care. What he's doing feels incredible, but as good as it feels, my center clenches, and a visceral need for more quakes.

"I need you. Now."

He looks up from between my legs, his fingers inside me, his breath caressing my most sensitive parts, and he dips his head down and presses his lips near my clit and sucks. A small scream escapes as my muscles quiver and my thighs press around his ears.

"Please." I tug on his hair, and he finally raises and kisses and sucks his way up my stomach, crawling as he works the buttons on his jeans and shoves them down. He sucks and bites a nipple, and I scrape my nails along his biceps, urging him forward.

"I should grab a condom." But he doesn't reach for his jeans, which are down around his knees. Instead, he's looking at me, asking.

"It's okay."

"I haven't been with anyone since you."

"Me neither. And I have an IUD."

And then he's kissing me and hovering over me, and then finally he sinks into me, stretching me. Forehead to forehead, we both moan.

"Oh, fuck, I've missed you."

Our eyes meet and lock, and his hips begin to move. He reaches for my good leg and lifts it, adjusting our angle, and my eyes flutter shut because it feels so damn good. He feels so damn good.

"God, Kate."

The muscles in his back strain beneath my fingers as I revel in his touch, in reacquainting myself with his body. I grip his ass and pull him closer, my hips rising to meet his. The bed frame hits the apartment wall, and he slows.

"No, it's okay. Don't stop."

"You are so fucking wet. You feel so fucking good. I'm not...are you close?"

He reaches between us, and those whiskey eyes seek mine as he slows his thrusts and kneads me. He watches me like I'm a guitar he's strumming, and all of my muscles tense, and a powerful, intense orgasm peels through me. He grunts as his thrusts become erratic. He freezes over me, pulsing deep inside me. And then we kiss, slow and soft, and like I've never kissed anyone before.

"Wow."

He rolls off me, onto his side, his chest heaving. His jeans are still shoved around his knees, but I don't care. His hands trace along my breasts and my stomach while I roam the hard lines of his abdomen, up along his chest and shoulders, and the slope of his neck.

Our movements are languid and relaxed, and it feels more right than anything I've ever felt in my life. He pulls me up against him, on his chest, so his heart beats into my ear.

"So, do we need to get you to an urgent care or something? For someone to look at that knee?"

"No, really, I'm pretty sure it's just a pulled muscle."

"There's a lot of swelling and bruising. You think we might need to get a professional opinion?"

"Not yet." I let my arm fall across him, and his heartbeat lulls me into an easy, relaxed state. "Worst case, there's a tear. But they wouldn't do anything until the swelling goes down. Swelling's already gone down some. If I still can't put weight on it tomorrow and the swelling has gone down, I'll go see someone. It's possible I'll need physical therapy."

The potential expense makes me nauseated. On the bright side, if that's the case, there'd be no reason to beat myself up over letting my insurance lapse, because my shitty insurance probably wouldn't have covered PT.

"I'd feel better if you saw a professional." The tips of his fingers glide along my arm, back and forth.

"Well, I was in med school. I know it's not the same as a doctor, but I'm not without knowledge."

His hand stills, and regret raps in my chest. I shouldn't've said anything.

"You were in medical school?"

"Yeah. Was."

"I thought you only wanted snow and mountains. Were you... were you gonna be slope side? Like one of those docs at the base?"

"Maybe."

"What happened?"

I let out a deep sigh.

"Hey." He tips my chin up until I'm looking at him. "No judgment. I just want to get to know you. Better."

I rest my head back down against him. It's easier to admit bad things without looking him in the eye.

"I hated it. I really, really hated it. I was miserable. And I just knew—"

"It wasn't for you?"

"Yeah."

"That's okay. I knew people like that in law school. Changed course."

"Yeah, but they probably got their degree so they could use it for something."

"Nah. Not all of 'em. How many years did you get in?"

"Two." One hundred and fifty thousand dollars in student loans. Money incinerated.

"Is there a medical aspect to ski patrol?"

"Some. That's what the red cross on their vests means."

"Huh." It feels like a loaded *huh*. "What exactly did you hate?"

"The smells. The formaldehyde. Blood. Needles. The subject matter. The videos. I'm just...squeamish. I thought it would get better with exposure. But it didn't. It got worse." His fingers stroke my arm once again with a matching slow back-and-forth rhythm. "I think I never wanted to be a doctor."

My chest aches at the admission. I've never admitted that to anyone.

"Well, damn good thing to figure out before you finished medical school and residency."

"Better late than never, right?"

"Abso-fucking-lutely."

"Would be better if I didn't have a ton of debt."

"True. But you'd have twice as much debt if you didn't pull out when you did. It's kind of like me and Collette. We lived together, and I didn't get out of that relationship Scot-free, but imagine if we'd been married."

"That's not quite the same thing." I pinch his nipple.

"Hey, what was that for? I'm being honest. And I was trying to make you feel better."

I laugh. Which is really crazy because I never laugh when talking about the biggest failure in my life.

"I take it Collette was your ex-fiancée?"

"Yeah. I guess I didn't mention her name before, huh?"

"No. And can we make a deal you never mention her name again when we're in bed naked?" He smiles his widest smile. He's so damn gorgeous. The hottest guy I've ever been with by miles.

"Deal." He holds out his hand to shake. "Now, what do we say we get cleaned up and get you packed so we can get to the Four Seasons? I've got some pampering and healing planned."

"Healing?" I grin, and he scrunches his nose.

"Sensual, baby." He slaps the side of my ass. "Come on, now. In the shower. We can shave those legs."

"Oh, my god. I told you." How mortifying. I really didn't think he'd be here this early. I expected a text with an arrival time or something.

"I'll shave them. You trust me?"

"You forgot how small my shower is, didn't you?"

"Come on. Up. I want to get you back to a bed that doesn't squeak and a wall we're not going to dent."

twenty-three

MAY 22

Oliver

Kate sits on the sofa, propped up with pillows behind her back. She's on the phone with her mother, the medical doctor. Her voice is low, and I get the impression she's taking care to keep it low. I'm in the kitchenette and busy texting away with folks back at the ranch and with my businesses. This wasn't exactly a planned trip, and I'm going to need to return home in the morning.

But I'm damn glad I made the trip. I searched on YouTube how to apply athletic tape to an ITB band injury. She griped, but after watching the video with me, took over taping it. I ordered about a case of the stuff, and it'll be delivered to her apartment tomorrow.

Sandra: Tell me about this girl.

I am sorely tempted to snap a photo and send it to Sandra. There's no telling how she got wind of my trip up here. Probably through the Drew fraternity connection. I'm almost positive she's not talking to Sam. I know Sam told Ian, and Sandra and Ian are good friends, so that's another possible avenue.

Doesn't matter how she knows. I probably should've mentioned her earlier, but with her living so far away, it didn't seem worth mentioning.

Me to Sandra: She's something else. Young, though. 25.

I watch both the phone and Kate. Kate's cheeks are gettin' rosy, and I meander over to the thermostat to see if I need to drop the temp. We have the fireplace going, even though it's warm outside.

Sandra: Age don't matter.

I chuckle. My friend is correct. Besides, I go older and younger. Age, to me, is a matter of heart.

Sandra: Any chance you can convince her to move to
Texas?

I frown. I already tried to convince one woman to overlook her heart's desire. There's no fucking way I'll ride that pony again.

*Me to Sandra: She's a mountain girl through and
through.*

If I were girlie, I'd add a sad emoji, but I don't do that shit.

Sandra: Any chance you'd move to Jackson?

Yeah, right, Sandra. She's got to know me better than that.

Me to Sandra: Not a chance in hell.

Three bubbles show, then disappear, then show. She's got a lot to
say. If I were in the room with Sandra, I'd be getting a piece of her
mind.

Sandra: Land won't keep you warm at night.

I flip the phone over. Sandra always wants the last word, and I'll give
it to her.

"Mom." The exasperated way that Kate belts out her mom's
name makes me think she needs a little more privacy, so I walk back
into the bedroom and into the bathroom.

When I come out, she's off the phone.

"How did it go?"

"Fine."

The sofa sinks when I sit down on it. There are two hickies on Kate's neck and probably a few lower. I don't think she's noticed them yet. I swear I did try to be gentle. I'm not a teenager. I don't know what came over me. I know better than to mark her, but I have to say, I do like seeing her with some branding of mine, if you want to call it that.

She looks up at me, and there's a whole lotta emotion behind glassy eyes.

"Hey, did your mom get you upset?"

"No. Not really. She was actually pretty supportive. I mean, when I told her I should've known better, she reminded me that doctors are infamous for doing things they shouldn't. She reminded me that every day at the hospital, doctors and nurses cluster outside to smoke."

There's a touch of a smile on her lips that doesn't quite fit with those glassy eyes. "So, what's wrong?"

"She told me I need to go to the doctor."

"All right, then. To urgent care."

"I'll go tomorrow. There will be a huge wait, and you're only here until tomorrow morning."

"Nah." Now it's my turn to grin. "I called yesterday and got us an appointment. It's in about thirty minutes, so we should probably get going. It's down in Jackson."

"You did what?"

"Did you really think I'd leave here without you seeing a doctor? Patty would skin me alive for that kind of foolishness."

"Patty?" Her mouth is kind of open, and then she gets it. "Your mom."

"Yes sirree. Now, what do ya' gotta do for us to get out of here?"

In less than ten minutes, we're in the back seat of the car service I ordered. I could've rented a car, but at the time, I thought I'd be spending the whole weekend in the hotel room.

There are quite a few people in the urgent care waiting room, but because we have an appointment, Kate waits less than five minutes. As soon as she's called back, I pull out my phone.

Me to Sam: Thanks again for your jet. You've got to tell me how much I owe you.

Me to Ian: You want anything from Jackson?

Me to Noah: I'm in Jackson. You need anything from Thai Me Up while I'm here? I just remembered you said you were making headway with them.

Me to Liam: I will not be going to that barbecue.

Me to Mom: How's the fishing going? You guys catch anything?

Ian: Who are you dating?

Noah: Maybe. Let me see if he's in town. I think I got an out of office from him.

Liam: Put your big boy panties on and stop whining.

Sam: Just glad everything's okay. Olivia wants to know more about Kate. She asked if you're off the market.

I'm sure Olivia did ask that. Olivia always seems to know a single woman when I visit the Big Apple. But she doesn't seem to understand that a big city girl is not for yours truly.

*Mom: Honey, Olivia told me about your friend. Is she
okay?*

*Mom: I sent Noah a seven-layer caramel cake. Do you
know if he got it?*

Me to Noah: Did you get a cake?

*Noah: I've gained ten pounds thanks to your mom. I'll text
her thank you now.*

Me to Noah: Ten pounds? One cake?

Yeah, I'm calling bullshit on that one. Patty uses some butter in her recipes but, come on, now.

*Noah: ONE cake? I've gotten lobster, steak, cupcakes,
fudge, barbecue, cobbler, frozen lasagna, pie,
unknown casseroles I have yet to thaw, Girl Scout
cookies, and I'm sure I'm forgetting something.*

I laugh out loud, and a woman waiting near me glances my way. I offer her a friendly smile.

Me to Noah: She thinks you're starving without your wife.

Noah: I will never show up drunk to your house again.

His comment reminds me that I need to get moving on building my home. The materials I've ordered should be delivered soon. I've got some workers lined up to help me too.

> *Me to Sam and Ian: Next time you're back home, please let's talk about property lines. I'm gonna start building soon, but I'd like to walk the potential lines with each of you.*

> *Ian to Sam and me: Whatever you want works for me. Do I know her?*

> *Sam to Ian and me: Ditto on plans. Ian, do you know anyone who doesn't live in Houston?*

I choose to ignore my brothers and respond to my mother before I forget.

> *Me to Mom: She's good. I'll be back at the ranch tomorrow by noon.*

> *Jason: Glad everyone's okay out there. Maggie has questions.*

> *Me to Jason: ?*

Jason: When do we get to meet her?

That's a question and a half. My auto response would be when are you coming to Texas, but he won't be meeting her in Texas. Jason and Maggie live in Chicago. Damnit, Sam. He goes and blabs, and now I've got to calm everyone's horses down.

Me to Jason: She's just a friend.

I switch over to the weather app, checking the outlook back at the ranch. The door swings open, and Kate hobbles out on crutches.

"Whoa. What did they say?"

She goes to the checkout counter, but I direct her away from the counter.

"I've got to check out."

The nurse behind the glass makes eye contact with me. I gave them all the payment information when I scheduled the appointment. Doesn't take a rocket scientist to know Kate doesn't have health insurance. The nurse and I agreed if she got there and provided health insurance, she'd only bill me what wasn't covered. But, as it turned out, she checked in, and as I suspected, no insurance card.

"Already taken care of."

"What?" She sounds alarmed, and a few folks waiting lift their heads from their phones.

I press against her back softly, urging her out of the place.

"You can't do that. I can pay for myself."

"What kind of friend would I be if I let you do that? Come on, now." She looks like she's about to pop, so I pull one from the Book of

Sam. "Hey, I have the means to pay. If the shoes were reversed, wouldn't you cover for me?"

"I'm not...I have money. I can pay my own way."

"I know you can. But if this makes your life easier, and I want to do it for you, why not?" We exit into the bright sunlight. She's slower on her crutches, and I cringe for her because I know those things hurt like a bitch. "Besides, I thought I'd be bringing you here kicking and screaming, so I figured the least I could do was pay for it."

That sort of softens the annoyed expression on her face.

"So, what did he say?"

"She," Kate pronounces the pronoun in a way that lets me know I just stepped in it, "said it's a pull, not a tear. But I'll need physical therapy."

Kate does not look happy with this news, and it hits me that some of her unhappiness isn't my fault.

"For how long?"

"Six months." We reach the car, and I take the crutches from her and she gingerly gets into the passenger seat. The driver smiles at us. Since it's a slow time of year, he had no issue waiting for us. When I scramble in on the other side, I ask the question I've kept the lid on.

"So, does this impact ski patrol next year?"

"Six months is the worst case. We'll see."

Kate's not a happy girl. We get back to the hotel room, and I suggest a nap. After all, I kept her up a lot of the night, and she readily agrees. When dinner time approaches, I wake her with my tongue, and I don't stop until she rewards me with a couple of Ol...lies.

After ordering room service, we make love again. And yeah, it's making love. It's slow and gentle because I need to be. Because she's hurting, and I want her to know someone cares. Everything I do, every time I touch her, every way I touch her, it's all about her. Helping her to forget herself, to give her a moment to forget the shit that's happened, to let all those endorphins do their magic. And afterward, I hold her against me while she sleeps.

In the morning, as we both pack our bags, I lasso the elephant in the room.

"How far out do you get your work schedules?"

"One week out. Except for the country club. That's two weeks out." She doesn't look up from folding her clothes.

"I'm thinking I'd like to come back in about two weeks. You think you could arrange time off? Or plan—"

"Come back?" She's looking at me like she's surprised, but the thing is, I don't know how she could expect anything else, not after the couple of days we just had.

"Yeah." I zip my bag and stare her down.

"Oliver, you know...I loved this. And it means so much you came here. But..."

"But what?"

"Come on. Where is this going?"

"I'll grant you that the long-term future might not look so bright, but let me tell you where I'm coming from."

I wait for her to lift those eyes and show me she's listening. After she smooths out a T-shirt, she gives me her attention.

"I missed you like hell." She nods, and I guess that's her way of saying ditto. I'll take it. "When that avalanche happened, all I kept thinking is, what if I never see you again? I wasn't ready to let that one week be our whole story. I just wasn't. I'm not ready to let this be it, either. I can't give you a five- or ten-year plan, but I can tell you that I want to see you again. Kate, one thing I absolutely know...I would not have been okay with not seeing you again. And now..." My hands fall to my waist, and I search for the right words. "You're important to me, Kate. I want to see you. I need to see you. What's between us is too good. I don't have a magic ball, but even if I did, I'd put about as much credence in it as that drunk fortune teller on New Year's. Can we just agree to keep seeing each other? When we can? Please?" Hell, I tried to fly away and not look back...but that didn't work out at all.

"Okay." She's still wrapped in a shell of sadness, but those lips turn up. Because of me. Because of us. And that lights me up on the inside like a multi-colored Christmas tree.

"Looks like we got ourselves a deal. You check your schedules."

"Okay. We'll keep seeing each other for however long. Just try not to break my heart too badly."

And, well, with that, the suitcases fall to the floor, and I make love to her all over again.

twenty-four

Oliver
June 11

The Guadalupe River streams by, smooth as glass in the early afternoon, and the bordering broadleaf trees reflect a haze of green over the far banks. Thanks to the positioning of the rock wall of the old gin mill, the sensation before the large panes of glass is that the river flows beneath the building. My vision is to lay white pine floors to add a level of warmth to the industrial design aesthetic.

Sam's heavy footfalls knock against the rotted wood beams. The gin mill and this portion of the property sit far away from any neighbor. The gurgling river, wind, rustling limbs, crickets, and birds coalesce in a daily orchestra. Once a week, a lawn mower or tractor blends into the background, and that's about it for manmade noises. To me, this is a slice of heaven. To my ex, this would've been hell. Life is all about perspective.

Sam's gaze travels across the space. "Is this buildable?"

"I've been working on the foundation for a while. It's secure. I've got the permits to run the lines for electrical and waste. Only thing is

I want to be certain you and Ian are in. I've got an idea of where we could split the property lines, you know…one day."

It should be pretty clear to my older brother where I'm going. Before I invest hundreds of thousands of dollars in building a house, I need to know we can agree on property lines, should he and Ian decide not to sell to me one day.

"If I'm going to be working the ranch, I'd like to live out here. And I don't want to keep living in our folks' house. Besides, one day, they'll tire of gallivanting, and San Pedro Island might get old. They'll want to move back. I love 'em, but I don't want to live with 'em. This way, I can be the one to look out for them."

"Right," he says. "So, you're really planning on living out here? Until you *die*?"

"That's the plan." I face him head on. None of this is news. I love it out here. Ranching life has always been it for me. I'm happier here on this parcel of land than anywhere else on Earth. It's in my blood. Four generations of Dukes have been born and bred right here. I have no intention of walking away from it. "Can we go walk the lines I'm envisioning?"

"Sure. But Ian and I already told you we're okay with whatever you want."

One glance at my big brother, and it's clear as day that's truly how he feels. And why wouldn't he? He's never loved it out here like I do. Growing up, he'd preferred to spend the day on a computer than outdoors. Sure, we could get him outside, and he always pulled his share, but the moment a lull arrived, he'd hop back into a book or on his computer. And now? He says he got lucky and created a backend system that powers online sales. Right time, right place kind of thing. He's humble like that. Billionaire wunderkind who can buy pretty much anything he wants, so if he decides later in life to leave the northeast, he can easily buy land…as long as some of it remains undeveloped.

"You should do what you want," Sam says. "I can't imagine Ian cares." Neither can I. Our younger brother is probably the smartest of all three of us. He's both a surgeon and some kind of medical venture capitalist. He's happier than a pig in shit over there in Houston at the world's biggest medical research park. "I doubt you'll get him to come out here and walk any lines. You might be better off doing a video and sending it to him." That's a good idea. Leave it to Sam. "But why are you taking this all on yourself?"

"This ranch, it's what I love. What I'm passionate about." Each of us found our own way in the world, and yeah, my passion isn't nearly as lucrative as my brother's, but it's as deep and as real. "I can't imagine being anywhere else."

"Well, just know if you need money. At any point in time—"

I shut him up with my hand in the air. "Got it."

"You don't need to shoulder expenses out here. And one day, our folks…"

"The Duke Family Farm is self-sufficient." He squints at me, questioning my statement. "I'm not bullshitting. I mean, yeah, we have lean years, but we cover the bills. And I've got other business-es." Truth is, small to mid-size ranchers these days often have sources of income that stem from outside the ranch. It's just smart business when your livelihood depends on something as fickle as the weather or commodity prices.

"Okay. Just know—"

"I know, you've got the bucks. If I ever need any, I'll come knocking."

I lead him out onto the property. I'd really like to have him walk the property line I'm envisioning, but he's slow and meandering, and it's a bit like herding cats.

"How're things going with Kate? From Jackson?"

"They're going." I step across a dip in the land that I'll need to landscape one day. "We talk every few days. Text pretty much every day."

Despite our agreement to see each other again within a few weeks, we have yet to schedule another visit. But that's partly because of our combined work schedules. My weekdays are pretty packed, and if she has any time off, it's typically during the week. There's no point getting stressed about it, as this LDR, as she likes to call it, has no potential end to the distance.

"I'm taking it day by day. Watch out for that," I warn, pointing to an older pile of cow manure that's partially covered in a clump of grass. "No expectations. Actually, I expect there's a time limit. We can't last forever long distance, but we're having fun. She's different."

That's an understatement. There's a connection between us that spans the distance. When I close my eyes, I see her. She fills both my dreams and fantasies. But, obviously, it's not just physical. If it were, we would've fizzled by February.

Our property borders the river on one side, although I bought the five acres across from the gin mill about four years ago to keep it from getting developed. I kept the purchase separate from Duke Family Farms. We head up to the fork in the creek, a spot that could mark one property line should we need to split the ranch three ways.

"How's she different?" Sam asks. A hawk flies overhead, his wide wingspan catching my attention as he disappears into the trees.

"One, she's not from here. She's a northern girl. But even though she's not from around here, she's a lot like me. She loves the great outdoors. She's got gumption. Pushes herself. Takes risks. She's not into highfalutin' parties. Her boots aren't heels. They're giant things that clomp through snow. She's a damn good photographer. Easy to talk to. Good listener. Makes me laugh. At the risk of sounding like I'm quoting Neil Young, she's got that heart of gold. I mean, make no mistake about it. She's still growing up, figuring things out. But aren't we all, to some degree?"

I become aware he's stopped walking yet again. At his pace, we are never getting down this line. When I turn back to him, he's got a weird smile on his face.

"Why don't you two go on a trip? Olivia and I bought a place in Costa Rica. Take her there. Tons to do outside."

"I wouldn't—"

"Ollie." He groans my name. "Come on. I don't rent it out. It's sitting there empty. Use it. It's a nice place. Next to the Four Seasons. Part of the Four Seasons. It's like a neighborhood portion of the resort. You're in a long-distance relationship. You've got to make time to be together, or it won't work."

I can't help but think of him and Sandra. "Speaking from experience?"

"You know I am. I mean, don't get me wrong. It all worked out the way it's supposed to. Olivia and I…"

His phone vibrates, and he pulls it out to read something, letting his sentence dangle. He doesn't need to finish his thought. I'm aware of where he was going. When he's done with his correspondence, I pick the thread back up.

"The thing about putting time in on this," I kick a rock, and it sails about a foot into a clump of grass, "is that there isn't a future." I want to go visit her on random weekends, but he's talking about getting away and going to another country.

"Since when did you become the guy who won't date a girl if it's not going to end in marriage?"

He's grinning at me in a way that pisses me off. That's not who I am, and that's not what I meant. But the wanker's right. I enjoy being with Kate. She could use a paid vacation. She works nonstop. As do I. And we have fun together. You can apply any name you like to it, but at the end of the day, we're dating. Why does it need to be more than that? And I'd bet she's overworking that sore leg of hers. If she doesn't give it a real break, she won't be ready to ski come winter.

Sam backtracks, and I give up. He doesn't have any interest in walking the property line. Back home, I send Sam and Ian both a map with the ranch and the divisions I'm proposing and tell them I'll video it if they have questions. And I also shoot off a quick text to Kate before heading over to the courthouse.

Me: Any interest in checking out Costa Rica?

* * *

Judge Stone contradicts his name. The man sitting behind a high-rise desk in the center of the small courtroom smiles, rubs his belly, and when he gets up during a recess, flashes his shiny black cowboy boots for the world to see. His boots remind me of an old law school joke. If you're in Alabama, and your lawyer shows up in boots, you're probably going to jail. But if you're in Texas, that just means your lawyer and the judge probably shop at the same place.

I am not litigating this case, but I am here as part of the legal team, observing the proceedings. Based on the boots, it's looking good to me.

After saying goodbye to my older brother, I showered and got glammed up for this glorious afternoon hearing. We're in a small courtroom in the new Austin legal multiplex. The benches on each side are only four rows deep. The Texas State Seal adorns the back wall, and flags hang at the corner of the room. There's a sliver of daylight through the narrow floor-to-ceiling windows on each side of the seal, presumably to remind us life exists outside these walls and to keep it brief so we can get back to it. But the subtle reminder appears lost on the hired legal eagles.

The plaintiffs sit on the other side of the aisle. The young boy who allegedly suffered greatly after falling backward and hitting his head on slippery-as-hell travertine sits in between two suits, his attention in his lap at a handheld gaming device. He's got some seriously thick black hair, but from where I'm sitting, his scalp looks just fine. His father's unbuttoned suit coat is a mite too snug on the shoulders. His greedy eyes dart over to the team we've assembled in our row.

We don't have a kid in our arsenal, but I've gotta say, the game boy they've got sitting there isn't about to cue the waterworks. I'd love nothing more than to put him up on the stand and ask him if he knew the pool was closed. Would love to see our lawyer ask if he knew he wasn't supposed to be there without an adult or lifeguard. To ask if he read the sign, or if he and his friends were fully aware they were trespassing and breaking the law.

But that's me. I'm told, given his young age, vilifying him won't sit well with the judge. I call bullshit to that, because Judge Stone looks like a good ol' boy who will see right through this sham lawsuit. But I'm not a litigator.

Really, it's annoying as fuck that they didn't take our settlement. Or, I should say, they didn't take our insurance company's settlement. Natasha Brown, said insurance company's legal representative, sits on the far end of our row, reading a car accident report. She's not concerned about this case, but she told me earlier that the father is going to regret not taking the settlement offered because he will not get that much from Judge Stone.

Apparently, a similar case four years ago netted $200,000 to the plaintiffs. But, as Natasha explained to me, that case held different variables. One, a liberal bleeding-heart judge presided over the hearing. Two, the apartment building was the girl's own apartment building. She hadn't been running, and her injuries stemmed from falling into a broken contraption beside the pool. Plus, the apartment managers knew the cover was broken and had failed to replace it in a reasonable time.

The jovial Judge Stone is, I am assured, a blessed conservative.

That may be true, but the parade of experts on safety ratings of pool landscapes remains unequivocally boring. I have half a mind to tap the game player on the shoulder and ask him for a chance to rotate in.

The door opens during one such expert's testimony, and Liam enters. He's smart enough to keep his head down, and he slides into the vacant row behind us.

"How's it going?"

Judge Stone glances our way, as do the folks in the other row and the jury members. I give him a discreet thumbs up. Two long hours later, Judge Stone announces the jury found Artisan Construction not guilty of negligence.

I stand, shaking hands with Natasha Brown and all of our lawyers. By the time I look across the aisle, the opposing side and their game-loving son are already out of the courtroom. It's a shame, really. We offered them $50,000 to settle. That amount would have covered all medical expenses and given them a nice bonus. But they heard about the other case. Or maybe their contingency lawyer decided his share of fifty grand wouldn't be worth his time, so he rolled the dice.

"We did it," Liam says, beaming, hand clasped on my shoulder.

"Five hours of my life I'll never get back. And that's just today." I could go off about the ridiculousness of our litigious society, but all I really want is an ice-cold beer. I check my phone as we head out into the hall and break out into a grin.

> *Kate: Costa Rica is on my list. The one year, not this year, list.*

Outside the courtroom, we meander through the parade of suits. We're on the fourth floor, and there's a gaggle of folks waiting near the elevator banks. A man in a light blue suit with a striped tie shakes hands with Liam and offers me his hand.

"Good case outcome, I hear." I have no idea who this guy is. He's got a small American flag pinned to his lapel. He raises his outstretched hand that I have yet to take, and the movement prompts me to take his hand, but after we shake, I really want to go find a sink and wash up.

"Congressman Taylor." He announces his name as he shakes my hand up and down. I'm trying to place the man, but no bells are ringing. It takes a great deal of restraint to not wipe my palm on my dress pants after he releases my hand. "I hope to see you at the next fundraiser."

"Jim," a woman in a red skirt suit and heels calls from down the hall.

"I gotta run." He angles his index finger and thumb and acts like he's shooting Liam while he clucks his tongue.

I wait until we're out of the building, and it's just Liam and me before I address the cold-blooded elephant.

"Did you bribe someone to win that case?" His mouth half opens. "We would've won that case no matter what. They didn't have a case. It didn't matter which judge presided."

"Calm down. Where do you want to get a beer?"

I stop on the sidewalk, suppressing the urge to strangle one of my best friends. He holds up his hands, palms splayed out, in a classic defensive gesture.

"I swear. I bribed no one. But…" *Oh, hell.* "I always make donations. Have for years. The judges and powers that be look out for us. There's nothing illegal going on. No direct bribes. But I don't think it's chance we got the best judge for our case. And that's why I donate. It's good business."

I'm not wearing a tie, but I wish I were so I could loosen it. I spin on my heel toward my car.

"Hey, what are you pissed about?"

"I'm not pissed."

"What about food?"

"Not hungry," I say, crossing the street and leaving Liam behind.

I do my best to stay out of politics. Which isn't particularly easy in our fine state. And I know there are weasels that walk both sides of the party aisle, but damn, does it make my blood curdle at the thought that we're greasing wheels. As a law school graduate, I find the entire concept appalling. An affront to the moral fabric of our society.

I pull out my phone and dial Kate.

"Hey, you." She sounds bright and happy. One familiar, friendly greeting, and my blood pressure stabilizes. All it takes is her voice.

"I need to get outta here. Get away."

"Something wrong?"

"Nothing that hasn't been wrong for centuries. But I still wanna get away." I need to see her. "How much time can you get off?"

"Well, summer is slow around here. I can probably easily get coverage 'cause everybody wants more hours, but I can't afford—"

"All expenses paid by my overly successful older brother." That statement is not the full truth. But I'm rolling some dice, hoping it'll make her say yes.

"You know, we both have overly successful older brothers." She has me grinning, and more of that annoyance that had me mentally grinding my molars dissipates.

"Yeah, we do. So, are we going to take advantage or what?"

A deep breath crosses over the line. I slow my steps.

"I do everything I can to not take advantage of my brother's success." I consider what she's saying. She could have capitalized on her brother's fame in Vermont, but she came to Wyoming to work her ass off to make it on her own merits. *Shit.*

She's like me. She earns her own ground. My thoughtless rolling of the dice made assumptions that made an ass of me.

"Poor choice of words. My older brother owns a place that's sitting empty in Costa Rica. He offered it up to us to stay. I'll pay for all of our trip expenses. With my hard-earned money. I was hoping you would come with me because when I think about all the people I know, and who I'd want to take, you top the list by a country mile. Not to mention, you work harder than anyone else I know, and you deserve some vacay. I'm also betting that leg of yours could maybe handle a little breather. What do you say? Spend some time with me? I haven't seen you in almost three weeks."

twenty-five

Oliver

July 12

Some would say July is a shit time to visit Costa Rica. It's called the rainy season for a reason. But, as I lie here in bed, thick, dark hair splayed out on the pillow beside me, and the sound of heavy rain pattering outside the expansive glass, it seems mighty perfect to me.

The rain won't last all day. We'll get some outdoor time in the sunshine this afternoon. Oversized umbrellas sit in buckets by any door leading outside.

Yesterday, we went on a hike to a nearby waterfall. Rain kept the tourists away, and we discovered a private swimming hole. The memory of sliding her swimsuit bottoms to the side, clearing the way for me to take her up against a rock, the warm rain coating both of us, dripping over her bare breasts, will go down as the most erotic moment of my life.

Yeah, I'd say so far, Costa Rica in the rainy season is doing us right. The crisp, white sheet crosses below her breasts. One of her legs kicks backward into mine, and her foot settles below my calf.

Rain pounds the window, and the dark sky veils the morning hour. Which works for me because we're on vacation, and I have zero desire to leave this bed.

I press my front to the curves of her smooth, warm back. Her lips transition into a smile, but her thick lashes stay put, closed to the world. She reaches back until her hand rests against my thigh.

"Morning," she says, her voice thick with sleep.

I press a kiss to the peak of her shoulder. Her smile deepens. My lips clear a path along her tantalizing skin and nestle into the crook of her neck. She's sensitive here. Goosebumps rise, and she moans as she presses her bare, luscious ass to my groin, eliciting a similar restrained groan. I cup her breast, and her hips undulate.

A dull clap of thunder adds bass to the storm outside. The light, unexpected touch of her fingers on my morning wood stimulates in the best kinda way. My teeth toy with the edge of her earlobe.

"What're you doing, sexy?"

Her fingers wrap around me in a tight grip that leaves no question that she indeed knows exactly what she's doing. She raises her thigh, resting her leg over mine, and shifts to position my tip at her entrance. Still lying on her side, she thrusts her ass back, rubbing my tip through her silky, soft warmth.

"You want me this way?" My tip dips inside her. She's so fucking wet. As if she was dreaming about this. She's so ready, and with one full thrust, I'm balls deep in her, luxuriating in what is fast becoming my favorite place on Earth.

From this angle, reaching her mound is easy, and my hand mirrors my pace. Little sexy noises spill from her. She tweaks her own nipple as my hand and hips work her.

"That's it, baby. Do what feels good."

This is one of those moments between us I wish I could film because I want to relive it over and over again. There's a large mirror on the opposing wall, and it provides the perfect view. It's an image I hope I never forget. Kate's eyelids are closed, her lips are pursed in pleasure, and her dark hair is spread out in abandon while her fingers coax her nipple.

Her little noises multiply, and my arousal grows exponentially. My balls tighten, and a surge up my spine warns.

"Fuck. I'm so close." Her hips buck up against me, and the added pressure and friction put me right on the precipice. My fingers thrum and she tightens and curves, and her walls pulse around me as she cries out.

One thrust, a second, and my release pours into her.

I collapse back onto the pillow, gasping for air.

"That," I pant, "is a good morning."

She laughs as I palm her breast. I want to hold on to her, touch her. No, I need to touch her and keep her close. She collapses against my chest, an arm sprawled out over me, one over the mattress. Seconds later, too quickly, she presses up and heads to the bathroom, giving me an absolutely gorgeous view of her backside. Her dark hair falls about halfway down her back and swings with the seductive sway of her hips. I am such a goner.

* * *

"Tell me something I don't know about you."

We're bundled in a light blanket on a low-lying sofa on our covered balcony. The rain falls in a soothing pitter-patter as the remnants of the storm system cling to the shore. We ordered room service for breakfast, but we have every intention of eating lunch in the poolside restaurant. If the weather forecast holds, today might be our zip-lining day.

"Like what?" Her smile lights up her face. She's got this natural, wide smile. She doesn't need lipstick or gloss or any of that stuff the ladies like.

"Whatever you want to tell me. Something that will let me know the ins and outs of Kate Oakley."

"I'm fairly certain after these last few days you know my ins and outs."

I pinch her, and her twisting and giggling beside me ends in the throes of a long, deep kiss.

Clusters of palm trees border the area in front of our building, offering seclusion. Off in the far distance, waves crash. Howler monkeys swing from palm to palm, shrieking from time to time.

With swollen lips and damp, wavy hair, I swear she's the most gorgeous woman I've ever held in my arms. She's wearing one of my old Texas T-shirts and shorts. I flick the tip of her nose.

"Come on. One thing."

"Hmmm. I wrote all of Hudson's English papers his senior year."

"Yeah?" That little nugget has me grinning, but in the back corner recesses of my mind, there's some judgment going on. "What'd you get in return?"

"He'd let me hang out with him and his friends when they watched movies." I squint in disbelief and, yes, judgment at her fuck of a brother. "It's okay. He needed help. School's never been his thing. And he was working so hard that year. Was on like two different ski teams and an event team. It's a lot."

"Yeah, I imagine it's a rough life. Skiing and boarding all day."

"He's so good at it. Lives for it." There's not an ounce of jealousy bleeding from those eyes. Only admiration.

"You and your brother are close, huh?"

She nods. "We are."

"Must've been hard for you to move away from him."

"Yes and no." She shrugs, and her gaze hits on the ceiling or maybe out along the tree line. "He travels so much. It was time."

"Time for you to move away?" It's interesting to me when people move away from the place they love. The people they love. I've watched people do it for eons, but I still find it to be worthy of a head scratch.

"Well, I moved away for college. I just never moved back."

She's twenty-five years old.

"How long did you say you've lived in Jackson?"

"It'll be a year in September." I went to grad school after undergrad. Finished up on the heels of twenty-five. Didn't go as far away. My ass stayed in Austin. Plenty of time on the ranch.

"I've got two questions." I brush her hair to the side and fondle her shoulder.

"Two? I tell you one thing you don't know about me, and it leads to an inquisition."

"This isn't an inquisition." I pop a fast kiss to the side of those swollen lips. "One, what was your major? And two, do you plan on moving back to Vermont?"

I rest my head on my hand, my arm stretched out as a brace. She's lying flat on her back, and she looks up at me. She runs her fingers through what I am sure is my wild and crazy bed hair.

"Are these tough questions?" Those dark orbs look up, her pupils so large it's hard to tell where her iris is. "I'll answer first. I studied Geography and Political Science in undergrad, then went straight on and got my JD-MBA, which is a three-year program. Never intended to leave Texas. Still don't." I push the hem of her T-shirt up and let my palm rest flat against her toned stomach. "Your turn."

"I'm the queen of changing my mind. Started off as an English Lit major, then Journalism, then pre-med, which for me was a biology major. Then two years of med school. But you already know that." Her head turns. There's a touch of color in those cheeks. She's embarrassed. "No one walks away from med school. If you flunk out, that's one thing, but after all that money, it's insane to walk away."

"You said you hated it." She gives the slightest of nods. "The definition of insanity would be to continue doing something you hate. You gotta stop beating yourself up over it."

"But med school is expensive. And there are options. If I'd stayed, I probably could have found something. Some way of using the degree that would help me pay off my loans." She's back to looking across the way. Her response sounds like a parental speech. Probably one she's heard more than once. "I let them know last week I'm not returning this fall."

"Who's they?"

"Virginia Tech. It's where I went to med school."

"And Vermont for undergrad?"

"Yep." I can't remember if she went to the University of Vermont or simply a school in the state, but it doesn't matter. It's not gonna be a school that Texas plays regularly, so there's not gonna be a rivalry.

"Well, darling, there are some life truths I hold sacred."

"Yeah?" Her expression softens into one of mild amusement.

"Yep. Listen and learn." I tap the tip of her lightly tanned nose. "One, there's a shit ton of paths to success. Ain't no one right way. Two, detours are the spice of life. Three, those who judge didn't read the commandments, and if they couldn't make it through a list of ten rules, then they are some ignorant fucks and should be disregarded."

Now she's on the brink of a smile.

"And I don't mean ignorant in a judgmental way. I mean ignorant because they chose not to comprehend. Your parents, I'm going to guess, have passed out judgment?" Her soft smile provides confirmation. "In their case, it's out of a heap of love and a desire for you to have the best in life, but sometimes even parents can be misguided. And it's your life. They got a chance to make choices for themselves. This is your time to choose. They had their turn. This is your turn." My palm travels up between her breasts, pressing flat to her sternum. Her heartbeat thumps steady and strong. "You are the only one who gets to choose your path. That was one of my truths a long time ago. Patty and Sam Senior had their own ideas, but Patty and Sam each got to blaze their trails. We're each given one life. Ain't no one going to choose my path but me. I think you're brilliant. You listened to this." I press down over her heart. "That'll pay off. Sure, you might be broke and living with a pain in the ass right now, but you're going to look back on these days as good times. Maybe the best of times.

You started down a trail and saw it wasn't right for you, and you changed direction. To me, that takes courage. A windfall of courage."

"Did you change direction?"

"Not career-wise. I had the good fortune to know from the youngest of ages what I wanted, and I set out to make it happen."

"Ranch life?"

"Yes, ma'am." To this day, I'm not positive Dad wanted that for me. You'd think he would. He seems proud and happy now. But there were times he pushed hard for engineering. Lord, that would've sucked balls for me. Sam and Ian might love it, but it's not my jam. "Always knew. But part of life on a ranch is finding some alternative sources of income. For me, saving up so I can one day buy out my brothers' shares. I mean, should they decide to sell. They might not, but I always wanted it to be an option. Set the plan in place a long time ago. But don't think for a minute I don't recognize I'm a lucky bastard. Never had doubts. Some people don't figure out their passion for decades. Now, one could argue that it leads to a lot of experiences and a more interesting life."

"A lot of detours," she says, and I dip my head to collect another quick kiss.

"Yep, detours. So maybe those people are lucky in their own way."

She exhales. "My mom says I latch on to something, then change my mind. She says I can't stick with any one thing."

"Harsh. It's not like there's a tremendous difference between English and Journalism. I'm gonna take a wild-haired guess that med school had been something your mom pushed?"

"It's stable, pays well, and helps society."

"But you hated it?" That should be all that matters.

"So much." Her grin is wide, but her voice drops. "But she says it because whereas Hudson had one hundred percent discipline and focus from the time he was three, I bounced around. Ballet, piano, soccer, horseback riding, lacrosse, hockey...you name it, I tried it all. Always excited...borderline obsession. Then I'd move to the next thing. Mom said I'd catch one butterfly and hold on until a different one caught my interest."

"You realize that that's what a normal, healthy childhood is, right? Exploring different things. Yours truly tinkered with Cub Scouts, baseball, football, soccer, tennis, and I can even..." I drop my voice to a discreet whisper, "ride dressage."

My dramatic interlude somehow leads to a sad expression. Her sadness squeezes at me uncomfortably.

"I worry, you know, that I'm going to get the patroller job, and I won't like it." Her whispered words are loaded. But her curveball's easy to catch.

"Oh, darling, if that comes about," I let my southern accent roll, digging us back out of this hole we inadvertently clambered into, "you'll just pick a fresh trail."

twenty-six

Kate

   July 16

All good things must end. It's a life truth. Unfortunately, life truths apply to our five blissful days in Costa Rican heaven. A bittersweet state of mind encompasses me. The end of our escape has me twisting inside. I don't want to go back to the real world. Thoughts of next week and juggling shifts and cleaning the apartment hold no appeal.

The sky outside is a mix of dark and light. The soft rain patters against the palm fronds, evident by the pools of water that gather on the broad green leaves before draining. Oliver joins me at the window, wrapping his arms around me and pulling me up against him. His rough stubble scrubs the side of my cheek.

"You ready to go get breakfast?"

We have a plan for our last morning. Breakfast poolside, overlooking the ocean, followed by one last hike along our favorite trail. Then we check out and climb into a car that will return us to the airport.

Slow, easy, rainy mornings, leisurely afternoons, and glorious nights have spoiled me. We spent one afternoon poolside with fancy drinks in covered chairs, one afternoon at the beach, one on a hike to the waterfalls, and one hiking and zip lining. The whole vacation has been an unexpected whirlwind dream, one I didn't expect but will never, ever forget.

Hand in hand, we stroll down the hill to breakfast. We pass another couple, and all four of us offer courteous nods. The other couple looks older than us, judging by the man's salt-and-pepper hair. Her ring finger sparkles. They are smiling and laughing, whereas I'm not sure I have a smile in me. Which is ridiculous because our trip isn't over. Not yet.

But I don't want to say goodbye to Oliver. I breathe easier near him. My skin hums. The attraction from the beginning has morphed into more of what I imagine an addiction is like. And the thought of the impending withdrawal brings with it all sorts of silly girl emotions.

"Think you can get away to come visit me in Texas?" He squeezes my hand. His smile goes all the way up to his eyes, where they crinkle in the corners. That smile tells me I am alone in my tidal wave of sadness.

"I told you," I say, half-heartedly playing back our running joke, "Texas isn't for me. Too red."

His skin is the same deep, tanned hue as when we first arrived, whereas my pale skin has traversed the range of pink to a shade more colorful than pale.

"I've told you once, and I'll tell you again, the cities are blue. Not everyone living here is in the Make Attorneys Get Attorneys party. Besides, now that you know yours truly, surely you can find your way to check out the greatest state. Can't knock what you don't know. And might I remind you Wyoming doesn't exactly qualify as blue?"

He's teasing me with his sexy smile and light banter. The highlights in his hair are blonder and brighter, and those whiskey eyes are set off by his summer tan. He's gorgeous and fun, and I absolutely love spending time with him. But as crazy as I am about him, what's the point in continuing to see each other? There's no universe where this works out. And won't visiting him at his home just deepen all these feelings? Inside my chest, sadness wells up, threatening to drown me.

We choose a small round table on an unsheltered patio. As we sip coffee and Oliver digs into his breakfast, I push the fresh mango around on my plate.

"What exactly is it about Texas politics you can't stand? I bet when you break it down, it's not so different from up north. I believe that, despite what the media would have us believe, we're really not all that divided."

"Guns." My chin sticks out in response to his startled gaze. He repositions himself in his chair and picks up a slab of bacon.

"You'll pry them out of my cold, dead hands." He grins his lazy grin that I love so much. Back home, this discussion would boil my blood, but he's got that grin, and my insides are suffering from a tsunami, so I don't bear even a hint of heat. I actually smile back at him as he chews, swallows, and continues. "But I believe the gun lobbyists have too much control. There's no reason to have cop killer bullets or assault rifles. But it's like the city folk forget guns serve a purpose outside of the city. We got panthers and rabid animals and shit...rattlesnakes." He opens his eyes wide, joking like always.

"I'm pro-choice. Adamantly pro-choice." I lift my eyebrows, daring him to disagree with me. If he does, the fire in me might roar through this wave of melancholy.

"Me too." Those whiskey eyes meet mine head on. It's good to know we agree on that. "But I'm not crazy about taxes."

I roll my eyes, so sick of hearing that argument. "No one's crazy about taxes. But tariffs aren't the answer. It's just another word for tax and it drives inflation."

"Touché." He taps his coffee mug against mine. And jeez, that sexy lazy grin gets me. I want to bottle it up and take it home. "What else ya' got?"

"What happened with you and your fiancée?"

"Whoa." He sips his orange juice, and his palm falls to his thigh. I half expect him to blow me off or turn it into a joke. "Already told you. She and I wanted different things. If I'm honest, having all the same friends probably kept us together a lot longer than anything else. Our parents liked each other."

"She was from your hometown?"

"Same high school, but we didn't date until toward the end of college. Undergrad. All through law school."

"She's a lawyer?"

"Yeah, she is. She's a big-time Dallas attorney. She loves it. She's married, and she's got everything she wants in life." He doesn't sound sad at all.

"You seem genuinely happy for her."

"Why wouldn't I be? We ended things before we hated each other." He leans toward me and taps my leg. "The easiest thing would have been for us to get married. Especially after six hundred invitations had been mailed."

"Six hundred?" *Holy shit.*

"Yeah. Right?" He chuckles. "Trust me, that wedding provided a lot of clues I was charging down the wrong trail. And I guess on her side, we couldn't agree on where to live."

"She wanted to live in Dallas?"

"Noooo. At the time, she wanted to live in Austin, about thirty minutes away from the ranch."

"Wow." He didn't want to be with her over a thirty-minute disparity. His *fiancée.*

"We always knew we had that disagreement. She always thought I'd change my mind. I always thought she'd change hers. We were two fools playing chicken."

"Who swerved?"

"I did, actually. Might not have, but I had the support of my dad. Maybe not so much my mom, but she came around. And my brothers. There's one guy, he's like a brother. Spent a lot of time with us.

Jason. He lost his parents when he was fifteen. Then he got cancer his freshman year of college. Crazy shit. He's more serious than Sam, Ian, and I all combined. But he's a big believer in the one-life philosophy. For a while there, he was big on that for everyone else but not him. Then his best friend, Maggie, she sort of made him see the light." A faraway look comes over his eyes, like he's thinking about their past. He blinks and returns to the table. "I think that's another contributing factor. I saw Sam and Olivia. And Jason and Maggie. And I knew I wanted what they had. And at some point during all those disagreements about the house, and location, and fucking tablecloths, it just became really clear I didn't have that with Collette."

"So, you ended things?"

"Yep. Smartest thing I ever did. Did I mention she's a divorce attorney?"

And just like that, now I'm laughing. Although it's a hollow laugh because his past underscores our lack of future. Our New Year's Eve fortune teller had it right.

One fat raindrop splatters on the middle of the table. I glance at Oliver, and it's like the heavens open up. We jump up and run for shelter below the overhang.

"Just a minute, sir, and we'll find you another table," the hostess says to us.

"I'm done. Are you?" Oliver scraped his plate clean, but he's questioning my full plate.

I nod.

"But you barely ate."

I shrug. "I'm good."

By the time he signs the check, the deluge has ended as quickly as it came.

"Still up for the hike? Is your leg okay?"

I nod because that's about all I have the energy for.

At the head of the trail, he bends down and applies athletic tape to the leg just the way the YouTube video says. Then he smacks his lips against my thigh and says, "It starts to hurt, and we turn around. Ya' got me?"

Once again, I nod.

The hiking trail loops through the jungle-like area bordering the ocean and on to the natural coastline, rockier and darker than the white manmade sand beaches. The scattered showers this morning have given us the gift of solitude. We're the only people out and about. A chorus of birds, crashing waves, and the crunch of the ground underfoot float through the underbrush. An earthy scent ascends from the wet soil.

"What's next?" Oliver's voice brings me back to the present. The place I should be. *Live in the present.*

The trail climbs up to the highest point along the coast. It's a narrow path, and Oliver walks behind me.

"What do you mean?"

"When you get back. What's next on your plate?"

"Well, I've gained all the certifications I need. I guess I'll keep working and hope to get called in for an interview."

"When do they do that?"

"Ah, September. Maybe October. Depends on how many open positions they have. Or that's what I'm told."

"How are they going to test your skills on a mountain before there's snow?"

"Well, Wyoming can start getting snow in October. But they could extend a provisional job offer. There's a lot of work the patrol team does before the resort opens."

"Seems to me you're a shoo-in. The head honcho even set you up training sessions, right?"

"A training session that ended in an avalanche." The memory only deepens my melancholy. For as long as I live, I pray I never endure another avalanche.

"Adds to your experience and skill set."

"From your mouth to god's ears." He stops, something I'm only aware of because I sense the distance between us. "What?"

"You're going to get it. It's your dream job."

"One of them, yes."

I spent my whole life receiving Hudson's photos, watching his live cams, living his life from the sidelines. Ski patrol offers a foothold into that life. But I'm here in Costa Rica. I don't want to think about that life.

"What about writing?"

"What about it?"

"Is that one of your dreams, Annie Oakley?"

"Oh, my god. You found my articles. It's just a way to make some extra money."

He wiggles his eyebrows and grins. "I was waiting for tips on how to survive an avalanche."

I smack his arm. "What about you? Are you looking forward to getting back home?"

"Ah, we're in the dog days right now. Hot as hell. I'll be looking forward to a break in the heat."

"When's that?"

"Maybe October? It's a guessing game. I suppose I can come up and visit Wyoming for a break from that heat."

I smile, even though he can't see it because he's directly behind me. My breath is getting shorter as the incline increases.

"I'd like that."

"Well, since a certain someone won't step foot in Texas..."

We reach the top of the vista. The rain mists, and a dark, eerie navy gray traverses the horizon. The narrow golden sandy strip of our resort marks the beach. A canvas of greenery covers the rest. It's so different from the beach towns in the US, where buildings and roads meet up with the ocean. Costa Rica has preserved nature, and in return, nature protects its shoreline during storms.

I snap a photo with my phone and text it to Hudson. Hudson responds to my photo with a downward view of a halfpipe and the tag, *current situation.* He's in Australia, partaking in an endless winter. For once, I prefer my current situation over his.

The mist transitions into droplets, and we seek shelter beneath a cluster of banana trees. The rain dampens my sundress. Oliver thumbs my nipple. The darker shade of my areola shows through the fabric.

"No bra?"

"Mm-hmmm."

"You don't like bras, do you? You like to be free."

It's true. I do. The mist coats his arms, and I smear it along his skin, up over his forearm, through his golden arm fuzz, and up around his elbow. He traps me up against a boulder, and his biceps flex as he partially holds his weight over me. My thumb glides over the curve of his bicep, and his mouth covers mine.

His kiss is warm, slow, and languid. I close my eyes, memorizing the feel. His damp hair tangles in my fingers. Our noses rub. I want to hold on to this moment forever. The thump of his heartbeat reverberates through my heavy ribcage. His thigh presses between my legs, and his hands cup my ass, pulling me higher, dragging my sensitive parts against his strength. His breath quickens, and his chest heaves.

"You might like being free, but you're mine."

His teeth graze my lower lip. His fingers roam up my thigh. He coaxes the sensitive skin above my panties, and I whimper.

"All. Mine."

He pushes the slip of cotton to the side and thrusts a finger in as his thumb works me over in just the way he's perfected. I tilt my head back and open my eyes. We're out in the open. On a public trail. Anyone could come by. But I want him.

I fumble with his shorts.

"Leave them on. Just take out my dick." His hot words skim over my ear. I release his dick, and fuck, it's like in one of those clothed porn episodes, hard, throbbing, and eager. My fingers wrap around him, gripping tight, and his hips thrust. I spread one thigh out.

Intoxicating whiskey eyes stare deep into mine. My breath

catches. With one thrust, he fills me, and the hard rock grates my back. I'll take the pain. All I want is him.

I want to be one with him. To feel him everywhere. Rain droplets glide down his throat, and I lick them, eliciting a primal growl. He lifts both thighs and surges up inside me, deeper than ever. "God, Kate, I love this." He grunts, and his thrusts transition into animalistic. My tears blend with the rain.

We shudder together, blanketed in soft, warm rain, my back against a painful hard boulder, our arms clinging around each other as if we're each other's life buoy.

I love him. My head chants those three words over and over and over. It's a pointless love. One that cannot endure. But I know I'm not the same person I was before him. He has forever altered the shape of my heart.

My fingers grip his hair, and his cheek presses to mine as he thrusts up over and over, pulsing out his release.

Slowly, he releases my legs. I cling to his shoulders until I regain feeling in my limbs. He presses his lips to my forehead. His thumbs wipe below my eyes. Then he tucks himself back in his shorts, straightens my panties, and lowers my dress.

"We'd better get back." Our clothes are soaked. "Gots to get dry."

Our hands swing back and forth in an exaggerated level of glee I'm absolutely not feeling. We only separate when the trail becomes too narrow. We're halfway back down when the trail widens, and he scoops up my hand once more.

"I may have gone a little caveman back there."

"It's okay." My voice quivers, and I stare off into the trees above, blinking back a burn. "I know you didn't mean it."

He stops. My feet continue, and I lurch back. He grips my hand, refusing to let go.

I force a smile and pull his hand to continue. We really are running out of time. We don't have time to stand in the rain and talk. And what we did, I wanted it, too. There's nothing to talk about.

"Kate. I want this." His stride matches mine. I carefully study the ground, given one wrong step and it's a steep slide down in mud which would wreak havoc for my recovering leg. "But I get you're younger."

I stop. This is bullshit.

"Let's be real. My age has nothing to do with it." Some of that anger I'd expected to percolate at the mention of politics earlier stirs. "We have no future. This is a fun-for-now thing. That, up there," I point up the trail for emphasis, "was fun."

This isn't how I wanted our week to end. There's no point in stewing, so I choose the first subject that comes to mind and continue down the trail.

"What have you got going on when you get back?"

"Oh, ya know. Little bit of this, little bit of that." His southern twang softens what I'm pretty sure is meant to be a response with bite.

"Seriously."

"Ah, well, my restaurant group is adding two more restaurants. We break ground on a new section of a neighborhood development this fall. And I'm working on building my house."

"How's it coming along?"

"It's coming along. Helps I have some fingers in the construction industry."

"God, you have it all together." I'm renting a room on a month-to-month basis, and he's building a house.

"I'm ten years older than you. Makes sense. Where do you want to be ten years from now? On a mountain? Patrolling?" His tone is lighter. We're back to all-out happiness.

His question sends my thoughts down a completely different path. Something other than us, which should be a welcome diversion. Since I quit med school, I haven't thought about a ten-year plan. I've been living day by day...but I don't know that I see myself patrolling ten years from now. I mean, there are those who do. It can be a career in a person's sixties or seventies.

I don't answer Oliver, and he doesn't press. We walk comfortably enough, hand in hand, back to the hotel. My mind whirs. I should approach life more like Oliver. Find alternative sources of revenue that feed my passion. I have my writing, but that pays worse than minimum wage. Claire has a dream of opening her own spa. That's why she went into hospitality. I don't have the money to invest, but maybe I could talk her into paying me for my time with stock or something. I enjoy bartending. I've had fun planning and coordinating club events. With more shifts, I could save the money to invest in Claire's dream.

Ten years from now. Thirty-five? Will I be a ski patroller by day, texting photos, and a bartender by night? Maybe a restaurant manager? Or a manager at the club? Or the ski rental place?

In the back of the van on the way to the airport, I curl up against Oliver. My head rests against his shoulder. When I'm thirty-five, he'll be forty-five. He'll probably be married and have children. He'll be a good dad. It's easy to envision him instructing a kid. His kids will probably run roughshod all over that enormous plot of land he loves. His heartbeat thuds in my ear, and he alternates between lifting my knuckles to his lips and weaving his fingers through my hair. Maybe one day he'll bring his family to Jackson, and I'll see them learning to ski or board. That thought hurts so much more than it should. I don't want to cry. The last thing I want is for Oliver to think I can't handle this. So, I stare out the window and use a meditation trick, clearing my mind of all thoughts.

When we arrive at the airport, we go through customs, and he walks me to my gate. It's a small airport, but his gate is on the opposite end.

I am heavy. My lower lip trembles. His index fingertips my chin up.

"Hey. Kate." He speaks so softly. "This little thing between us—"

"What are we doing?" My question comes out sounding like a little girl's whine.

"We're exploring a trail...seeing where it goes. Why don't we say we'll keep on keeping on until it's not fun anymore?"

Until we grow apart. Until we end. That's what he means.

My heart hurts. The pain is too intense. This isn't fun. But I nod and force a smile.

"Call me when you land." He presses his lips to mine. And I watch him disappear, hurrying off to catch his flight.

The crowd blurs, and my heart implodes.

End of Part 2

twenty-seven

Kate

September 1

> *Ol...Lie!: Any chance you can get away for a couple of days*
> *soon?*

> *Me: Assisting with an upcoming 10K and a triathlon on*
> *my days off.*

Guilt wracks me as I hit send. But I have to be truthful. Honesty is a critical part of a long-distance relationship. I know this because I researched and wrote an article titled "How to Thrive in a Long-Distance Relationship." I also earned a whopping $250 for the article last month, which has surfaced on multiple sites through repeated distribution.

*Ol...Lie!: If I didn't know better, I'd say you're avoiding
me...*

A million excuses come to mind, but first and foremost is that I'm an hourly employee, and I need to eat. He needs to appreciate that I took almost an entire week off work without earning any income to spend time with him. And yes, maybe my leg benefited from not standing all day every day, but it was time without any income. Yes, I had a couple of days here and there in August without work because it was a remarkably slow time of year, but I needed some distance to get my head back on straight after sobbing for an entire plane ride. A mother of a young child sitting on the opposite row kept leaning over and wordlessly offering me tissues.

Oliver and I still text photos to each other, similar to how I do with Hudson. But I now keep my phone in the employee locker when I bartend at night. It reduces the temptation to text Oliver during slow off-season nights, and it gives me some much-needed space to try to figure all this out.

Did that need for space figure into my LDR hot tips? Absolutely not. But I've never cared for anyone the way I care for Oliver, and it's unnerving. In the best of all worlds, we'll continue having fun and then slowly and easily grow apart until we morph into just friends. But how does one pull off that kind of trickery?

There's no easy answer. But the beauty of a long-distance relationship is that it is easy to focus on my life priorities. It is easy to not answer a text or to buy time and say we'll talk the next day.

Yesterday, I handed proof of all my certification requirements over to Bill Woodland, along with my official job application, two weeks ahead of deadline. He didn't tell me to forget about it. He didn't ask me about my leg either, and I know he's aware because it's a small community. He didn't actually say much other than a cordial hello and thank you. The office assistant said he'd be in touch about training sessions. So, I'm cautiously optimistic.

Ol...Lie!: Can we talk tonight?

Oliver's not an idiot. He knows I've been putting distance between us. I haven't had the strength to completely cut off contact. But I fell for him. My epic breakdown on the plane proves it. But where I keep getting hung up is that it would be one thing if there was an end in sight to the distance. That's one thing every single article I found said about LDRs. You've got to have an end in sight. It can be a couple of years, but there needs to be a path to being together without distance. And that path simply doesn't exist for Oliver and me. Which means if our relationship strengthens, it will hurt even more than the airport goodbye.

Oliver originally planned to come and see me two weeks after I saw him in Costa Rica. But life threw a curveball. His ranch manager had a heart attack. Thankfully, it was a mild one, but he can't put in the hours on the ranch that he used to. And they've apparently had a spate of turnover at the ranch, and he's got too many hired hands who aren't reliable. He hasn't felt comfortable flying to Wyoming. Which has put us getting together squarely on my shoulders. Or, as Oliver would say, the ball's in my court. Which is good because, again, I need both time and space.

My phone rings while I'm staring at Oliver's text, debating if and how to respond. The name on the screen reads Dr. Oakley. *Mom.*

I answer with a heavy heart, but attempt an upbeat, "Hey, Mom," in order to avoid the inquisition.

"Honey. Glad I caught you while you're up."

"Mom, it's almost ten in the morning."

"Oh, right. We're in Sydney. Australia. I'm screwy with the time zones."

"Why are you in Australia?" Hudson had been out there for the Australian winter, but to my knowledge, the good snow stopped in early August.

"Hudson was in a car accident."

"Oh, my god!" My peripheral vision blurs, and I automatically place my hand over my other ear to be certain I hear every single thing she says.

"Your dad and I got the first flight we could and have been through traveling hell."

"Why didn't you tell me?"

"I thought about it, honey. But I didn't want to worry you. Not until I was here and I could tell you what's really going on."

"How is he?"

"He's good. But he did a lot of damage to his left leg. His femur shattered."

I've been so wrapped up in my mental distance game with Oliver that it hadn't even crossed my mind I hadn't heard from Hudson in days. Plus, with him being in Australia, our texts had declined in frequency. My already heavy heart somehow sinks lower, and I gasp, open-mouthed for air.

"His career."

"He was topping out, anyway. You know that."

I knew Mom thought that, and I knew professional boarders rarely continue into their thirties, but some do. Hudson definitely didn't think he was about to top out. He was aiming for the US Snowboarding Team again.

"How is Hudson taking it? Are you with him?"

"I stepped outside the hospital to call you. I can't get a signal in his room. Honey, he's so lucky. It could've been so much worse. When we first got the call, he was in surgery. And we didn't know for sure he would make it."

"And you didn't tell me?" Hudson is my brother. *My family.*

"What would've been the point? I had to get to Hudson. Leaving you so worried you might wreck or hurt yourself wouldn't do any good. Both of you have always been such daredevils."

There's no point in arguing with her. "But he's okay? He's going to be okay?"

"He's got a long recovery ahead. He'll need to come home and live with us. We're going to have to pay off a lot of the debt he's accumulated out here. But he's already talking about transitioning to life as an instructor."

"Why hasn't he called me?"

"He's so doped up on drugs, honey. And his phone was destroyed in the wreck. He won't have money for a new one for a while." I recognize Mom's tone. It's the tone that says she's going to whip him into shape.

"Mom, he's almost thirty."

"And isn't it ridiculous he still depends on his parents?"

"He earned a living." She's wrong. He has sponsors.

"Not enough to cover his expenses. Why do you think he lived with us this past year when he wasn't at competitions?"

"How did the accident happen?"

"He and his friends were stoned and drunk. It showed up in his blood. I don't think he'll be welcome to return to Australia ever again. It's a good thing he got in several months here on this trip."

"Shit. Driving while impaired?" Hudson totally knows better.

"Well, he wasn't driving, but yes."

"Who was driving?"

"A Damien Oseguera. Do you know him?"

"No." I shake my head slowly. But that's not surprising. It's been years since I hung out with Hudson's friends.

"Well, what can I do? Should I send flowers? Cookies?"

"Honey, save your money. We're in Australia. You can send something when we get him home. But no. You know what you can do?"

"What?" I scan my bedroom for a pen.

"You can return to medical school. Make us all proud and make something of yourself." Her statement hits like a punch. The window to return to school passed. I am officially withdrawn.

"Mom, no."

She says nothing, but I can hear her disappointment through the line. I can see her face.

"I'm sorry," I say out of habit.

"What are you going to do? You know, your brother and you both need to realize that your dad and I aren't made of money. You need to make something of yourself."

"Mom, that's not fair. I haven't taken money from you and Dad in years."

My medical school loans are all on me. I would never take money from my parents. I work my ass off to be independent. A lengthy sigh transpires halfway around the world.

"I know, honey. I'm just...I didn't sleep on the plane. We came straight here to the hospital. A part of me wants to strangle your brother. I'm taking it all out on you, and I shouldn't." Again, she sighs. "I'm the one who should apologize."

I lift the phone from my ear and stare at it. That's the first time in my life my mother has apologized to me.

"Ski patrol?" she asks. "That's what you want to be doing ten years from now?"

What is with this ten-year question? Why is everyone going on about ten years?

"We'll see. Training starts this month. I've passed my certifications. Nothing is definitive, but it looks likely."

"Of course you passed your first aid certifications. You were in medical school." *Were* being the operative word. Her exasperation comes out in full force. "What about your leg? You know, all of these physical careers come with great risks." Another sigh. I think she even mutters the word *Jesus*. "I'm sorry. I'm gonna go now. I need sleep."

"Will you and Dad keep me updated on Hudson?"

"Of course. I've got to meet with more of his medical team, but

I'll let you know when it looks like we can get him home. In case, you know, you want to visit. You haven't been home in over a year."

The pointed jab hits where she intends. My first thought is that I can't afford the flight, but after this conversation, I'm not about to say that.

After the call ends, I fall back onto my bed. Jesus, Hudson could have *died*.

There's a knock on my door, and before I can answer, Paisley barges in and plops onto the end of my bed.

"You working today?"

"My shift starts at noon."

"Until what time?"

"Four."

"Short shift?"

"Yeah. There's some business tourney, and I'm manning one of the drink stations."

"Any interest in covering for Lainey at six? She needs to cut out early."

"Sure. No problem."

"Six to close?" she asks for confirmation.

"Sure." She beams her constantly upbeat smile. "Hey, Paisley, where do you plan to be in ten years?"

"Well, in ten years I'll be thirty-three. I hope to own my spa by then, be a certified yoga instructor, which I'm about one year away from, but I'm saving for the last stint, and maybe a doula."

"A what?"

"You know, someone who helps women give birth naturally? It's something I think would integrate well with a holistic women's center that offers spa treatments, yoga, and childcare. And in my ten-year plan, I'd love to be married, but that may not happen. I'd say if I'm not married by thirty-five, then I'll be looking at other options for having a child because I definitely want to be a mother."

"You've spent a lot of time thinking about this, haven't you?"

"Well, yeah." The expression on her face says, in a nutshell, duh.

"What about you? You think you and your Texan will be together in ten years?"

"He'll never leave Texas. He's got, like, land there. It's like…it's actually crazy."

It's crazy to me. My parents moved three times when I was growing up. I have no idea where my great-grandparents lived. I'm not even positive about which state my grandparents were born in. And Oliver knows where the Duke family members are buried six generations back.

"Well, I don't think too many people are with their forever partner at our age. That's fine." The mattress dips as she bounces. "But you have a plan, right?"

My plan has been far too short-sighted. My plan had been to take a year, and that year has basically come and gone. And I have stealthily avoided all long-term planning, focusing only on the now.

After leaving medical school, I could only carry the burden of so much self-hate. But maybe it's time to let some of the driven Kate back in. At least back in enough to consider what I want from life and what I need to be doing to make that happen. Because ski patrol offers one path, but what if I'm injured again? Mom may be infuriating, but that doesn't mean she's wrong.

Re-injury is common. I need options. A line from some motivational book I read comes to mind. The saying is something along the lines of a successful apple farmer doesn't rely on a single apple tree. Like Oliver.

What do I want from my life? Where do I want to be? Those are big questions, and thankfully, they don't require answers.

Before I head to the country club for work, I allow myself one text to Oliver.

> *Me: I'd love to talk tonight. Hudson was in a car accident.*
> *He's going to be okay, but…I'd really love to talk. Is 11*
> *your time too late?*

twenty-eight

Oliver

September 5

Compared to winter, the hotel in Jackson Hole is deserted. The lobby seats are vacant. You can easily get a seat at the bar or the restaurants.

Outside, it's a brisk, sunny, sixty-eight degrees, and heavy pavers prop the doors open to let the fresh air inside. The vibrant leaves across the mountainous horizon attract tourists, but not on the same scale as the winter playground.

The fall vibe here reminds me once again of the vast difference between Wyoming and Texas. Back in Texas, the AC pumps and sweat drips if you spend over five minutes outdoors. Of course, in Texas, our temps are currently higher than average in a late-season heatwave.

Here, there's a chill in the air that promises the change of seasons, and the shadow of Old Man Winter hovers. My first weather alert upon landing warned of frost tonight.

As I cross the green quad, my nerves are on fire. There's no telling what kind of reception I'll be getting from Kate. This is the second time I'm surprising her, and yeah, I'm second guessing this wild hair. She's been hemming and hawing about getting together. Part of me thinks I should just take it for what it is. Accept that she's not interested. But that's bullshit. We still talk pretty much every day. With all the photos I send her, at this point, she knows the ranch better than my brothers do these days.

I'm a confident guy, but my gut's telling me there's more going on here than she's letting on. Not just my gut. I follow Annie Oakley on *Medium,* and they alerted me when she posted all the ways to succeed in a long-distance relationship. She did the research and mapped out the steps. So why, exactly, isn't she following through on her own advice? Why is it so damn hard to lock her down for a visit? Hell, even to talk to her regularly.

Long distance sucks, but it sucks all kinds of balls if there's uncertainty if the other person wants you in the picture.

The carpeted hallway to Kate's apartment reeks. I can't quite pinpoint the odor. It's not beer, cigarettes, or vomit. Those are smells I grew to know well when living in a fraternity. I'm pretty sure it's simply the smell of old, worn-down indoor-outdoor carpet tossed with poor ventilation. The architecture of this apartment building is circa 1970s or 80s. It's a surprise the entire building hasn't been torn down and rebuilt with a snazzy resort hotel, but I suppose the resort owners recognize they need some employees nearby. After all, they love to hire international and college interns, and they don't always have cars.

Knock. Knock.

My fist raps against the faded red wooden door. Someone propped the door to the building open with a good-sized rock, so there was no need to buzz up. A few heavy footfalls sound through the door. By the deep thud against the wood, I'm guessing it'll be Nash who opens the door.

The door swings wide, and a shirtless Nash greets me with a wide grin.

"Hey, man, haven't seen you in a while. You here to see Kate?" He kicks his leg out to prop the door open for me to enter. "She's not here, but come on in. I think her shift ends soon. Have you spoken to her?"

"No, why?" I enter the apartment, and he shuts the door. The faint smell of lemon fills the space, but the underlying mildew scent leaves an overall unsavory olfactory experience. The windows are wide open, as is the sliding door that opens onto the narrow deck.

"Chopra mentioned he might call her in to bartend tonight. He was looking at the schedule and realizing he might be light. There's a bike race or something like that. But I don't know why he's worried. I doubt they'll make it here after it's over. They usually stay down in Jackson."

Kate had mentioned she'd been picking up shifts at a bar. And working with her roommate Claire at a resort spa, in addition to doing everything from waiting tables to helping on the golf course at events at a nearby golf club. I glance around the place. I haven't met Paisley yet. She's the one who set her up with the golf course job.

"Is Paisley here?"

"Nah. She's working. She's a manager. Pretty much has to be there all day."

I meander over to a narrow table that's back up against one wall. It's still loaded with photos in frames, four or five deep, stacked haphazardly all along the table. Dust lines the corners of some frames, and some look brand-spanking new. I pick up a photo of Kate and a group of guys, all decked in ski gear.

"What're you doing in the off-season?"

"Bartending. Got Kate the extra gig. Since you're here, if Chopra needs her, I can cover." He plops down on the sofa, and it creaks when he lands. "So, you're here when there's not a speck of snow on the ground. Does that mean things between you and Kate...you guys serious?"

I set the photo down and pick up another. It's a newish looking one, and it's one of Kate and another woman smiling and clinking beers.

"What does Kate say is going on with us?" I don't turn my attention away from the perusal of all the party shots, but if I had a horse's ear, it'd be pinned in Nash's direction.

"Nothing much."

I set the photo down and back up to the sofa. My ass rests on the back of the sofa, and I continue to stare at the lineup of frames.

"Don't take it the wrong way, man. Kate...she's not one to talk much."

I have nothing to say to that, so with two steps, I'm back at the table, picking up another frame. The fact she says nothing about me rattles around in my brain. All those in my close circle know about Kate. Hell, Sam asks about her in every single phone call. Sandra, Noah, and Liam all know about her. Even Drew, who I see twice a year, knows about her and asks. My parents ask about her. And she doesn't talk about me to her roommate.

"Hey, don't read into those photos too much." Nash's comment has me giving the frame in my hand a second glance. She's outside at a bar with a table of friends. "They're all Insta."

"What does that mean?"

"Posed. I've got one of those little printer things in my room, so I'm the one who rotates the photos." He scratches the back of his neck. "I like to have photos of friends who come over to hang out."

"Nice." Gotta give it to Nash. He's the hostess with the mostest. I set down the photo in my hand.

"Kate will come out for one drink after a shift ends, but she almost always goes home after. She's the hardest-working girl I've ever met. Up early at the gym, multiple jobs. She wants that patroller gig. I think she's gonna get it, too."

"But not you?"

"What do ya' mean?"

"You don't want to be a patroller?"

"Nah. I like teaching. It's the perfect lifestyle for me. If I was good enough, I'd teach tennis or golf in the summer. I'm thinking about applying for one of the white water rafting positions somewhere next summer. I'm pretty good at it, and that's a lot like teaching. Plus, you're outdoors, fun times in the river."

The apartment door swings open, and Kate's eyes widen and her mouth forms a little O. Then, with a squeal, she leaps forward, knocking me back against the sofa frame.

"What're you doing here?"

"Got away."

She smiles a wide, open, honest smile that sets everything in my chest to rights and calms those skittish nerves. There's no doubt this woman is happy to see me.

A door clicks, and I scan the room. Nash has made himself scarce. He's a good guy.

I weave my hand through her hair at the nape, tilt her head back, and sink into her kiss. Her kiss does things to me I can't even describe. I breathe easier. My world brightens. It's like a Disney movie on steroids. A kiss from this woman is like coming home after a long trip away. No, it's better.

And as if my body needs to drive the point home, my shorts are tented by the time she breaks our kiss and takes my hand to lead me back to her room.

"Can you maybe...pack a bag? Come stay with me?"

"You've got a room?"

"Better than a room. The room. Room 248."

"You don't want to..." Her lips are swollen, her cheeks flushed, and my demanding fingers rumple her braided hair.

"Oh, I want to. But you've got roommates. I want to get you all to myself."

As she packs, I sit on the edge of her neatly made bed.

"How's Hudson doing?"

"He's cleared to fly. They leave in a few more days. They saved a lot of money on their flight by booking flights further out."

"He's lucky your parents could take so much time off."

"Well, Dad flew back after they realized his life wasn't in danger. Mom had the days with the hospital, and she's worked there for so long. I mean, most of my life. They're working with her."

"Your brother is lucky to have them." Those brown eyes meet mine, and there's an undercurrent of something there, but I can't quite decipher it. "And you too."

She zips her overnight bag.

"You ready?"

The second my hotel door clicks closed, I'm all over her. Control be damned. Yeah, there's a part of our relationship that's too eerily similar to Sandra and Sam. The person in pursuit is me. I'm the one who will be left behind as she pursues dreams that don't have room for me. I'm the one who's going to yearn for her something fierce when she moves on.

But as she wraps those lean legs around my hips and I thrust inside her against a wall two feet inside the hotel room, god, I don't fucking care. She is heaven.

At least, that's how it feels as she quivers around me and I come so hard I almost black out. My leg muscles tremble, and it's only by resting our weight against the wall we remain upright, panting, half-clothed, half-naked. She presses her lips to my throat, and my hand finds its way up to her breast. We cling to each other. Once our breathing stabilizes, she laughs. Her laughter cracks me up. It goes like that until we stumble through the small suite, and I pull her up onto the bed and remove her tank top. She removes my shirt and runs her fingers through my chest hair.

We're half-dressed, on top of the comforter. The windows offer a fantastic view of the reds, golds, and greens. Later on, we'll flick on the fireplace in the den and debate ordering in or venturing out.

"When's your next shift?"

"Tomorrow. I have to be at the club at eleven. And then I have a bartending shift, and I close." She grimaces.

I press my lips to her forehead. "No worries. I was rolling the dice with this surprise." There's a light blanket that I pull over our waists, then I settle against the pillows, pulling her to me. "You bartending more these days?"

"He's giving me more shifts. It's fun. I mean, it can be tiring, but I like it. You get to meet all kinds of people and listen to good music. When it's busy, the time flies, and there's a bit of a challenge to it, depending on what people order. How's your house coming?"

"Windows installed last week. Floors are done. Next week, I've got a crew coming in to help install cabinets and counters in the kitchen and master bath."

"You think you'll be moving in soon?"

"Eh, maybe. My current plan is to get the living area and my bedroom done, then move in while the rest comes together." I suck in one of her nipples and twirl my tongue around the delectable nub.

She exhales and moans. Her fingers toy with my hair. "I'm glad you came." She gives me a teasing smile as I press my lips to the smooth skin along her stomach.

"Is that a double entendre?"

She giggles, and I kiss my way back up to her breasts, fondling the peaks I so often dream of as my dick comes back to life. It's like he knows we're back with her and under time constraints.

"Maybe one day I can get you down to Texas."

"Is that a double entendre? Because if so..." And I rest on my back, letting her settle into her own exploration.

twenty-nine

Kate

October 3

Bill Woodland stands a good foot and a half taller than the hostess. It's a slow period before the dinner crowd hits, and I'm wiping down the counter. The guy who trained me told me the owner is a big believer in the "if you've got time to lean, you've got time to clean" motto, so even though the counter is spotless, I wipe. I've already stocked the glasses and double-checked stock supplies.

While I am fully aware it's rude to stare, I can't seem to stop staring at Bill. He's got a beard, and he's wearing a baseball cap, so I can't quite tell if he sees me. But he nods and points my way, apparently telling the hostess he'll sit at the bar. *Be cool.*

Job offers are being extended this week. They extended offers to last year's crew first, but of course, for those guys, it was more of a formality. They made verbal offers to the existing team in the spring. The fall is when Jackson Resort finds out who may have gotten a better deal or a change in life plans over the summer.

"Kate." Bill says my name in a low, gruff tone.

"Hi, Mr. Woodland." I lay a menu in front of him. We've gone to the electronic menus here, but we have paper menus available in case someone can't get their Wi-Fi working, which happens with out-of-towners for whatever reason. "What can I get you?"

"I'll take a Snake River Pale Ale."

"Sure thing." I smile brightly, showing him my best hospitality smile. I've made it through all the trainings they hold. Trainings are varied, but include rescue toboggan handling, communications, avalanche, search and rescue, and lift evacuation support. He assessed my ski and boarding skills last season. Bill hasn't specifically said that, but I know he did. I know that my time with Matt provided him with an additional perspective. I carefully set his golden ale down before him on a coaster. "Anything else?"

"This is good for now. My wife's running late. We'll get a table when she gets here."

"Sounds good." My smile is too bright, too forced. As aware as I am of this, I can't fix it. I pull out a rack of water glasses and pretend to be confirming they're clean. I need to look busy and not stare.

"Didn't know you worked here," Bill says.

"Yes, sir. Started a few months ago. I also work at the country club and at the Jackson River Spa."

"Can be hard to make ends meet in the off-season." He's right. It can. But one good thing about a small mountain community is business owners look out for staff. They ask around as seasons change. "You gonna keep bartending when you start patrolling?"

The glasses clank as I shove the rack back on the shelf. He said *when*. Time slows as I turn around, wiping my palms on my black polyester waist apron.

"*If* I get the patroller job, I imagine I'd be too tired at the end of the day to have another gig, especially one that closes down at around three in the morning."

He sips his beer and sets his beer down. One arm rests casually on the bar.

"Well, you might want to go ahead and give your notice, then."

"I'm getting the job?"

"Sure. Did you doubt it? You've proven yourself."

I do a full-on jump, both knees lifting to my waist, arms sky high, and scream out loud. Jo, the hostess, puts both her hands over her mouth, laughing at me. Bill smiles. I think it might be the first time I've ever seen the grizzly bear smile.

Yes! I fucking did it!

All that negative talk. I'm too slight, not strong enough, can't get everywhere on the mountain. It's too tough of a life. I can turn around and tell all those skeptical ninjas to suck it.

No one can dim my ray of light. I am happier than when I got into medical school. And, truth be told, I'd been pretty fucking thrilled then. This elation ranks with our high school ski team winning the state championship.

"Word of advice. Review the offer before you cheer. It's going to be hard for me to take any counteroffer from you seriously."

Who is he kidding? No one really negotiates the first-year offer. And I'm nursing an injury. I hold my palm out for a high-five. Our palms slap as the door opens. He spins on the stool and waves his wife over.

"You can sit anywhere," I tell him.

"Yeah, Jo told me. Stop by my office tomorrow and we'll make it official."

The kitchen door swings open, and Bradley, the owner of Thai Me Up, joins me behind the bar.

"What was all that about?"

"I did it!" I squeal, bouncing on my heels. "I got it!" His brows thread together, confused. "The patroller job. Ski patrol. I made the team."

"You look excited." And he looks a little puzzled.

"So. Excited."

I don't know Bradley well. Nash got me on the schedule by putting in a good word for me, but for weeks Bradley didn't come around because he was off at other locations. He's the owner, but he owns other places, too

"Damn," Bradley says after I'm done with my little happy jig. "I had a managerial job opening I was hoping you'd be interested in."

"Really?" The frequency of my shifts has increased, and I've even pulled hostess duty. Plus, I joined a select group to help with some menu decisions for this upcoming season. But I'm hardly management.

"Guess you won't be interested now."

"No. But I'm totally flattered you'd think of me."

"All right, well. Good luck. I'll look for you out on the mountain."

"I'll be the one in red."

"Damn, girl. That is one happy smile. I'd buy shots for you, except you're on shift."

There are bars where the bartenders take shots. It's an experience for the patrons. Bradley won't have any of it. He wants his bartenders sober. Which, honestly, this place during peak season can get so packed, I can't imagine how anyone could handle the orders with the slightest level of intoxication. But I do have an idea for this place that I'd wanted to mention.

"You know, if you went for the experience angle, you could keep one of these glass bottles back here with water in it. Maybe use blue dye or something...pink, whatever. And let the bartender take shots of that. The crowd wouldn't know the difference. You'd get that experiential vibe. You'd probably increase the number of shots sold in a night."

It's no secret that restaurants like Thai Me Up make their gold in alcohol sales. Anything that increases alcohol sales is a winning strategy.

"You think we could pull it off? Folks wouldn't get wise?"

"They'd be getting drunk. People getting drunk don't get wise, much less remember. Just, when you hire, look for people who can pull it off and play into the experience."

"Hmmm." He crosses his arms and smiles at me in a way that has me taking a step back and searching for the rag to wipe the countertop.

"How's Lucy?" His girlfriend comes in some nights when he's here, and I've gotten to know her because she sits at the bar.

"She's good." He raps the bar with his palm and heads back to his office as he calls out, "If things don't work out in ski patrol, come talk to me."

Oh, it's going to work out. I mean, there is a trial period. But it's going to work. I hope it's going to work. I spent a year out here doing odd jobs pursuing this job. That can't be for nothing.

A typical off-season night follows at the bar, and I make about two hundred bucks in tips. It's a weeknight, and there's no bar crowd, so our manager closes up at ten.

The second I walk out of the place, I have my phone in hand. I dial the one person I've been dying to call the whole night. The one person who has never tried to talk me out of this endeavor.

"Oliver? Guess. What!"

thirty

Oliver

October 22

Kate sent me a selfie last night. No caption, only the photograph. She's lying back on pink and white pinstriped sheets, her hair artistically cascading over the pillow. She's wearing a dreamy expression and nothing else. The photo cuts off right below her breasts.

I fell asleep early last night and didn't get the text until this morning. My thumb has a mind of its own and keeps flicking back to the photo. You'd think the photo would be an enormous turn-on, and it is. Definitely brought on a semi. Maybe it's the change in seasons as Halloween approaches, but it's also a downer. Or perhaps the photo isn't the downer. It's a grand thing she's feeling comfortable enough in us to send this over. She trusts me. But what does it mean? Sure, I feigned happiness when she called about her dream job. I mean, I am happy for her. She worked her tail off for that job.

It's Saturday morning, and there's a slight chill in the air, but nothing a steaming cup of coffee can't handle. Today the high will hit eighty-five, but the nights are getting cooler. Won't be long before the leaves transition to hues of yellow and gold.

"Hey there, cowboy." The screen door creaks as Sandra pulls it.

"You want some coffee?" I don't much feel like getting up off the sofa, but I will for Sandra.

"Already had mine." She sits down on the opposite end of the sofa, kicks off her flip-flops, and pulls her feet up under her. "Why the long face?"

"No long face. Just a slow mornin'."

She squints, studying me, then lets the lie pass. "I heard from Randy you guys are developing Phase II. And you won that case."

"We won that case a while ago. How've you been?"

"Oh, you know, same ol', same ol'." The way she's sitting, knees up in the air, I could probably catch a sliver of her panties if I lean in her direction. High school me would have totally leaned. "How's the girl from Jackson?"

"Kate?" She nods. We're both grinning. It's a thing with Sandra and me. We grin when we talk about the other folks we date. "Kate's good."

"This sad face you've got going on. It's about her."

"I don't know what the hell you're going on about. I'm smilin'."

"No." Her fingers wiggle, and she shakes her head. "You've got a look when you're in a funk. You didn't even bother with gel."

For that dig, I shove her.

"I don't wear gel." She opens her mouth to argue. "It's Saturday morning."

"I'll take that coffee." She gets up and goes into the kitchen.

Off in the distance, a hawk flies overhead. Nearby birds chirp loudly, and I wonder if their volume spiked because of the hawk or if I just wasn't hearing them earlier.

Sandra returns with a fresh cup of joe and sits. This time she sits with her legs open, and I have a full-frontal view of dark panties.

"Sandra, you're giving me quite a view."

"What do you care?" she asks, but she grabs a throw pillow

and puts it between her legs. She's right. We're basically siblings at this juncture. I don't really care. "Is long distance getting you down?"

"It's not exactly a blast. I was gonna go up and visit last week, but her schedule changed. She's finishing up summer jobs and agreed to take on extra shifts to end on good notes." It makes sense. She can't afford to burn bridges, but damn.

"She's younger, right?"

I nod.

"Is she a partier?"

"No, not really. Just loves the mountains and snow."

"Long distance sucks." She sips her coffee and eyes me over the mug.

"Probably a lot harder when you were in college." It's no secret she blames the long distance for the end of her relationship with Sam. We've never discussed it, but I suspect there were other issues at play.

The nearby birds chirp, and a toad somewhere nearby joins the ruckus.

"You know, this might be blasphemy," Sandra says, "but there's nothing that says you're tied here. No one else in your family feels tied to the ranch."

Sandra knows me well, and she should be able to read the facial expression I give her that basically says *no fucking way*.

"No one says you can't let it go for a few years. Let the ranch run on auto. Hank can run the place. Hell, you're only working out here part-time as it is. I hear real estate in Wyoming is heating up. You could oversee a development near Jackson. I read this article about how with global warming, Jackson's going to become one of the more reliable places with snow. You could copy the community formula you're putting in place down here. Do it for a few years. See what happens. Plan to come back later."

"She has no plans of leaving the mountains." Ever. She lives and breathes alpine air. I could also share that she bleeds blue and doesn't want to cross the line into Texas in her lifetime, but that's a bit much to share over coffee.

"Do you know that for a fact, or are you assuming it? One thing I know from experience is that communication is doubly important in a long-distance relationship."

Communication. Interesting word. After Costa Rica, Kate pulled back big time. Holding out our communications like they were baby carrots. She's freer now and more constant. But...hell, I don't want to think about it. I swipe my hand through my hair vigorously as if a fly landed in it and shake my head. A change of subject is needed.

"What about you? What are your plans, Sandra?" I drawl out her name, and she laughs.

"You're probably looking at it. Stay right here in Hill County. Why would I leave? I've got everything I want. Horses. Land. Austin is close. Family. A job I love. Might it be nice if I found someone? Sure. But you can't get everything, and I've got a lot."

A text from Ian comes to mind. "Didn't you go to Houston recently?"

"I did." She grins. "Hung out with your little brother."

"How's Ian?"

"He's good. Working too hard. He's got the same Duke boy affliction."

"What's that?"

"Workaholic."

I chuckle at that. "Yours truly does not suffer from that affliction."

"Bull. Shit," she spits out. Her eyes narrow. "What about you?"

I raise an eyebrow. She's gotta be more explicit.

"Have you got everything you want right here? Because I'm not sure you do."

She might be right. But my life is pretty damn good. And yeah, this year I got wrapped up in a girl and haven't quite been myself. But things'll come around. They always do.

"What're you planning to do to celebrate the big three-six?"

"Aw, hell. Things you did not need to bring up." She laughs, and I stand. "Get on out of here. I've got to get to work."

"See, workaholic." She hands me her half-full mug. "Take care, Ollie."

"See ya, Sandra." She starts to head out, and I ask, "Have you talked to Noah lately?"

"No. But, you know Jocelyn is living with her baby daddy in their house. I met up with Natalie and Liam, and Natalie said he is not too happy about that."

I shrug. It sounds like she's getting the house, and she's having a baby with this guy. "That's gotta suck for Noah."

"He's not pleased," Sandra says, slowly shaking her head. But her lips tweak, and I recognize that tiny smile. She's got the scoop.

"What?" I prompt.

"He's seeing someone."

"Really?" I know he's been having a lot of hookups, and in this little suburban town, that could get miscommunicated real fast.

"He made sure Jocelyn knows. And she's younger. Someone he works with."

"Oh, shit." She laughs. "Please tell me she's over eighteen."

"I don't know much about her. I think she's a waitress at one of the locations, so I'd assume she's legal. We all think he went younger because she did."

"Her baby daddy is younger?"

She grins like the cat that ate the canary. "Yeah, he is. Not crazy younger. But younger."

"How, exactly, did he make sure Jocelyn knew about his most recent hookup?" I kinda don't want to know. Those two have acted like dumb knuckles for as long as I can remember. Going back and forth, getting each other riled up. But I must say, Jocelyn knocked it out of the park with the baby bit.

"He walked by her office holding hands." Sandra's cheeks are rosy. Sharing gossip practically makes her glow. Of course, I don't know why Jocelyn would care if he's seeing someone else. Or why he'd care enough to try to goad her.

"I'll lob a call to him. Check in."

"You do that. I'll see ya later." She presses two fingers to her lips and blows me a kiss.

At the sink, I set the phone down and stare at the dark screen as I rinse the mugs and put them in the dishwasher. I have a choice with Kate. I can play games and wait a few days to respond to her provocative image. Leave her hanging. I could do that. Make her squirm. See how long it takes before she calls me.

Fuck games. That's the kind of bull Noah and Jocelyn pull.

Me: Damn, girl. You know how to make a guy drool.

For good measure, I send a follow-up too.

Me: Miss you.

thirty-one

Kate

November 28

Thanksgiving marks Jackson Hole Resort's opening day for ski season. Four days ago we opened, and Christmas music plays in speakers everywhere you go. Holiday lights are strung, Christmas trees are decked out, and holiday-themed decorations feature in every store window.

Snow in November is finicky, but we've lucked out. Twenty-one inches plus the snow machines are pumping the second the temperature dips below freezing.

As all the fresh snow falls and settles, avalanche risks rise. So, in addition to skiing the area, I've spent a good amount of time helping to post signs and warning fences. It's a lot of mind-numbing physical labor.

This early in the season, locals and annual pass holders dominate the mountain. Snow forecasts are the number one topic of conversation. There's a system coming through this coming weekend, and the excitement in the air pops like corn kernels on a stovetop.

Today, the high will be twenty-eight at the base, which means farther up the mountain, temps will be colder. My duty this morning is to shovel snow near the lift. During the season tails, we have to do a bit more of that, as keeping a snowpack through the lines and lift is more challenging. It's not an Instagram-worthy shot by any stretch of the imagination, but I snap a shot of the base lift where I'll be assisting and shoot it off to Oliver. My caption reads, "Bet you're jealous."

He invited me down to Texas for Thanksgiving, but I couldn't exactly beg off on opening day. Plus, as a newbie, I'm guaranteed to get the days no one wants. Only three lifts are open right now, but there's snow on most of the mountain. They'll wait for a few more good dumps to open more of the lifts.

My phone rings and disappointment smacks when I see it's not Oliver, but I shake it off.

"Hey, Hudson. How's it going?"

Hudson has been calling more frequently now that he's short on awe-inspiring videos. The best photos he sends are of the inside of our childhood home. I'd expected he'd resort to memes, falling into the scrolling trap instead of outdoor activity, but he doesn't seem to visit his social world often. I suspect it's a little too heartbreaking seeing everyone else gearing up for ski season.

"Hanging tight. What're you up to today? I saw only three lifts are open."

"It's a small crowd, and you know how it goes. We're optimistic we'll be fully operational by Christmas."

"Yeah, there are two different storm systems coming through next week."

I have a good ten minutes before I need to hike up the hill, so I kick a heel out and do one of my leg stretches.

"How's rehab?"

"It sucks." That's his standard answer.

I let out a compassionate sigh, one I feel deeply, given I did physical therapy most of the summer. "It'll get better. You'll be back to boarding in no time."

"I'm not sure I will."

"What?" I'm careful to avoid flat-out arguing with him, because he's been seeing medical experts. There was always a chance he wouldn't board again, at least without pain. It's conceivable this is the new diagnostic conclusion.

"Kate. I'm thirty fucking years old, and I'm living at home. My health insurance is the basic plan. Do you know what that pays for?"

"No." I now have health insurance, but Hudson's medical issues are a world different from mine. I don't have a good grasp on what the lowest level of insurance covers.

"Well, let me tell you. It's not paying for my physical therapy. It didn't pay for much—"

"But Mom and Dad?"

"I don't want to keep taking from them. And, honestly, spending my days mid-mountain teaching ski school isn't worth it. With the debt I have, I'll be living at home for years. I mean, don't get me wrong...I loved competing. But I'm ready for something new. Are you sitting down?"

"Yeah," I lie and switch legs, kicking my other ankle out to stretch the other leg.

"Next week, I'm going to join Dad and work in the office. Once I'm able, I'll join the construction crew."

"You hate construction."

"It's not that bad. Dad wants to work less."

"But that's not what you want to do..."

The Hudson I know would never agree to this. He lives an unrestrained life.

"Well, things change. I figure I spent my twenties having the time of my life. Maybe now it's time for me to figure out the next stage. I'll start with Dad's company. I'm also looking at some classes at UV for architecture."

"Architecture?" I vaguely recall he'd been interested in under-grad, but he ultimately skated by with a business degree.

"Yeah, Chloe's brother is an architect. He does some cool stuff, and it would complement the construction business."

"Who's Chloe?"

"She's my physical therapist. We've been hanging out."

"Hanging out?" I remember Mom mentioning that Hudson hasn't been spending a ton of time at home. I had assumed he was hanging with our high school friends. "Spending a lot of time at her place, huh?"

"As much as I can."

My mouth drops. No denial?

"You really like her?"

"I do. She's not like anyone I've ever known."

Holy shit.

"And you're going to work for Dad, and looking into architecture classes?" Dumbfounded, I repeat his statements back to him. Mom must be ecstatic.

"That sums it up. Enough about me. What's up in your world? Is ski patrol everything you dreamed?"

Is it everything I dreamed? What did I dream? Photos from mountaintops, first ski down of the day? Skiing nonstop, every day.

"We're less than a week in." Most of the mountain is still closed.

"You'll have fun. At least for a few years. It's a fun life, but it's a hard life too."

"You're really giving it all up?" I can't quite wrap my head around this turn of events.

"I'll be out there on weekends when I can. Probably on skis. Not sure my leg will take the workout of a board. Maybe I'll be a ski patrol volunteer when I can. Chloe does that, and she has fun. I'm not planning on dumping my equipment at Play It Again Sam's just yet." The smile in his tone comes through loud and strong. "I'm proud of you, sis."

"Me?" *Why?* Then it hits. "You didn't think I'd ever be good enough for ski patrol. Right?"

"What? Shit. No. Everyone knew you could do it. You have the skills and determination. No, I'm proud of you for walking away from med school. Redirecting your life when you realized you weren't happy...well, I know firsthand how hard it is. And you had it doubly hard. Standing up to Mom. Realizing two years in you hated what you were doing. I'd bet there are people all over who hate being doctors or lawyers or even preachers...but they invested so much to be that thing and they refused to change course. You did it. You changed course."

"After sinking two years of tuition."

"Could have been four. Or more." He's correct about that. "Anyhoo, I'm proud of you, little sis. Send me photos. Let me live vicariously through you."

"Yeah, well, today I'm monitoring the base and yelling at newbies coming in at uncontrolled speeds. You want a video?"

"Ah, you're in cop mode today. Have fun, sis."

"Good talking to you, Hudson. Thanks for calling."

All the way up to the lift, I replay our conversation. Hudson's got a girlfriend. He's going to work for Dad. Talk about a change in life direction. That's one I didn't see coming.

The snow piled up at the lift is manmade snow, and a backhoe delivered it during the night. Three shovels into the icy, hard stuff, and the first bead of sweat drips from my temple. My hands are moist inside the gloves, but I'm not about to take them off. The skin on the underside of my hands needs the protection.

After about an hour and a half of shoveling snow, a man in a red ski patrol suit approaches.

"What're you doing?" At the sound of my boss's voice, I look up into the sun.

"Moving the snow around to some of the lighter spots in the line and below the lift." My job.

Bill lets out a sigh.

"Brandon. Get your crew out here to do their job." The three guys working the lift break out into laughter. I am officially confused.

"That's their job. Don't fall for their shit. I need you up about midway at the first slower sign." There's a junction farther up the slope where three different runs converge. We posted a red slow sign in front of a fairly bare stretch of hill. Flagging speedsters is an important part of the job. A few years ago, a young girl died when an out-of-control skier took her out near the base. Signs in the lift line memorialize the event and warn speedsters.

"Yes, sir. Sorry for misunderstanding." This is my third day of shoveling snow before heading up to my station by the sign. *Those jackasses.* "Ahm, am I supposed to be staking signs where you need them at the start of the day?" I might blow a gasket if he says no.

"Yes, that you should do. And it's not unheard of for ski patrol to help with this. But when you see three lift guys hanging out shooting the shit, you know they're fucking with you."

Right.

I shoot the younger guys a glare. They snicker. One of them shouts, "Great work!"

I resume my post by the mid-slope sign. It's funny how the mere presence of a red suit helps to control speed. It's a light day on the mountain, but three different adult skiers go into a pizza wedge to slow down. And, if they need to pizza wedge to slow down, it's a good sign they're novices and probably at risk of hurtling out of control.

My leg muscles burn. My mind wanders. People ski or board by, but there's not much conversation. There's static on my CB.

I can hear ski patrol assists being called over the mountain. One broken ski needs patrol. Someone is too scared and needs an assist. There's a leg injury not too far away from me.

Static comes through the line. Injury? Equipment failure? I wish we could place bets.

"Oakley. You still at your post?"

"Yep," I say brightly to whatever male voice is coming through.

"You're closest. Got a call with an injured skier. Near Casper Restaurant. They're saying it's lots of blood. Cox is bringing up the toboggan. Code red."

I tug my poles out of the snow where I jammed them hours ago and shove off. Through a path in the trees, a group of skiers huddles. My adrenaline spikes. I weave through the gathering onlookers.

"Ski patrol. Coming through."

On the ground, a young person lies flat in the snow. Her skis aren't on. Below the juncture of the back of her knee, there's a clean line on both legs. The shine of white exposed bone gives rise to nausea. Small black dots bounce on my periphery. I suck in air.

"What happened?"

The young person is quiet. The helmet is facing sideways, like he or she is resting. I don't see any tears. Cheeks are pink. A hand moves. The person is conscious. Over by the edge of the trail, a man retches into the trees. The sound of someone vomiting gives rise to my own in the back of my throat.

"What happened?" I repeat.

A woman runs out of the nearby mountain restaurant with white towels. She bends down and places them on the backs of the girl's legs. Red spreads over the snow.

"A snowboarder whipped by. She was just standing here. He went up on the edge of his board. The edge sliced her legs."

"Where is he?"

"I don't think he knew he did it. She fell forward after he hit her. We didn't realize what had happened. When we went to help her up, we saw the blood. We called ski patrol, and I ran to get towels. Her father can't handle blood. He's over there."

The man from earlier has a palm placed against a tree. His back is to us.

"Okay. A toboggan is on the way."

I lift my radio. "We're going to need an ambulance at the base. Severe injury."

The medics at first aid can do a lot, but I saw bone. She's going to need surgery.

"Okay. What's her name?" I bend down to her and take over pressing the white cloth against the backs of her legs. The white slowly morphs into red. I breathe in deeply and exhale. My throat tightens.

"Monica," her mother says. She's at the girl's head now. The girl is blinking, but she's not crying. "Why isn't she saying anything?" the mother asks.

"She's in shock. She'll feel it soon enough."

Two members of ski patrol join us. We have to get her down fast. She's bleeding out quickly. I lift the red rag to show the two medics what we're dealing with. We need to pack the wound, get her flipped, get her down and loaded into an ambulance.

I grab a white towel but look into the wound through the sliced ski pants, taking in the sliced muscle, tendons, and the exposed bone. The dots in my peripheral version merge into a solid sheet of black.

* * *

Tears run down my face as I tell my mom everything. My first rescue. How I fainted. A young girl suffered one of the most serious injuries the mountain has seen in years, and I fainted during rescue.

"Honey, some people don't react well to blood. It's a physical reaction." I dab my runny nose with a tissue. "Why didn't you ever tell me?"

"Would it have made a difference?" I already know the answer. I told her formaldehyde made me nauseated, and she told me to suck it up and get over it.

"Oh, honey. You've always been so stubborn. If you had told me you faint when you see blood, I wouldn't have pushed you toward a career in medicine. I'm not a monster. I always thought you quit med school to prove something. Or that maybe I slipped up and told you what to do. You've never responded well to being told what to do. But there are techniques for dealing with an aversion to blood. If you want a job in medicine, there are options. You don't have to be near blood."

"Mom, I wanted med school for you. To make you proud." The aversion to blood was problematic, but it wasn't the only reason I left med school. I truly hated it.

"I think deep down I knew that. Science has never been your passion, has it?"

"I like biology and chemistry well enough. But I hated med school. I hate hospitals. I don't like being around sick people."

"Yeah, medicine is probably not the right career." We both laugh. It's not particularly funny, but it lightens the mood, and tears spring to the corner of my eyes. "Your favorite classes were always English and history. I can't deny it surprised me when you called and said you were applying to med schools."

It thrilled her. My call to tell her I was dropping out did the exact opposite. "And now I don't even know if I have a job."

Johnson, a senior member of ski patrol, insisted I wait for another toboggan to be carried down the mountain. Bill sent me home. His expression had been unreadable as Johnson unzipped me.

"Well, I imagine a woman fainting on the mountain has them suspecting pregnancy."

Her comment brings out a snort. "Why?"

"Well, I imagine your boss won't assume a prior med school student faints at blood. If a woman faints, I always give a pregnancy test. Any chance you're pregnant?"

"Mom. I promise you. It was the blood. Well, the blood and everything else."

"It sounds like a gruesome accident. But honey, I have to ask. I thought the whole point of ski patrol was the rescue aspect. With a reaction like yours to blood, why would you pursue ski patrol?"

"I don't know." I hold my hand up in the air. Not that she can see it. "I wanted to apply what I learned in med school, I guess? I just thought it would be like muscle injuries. Or broken bones." The visual of the poor girl returns full force. I blink rapidly, trying to clear the vision. "And I wanted to be the first one on the mountain."

"Like Hudson?" She's soft with her question.

"Yeah. It just seemed like...." I wanted that uninhibited freedom. "I didn't expect I'd come across much blood."

I mean, sure, I see splotches of blood on the snow from time to time, but small amounts.

"Honey, didn't they cover in your first aid work that compound fractures are common on the mountain? Very often that's bone sticking through the skin." I rub my forehead. Yes, they went over this. I had to look away and breathe deeply. "That's bloody."

"I know."

"You've spent so much of your life chasing Hudson. That's my fault. We hauled you around to all of his events because, at first, you were too young to do it yourself. And then..."

"I sucked at it, so you still had to haul me around."

"You didn't suck at it." I roll my eyes. I totally sucked at it. "You weren't a natural like him, but you worked twice as hard. You did well. Your high school ski team won states. You could have skied for a college team. That's not sucking."

I could have skied for a college team, but not for Vermont, which is where I wanted to go. Mom sighs into the phone. It's late for her, and I should let her go.

"What are you going to do?"

It hasn't been too long since Thai Me Up mentioned a managerial position. I suppose I can go back with my tail between my legs and ask if Bradley still has anything. Claire also has some interesting ideas about businesses. If Hudson can change and find a path forward in business, so can I.

"If you need money—"

"Mom, it's good. I'll find something." I will not be like Hudson in that respect.

"I doubt they'll fire you, honey."

"Well, technically, we're under a review period. So they don't have to fire me."

"Still, I doubt they'll let you go. I think the bigger question you need to be asking yourself is if this is what you really want to do."

"Look at that. I'm finally just like Hudson."

"Well, your brother has fallen in love. Love changes priorities. I'm afraid to tell you what I think is going on with you."

"Tell me." I don't know what's going on with me, so I might as well listen to her theory.

"I think you essentially married med school. And this ski patrol gig was your rebound. Now, you've got to do some soul searching to figure out what you really want. And, you know, honey, I think it's worth mentioning that career doesn't define you."

I know that. It's on the tip of my tongue to bite back at my mother, but the sting of defeat weakens my defenses. Career doesn't define anyone.

"I wonder sometimes if your dad and I pushed you and Hudson too hard as kids. I feel like Hudson kind of stumbled into love, and it's made such a huge difference. He's so much happier. And you know, that's really all your dad and I want for you."

All of her comments over the years about money come to mind, but instead of getting angry, amusement bubbles up. She doesn't want us to starve. I can't fault her for that. She and I don't usually talk about my dates or boyfriends. But maybe it's time for that to change.

"I am seeing someone." I hold my breath, waiting. She could scold me, tell me that I need to get my feet on the ground first. But she just says...

"Who? Tell me about him." There's genuine excitement coming through the line, and for the next thirty minutes, I tell her all about Oliver Carson Duke.

thirty-two

Oliver

December 7

From one angle, the tree stands erect and straight. Two feet over, and there's a lean to the right.

Knock. Knock.

"Ollie? You—Oh, wow. What a gorgeous tree!"

Sandra's carrying two red and green cups with white plastic lids. She's barefoot, as she kicked off her shoes at the door.

"It's leaning."

"Is it?" She cocks her head and circles the outer rim.

My folks are spending most of the month at the family home here on the ranch. I haven't completely finished the renovation on the mill, but it's livable. The kitchen and living area are mostly done, and my bedroom and bath are too. Living here, I'll be able to finish up at my pace and in my off hours.

I put the tree in a corner against the window. I like it there because it's near the fireplace on the back wall. The only drawback is it covers up a portion of my back wall window, and I love that view out over the river and riverbank. But most of those trees are bare now. I'm hoping this tree will add some brightness to the dreary outside.

I've had a case of the bah humbugs, and I'm ready to break out of it. It's not like me to be in a funk for too long.

"I just love what you've done to the place."

Sandra moves on to the kitchen, then circles back to my living area. She offers me a cup.

I take it from her but ask, "What is it?"

"Gingerbread hot chocolate."

That sounds like liquid sugar. "Thank you." I take it from her but don't bother with a sip and instead place it on the kitchen counter. "I'll save it for later. You think it'll reheat?"

I plan to dump it as soon as she leaves but let her think I'll drink it.

"It should. There's no whipped cream in it, so you can add that later."

"If I add anything, it'll be whiskey. You wanna spike yours?"

"No, thanks." She sips her concoction then points. "Are you going to decorate that tree?"

"Nothing more than lights. This weekend I'm going with my folks to select a tree for their house, and since I'm the best son, I'll help her decorate it. That'll cure any decoration desires for the season."

"I hear you. I bought my tree over Thanksgiving. It's half-decorated."

There's really not a point in decorating a tree if you don't have kids, in my book. I moved in here Thanksgiving weekend. Wouldn't have gotten a tree, but with it being a new half-furnished home with an unfinished upstairs, it feels too empty for my taste. Holiday crapola will fill some gaps until I can con Sandra or Patty into using their feminine wiles to give it a homey feel.

"Here. You stand here and tell me which way to move the tree."

She does as I tell her and goes about directing me.

"Left. Too much. A little right." The directions continue until I don't give a damn anymore and screw the tree in place.

"What's your Jackson girl up to?" Sandra asks while I'm on my knees, reaching under wide branches to get the screws on the stand in nice and tight. Sandra's question reminds me I didn't receive a photo this morning. But Kate's been off on texting photos ever since the incident on the mountain.

"Working, I imagine." She works all the damn time. She could give Sam and Ian a run for their money on the work front.

"How's she liking ski patrol?" I told Sandra and all my friends when she'd gotten her dream job. But I didn't tell them she was now exploring options in hospitality.

"I don't think it's all she cracked it up to be."

"Oh, really?" Sandra cuddles into one of the double-wide armchairs.

"Yeah. There was an incident on the mountain. Young girl injured. Shook her up."

"I never knew what she saw in it to begin with. Seemed like a lot of manual labor to me."

"That's why you don't get why I enjoy ranch work."

It's not just Sandra. No one gets it, but I am happiest outside. This place I built feels like you're sitting outside, thanks to the floor-to-ceiling glass and being perched right on the edge of the river. The stone base lifts the building high enough that even when the river rises, the house sits high above the raging river. Not that we get too many raging rivers these days. We're in the throes of a multi-year drought.

"So, does that mean she's going to come down here?"

"Still loves the mountains. I've been thinking about what you said."

"*Moi?*"

"Yeah. You. That I could go up there and lay the groundwork for a new development. I've given it some consideration. I had to hire a full-time ranch manager since Hank had his heart attack, but he's working part time. So, there's a lot of staff right now. Figure I can go up and spend a few winter months up there. Scout the land."

"Holy shit. You're thinking about moving for her." Sandra's wide eyes and open mouth put her dismay on display.

I chuckle as I sink into the other oversized leather armchair. I have a sofa coming, but it's on backorder, as is my wide-screen television, which is a much larger concern.

"I wouldn't move forever. Texas is my home. But moving away for a while won't kill me. I did it for college. Came home on breaks. I think we've got a good thing, but we've been long distance. I hate the distance, but I dig her." Hell, I love Kate. Fallen hook, line, and sinker. Can't stop thinking about her, and the distance is making me borderline miserable. "Might as well see how we do living in the same place." If I get up there and after a week or two, it fizzles, I haven't lost anything. Maybe just learned something. Maybe scouted some good investment opportunities.

"I hear you." She smiles over the rim of her sugary Starbucks concoction. "No commitment quite yet. Just move and feel it out. See how it goes."

I chuckle. "Yeah, something like that."

Hell, you never know. Fizzling out like soda pop is a real potential scenario. But it's been almost a year, and I don't see that happening. My gut tells me if we can keep it working with the distance between us, we'll be more solid than the foundation of this old gin mill if we're together every night. And if I'm right about that, I'll have to sell her hard on the benefits of southern living. We're in the Austin suburbs, but our neck of the woods is like a small town, and we've got all the outdoors she could ever want. It's just the mountains and the snow...but maybe, just maybe, with all the recent developments, snow is losing some of its luster.

Knock. Knock.

"You expecting anyone?"

"*Nada*," I answer as I head to the door. "But Patty and Sam Senior are on the ranch."

My front door is wood with glass on each side. Whoever is at the door is standing in front of the wood. Probably Patty with an arm full of food.

I swing the door open and blink. My heart does a full shimmy. *Kate.*

"Kate?" No matter how much I blink, she's still there. This is not a hallucination.

Her beautiful, stunning smile brightens her entire face, not to mention the gloomy December haze.

"Surprise!" She bounces on her heels and holds her arms out.

"What?" My mouth is open. My brain function stops. "Did they fire you?"

It's the only thing that makes sense. And that's really fucking wrong if they did. She worked her ass off for that position, and two legs being almost sliced off is not a normal day on the mountain.

She half-laughs. "What? No." She's grinning at me like I've lost a marble, but she had been worried about that. "No. The review period goes two ways, you know? I had to decide if that's what I wanted. And I went, and...Can I come in?"

"Oh. Yeah." I swing the door open. "Have you got bags?" I mean, if she's here, she's spending the night, and she's staying with me.

"Yeah, out in the car."

"The car? Why didn't you call me to pick—"

"You keep surprising me. I wanted to surprise you. And I'm not paying for the rental. The company that flew me down here preferred..."

Sandra approaches the door, barefooted, eyes wide and mind nosy. Kate freezes, taking in Sandra in her barefoot glory.

"Kate, this is Sandra. Sandra, this is Kate. Kate's my girlfriend." It's the first time I've introduced her to anyone that way, and it has a nice ring. So nice, in fact, a need to touch her mounts, and I wrap my arm around her, pulling her into my side. She looks up at me with enough warmth to thaw the iciest winter day.

"The girl from Jackson," Sandra says while holding out a hand. "I've heard a lot about you. Nice to finally meet you in person."

Kate and Sandra shake hands as they size each other up the way women do.

"I'm gonna get on out of here," Sandra says.

"You don't have to go," I'm quick to say, out of politeness, but I keep the door open so she can head right on outside.

"No, I promised Patty I'd stop by, and I'm behind on shopping."

The second the door closes behind Sandra, I tug on Kate's hand and trap her up against the door. A glass house works just fine out here with no cars or neighbors, but I have just enough presence of mind to know that any place other than against the door can be viewed by Sandra, at least until she drives away.

My lips claim hers, and damn, my girl tastes good. Minty and sweet, and god, she feels heavenly. I can't believe she's here. In my house. In my arms. Everything goes surreal, like I'm dreaming. If I'm dreaming, I don't want to wake up from this wonderland. My body overrides my mind. I want her. I need her. And taking her right up against my front door feels like just the thing to do.

She's wearing this suit jacket, and the fabric is everywhere. I have to break the kiss to see what I need to push aside so I can remove this blouse and touch her skin. Her fingers still against my jaw, and she licks her luscious, swollen lips.

"I have an interview I need to get to. But I had time to spare and was too excited to not come here first."

My breathing slows, and my brain kicks into gear. My erection is so fucking hard it hurts, so I rock against her as I slow myself down and thoughts coalesce.

"Interview? Here?" I blink. There's really nothing around Whispering Creek.

"Well, in Austin. I probably shouldn't have driven out. But my flight got in early, and—"

"Best surprise of my life." I smack my lips against hers, intertwine our fingers, and lead her into the living area, where I pull her down on my lap in the oversized armchair. "Give me the rundown—how long are you here?"

"My return flight is on Sunday. The company would have sent me back tomorrow, but I asked if I could pick my return date, and they said yes."

Holy shit. I get an entire weekend with Kate. I lift her knuckles to my lips. There's a part of my brain that is still registering she's here. In my lap.

"What company? I might know someone...are you thinking about moving to Austin?" My squirrelly brain gallops off in too many directions.

"Maybe," she says, her tone high-pitched as she shrugs. "Bill said he'd seen bigger men than me vomit at what I'd seen...but I'm seriously second guessing the patrol gig. And I don't think I told you, but Thai Me Up asked if I'd be interested in a manager's role about a month ago. Well, I doubled back to them after, well, let's call it the incident, and that position had been filled. Of course. But he knew about another position. Down here in Texas. Said they'd called him asking if he knew anyone. And it's kind of perfect for me. They're opening a new restaurant down here, and I could be a part of the team opening it. And then, if I like it...and, well, they like me when I interview.... I could stay on as manager. But they plan to open more locations, and they have management positions, too."

"What's the company?"

"Good Foods. They own a lot of different restaurants." That's Noah's firm. One look at her glowing expression, and it's clear as day she doesn't know I have a connection. But I'm an investor and general counsel for the company.

"Is this what you want to do?" It's a big shift from life on a mountain.

She lets out a loud sigh. One arm loops around my neck, and both her legs drape over my lap. She leans back a smidge, and those chocolate eyes look straight into mine.

"Is it okay to say I don't know? I mean..." She sighs and lifts her shoulders. "I don't know. I've never wanted to spend my days chained to a desk. Neither of my parents were chained to desks. I think that's one reason I thought medicine might suit me. But it doesn't. And...I think I romanticized ski patrol. I envisioned...well, it doesn't matter what I envisioned. I guess my brother's accident drove home the idea that nothing's guaranteed, and my leg...I could reinjure it so easily."

"I thought you wanted a life skiing every day." This turnabout confuses me, and I'm having trouble mentally following her path to my door.

"I did, too. But if I'm honest with myself, I forced myself on that mountain because of the challenge. I didn't love every moment. I find posting signs and checking for dangers and watching for speeders to be, well, boring. Which is crazy because I spent a solid year pursuing this. Which is better than the two years I spent pursuing a med school degree. So, I don't know. Is it okay to say I enjoyed bartending? I like the restaurant industry. Paisley has me intrigued by the possibilities in hospitality. I mean, based on this phone interview, it sounds like this company could be perfect for me because there are several options. So, I could get in and work on launching this restaurant, then I could move on to open another restaurant, or move into exploring franchises, or...I don't know. There are options." She scrunches her nose. "They may hate me. The phone interview went well, but...you know, in person is different, and I'm sure they are interviewing a lot of other candidates. Either way, it's a free weekend down here to surprise you."

"Color me surprised." My hands continue to roam her because my body is on autopilot while I wrap my head around all that she's saying. I could tell her the position is guaranteed if she wants it, but my gut says that's not a good plan.

Kate is a strong-willed, stubborn woman. I didn't have a damn thing to do with her interview. Now, maybe Noah heard her name, and he jumped on it. He's a good friend like that. But I don't want

Kate hearing about this connection and skedaddling out the door. She's pretty big on independence.

"Did you have other plans this weekend? Am I...Good Foods offered to get me a hotel—"

"Absolutely not. You'll be staying here. With me. Now, if I can't welcome you to Texas the way I'd like," I wiggle my eyebrows for effect, "would you like a tour of my new home? You'll have to keep your shoes on because upstairs is a construction zone. Then forget that rental. I'll drive ya to your interview. Be sure to take you along the best routes."

"You don't need to—"

"Need?" I stretch out that word like it has four vowels. "Now that I got you here, I've got to sell you on this great state. There's not another one like it."

"Ugh. The big, giant red state." She's teasing, but there's a hint of truth in her chagrin.

"Look at it this way. One more blue vote. And you'd be here with me."

Horse people like to say to never put the cart before the horse. And I know Kate has yet to spend one night here in the land of the Alamo. But I can't help but qualify this turn of events as outstanding.

thirty-three

Kate

December 7

My interview starts with sweaty palms, but within ten minutes, the interview with Jessica Brown eases into an easy conversation, with my asking more questions than she asks me. I learn all about the different restaurants the Good Foods group owns, three of which are franchises, and she openly shares expansion plans.

"Do you have any more questions for me?" Her question stumps me, partially because I can't believe thirty minutes have flown by.

I counter with, "No, it all sounds great. Do you have any more questions for me?"

She laughs. Like, full-on laughs. "No, I have a list that I printed out from a website about great questions to ask an interviewee, but honestly, I think some of these are crap. I mean, really." She holds a piece of paper up and reads aloud, "What are three words friends or colleagues would use to describe you?" Her face contorts, and I laugh. "Who comes up with this? I haven't been trained to interview people, but personally, I prefer to just see how easy someone is to talk to because I'm going to have to work with them. It's not like what we're doing is rocket science. But you asked good questions," she shrugs, "and I like you. Anyway, are you ready to meet Noah Alden? I think you already met on the phone?"

"We did." I follow her across the hall, and she taps on the door.

"Huh. He's not here. Let me go find him."

A few minutes later, Mr. Alden enters his office where I'm waiting for him. He holds out a hand, and as our hands follow professional courtesy, he says, "It's nice to meet you in person."

He sits in a chair across from his desk, right beside mine. His eyes narrow.

"Now, tell me. Are you really open to moving to Texas?" The unspoken question hangs in the air. *Are you wasting our time?*

I exhale, cross my legs, adjust my skirt, and give myself a moment to collect my answer.

"Yes, I'm open to it." Noah's bright blue eyes peer down at me, and I feel compelled to add more to ensure he really gets who I am, which is probably not recommended in interview situations, but Jessica seemed so down to earth and real, and it's not like I have a lot of interview experience to fall back on. Pretty much every job I've gotten has been because I know someone. "I'm going to be honest with you. Since graduating from college, I've pursued a few different career paths. I'm still figuring out exactly what I want to do."

"Totally get that," he says. He crosses one ankle over his knee, more or less mirroring my position, and that's when I notice his scuffed cowboy boots. "Can you tell me what you don't want to do?"

I smile because that's something I've always been somewhat clear about. "I don't want a job where I'm behind a desk all day." I think about my med school experience. "I'm not good with blood. I can't stand hospitals. But I like working with people. I like coming up with ideas for events. At the golf club, I organized several of their tournaments, and I enjoyed planning out the different elements and overseeing the execution."

"Bradley said you're great with the customers. He also said you're a hard worker. Honestly, with just those two attributes, as fast as we're growing, we could use you. But what would your long-term plans be? Work here and then move back to Jackson?" He leans back in the chair, and his fingers lightly tap the wooden armrest. "If that's your plan, it works for us. We can keep an eye out for locations in other states. But I'm curious."

"I'm kind of scared to say." I look him straight in the eye as I answer. "Plans change. I don't know how I'll like living here."

I've always prided myself on putting career first. A guy has never registered into my plans. But, if it weren't for Oliver living here, I would have never considered moving to Texas. It's not a particularly pro-woman state. But Oliver is here, and I wanted to see him. Noah studies me with his fingers steepled and pressed against his lips.

"Well, I give you big points for honesty."

He asks a few more questions, and I ask him some. He wraps up with a straightforward, "We're still interviewing candidates, but I expect I'll be in touch. You got any plans this weekend?"

"I'm staying with a friend."

"A friend." He nods slowly, and I force a smile as awkwardness creeps into the room. "Well, I hope your friend shows you the best parts of Texas."

Jessica leads me back out of the building, and she gives me a warm smile and more or less shocks me when she pulls me in for a hug.

"I'm southern. I'm a hugger." She smiles her warm smile like it's totally normal to hug someone you just interviewed. "Hope to see you again soon."

When I exit the office building, Oliver gets up off a nearby bench.

"How'd it go?" he asks.

"Good," I answer, still a little blown away by how friendly and easygoing the interview process was. I'm not sure what I expected. Maybe a series of, like, ten interviews. They flew me down here, after all.

"Nice. So, what kind of food are you in the mood for? I've got reservations at three different hot spots. I also got this little travel guide on Austin." He holds out a thin book. "Figured you could look through it and see what intrigues you the most, and we'll plan our day tomorrow over dinner."

My head spins. Pedestrians hustle by on the sidewalks, and cars slowly pass on the congested street. There are more trees along the street than I expected, but otherwise, it feels like a city to me.

"I'm a little tired from being at the airport so early and traveling all day. Do you think we could maybe just order something to take back to your place?"

"Yeah, sure. We can do that."

His fingers weave through mine as we make our way through the parking lot to his pickup truck.

"Tomorrow, I'd really like to spend time on your ranch. I want to meet the goats and the horses. Did you ever name the babies?" One of his goats had two little baby girls.

"Mary Sue and Mary Ellen."

"Seriously? You named them both Mary?"

"Less to keep track of. They'll come when I call them." He winks at me then pulls me into his side, and I sort of meld into him. "You can change their names if you like. Or, I'm pretty sure one of the barn cats is expecting. I'll give you naming rights."

As we drive home, the sunsets and the lights on the roadway blur into hues of red and yellow. The temperatures are somewhat warm, but there are holiday decorations hanging from all the streetlights. On the radio, holiday music with a country twang plays, and it sounds better than I would have thought. Oliver doesn't stop touching me the entire ride back to his place, and the farther we get from Austin, the harder he presses the accelerator.

On the way home, he stopped by a rustic restaurant and purchased far more barbecue and southern sides than the two of us could ever eat because he swore, "you just have to try it." I told him I'd actually eaten barbecue before, as well as collard greens, fried okra, and mac and cheese, but he ignored me, saying, "But not from Texas."

Back at his house, I set the brown paper bags on the kitchen counter and pull him away.

"Let's eat later." He grins, and so do I because that's really all I have to say.

He lifts me onto the center island. It's a thick, smooth wood block. He steps between my legs, and I knit my hands into his hair. His hands roam my backside, pulling me close, so close I can feel the thunder of his heart.

"I have missed you."

"You too." And god, I really have. We text every day and FaceTime at night, but that's all a poor substitute for having him near.

He angles my head and kisses me like his life depends on this, on us. And then he slows as our fingers roam, reacquainting ourselves with each other. He pushes my blazer off first, taking care to fold it and set it aside.

Those whiskey eyes twinkle as he unbuttons my blouse. Behind him, the river gurgles, and a mix of pine and bare trees blend into the scenery through the window. He cups my breast, and the warmth of his mouth covers my nipple. I gasp, closing my eyes.

My bra falls away, and he pushes me back on the island and begins the process of working the remainder of my suit off my body.

"Is this...can anyone see inside?"

"No, baby. No one's out here. It's just us. Only us."

And then he proceeds to remind me, over and over, with his tongue and his fingers, exactly how well he has learned my body over this past year.

"I'm so glad you came here, baby. It's about time I christened my kitchen."

I slide off the island and fall to my knees in front of him. I maneuver his jeans down, and his cock springs out. He backs up to the island, grips the edge of the counter, and tilts his head back, moaning as I show him I've learned a few of the things he likes, too.

He loves how I lick his shaft, and he especially loves when I take him deep and cup his balls. The action earns a deep, guttural groan. He expands in my mouth, so close.

"No, baby. Not like this." He pulls me off him and lifts me onto the island, an island that happens to be the perfect height. With expert precision, he takes us both to the precipice.

"God, I love you, Ollie," I gasp right before my body quivers and quakes as we both find our release. His damp forehead falls to my chest, and his back heaves as he sucks in air.

He presses his lips to my temple, to my forehead, and to the top of my head. Then he cleans me up and gets me one of his flannel shirts to wear, and he takes me through his favorite barbecue selections. And I have to admit, the barbecue is really good. Maybe a little sweet for my taste, but this far surpasses any pork I've eaten in Vermont or Wyoming. The way he beams when I admit this fact would make you think he cooked it himself.

After dinner, we snuggle in his oversized armchair beneath a blanket. Lying in his arms, looking out over the barren, dry winter woods, happiness bubbles and overflows. I am happy. Maybe happier than I have ever been.

thirty-four

Kate

December 8

"Now, Katie, sweetie, are we going to see you at Christmas?" Mrs. Duke holds me in a bear hug, and I half expect her to reach up and pat my cheek.

She began calling me Katie within ten minutes of meeting me. Oliver corrected her, but I told him it's fine. To Mrs. Duke, he's Ollie, so I can be Katie. His mother took me aside and told me she recently let her hair go gray after years of coloring it. One thing about the color is that it makes it very difficult to see her as the stern mother of three boys Oliver told me about. The gray transforms her into the soft grandmother one wants to hug and bake cookies with. I can't imagine her being strict with anyone.

"Ah…" Her question about Christmas plans has me searching for Oliver. We haven't discussed Christmas. It's weeks away, but I've had much bigger things on my mind.

Oliver and I spent the better part of the day that we didn't spend in bed riding horses. We didn't go much faster than a walk since I hadn't been on a horse since summer camp. The Duke family ranch is peaceful and gorgeous, but I think what I loved most is listening to Oliver share his childhood stories. He practically glowed with pride.

"I'll probably need to work. Christmas week is one of the busiest of the year."

"Well, we don't have to go to Aspen this year. We can go to Jackson. Or we can split our week." She lets me go, but her hands ball into fists and she rests them on her waist, staring down the two Duke men in the foyer. Photos of the Duke family fill the entire wall behind her. In the dining room, there's one formal portrait taken when the boys were around middle school age, but these are candids, and almost all are outside during some kind of activity like hunting, fishing, skiing, or riding horses.

"All right, Patty, calm your horses," Oliver says, stepping between me and his mom and positioning us closer to the door.

"Ollie Carson Duke, I am your mother." She reaches over with her fingers, prime to pinch.

"Ollie, don't rile your mom up," Sam Senior says from his perch, leaning against a doorway. "Patty, he's right. We'll let the kids tell us where we need to be."

"Much appreciated, Dad."

Oliver's wide smile is full of love. In this home, he is happy and relaxed. The way he interacts with his parents isn't that different from how Hudson and I are with my parents. Our mothers are very different, though. Whereas my mother is more reserved, and there's a professional air about her even when we're at home relaxing, his mother is like a force to be reckoned with, a tidal wave of exuberant love.

Oliver had to cancel reservations at a restaurant in Austin, but apparently when his mom found out I was here, she didn't give him a choice. Well, she did. The choice was dinner with them Saturday night or church and lunch Sunday morning. So, Oliver and I agreed to dinner. I need to arrive at the airport early Sunday afternoon, and I'd like to have a slow, easy Sunday morning.

"Katie, it was lovely to meet you, dear." Mr. Duke stands straighter, hands in his loose jean front pockets. I imagine he's ready to go sit down on the sofa and watch television.

"Oh, it sure was. Katie, I know we're going to see a lot more of you. I just know it." Mrs. Duke hugs me again.

Mr. Duke's hand covers his wife's shoulder. "All right, Patty, let's let the kids go."

Oliver rolls his eyes and holds the side door for us. "Mom, I'm trying to sell her on Texas. Not make her move her flight up to an earlier time."

"Oh, Ollie." She shakes her head, but her smile matches her son's. "Dear, I'm going to pray you get that job offer. I'll have my church pray for it, too."

"They even remember who you guys are?" Oliver asks, but he doesn't stand around to hear the answer. With his hand on my lower back, he guides me outside.

"We attend virtually. Do you?" she asks.

He tosses his hand up and waves, but his back is to her. I turn, waving as I thank them once more and call out my goodbyes.

We walked here. The place he's built is about a mile from his parents' place by car on a gravel road, but by foot it's closer.

"Keep walking," Oliver says under his breath. "Patty'll keep us here talkin' for another hour."

"I heard that," she calls.

"See you soon, Katie," Sam Senior calls, and then there's the sound of a door closing. Crickets chirp off in the distance, and there's a deep *whoo* winding through the trees.

"We've got some owls in the woods," Oliver says. "You hear 'em?"

"Yeah." The nearly full moon lights the path back to his place. The stars canvas the sky, and the limbs bristle in the breeze. "I like your parents."

"They're good people." Pride seeps through his words. His fingers tangle with mine. "One day, I'd like to meet your family. I feel like I already know Hudson."

"Hudson's changed. He's not the guy I grew up with."

"How do you mean?"

"Well, before the accident, the only thing that mattered in his world was boarding. The next competition. Now he's...well, he's saying he'll be a weekend boarder." That still blows my mind.

"Maybe it's his new reality."

I understand why Oliver might assume that given he's in physical therapy. But there's more at play.

"Mom says it's because of this new girl."

"I've been told a time or two life changes when you meet the right woman."

"Is that right?" I side-eye him. He's almost thirty-six. It is shocking he's still single. But he was engaged at one point in time. After having met his parents, my bet is his parents have been the ones counseling him on life changes.

Twigs snap and leaves crackle beneath our footsteps. The nearly full moon overhead lights our path.

"Will this be your second year being away from your family on Christmas?"

"Yep. I'd hoped they'd come out to Jackson, but then the accident happened."

"Your brother can fly now, right?"

"Oh, yeah. It's...that accident was expensive. I don't think my parents want to spend more money right now. They offered to fly me home, but I assumed I'd be working. Flights are insanely expensive now."

"You know, we could, if you're up for it, spend Christmas with your family, then the rest of the week in Aspen. If you take this new job." My feet stop moving. "Just throwing it out there."

The vision of spending an entire week with Oliver and our families fills me with warm, sugary holiday vibes. My family would love him. He and Hudson would hit it off. And skiing or boarding for fun brings back memories of Oakley vacations before competition madness.

He tugs my hand, encouraging me to continue down the moonlit path that weaves along the strip of woods bordering the pastures.

"You're getting ahead of yourself. There's no way I'm the only person they're interviewing. And I have zero experience opening a restaurant. Realistically, I will not be the strongest candidate."

"I thought you said this role would assist someone opening it, so you could learn the ropes, and then if you like that, move on to open other locations?"

"That's what they said. But don't jinx it. We can't plan on me getting this job." I haven't planned on it. I've got five shifts bartending at night next week, and I'm picking up two extra lunch shifts at the country club, plus four morning shifts as a cashier at the spa.

His grip on my hand tightens. It's not an uncomfortable hold, but it's firm enough that I wiggle my fingers. There's a long limb that fell over the path, and with his free hand, he picks it up and sends it sailing.

"I think I need to cop to something."

His tone puts me on alert. It's the tone someone uses when he's about to confess to something bad. Has he been seeing someone else? Is he questioning the wisdom of my moving here?

"Are you going to speak up, or are you going to leave me guessing? I know I sprung this on you. If you're seeing someone else—"

"How'd you get to that?" There's heat in those amber eyes. He angles his head to the ground and grits his teeth. "It's nothing like that. I haven't been with anyone other than you. You know that."

He's right. He told me that. And I trust him, so I shouldn't go there.

"You're right. It's just the distance. And we went so long without a commitment."

The light to his front door is on, and it glimmers through the trees. The river gurgles nearby, and another *whoo* weaves through the woods.

"Darlin', my word is good. I told you I wouldn't date anyone else, and I haven't. No, this isn't about that. But what I need to tell you might piss you off, so try your best to keep your horses calm."

"Would you just say it?" He's speaking in near riddles.

"I'm a partner in Good Foods. But. I had nothing to do with you getting called down here for the job. That was all you. And Noah."

"Noah Alden? The man I interviewed with on Friday?"

"One and the same. He's a buddy of mine from way back. Elementary school, actually. I'm basically an investor and General Legal Counsel for Good Foods. Technically, I'm a partner. But I really do nothing with day-to-day management. We've been talking to Bradley from Thai Me Up to see if we can work together to create a franchise with the Thai Me Up brand. One of our managers filled that role in Jackson. Worked out for him, as he had wanted to move. Anyway, that's how Bradley knew about our open role down here."

"So, when I went and talked to them, Bradley forwarded my resume to your company. Did Noah know about you and me?"

"Yeah, he did. He recognized your name. Asked you down for an interview as a favor to me." I shoot him an irate glare, and his palms fly up in defense. "I did not know about it. He said Bradley spoke so highly of you he'd have considered you anyway. Maybe done an interview via Zoom. The flight down was my holiday gift from him." He shrugs. "Anyway, if you want the job, it's yours. He's already checked in, asking if you're going to want it. And what he said about if this role doesn't float your boat, and there are other roles you could move into...that's all true. He has eight different restaurants under management now, with plans to double that over the next three years. He's also got a test restaurant he believes could be franchised."

"Sweet Magnolia Bread & Bakery. He told me about it."

We arrive at his door. "Whatever you decide, I'm good with it. I just wanted you to know sooner than later that I am, coincidentally, connected to your potential employer. And let there be no doubt, I'll be thrilled if you take the job. But if you don't, I'd been working on a backup plan, anyway."

"What do you mean?"

"I was looking at options for me to move up there. Working with a different company, actually. Artisan Construction Group."

"The company that had the lawsuit earlier this year?"

"One and the same." He holds the door open, but I find it hard to move forward.

"You'd move for me?"

"I think it's worth giving this thing between us a fair shake. And the one obstacle we have is no end in sight to the distance."

"You'd move for me?" I repeat this because I can't really wrap my head around it. This place, this land, it's a part of him, the fabric of his being.

"Not forever." He cups my face and pulls me up against him until his heartbeat vibrates through my core. "But I figured I could do it long enough to win you over. Let you get the ski world out of your system and sell you on Texas."

"That's a mighty big gamble, Mr. Duke."

"Well, you know what they say...some gambles are worth a roll of the die."

The shadows darken the lines around the eyes I envision each night before I fall asleep. But the truth is, it doesn't matter that the moonlight doesn't shine on all his angles, because I see him, even with my eyes closed. I am in love with him.

"Honestly, it's crazy. But I like what we have. I want to see what it's like living in the same place."

Have I changed my mind about life decisions in the past? Absolutely. But Oliver's right. Some risks are worth the gamble. I'm going to take that job. And I'm going to test the waters on a career in hospitality. But I'm also going to explore living every day with Oliver.

"You know, I might hate it. The job. Texas."

He nods. "Fully aware. But you might love it, too."

All thoughts of what might be disappear when his lips brush

mine. His rough callouses ignite sensitive skin, and tendrils of need curl through my core. His hands grip my ass, pressing me against him. Our tongues clash, on the border of frantic. When he breaks the kiss, with a tender touch, his thumb swipes my swollen lips. We're both breathing heavily, clutching each other. It feels like our relationship has crossed a bridge, yet we have said little. All we've admitted is we want to give ourselves a chance living in the same place. We don't need to cling as if we're about to say goodbye, because time will be ours.

He dips down, and I gasp as he swings my legs up off the ground.

"What're you doing?" He crosses the threshold as I complain. "I'm too heavy."

"You're perfect." He kicks the door with his heel, and it slams behind us. He's carrying me like a bride, and shivers loop and circle at the sensation of being carried across a threshold. His boots clod on the smooth concrete floors and up the stairs. With the utmost care, he sets me down on his bed.

Behind us, the moonlight lends a golden glow to the black swirling river and the shapes of trees along the riverbank.

He unbuttons his shirt, one button at a time.

"Take off your clothes."

I'm wearing a sweater dress and boots. Using my toes, I kick the boots off, one by one. His hungry stare has me feeling self-conscious, and I glance back over my shoulder at the scene beyond the glass wall.

"You may need to get some window treatments."

"I'm hoping you'll help me design the master bedroom."

A bed is the only furniture in his bedroom. His clothes hang in an oversized walk-in closet or lay folded on shelves.

"So we can make love below the stars?" There's a massive skylight over his bed, and I can imagine the pitter-patter of rain on a rainy night. But on a clear night like tonight, a million stars twinkle.

"Every. Single. Night." His briefs hit the floor at the same time as my dress.

Corded and tanned arms circle behind me, unsnap my bra, guide the straps over my shoulders, and let it fall to the ground.

"You are so damn gorgeous." I could say the same thing to him. My fingers roam the planes of his chest and farther down to the dips and curves of his abs and over the light smattering of hair that trails down. His firm erection probes forward, and I reach for him, wrapping my fingers around him.

I bend to my knees and gaze up into whiskey eyes full of approval. His eyes flutter shut as I lick him, then take him fully into my mouth. His sharp intake of air spurs me on.

I love bringing him to this edge. I love how much he wants me. Needs me. His hips thrust forward as his hand gently guides the back of my head. His width expands in my mouth.

"No." He gasps. "Too close."

With a pop, I let him go. He nudges me to stand and holds me tight against him, so tight his erection presses into my belly. I feel his touch everywhere, along my back, my ass, the sides of my breasts. The tug on my hair breaks our unhurried kiss, and he directs me onto the bed, over the comforter, back on the stacked pillows.

"Spread those legs."

I do as he says, and he stands before me, taking me in. For the last twenty-four hours, we've made love so many times it's astounding he can still have this much hunger. But this time is different. Because in my heart, I know I'm going to give this a chance. A real chance.

He crawls onto the bed. His fingers cover my panties. The warmth of his skin, of his touch, has me squeezing my thighs. Gently, he shifts the fabric to the side. Tenderly, he kneads me, and one of his long, calloused fingers enters me.

"Christ. You're drenched." His fingers slip beneath the sides of my black thong, and he slides it down my thighs, over my knees, and lets it fall to the floor with our other clothes.

He climbs on the bed and lavishes kisses up my thighs to my apex. My hips surge at the cool entrance of his tongue. I tilt my head back and gasp as he delivers the most amazing sensations. His fingers join in, and within minutes I'm on the precipice, about to come.

His fingers slow.

"Look at me, baby." I force my eyes open. "Close?"

"So close." My muscles vibrate beneath his knowing touch.

"I need to feel you come on my cock. Can you do that for me?"

With one hard press of his lips to my center, he pushes up on his hands and rises over me.

I spread my legs, making room for him. He positions his tip at my entrance, and we both watch, mesmerized, as he moves it up and down, flirting with my folds.

"Please." My core aches with need. "I need you."

And then he fills me with one thrust. Stilling over me, he brushes the hair away from my face, and those tender eyes seek mine.

"I love you." His hips move, and my body inches upward. "God, I love you, Kate."

We devolve into two sweaty bodies, roiling into each other. Each thrust sends shock waves through my sensitized clit, clenching my muscles. His tongue alternates between my nipples, along my neck, and in my mouth with impassioned kisses.

"Ollie," I call out.

"Yes. Say it again."

"Ollie. Ollie." I pant and moan.

He pushes my legs down so they lie almost flat below him. In this position, our bodies align. Sweaty skin touching sweaty skin on every point of contact. The pressure on my core magnifies and carries me to the brink of delirium. I'm on the edge, looking down. We both are.

His hips jerk as wave after wave of pleasure crashes over us. His forehead falls to my shoulder, and I clasp him to me, my arms wrapped around him tightly as our chests expand rapidly, seeking air.

"I love you, too." It's a soft whisper, but everything pouring out of me says so much more.

In the morning, we wake tangled in each other. When he returns from downstairs with coffee, he has his laptop. Beneath his skylight, we lean back on pillows.

"Want to show you this." He opens it to design mock-ups. "These are some ideas I've been throwing around for the second floor. The place is a work-in-progress." He shrugs. "As you can tell. Still a lot of work."

"I think it's amazing." It truly is. The floor-to-ceiling windows on the back wall give the sensation of being outdoors. The brick walls are original to the building. He clicks to another concept. He's using a software program to lay out ideas.

"I'm limited by the software. So, it wouldn't be this color wood." He touches the screen. "This is far boxier than what I'm envisioning. But, you see, I'd like to add a fireplace in this room, on that wall. Gas, like we had in our room in Jackson."

"It'll be amazing," I reassure him. "Any of these concepts."

"Well, I'm sure ideas will continue to evolve. Plumbing and electrical are already in, but anything else can change."

"Really, it's great." He's looking at me like he wants me to guide him, but he's got to remember I still live like a college student.

"I suppose the priority is decorating the living spaces. Will you help me with that?"

"I will." He hasn't shaved, and I rub the copper-hued stubble. "Did you know that your beard growth has more red in it than your hair?"

"See? Katie, my girl, you think you know everything about me. But there's still plenty to learn."

"Maybe so."

"Oh, darlin'. I promise to keep you entertained."

On the drive to the airport, he toys with my fingers as we discuss our upcoming travel options. It's premature to plan anything without first receiving the job offer. But, assuming I get it, I'll talk with my current employers and confirm I won't be leaving them in a lurch. But it doesn't really matter whether I can get Christmas week off because we've got plans and backup plans. And all of our plans involve being together.

He walks me to the security line and lifts me off my feet as he gives me a deep goodbye kiss. This kiss says he loves me, he'll miss me, and he's going to see me again very soon.

"I love you," I tell him. With reluctance, I pull my suitcase behind me, stepping into the security line.

"Love you, too. Call me when you land."

thirty-five

Oliver

December 25

"They're here! They're here!"

Mom, in all her Patricia Duke glory, throws her arms wide, running down the front steps of the Duke family ranch house. My nieces charge forward, nearly tackling their grandmother. Kate and I are in the third row of the super-sized van that picked us up from the airport, and she intently watches the scene through the glass panel.

Through the open front door of the ranch house, a lit Christmas tree stands at the back of the foyer, and another lit Christmas tree lights the window near the front door. Mom loves trees. I should know. I helped her deck out all five trees that grace her house, all themed. As I pointed out to her, and do every year, I am her only son who shows up to assist. Dad always makes himself scarce, Ian never comes home, and Sam, if you asked him, would offer to hire someone to do it. Patty would go into cardiac arrest at the mention of someone coming into her family home to decorate her beloved memory trees.

Olivia and Sam scramble out of the van after their kids. The driver of the van slams the door closed as he heads to unload luggage.

"You ready for this?" I ask Kate.

"Absolutely." She beams up at me, and my heart goes on a full pitter-patter skitter.

We spent the last four days with her family in Vermont. I finally met the infamous Hudson, and we both met his new girlfriend. As expected, her brother and I hit it off. If we'd gone to the same college, we would've been thick as thieves.

Kate's parents never criticized her for her career change, something she'd worried over. She prepared herself for an inquisition. But from my armchair perch, it seemed to me her parents supported the change without question. Maybe a lot of the parental criticism had been in her head over the years. Self-directed criticism can be a gnarly beast. Regardless, I never had to get defensive on her behalf, and we had a blast with her family. We spent one day boarding at Killington, and I have to say, her pro brother is about ten times more considerate of a boarding partner than my friend Drew.

After spending Christmas morning with her family, we met up with Sam and joined his crew on his private jet down to Texas for Christmas dinner with the Dukes. The private jet blew Kate's mind. It's a way of life I don't aspire to, and I warned her commercial is my norm. I do well, but billions isn't on my radar.

Looking at her oohing and aahing, I felt compelled to tease her a bit. "If this jet gives you the goo-goo eyes for my big bro, just remember, he's already taken."

"This right here is the only Duke brother I want." She gave me a kiss that had me wishing we were the only ones on the plane and had one niece shrieking about kissing.

We separated for takeoff, but once we hit altitude, I pulled my girl right back up next to me.

We'll spend Christmas dinner with my family, and tomorrow I'll test my niece's riding skills. Then the next day, we'll fly up to Aspen and stay through the first.

Jason, my brother from another mother, will meet us all in Aspen. He'd been a friend of ours for years, but his parents died when he was a teenager, and Patty and Sam Senior basically adopted him. Jason and his wife Maggie always spend part of Christmas week with us in Aspen. Except for last year, that is. Hand, foot, and mouth disease altered all the family traditions.

Thank the gods. Otherwise, I wouldn't have met Kate. My hands rest on her hips as I stand before her, assisting her out of the van. Just goes to show, altered plans are part of any journey. And sometimes, the unexpected fork in the road delivers the best parts of the trip.

Behind me, Christmas music filters out of the house and mixes in with excited greetings. Before me, Kate looks up, eyes sparkling, and my chest overflows with warmth. It's kind of becoming a standard sensation, but it's one I hope I never take for granted. I brush my lips across hers, treasuring this moment before we're immersed in the Duke family shenanigans.

"Just remember, no matter how crazy it gets, I love you."

She laughs.

I feign seriousness and warn her once again, "And don't take offense, but we play second fiddle to the grandkids."

"What are you telling my Katie?" Patty's loud voice booms from the front yard. I palm the curve of Kate's sweet ass, kiss her cheek, and head to the back of the van to help unload our luggage. Olivia and Sam will stay here at the ranch, but after dinner, we'll get a ride back to the gin mill. Or maybe I should say our place. She agreed to move in with me. She was hesitant, but it makes the most sense. I have zero intention of spending nights apart, and she can put her rent money toward paying off that school debt she worries so much about. She starts her new job right after the new year on January third.

It ended up that none of the businesses where she worked part-time had counted on her for the holiday season, as they expected she'd be working full time as a patroller. It bothered her that Bill didn't seem surprised when she backed out of patrolling during the trial period. She said he kind of expected it, and she worked herself up into a frazzle over it. But if you can't let something go at Christmas, when can you?

By the time Sam and I have unloaded the luggage, the entire Duke clan is inside, Kate included. Together, Sam and I move his luggage into Sam's old room. It's a fancy-schmancy guest room now. His girls are staying in my old room, which is a study-slash-guest bedroom. Didn't take Patty long at all to take down my guns and deer heads from the walls. Ian's expected home at some point tonight, and the night light's on in his old room, ready for him.

Sam slaps me on my back as I roll in the last enormous suitcase.

"I like Kate," he says.

"That's a good thing." I grin. "I like her, too."

Hell, I love her. She'd been going on about what to get me for Christmas, but I was all kinds of sincere when I told her she'd given me the best Christmas gift of my life by agreeing to move down here and give us a shot. Agreeing to live with me is like the sparkly star on top of the tree.

"When it comes time, remember I've got a diamond guy." Sam has a guy for anything and everything. But what he means is he buys directly from a guy in the New York diamond district and avoids paying the retail markup.

"Thanks for the reminder."

"Don't give me that look," he says. I don't know what look I'm giving him, but I feel the need to set him straight.

"There's no look. She's it for me. I won't deny it. But she's still figuring things out."

He grips my shoulder in the hold he's loved for as long as I can remember. It's the one that says, *here, now, little brother, I'm older and smarter, and you can learn from me.* "Marriage doesn't mean everything is solved. It just means you figure things out together."

Our evening progresses like a Duke Family Christmas special.

Christmas songs play nonstop, the low flames from the gas fireplace glow, and the kids are lit up brighter than the multi-colored lights on the back porch tree.

After dinner, we exchange gifts. I have to give it to Patty. She orchestrated the gift exchange and ensured Kate, the newest member of our family, received a gift from every family member. Mom got wind that Kate would need a new wardrobe for her new job, and she and Olivia went all out. It's a good thing we planned to drive back to our house because we'll be loaded down.

After presents, we Zoom with Jason and Maggie. It's snowing in Chicago, and the sight amps up my jacked-up nieces. Kate ends up trapped on the sofa during the Zoom call, with one niece on her lap and one niece on Mom's lap, with Ian beside Mom and Olivia beside Kate. Dad snaps a photo of them on the sofa while Sam and I stand off to the side.

My phone dings and I pull it out, expecting a Merry Christmas text from Liam, Noah, Drew, or Sandra. But it's a shared contact from Sam. The note says, "My diamond guy." The smug guy winks at me, and I just grin.

It's late when we finally make it back home. Thanks to the miracle of timers, my tree sparkles with tiny white lights. There are no ornaments on this tree.

I open my suitcase and pull out two of the gifts Kate gave me early this morning when we woke at her parents' place. She gave me photo ornaments, and I love 'em. One is of us at the Mangy Moose. Apparently, Nash snapped a photo of us that first day when Kate and I sat across from him and Drew. I don't remember him taking the photo, but we're posing, leaning toward each other. The caption on the ornament reads, "Our first Christmas." The second ornament says, "Christmas 2022." My mom snapped this photo of us in front of her Christmas tree on the day my parents met Kate.

As I hang my two ornaments on the tree, I say, "So, we survived our first Christmas with our families."

My comment earns a laugh. "That could be another article. How to Survive Christmas with the Family."

"Oh, man. Think of all the articles in front of you. A northern girl's guide to life in the south." I pull her to my side so we can appreciate our two ornaments. A white light bulb shines above each ornament, and the glass front sparkles beneath the warm yellow glow.

"How to survive your first day at a new job," she adds.

"How to survive moving in with your boyfriend." She squeezes my love handle, so I return the favor, and she squirms. "How to survive decorating a home with your boyfriend."

This gets her laughing. "How to survive a vacation with your boyfriend's family."

"Yeah, that one's not far away at all, is it?"

She presses her lips to my throat, and my insides nearly explode with the realization this is the best Christmas of my life, and we've got so many more fantastic holidays in front of us. Everything is in front of us, and there's not a bit of me that's scared. Hell, I'm eager for it all.

"You know, you could take a theme like surviving wedding planning and turn it into a full book." I brave a glance down, gauging her reaction. There's a rosy gleam to her cheeks, but she's silent. "Did I scare you?"

It could all be in my crazy head, but with the warmth oozing from my chest, the love between us is tangible.

"No. I mean, it's terrain I've never navigated before, but...it feels right."

"That's because it is right. And there's no need to be nervous. We're gonna figure it out day by day."

"Together. Wait...hold up. I just got another idea for a listicle." I find a notepad and jot it down before the idea slips away. "How to roll the dice and win at life."

epilogue

Kate

Three Months Later

"Kaaaate!"

A fit of giggles erupts. Oliver found my babies. His boots clomp down the path where I'm loading up the back of a four-wheeler.

"What the heck, Kate? Those are barn cats. The operative word being 'barn.'"

"But Peggy Sue had babies. Aren't they so cute? And there's a heavy rainstorm expected tonight."

"And they would be as safe as can be in the loft over the horse barn."

"Did you see the tiny one with a black face and white button nose?"

"Kate, babe." Oliver steps up behind me, lifts my hair out of the way, and trails kisses up my neck to my ear, leaving a wake of goose-bumps. "Those kittens are going to grow up to be my rat hunters."

I twist around, looping my arms over his shoulders. I give him my best pleading eyes and wiggle against his crotch.

"But while they are babies, they can live with us, right?"

His upper teeth sink into his lower lip in a failed effort at biting back his smile.

"I love you," I say. Then he gives me a long, slow, deep kiss that says he loves me, too.

With a playful slap to my ass, he breaks the kiss and peers over my shoulder.

"What have you got on here?"

"I thought I'd bring some fresh strawberries. And I just put together a few other things."

His brow crinkles, and he lifts the towel I've laid over a few of the dishes.

"You're bringing food to Mom's for dinner?"

"Well, it's just that...she said she's having strawberry shortcake, and her strawberries aren't fresh."

"Sure they are."

"No. They're in syrup."

"Baby, she adds sugar to them. That's not the same thing as syrup."

"Why on Earth would she add sugar? Is that why her peaches are mushy?"

"What did you think?"

"I thought maybe she...I don't know. Didn't get a chance to buy fresh fruit. Why would she add sugar? That's so unhealthy."

"Honey, you've been living in the south for three months now. Butter, sugar, and salt will be added to everything in some combination."

"And vegetables are fried." I pat his extremely firm abdomen. "I don't understand how you aren't twice your size."

"Do you not see how much work I do on the ranch? I can eat anything I want for the rest of my life."

"Yeah, tell that to your arteries."

"Hush your mouth. The bacon might hear you." He's teasing me. Although, food has been our biggest adjustment since moving in together. It's one thing to order off a menu together. It's quite another to grocery shop and cook together. I've been slowly convincing him that bacon every single morning isn't a good long-term health strategy.

He looks over the dishes I've loaded up to take to his parents. They're in town for the week, and they invited us over to grill out with them.

"You made your own butter beans."

"She adds bacon!" He looks skeptical, so I add, "I told her I'd be bringing this. She isn't going to be surprised."

"But don't the butter beans negate any bacon negatives?"

"Your mother adds bacon grease to those butter beans. Bacon grease!" He shrugs and lays the towels back down over the covered dishes.

"I'm sure with a little Tabasco sauce, your butter beans will taste good too."

I reach over and pinch him. "I want you to be alive for decades to come. These are little changes."

"I like the sound of that."

My cheeks heat under his gaze. We just stand there, holding on to each other. My insides flutter under his inspection. There's something there, maybe some serious thoughts going on behind those whiskey eyes. His thumb brushes my bottom lip, and he caresses my cheek. I think he's going to say something, but instead he palms my butt cheeks the way he likes to do and pulls me into him, kissing me until I'm practically panting.

With a slight groan, he breaks our kiss and rests his forehead on mine. "All right. Best not be late to dinner. People are waiting."

He climbs on the four-wheeler, and I hop on behind him, wrapping my arms around his waist and lying my head against his back. When we're not on horses, we ride four-wheelers around, but I prefer sharing one with Oliver.

Moving here has been the best decision. I love it out here on the ranch with the wide-open spaces and rolling hills. Land we share with an abundance of cows, horses, goats, and cats.

Oliver and I go on trail rides on my days off, which are Sunday and Monday. The days are getting longer now, so he says we'll be able to go on trail rides after dinner soon. My hours mesh well with Oliver's. I work morning and lunch shifts, so I'm home by late afternoon. The work varies, making it fun and interesting. The people are super nice, I'm learning a ton, and I'm optimistic about Sweet Magnolia Bread and Bakery franchise potential.

Ironically, I've skied more this past season than I did the year I lived in Jackson. We went skiing every day in Colorado with his family and in Vermont with mine over the Christmas holiday, and we just got back from a one-week vacation in Jackson. It was great to see my old friends, and awesome to be out on the slopes all day as a vacationer and meeting up with them for après ski.

Paisley plans to relocate to a resort in Breckenridge, Colorado this summer, and Nash has a gig as a river guide that starts in a few weeks. To put it in his words, he's stoked. Claire moved to the Utah side but still works in Jackson. She promises to come visit as soon as ski season is officially over and things calm down.

I can't wait to show her around. This place has a special magic to it. There's a peace to undeveloped land far away from roads and unsightly power lines. Deer regularly bound through the pastures, grazing right alongside the horses, cattle, and goats. We had a fox come through a few weeks ago, and Oliver and Hank jumped on horses bareback, shotguns in hand, chasing the animal off the property. That was an exciting day, but mostly our days are pretty calm, peaceful, and perfect.

When we arrive, Ian and Sandra are sitting on the front steps.

"Hey, bro. How's it going?" Oliver asks the moment he cuts the engine. Ian bows his head and walks over to his car with Oliver on his heels.

"Sandra, glad I saw you. Do you want to ride together to the Lillian's List meeting next week?" It's a group in Austin working to nominate more pro-choice candidates to the Texas legislature. I said when I moved here I'd work to improve things, and I love that Sandra introduced me to this group.

Oliver joins me at most of the meetings, which makes me love him all the more. He said he typically stays out of politics, but he agrees this is important. He says women's health isn't just a women's issue, that he loves me, and therefore it's his issue, and when we have little ones, it will continue to be his issue. He says he hates the extreme direction his state has gone in, but he'll work to put it to rights.

Sandra wipes her hands below her red-rimmed eyes.

"Are you okay?"

"Yeah, I'm fine. Just...allergies," she says, sniffs, and turns her back to me. "Ahm, I'm, you know, not feeling that great. I think I'm going to cut out. Will you tell Patty?"

Gravel crunches as Ian's car drives away. Sandra's palm flattens against her stomach, and with her head down, she heads to her Jeep.

I join Oliver at the back of the four-wheeler as he calls out to Sandra, "Hey, girl, where are you off to?"

"Let her go," I whisper.

Sandra waves her hand in the air and says, "It's all set up. Take pictures."

"What's she talking about?"

"Who knows? Crazy girl, that one."

We watch as she reverses and steers out of the drive. "Is she dating Ian?"

"Nah, babe. Never." I cock my head at him because something tells me he wears blinders when it comes to Sandra. "That would never happen. She'll never get over Sam."

I'm not sure why he keeps saying that, but there's no point in arguing about it. This is his family, and I'm still learning how to navigate the Dukes.

Patty swings the door open, a huge smile on her lips. George Strait's deep twang spills out of the house. Identifying country musicians is a new skill I've picked up since moving in with Oliver. I've always been more of an alternative rock kind of girl, but he's been introducing me to what he calls "the classics." He listens to pretty much anything, but he says now that I've moved here, I need to expand my musical horizons.

"Hey, Katie," Mrs. Duke says, and a brown ball of fur trots out between her legs.

"Oh, my god, you got a puppy!" I squeal, immediately forgetting the food and dropping onto the ground as the puppy rolls down the two steps to the ground, its fat little tail flopping back and forth.

"Jesus, this family." Oliver tilts his head back and places his hands on his hips.

"Where did Sandra and Ian get off to?" Mrs. Duke asks.

"Mom, what're you doing?" he asks with far too much attitude.

"Hush!" I say, throwing one of his favorite words right back at him. "Look at this cutie pie."

"Kate, that girl is yours. We had an entirely different plan, but apparently, we have suffered a plan malfunction." I'm sure he's glaring at his mom, but the puppy is on my lap, licking my face, and I'm not giving grumpy Ollie any mind.

"The puppy piddled on the floor, and your dad asked me to take her outside."

"Do you like her? Give her a name," Oliver says.

Wait. What?

"What do you mean?"

"She's yours. That's why it would be better if we kept the cats at the barn, but I suppose we can see how they all get along. Maybe set the kittens out on the covered screened porch?"

"You got me a dog?"

"Well, you gallivant all over, and it'll be safer with a dog trailing you. They're good at keeping an eye out for snakes and such. This one here is a lab. They're good dogs. Loyal."

Tears well up. I sit flat on the ground, cross-legged, and the squirming puppy attempts to climb up my chest.

Patty wiggles her fingers and backs into her house, a beaming smile on her face. "We'll be waiting for you on the porch." The screen door creaks shut.

"You got me a puppy?"

"Yeah. Doing everything I can to sell you on Texas. You know, we don't have mountains or snow, and yeah, it's not a perfect state... there are some big issues, but..."

"Oliver, I love you. You didn't need to get me a puppy."

"Ah." He crouches beside me and lets the puppy gnaw on his finger. "We needed a dog out here. We used to have a lot of them and...I don't know. They went off to doggie heaven and we never replaced them. But it's time. A ranch needs dogs."

"And cats."

"Yeah. We never got rid of those."

He lifts my hand with his free hand and presses it to his lips.

"This ranch needs you. I need you."

"You don't have to bribe me. I'm pretty sold. I mean, I don't think I'll ever be able to drink your mom's sweet tea without my teeth hurting, but moving here was the best decision I've ever made."

He sits down beside me, legs splayed, and pulls me and the puppy between his legs.

"We can't bring her home quite yet. She's one of Hank's pups. In about two weeks, she'll be ready to wean, and she can come live with us. It's been hell keeping her a secret from you. What do you think you'll name her?"

I scratch behind her ears. She's got short, stout legs and big paws. She's got to grow into herself. I settle my back against Oliver's chest, petting her.

Out here on the Duke ranch, they love all the two-name southern names. His childhood dog was named Daisy Duke. The black lab's photo hangs in the hall. Given her prominence in Duke family history, it's clear that's a name that can't be reused. Maybe there's an article there...top childhood pet names.

But no, this little one here is Oliver's gift to me. Our first in what, if I'm lucky, will be a long line of ranch dogs. And it comes to me.

"What do you think of the name Fling? Is that too...?" I let it dangle out there, wondering if he'll get it.

"Fling, huh?" He reaches forward and jiggles the puppy's bright red collar. "Flingy doesn't sound too good."

"Or Holly, for holiday."

His fingers maneuver her collar, and I gasp. A diamond solitaire dangles from green wrapping ribbon looped around her red nylon collar. There's a handwritten note attached that reads, "Marry us, please."

"If we're going to flaunt our humble beginnings to the world, maybe you'd consider wearing this? Just so, you know, everyone knows..." I sit there, processing what I'm seeing, as the puppy meanders down to my boot and promptly sets her teeth to the pointed toe.

"Marry me, Kate. Please? Spend your life with me. We'll spend lots of it here, but we'll travel too. We'll get a mountain house, and I'll take you to the snow. Let me spend my life working to make you happy, make your dreams come true."

"Yes." My answer comes readily. There's no need to second guess myself. "A thousand times yes. But only if I get to make your dreams come true."

He presses his lips to mine and holds me tight. "You already do. But, ya know, if you want to write out a list of a thousand ways to say yes, I'm game."

Coming in 2023

Always Sunny (Ian and Sandra)

Arrow Tactical Security Series

Better to See You (Wolf and Alexandria)

Sure of One (Jack and Ava) - Coming in 2023

The Twisted Vines Series

Crushed (Erik and Vivi)

Breathe (Kairi and David)

Savor (Trevor and Stella)

Haven Island Series

Rogue Wave (Tate and Luna)

Adrift (Gabe and Poppy)

First Light (Logan and Cali)

The West Side Series

When the Stars Align (Jackson and Anna)

Trust Me (Sam and Olivia)

Walk the Dog (Delilah and Mason)

Lost on the Way (Jason and Maggie)

Chasing Frost (Chase and Sadie)

Misplaced Mistletoe (Ashton aka Dr. Bobby and Nora)

My editor, Lori, added a note to her edits for this one. Straight and direct, as is her style, she said "You're going to get some pushback on the political element, but I don't know how you can have someone move to Texas without addressing it."

"It" obviously being the elephant in the room. The elephant in the room that exists in any group setting where you aren't quite positive you're with like-minded individuals, so you refrain from speaking.

So why did I do it? Well, for a few reasons.

Like my editor said, how could I not address it? I know readers read fiction for an escape, but the perspectives expressed would be true to these characters. (And, this might be a good time to add the reminder that a fictional character's point of view does not always align with the author's point of view.)

Aside from that, one of the things that I love about contemporary fiction is that it's a reflection of our times. It's worth noting that many of the classics of today, when written, were contemporary works that only now are historical. And, for better or worse, differences in opinion regarding politics are a part of our lives.

I read that a poll found 40% of Republicans want a civil war, and

32% of Democrats want one. I hope it's not true, but let's pretend we buy it. *How crazy is that?*

I grew up in the south with Civil War history buffs for parents. And what hit home to me was how families were torn apart. Cousins killed each other. Siblings killed each other. Is that really what we want?

I hope not. I have friends and family who disagree with me. And yes our disagreements can become heated. But I don't want to physically harm them or force them out of their homes and into a different state.

News channels earn more money when they anger or scare people. Politicians raise more money with emails designed to stoke anger and hatred and desperation and fear. On social media, the most polarizing viewpoints gain the most traction.

Is that the world we want to live in? I hope not.

In my happily ever after, we'll find a way to the middle ground. We'll find a way to disagree respectfully and truthfully. It's like we're back on the elementary school playground. In my HEA, we're going to find a way to get along.

Isabel Jolie, aka Izzy, lives on a lake, loves dogs of all stripes, and if she's not working, she can be found reading, often with a glass of wine. In prior lives, Izzy worked in marketing and advertising, in a variety of industries, such as financial services, entertainment, and technology. In this life, she loves daydreaming and writing contemporary romances with real, flawed characters and inner strength.

Sign-up for Izzy's newsletter to keep up-to-date on new releases, promotions and giveaways. Or stalk her on your favorite platform. Feel free to send her an email...she loves to hear from readers!